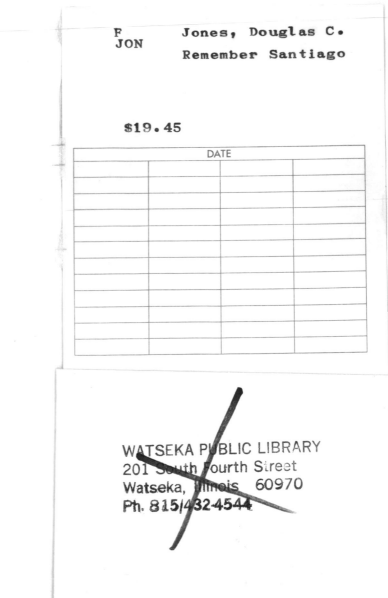

F   Jones, Douglas C.
JON
        Remember Santiago

$19.45

DATE			

© THE BAKER & TAYLOR CO.

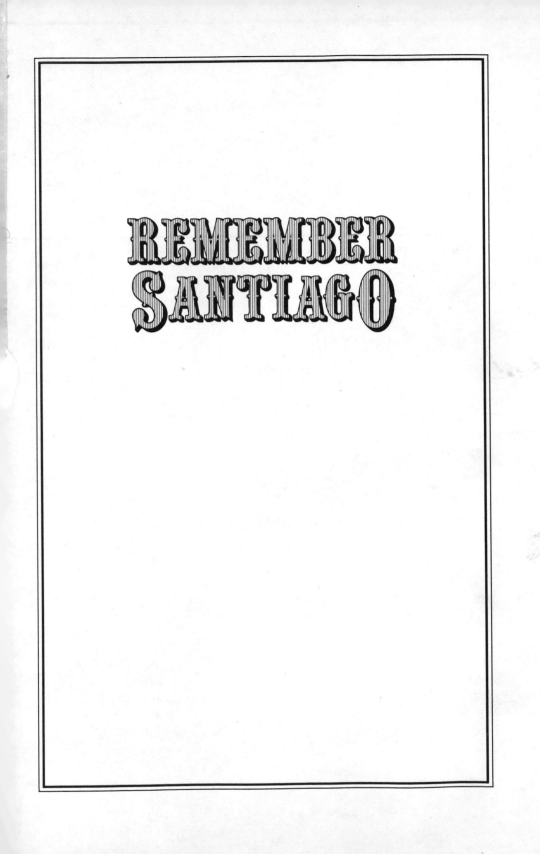

REMEMBER SANTIAGO

Other Books by Douglas C. Jones

REMEMBER SANTIAGO

DOUGLAS C. JONES

Henry Holt and Company, New York

Published by Henry Holt and Company, Inc.,
115 West 18th Street, New York, New York 10011.
Published in Canada by Fitzhenry & Whiteside Limited,
195 Allstate Parkway, Markham, Ontario L3R 4T8.

Library of Congress Cataloging-in-Publication Data
Jones, Douglas C.
Remember Santiago / Douglas C. Jones.—1st ed.
p.   cm.
ISBN 0-8050-0776-8
1. United States—History—War of 1898—Campaigns—Cuba—Fiction.
2. Santiago Campaign, 1898—Fiction.   3. Cuba—History—Revolution,
    1895–1898—Fiction.   4. Osage Indians—Fiction.   I. Title.
PS3560.0478R4 1988
813C.54—dc19   88-10310
                                                                  CIP

First Edition

Designer: Liney Li
Printed in the United States of America
1 3 5 7 9 10 8 6 4 2

CONTENTS

AUTHOR'S NOTE

This novel is dedicated to all my children, none of whom have the vaguest notion of how badly things can get screwed up.

The historical events described in the following pages really happened. Only the principal characters are fictional. Some of them you have met before. Some of them you will meet again. They are all part of our growing family. A sometimes brash but lovable breed. I hope.

HISTORICAL NOTE

At the time of the Spanish-American War, there was no Thirty-seventh Infantry Regiment on the active list of United States Army units. The Thirty-seventh in the following pages, along with its officers and men, is fictitious.

All other units mentioned actually existed and were a part of the Cuban campaign as described. The principal officers of these units who play a part in the narrative were real.

The Thirty-seventh Infantry Regiment is placed in a factual setting as a subordinate element of the Second Infantry Division, Brigadier General Henry W. Lawton commanding.

I.

OUR SPLENDID LITTLE WAR

Joe Mountain

My great-grandfather sometimes painted his face yellow and black and went out to capture a few Caddos to sell to the French. That was a long time ago. It was when the French were coming up all the rivers like the one called the Arkansas now. The French needed slaves to work their cane fields in those islands they had south of Florida. Anyway, that's what Eben Pay told me.

And he told me that the Caddos and those other people the French bought died off trying to work the cane fields. So the French stopped buying slaves from my great-grandfather because now they needed the black men from Africa, who were the only ones who could work the cane and not die off fast.

One time, my great-grandfather got a needle for making tattoos from the French. His people had known for a long time how to do tattoos on a man's skin. But the French needle made it a lot easier.

So when I was a little boy, my father tattooed a line of dots on my face, like black raindrops running from my hair down to my jaw. It hurt like hell. But I didn't say anything about that to my father.

My little brother Blue Foot says those dots are the only things I've got left that are Osage. All the rest of me, Blue Foot says, is white man. Blue Foot, he's an old-line Osage. Hell, he still roaches his hair!

Maybe Blue Foot's right. My father told me, after he put those black dots on my face, that a man could live swimming with the big fish or die swimming against them. And he said the white man was the biggest, hungriest fish there was. Worse than a big river gar. Worse than a Kiowa.

So when the white man sent all those people in soldier suits and tall beaver hats and string ties into our country, my father swam with the big fish. He learned the white man's language. He already knew a lot of French and he knew Caddo words and a lot of Comanche, so learning a new string of words was easy.

Maybe that's why my father put those dots on my face. So no matter how much I was swimming with the white man, every one of them who looked at me could see that I was really an Osage.

Anyway, when the white man set up a fort where the Arkansas and Poteau rivers come together, my father helped. He was an interpreter. Even to the Cherokees, a people he hated like he hated the Kiowas.

The white man set up that fort mostly to keep the Cherokee and Osage from making war on one another. And my father understood that. So my father helped build Fort Smith. Maybe he was right. Maybe he was wrong. I don't know.

Later, I knew all the things my father knew. Because he taught me. I was an interpreter, too. And when they made the Indian Nations with all those tribes they brought in from the east and gave the Osage a little chunk of land right amongst them, I taught the white man's language for a long time in one of the Osage academies for boys.

I was swimming with the big fish.

When old Judge Parker came to Fort Smith, I went over there and got to be a scout and tracker for some of Judge Parker's deputy marshals. Those marshals were trying to keep order in the Nations. Sometimes, if a man wanted to resist arrest, I helped convince him. Sometimes the convincing was fatal to whoever it was if they just kept on insisting they didn't want to go into Fort Smith and get hanged for murder or rape.

It was mostly white men who got hanged or who needed convincing over in the Nations. There were a few Indians or halfbreeds and a few colored men, but mostly, they were white men.

None of that made any difference to Blue Foot, my little brother. He was just an old-line Osage. He kept calling me a white man because I'd cut my hair.

It was like Blue Foot thought time was standing still and we

[4]

could all go out west of the green country onto the flat land and hunt buffalo and fight Kiowas—all the things Blue Foot had heard our fathers tell about the way it was in the old days, when we were the only ones living in the hills where the tree grew that made good bows. Those were good trees. The French called them *bois d'arc*. Later, they were called bodarc. And then Osage orange. And they gave that place its name, for us first and then the French: Place of the Bows. Now everybody calls it the Ozarks because that's the way the English-speaking white man said the French name. But it wasn't a French name. It was really Osage.

Blue Foot doesn't even know all that. But I do. And he says I'm not even Osage. I know a lot of things Blue Foot doesn't know. But maybe he knows a lot I don't know, either. Being an old-line Osage, like he is.

Anyway, those Ozark hills were full of white men and railroads and Baptist churches. But Blue Foot didn't want to believe it. Because he lived in his mind what the fathers had built. Not in the real land. Even when he came to Fort Smith and we were together and he helped me track and scout and convince those hard men in the Nations to come on into Fort Smith and get a rope around their necks.

Finally, while I was working at Fort Smith, Eben Pay came. He was just a little white man. Well, most men to me are little because I stand a head or so taller than any of them. He was just silent at the right times, and said something where it needed saying. And the first time I ever saw him, I knew he understood my tattoos.

Eben Pay came to Fort Smith to be an assistant to Mr. Evans, who was United States Attorney. Which meant he worked hard to help Mr. Evans send arrested people who had done murder and rape to that gallows Judge Parker had built. Me and Eben Pay got along good.

I rode with a lot of white men out of Parker's court. Some were all right. Some were very bad. Eben Pay was different from all the others, not just because he was young. He could look at you and not say a word but the way his eyes worked made me think of my father. Sometimes when we were out, away from

Fort Smith, Eben Pay would hold his horse in and listen. I don't know what it was he was listening to but I always tried to hear it, too. I never did.

Once, just before Judge Parker died, me and Eben Pay were over in the Creek Nation on some court business. There was this Cherokee man selling stock at a horse race. This Cherokee man had a daughter whose name was Missy Bishop. Eben Pay took one look at this Missy Bishop and started acting like one of the horses had stepped on his head.

Missy Bishop was all right for a Cherokee. But Eben Pay acted like she was the only woman in the world.

She was a pretty little thing. I always liked my women a lot bigger than that, with some meat in good places. But Missy Bishop was fine to look at and she'd been at one of those girls' academies in Talequah or some such place and she knew how to talk English almost as well as Eben Pay and she had these tiny little ears with a big pearl in each lobe. I always liked ears pierced at the top but the Cherokees had been doing white man things for so long that most of them wore their earrings at the bottom.

Eben Pay didn't care where Missy Bishop wore her ornaments. He wasn't thinking about ornaments.

He pert near wore out that ferryboat going back and forth from Fort Smith to the Cherokee Nation. Taking oranges and fruitcake and stuff to that farm where Missy Bishop lived up close to Going Snake. I always went with him because Mr. Evans said he didn't want his best assistant wandering around in Indian Territory, all by himself. Of course, I never went into that farmhouse with him where Missy Bishop lived, me being an Osage and all. So I'd just stay in the woods and wait until Eben Pay came out then we'd ride back down to the ferry and Eben Pay would have this big grin on his face and he wouldn't talk about anything except maybe the birds and the way the honey locusts smelled and bullshit like that.

Well, there's not much you can do when a man gets snake bit the way Eben Pay was. So before long, he brought Missy Bishop back to Fort Smith with him. I think he may have paid her father a few horses. I don't know. I never asked. I reckoned it wasn't none of my business.

So they got married and Mr. Evans stood up beside Eben Pay, like they do in white man's weddings. It was a sad thing that old Judge Parker had died a couple of years before because if he'd been alive he might have stood up there himself beside Eben Pay. And if he had, maybe more people would have come. There wasn't very many who came to see Eben Pay take his wife. And they wouldn't let me in the church. Being an Osage savage and all. So I stood outside and even didn't get to see Eben Pay and Missy Bishop leave by some back door and go off to celebrate their wedding.

Missy Bishop had this little baby about a year later. A little baby boy. He looked like a boiled peach, so light and fuzzy. Not a good healthy brown like Osage babies. So many of those Cherokees were whiter than the white man, and Missy Bishop was like that. But he was a nice little baby even though he cried a lot and when he did Eben Pay would pick him up and pat his bottom. Hell, we always let ours cry until they stopped. After a few times, it didn't take long for them to figure out crying was a waste of breath.

Anyway, they called the little baby Barton. And the day he was born, Eben Pay strutted up and down Garrison Avenue buying whiskey for everybody in the saloons and giving strangers cigars. I went along to be sure none of that Garrison Avenue trash didn't take advantage. Those white man saloon drinkers didn't like me worth a hoot but none of them ever bothered Eben Pay when I was with him.

But the next day one of the worst things I ever saw happened. Missy Bishop died of the troubles she'd had bearing the baby. Eben Pay almost went crazy. I tried to get him drunk but he wouldn't drink anything. We'd go down by the Poteau River and he'd just stand there and look at the water and we'd hear the wind in the sycamore leaves and I'd watch him to be sure he wasn't going to jump in that muddy river.

I tried to get him to go with me to Henrietta's or Pearl Starr's, two of the whorehouses down in the rail yards, where we could sip a little gin and beer and get folks to talk with us, but he wouldn't go. We'd just sit in his house on B Street, him looking at the wall and making fists with his hands and this lady he'd hired to wet nurse and take care of little Barton in the back room singing these Baptist hymns.

Maybe it was good the war came. The war with the Spaniards about Cuba. Eben Pay said he had to go. He waved newspapers in my face where they told all these things about it. And he said his daddy in Saint Louis, who was a federal judge, had got him this job in the war with a man named Teddy Roosevelt.

Well, I reckoned his daddy in Saint Louis never liked the idea of Eben Pay getting himself a Cherokee wife. And he didn't like the idea of that baby, either, half Cherokee. Like the whole business was a bloody mark on the family blanket. That judge never came to Fort Smith. Him or Eben Pay's mother, either, when Eben Pay got married or when Missy Bishop died.

All that judge did was get a place for his son in the war.

And everybody in Fort Smith seemed like they were just happy to have Eben Pay go off to war. Mr. Evans and his woman said they'd take care of the baby. And the new judge at the federal courthouse, he said it was Eben Pay's duty, being a red-blooded American like he was. Maybe all them white men were ashamed of Eben Pay. He was a big man in the town now, a real prosecutor in the court of old Judge Parker. And there he'd gone off into Indian Territory to find a woman and brought her back to Fort Smith. And had a little half-blood baby.

Hell, I don't know.

All I know is that Eben Pay decided to go off to this war and when he told me I said I'd go with him. And he got mad and yelled until he was blue in the face and said there wasn't anyplace in this war for a big, ignorant, savage Osage but I knew it was all because he was troubled in his soul because of Missy Bishop.

So I said to Eben Pay that if he tried to go off to this war or any other war without letting me go with him, I'd catch up to him and break both his legs.

Eben Pay looked at me for a long time. Then he came over

[8]

to me and put his arms around me and we hugged. I guess it was the first time we'd ever hugged. My chin was on top of his head and I felt him shaking but I didn't know if he was laughing or crying. But one thing I did know. From then on, wherever Eben Pay went, I'd go.

When I told Eben Pay that, he laughed. It was the first time I'd seen him laugh since Missy Bishop died. And he said, All right, so from now on I guess I'll have to call you Ruth.

I didn't know who the hell this Ruth was, but if it made Eben Pay laugh, it was fine whatever he called me.

CHAPTER 1

IT was May in San Antonio. The river, coiling through the town like a speckled brown copperhead snake seeking low ground in the south Texas hills, gave off a scent of lily pads and green frogs.

It had been a long time since rain. Horses and wheeled vehicles in the streets lifted a fine, amber-tinted grit. And in most quarters of this community of almost fifty thousand souls, the smell of acrid dust mingled tantalizingly with the pungent odor of chilis and suet and tomatoes and cornmeal being cooked individually or in strange combination.

Old Mexico was not very far away, as distances were measured in the Lone Star State, and the faces of her progeny gave black eyed, brown skinned testimony to that fact. Along Flores and Saint Mary's streets were the sounds of their music.

At the Alamo Plaza bandstand, music of a different kind, heavy on brass and bass drum, the players all soldiers come in from The Quadrangle, now called Fort Sam Houston, which stood with its tall watchtower on the lift of ground just to the northeast of the city.

The bells of the Mexican missions and those of the newer Anglo churches rang to mark the hour and the setting of the sun and their notes could be heard at Turtle Creek in the west, where the green roll of hills was penciled across by the old Spanish military road to Val Verde County and on to El Paso, almost five hundred miles away.

It was early evening when Eben Pay and Joe Mountain stepped down from their Southern Pacific coach and into the bedlam of streets choked with every kind of vehicle imaginable, from donkey-drawn two-wheel carts to clanking, rattling, ringing trolley cars swaying and lurching along tracks set in the major thoroughfares beneath overhead electric wires.

"Seems like they enjoy loud colors down here," Joe Mountain said.

A passing streetcar was painted canary yellow and immediately behind it came one in startling, brilliant cock-cardinal red.

Color was everywhere, undimmed by coat of dust. Many of the buildings glowed adobe pink in the last light of day and sidewalk lamps, just flickering on, threw splashes of orange across sienna sandstone or rust-brown brick façades. The people were like clouds of slowly moving confetti, scarves and shirts and blouses and serapes and skirts, red and blue and green thread embroidered into it all. Scarlet and gold. Black and silver.

And frock coats, too, and planter's hats light tan with yellow bands, and flowered bonnets and slightly bustled taffeta gowns. A sprinkling of soldiers, too, walking jauntily and calling to one another, with khaki jackets and duck trousers tucked into lace leggings and flop-brim campaign hats.

"By God, Eben Pay," said Joe Mountain. "It looks like Muskogee when the Creeks are havin' a carnival."

They admired the saddle horses moving up and down the streets, and more of the garish painted trolleys, and once a group of soldiers rode past, bareback on half-wild horses, yipping like plains Indians. As Joe Mountain and Eben Pay stood on the sidewalk watching the passing cavalcade, a man in silk bowler and a flowered vest paused beside them.

"Army bought some more horses out at the fort," he said, displaying two gold teeth as he leaned toward Eben Pay. "Now the good boys are riding them down to their camp at Riverside Park. From the suitcases this servant carries, I assume you just arrived in town."

Eben Pay looked at him once and then turned away.

"You like to play a small game of poker?" gold teeth asked.

Eben Pay started to walk down the sidewalk, quickly, avoiding the other people.

"You like some fancy lady companionship?" gold teeth asked, following along, leaning toward Eben Pay. "Very fancy, sir. Very cheap."

Joe Mountain, a valise in each hand, moved in front of the man and stopped, not smiling now.

"We're takin' the kinks out," Joe Mountain said. "Gettin' the bruises off our asses from ridin' trains. So you go off someplace, mister."

Then in three quick strides, Joe Mountain was back beside Eben Pay, dodging through the pedestrian traffic.

"Joe, you don't have to protect me."

Joe Mountain laughed and his great teeth gleamed. "Hell," he said. "I was protectin' me."

And so taking the kinks out, they saw some of San Antonio at its best and most glorious time, the sun just gone, its lavender light still above yet shadows deep enough to make the lamps and the bright rectangular windows and the sparks from trolley wheels on lines overhead cast a new, artificial light, as though this man-made illumination promised to retain the life of the sun until it had rested and then been born again with dawn.

There were kinks enough to take out. They had started two days before in Fort Smith riding the Frisco line to Paris, Texas, then a feeder to Fort Worth and there on to the Southern Pacific. Smoky, rumbling cars filled with drummers and whores and men whose hats grew larger as Eben Pay and Joe Mountain traveled south. And the ubiquitous news butches, the lads selling the latest newspaper sensation about the cruel Spaniards. And apples and peppermint candy and chewing gum from trays they carried suspended by straps from their shoulders.

There had been time to eat only once, when their train paused in Austin and they bought a dozen tamales from a Mexican boy who could not have been over seven years old. Peeling off the husks they found inside only boiled cornmeal and no meat, but by then the locomotive ahead had lurched forward to take out coupling slack and the boy was gone in the platform crowd and Joe Mountain was leaning out the window, pushing cornmeal into his mouth, and shouting obscenities in Osage.

After he settled back into his seat, Joe Mountain shook his head and there was a black, deep light in his eyes.

"Little bastard," he said. He offered one of the oily, meatless tamales to Eben Pay. "You want some real good cornmeal?"

They both laughed and then on to San Antonio.

So they saw the heart of Bexar County's seat of government: the old cathedrals and the streets sometimes paved with cobblestones that had been laid down before Texas was a republic, and the winding river that held the city in its loops, and Doloria and Villita streets and Mexican vendors selling beans and tortillas or great sprays of gladiolus and the staid German farmers in from just north of the city to shop and the high-cheeked, gray-eyed women who wore old Spain in the coils of their shining hair. And the thin-lipped, long-jawed blond men, Scots-Irish Presbyterian, whose fathers had come out of Kentucky and Tennessee and were the New World's most vicious fighting men, come to stand against Comanche or Apache or Santa Anna or anyone else who stood in their way.

And finally, the Alamo Plaza.

"A lot of men died there," Eben Pay said as they stood on Alamo Street looking at the face of the old mission.

"What happened?" Joe Mountain asked.

"It's a long story," Eben said. "But the Spaniards built that mission."

"Well, I hope when we get to wherever the Spaniards are now and start to fight 'em, we don't get penned up in some old white man's church like that. It's better to be out where you can move around a little."

He drew a deep breath. "Eben Pay, I'm hungry as hell."

"Me too," Eben said. "And right there's the Menger Hotel,

so let's get our rooms and eat and see if we can find Mr. Roosevelt."

On that first evening in San Antonio, finding Mr. Roosevelt was indeed easy. Having just arrived in the city that day, and taking up temporary residence in the Menger on Alamo Plaza, where the second-story veranda overlooking the street was framed in wrought iron that would have done New Orleans proud, the just recently assistant secretary of the navy and now self-proclaimed leader of light cavalry was holding forth in the rotunda of the lobby.

The place was a madhouse. Newspaper writers, enough of them to form their own regiment, shouting questions. The city officials of San Antonio in starched shirts and winged collars and sweating. Officers of the regular army from Fort Sam Houston, blue waistcoats in sharp contrast to the tacky duck jackets of the newly commissioned First Regiment of United States Volunteer Cavalry, which the newspaper scribes, with their eternal love for alliteration, were already calling Roosevelt's Rough Riders. A furtive little man with a goatee and monocle was sliding about through the crowd, whispering that he would give the first man who captured a Spanish flag $1,000 and half the ownership in his liquor store at the corner of Forty-seventh Street and Third Avenue in the city of New York.

There, too, were ladies in hats large as umbrellas, ladies attached to the arms of swallowtailed dignitaries but others fresh faced and rouged and laughing and ready to be attached to anyone who expressed loneliness. A harried hotel assistant manager with sleeve garters and a fistful of room assignments on little pieces of paper that he clutched in each hand as though they might be yellow birds about to escape him. A group of large-bellied men, gold watch chains shining, looking very Republican. A wind-bronzed cowboy with a quart bottle of rye whiskey in one hand and at his waist a sheathed machete, which was standard issue for members of these Rough Riders.

In one corner, three pink-cheeked and bowlered young men, in striped shirts, their noses in the air, and speaking in accents understood only in Newport, sipping champagne from stemmed glasses.

[14]

Nowhere to be seen were the pinched features of Colonel Leonard Wood, commander of this already legendary regiment. An army surgeon turned tactician, he had the one qualification required for his job: he was a close friend of Teddy Roosevelt.

And Teddy Roosevelt, the second-in-command, was there beneath the rotunda of this Texas hotel, and some thought perhaps already thinking of another rotunda, the massive dome on the banks of the Potomac. The new electric bulbs in the brass fixtures about the hall sent dazzling reflections across his glasses and the ranks of teeth which he exposed beneath a mustache that bristled like old bronze wire, as bellicose as his voice, as barbed as his words.

Each time he threw back his head to laugh, which was often, his glasses flashed like lightning. His eyes were slitted, yet wide open, and seemed to produce their own fire of inner enthusiasm. The very sight of him brought the unmistakable odor of gun oil and bay rum and waterfalls.

"We will be first upon the firing line," he shouted. Everyone applauded. "We start here on this hallowed ground, where men once stood . . ." and he pointed in the direction of the Alamo, ". . . to fight for freedom. We go to do the same for our neighbors, downtrodden in Cuba and under Spanish yoke. And now gentlemen, I will receive visitors in my suite. Please see my adjutant."

But before he escaped completely, Eben Pay was before him, introducing himself.

"Oh yes, young man, your father, a fine, fine man," and Mr. Teddy clapped both hands on Eben Pay's shoulders.

Mr. Teddy could not help but see Joe Mountain, looming behind the young man before him, and he shouted a few words, unintelligible to all. Joe Mountain grinned and shook his head.

"That's Shoshone," Mr. Teddy roared, the blood vessels in his neck bulging over the tight collar of his khaki military jacket, for he was already in uniform, with flared riding breeches and leather puttees shined to glossy brown. "Shoshone. I learned that in Wyoming when I was there shooting bighorn sheep."

Joe Mountain's grin grew, exposing his enormous eyeteeth. He shook his head.

"Well, Cap'n," he said. "I don't parley much of them blanket-ass northern tribes. You got some Osage or Pawnee, I could keep up with that."

Mr. Teddy's face clouded, quickly, violently, like a storm over the Powder River. Eben Pay quickly mentioned Judge Parker.

"Yes, yes of course, Isaac Parker, a fine man," Mr. Teddy said, still glaring at the Osage. "Much maligned in the newspapers."

Then, in a lowered voice and bending near to Eben Pay's ear, he said, "Damned newspaper writers. Always making a hash of things."

It suddenly crossed Eben Pay's mind that perhaps Mr. Teddy would not be where he was had it not been for the damned newspaper writers of Mr. Pulitzer and Mr. Hearst, but he nodded.

"Yes sir. That's true."

Then the just recently assistant secretary of the navy and now self-proclaimed leader of light cavalry was gone, abruptly, rudely, Eben Pay thought, and leaving a vacuum in the rotunda lobby where the noise now seemed to swirl around aimlessly.

"Joe," he said. "Let's get a drink."

"Why hell, I'd be willin' to do that," the Osage said and he followed Eben Pay through the crowd, still holding the two suitcases in either hand, bouncing them off the protesting butts of whoever failed to see him coming and get out of the way.

It was a nightmare of encounters. With someone calling himself Mr. Roosevelt's adjutant they stood at the registration desk. The desk clerk, hair down across a damp forehead and cursing to himself.

"I never saw so many goddamned Republicans."

Jostling people at the desk while a man calling himself night manager came out to inspect Eben Pay's telegram message confirming his accommodations. A Mexican bellboy, to whom Joe Mountain refused to surrender the suitcases.

"For God's sake, Joe, let him take the baggage," Eben Pay said.

"I'd rather carry it than let one of these sons a bitches touch it," said the Osage. "Remember that little thief who sold us cornmeal without any meat in it."

The barroom was impossible of entry. They went to the dining room. A waiter with a drooping mustache, dripping perspiration, explained that normally Indians were not served in the Menger, but in view of the circumstances, he would overlook Joe Mountain's obvious lack of Anglo blood, but there was nothing left in the kitchen but a few baked sweet potatoes and some longhorn rump roast, which might require one of Mr. Teddy's machetes for slicing.

At last, they were in their room. And there were two beds, a great blessing to Eben Pay, who had been thinking for some time how he could accommodate a decent night of sleep in a single bed beside an Osage Indian who was six feet seven inches tall and weighed all of two hundred and seventy pounds.

Lights from Alamo Street below cast a wavering glow across the ceiling. And with that came the sound of a guitar, accompanied by occasional blasts from a brass cornet, and a great deal of laughter and Spanish language.

"Joe?" Watching the dancing ceiling.

"I'm awake, Eben Pay."

"That little bastard who came whispering to me. In a major's uniform. He said Mr. Roosevelt said we'd get assigned to the staff of the commanding general. Whoever that might turn out to be."

Joe Mountain didn't say anything. Eben watched the lights moving on the ceiling and heard a trolley coming near, clanging. Laughter from below. Glass breaking.

"Joe?"

"I'm awake, Eben Pay."

"You know what he said? He said Mr. Roosevelt's regiment was full up. Hell! You know what I think?"

"No," Joe Mountain said. "But I think you're fixin' to tell me."

"I think they know I'm a Democrat. And this Rough Rider thing is straight-out Republican. A goddamned political club. And you know what I think, Joe?"

"What do you think, Eben Pay?"

"I think a big war hero can look to a lot of votes someday. That's what I think."

"Well, I don't know nothin' about this politics," Joe Mountain said. "And you talkin' about it just makes me wonder why the shit we left Fort Smith."

Eben Pay sighed and rolled onto one side and thought about sleep. But he was awake, wide awake. Listening to that music from the street below.

"So because I'm a lawyer, I'm going to some general's staff."

"Well, you're a lawyer, all right."

The streetcar rumbled and clanked along the street below.

"God, I wonder if those things run all night," Eben said. He lay for a long time, thinking about Fort Smith. Thinking about Saint Louis and his mother and father. Thinking about Missy Bishop.

"Joe?"

"I'm still awake, Eben Pay, but I ain't gonna be for long so you better say it all fast."

"Don't call Mr. Roosevelt captain again. I don't think he liked that much."

Joe Mountain started laughing, a low gurgle at first, then building to a cascade and finally making his bed shake.

"Hell," he said. "All these army men are captains to me."

And Eben Pay, turned on his side away from the Osage, was laughing, too. And when they'd finished, Eben Pay said, "Joe, you know this old hotel? Sam Houston and Robert E. Lee stayed here."

"Well, now," Joe Mountain said. "I've heard of them men. I wouldn't call them cap'n. I'd call them sir."

So they had their laugh again, soft and long but with an understanding that men sometimes have in little jokes that mean nothing to anyone else. The lights on the ceiling wavered and flamed and the sounds from the street below surged and then quieted, surged again, but less so, and then began to die.

"Maybe it's a good place to start a war," Eben Pay said, quietly, not even expecting Joe Mountain to be awake still.

"Not with them rifles I heard they started givin' out," Joe Mountain said. "Bolt actions. Shit! I'd want me a Winchester."

"Kraig Jorgensen's," Eben Pay said.

"Yeah, bolt actions. Them Gatling guns everybody's talking about, I never trusted them fast shooters."

"Joe, where'd you ever hear about Gatling guns?"

"For God's sake, Eben Pay. I can read."

"Go to sleep, Joe."

"Yeah. That bunch we seen down there tonight. What kinda war can that bunch fight?"

"Joe, go to sleep."

"Yeah, all right."

It was a long time. The noise from the street below had tuned down to only a murmur. When Joe Mountain spoke, it was only to himself. But aloud.

"That damned meat we had for supper. In the Territory, dogs wouldn't eat it."

"Joe. Go to sleep."

"Yeah. All right. But you know what Eben Pay?"

"What Joe, for God's sake?"

"That Mr. Roosevelt. He got the ugliest teeth I ever seen."

And so they laughed together and had their only night in San Antonio and the next day entrained with appropriate papers from the hand of Mr. Teddy Roosevelt himself, entrained for Tampa, Florida, leaving behind the First United States Volunteer Cavalry Regiment and its hectic scrambling to get to the war, hectic even to the extent of loading their horses in railroad day coaches, not knowing that most of those same horses would never get to Cuba.

But, Eben Pay said, it was a good place to start a war.

Carlina Bessaford Newton

My mother was a Rhode Island Bessaford. Her father had immigrated from the English Midlands, along with his three brothers, in the year before she was born, to establish a textile mill on the Blackstone River near Woonsocket. They were what might be characterized as a modestly successful group of businessmen. They were Unitarians, in a rather casual sort of way.

My father was a Fitchburg man who proudly laid claim to a lineage that stretched back to the first arrivals at Massachusetts Bay Colony. There was nothing at all casual about his fundamental Calvinism.

It was a strange mating, indeed. One in which it must be supposed was, at least initially, a physical passion intense enough to overcome the contradiction of a Unitarian and a Calvinist contracting to live in harmony together under the same roof without committing murder on one another.

I could never imagine either my mother or my father submitting to carnal lust. Not mother, because she was so meek and withdrawn that it was difficult to conceive of her reaching for a crust of bread even were she starving.

Not father, because he was constantly making stern pronouncements to the effect that the pleasures of the world were nothing more or less than traps set by the Devil which must be shunned and abhorred in order to have any chance of Paradise.

In any event, the union was made and I was the result in the year that Rutherford B. Hayes was elected to the presidency. So on at least one provable occasion, my father and my mother indulged themselves of human instinct which may well have been so distasteful to them that they never did it again. At least, I was their only issue.

Of course, my father would never admit even to himself that base passion was involved. Rather he would put it all down to a resort to wickedness solely for the purpose of propagating the race. Long before I discovered on my own initiative how little children were begun, never having had any such instruction at home, my father would sit at table or on his high-backed chair in the parlor, and make resounding discourse to the effect that we were all the product of Original Sin, for which we must spend the rest of our lives trying to atone in order that we come to Grace.

My father always said Grace with a capital G. He gave the same distinction to Original Sin. At the time, I hadn't the vaguest notion what either term meant. And I am not completely sure that I do now.

From my earliest recollections, it seemed that there was a struggle for my immortal soul in that drab house in Fitchburg. Father reminded me daily that salvation could come to me only when Jesus revealed Himself as a result of my constant study of the Bible and a steadfast refusal to fall victim of worldly temptation. And that such a Revelation was already predetermined and so all left for me was to pray and hope that someday the Holy Ghost would arrive and touch me.

And after some of his most impassioned sermons, I would go up to my room and Mother would come and sit beside my bed and say in her very small voice that really Jesus was only a man and not a god and that there was no Trinity and that if I was good throughout my life then I had a wonderful opportunity for Heaven.

Being pushed and shoved in these various spiritual directions, my appreciation of the Christian faith was understandably confused and fragmented.

In all of this, my father's greatest ally was Mr. Theophilus Compton, a bachelor who owned a number of undertaking establishments throughout the state. He was not himself a mortician. Rather, he owned these establishments and my father was an undertaker in one of them.

I slowly came to understand it was this profession of my father's which announced his presence in our home by the rather distinctive odor of formaldehyde.

[21]

Mr. Theophilus Compton was not only an entrepreneur of the dead, he was ordained in the Calvinist persuasion. And it was in that capacity that I came to know him, sitting spellbound on a footstool in our parlor as he talked, his great flare of muttonchop whiskers seeming constantly to attempt escape from his jowls. They were red muttonchop whiskers, although the hair that remained on Mr. Theophilus Compton's head was snow white.

He spent many hours at our board and in our parlor. He extolled the virtues of Oliver Cromwell. He raved against the deism of our Founding Fathers. He raved against the study of pagan Greek in our schools. He raved against the sin and corruption to be found on the pages of books at the public library.

It seemed to me, even at that innocent age, that he raved against vices and left virtue to the imagination.

Well, on many occasions, he chastised me for reading some of those same books he condemned because very early I had learned to read and did a great deal of it. I think he had spies in the library.

At any rate, this punishment came in the form of spankings. Sitting in my own father's chair in the parlor, he would call me over and turn me across his knees and administer his palm to my bottom. Explaining as he did that it hurt him more than it did me and that it was all for my own good and other accepted bromides, and always with the admonition that there was only one Book in which there was to be found everything appropriate to a young girl's enlightenment.

There was no pain involved in these punishments. Only the humiliation of having my bloomers revealed to Mr. Theophilus Compton and to my parents who always sat through these executions, my mother about to cry and my father nodding his approval that such an august hand should be applied to my posterior.

It would have been better, I think, if there had been pain. But each time, the palm of Mr. Theophilus Compton did not punish so much as caress. At the time, I thought it strange. Now I understand it.

The spankings ceased when I was nine years of age. By then I had read a great many of the books that were condemning me to Hell, by the lights of my father and his mortuary mogul, which provided me with a delightfully secret kind of rebellion. But the spankings did not cease because I had forsaken my lovely printed words. They ceased because Mr. Theophilus Compton died of a stroke.

If, as he had always said, everything was preordained, the schedule for his demise was well conceived. It occurred as he was in the pulpit denouncing a government without Christ that had allowed too soon the end of federal troops occupying the South.

This having been a day that I was confined to my bed at home with a rather mild case of scarlet fever, I was not in the church when the event later described as catastrophic occurred. It was said about Fitchburg afterward that Mr. Theophilus Compton's face turned a livid shade of purple and that he staggered toward his right hand and fell into a group of Puritan ministers who had come to hear his preachings. His words had by then become famous throughout the state, giving the sense of a spiritual power strong enough to detach the head of an English monarch simply because he had dared to take Jesus in some direction other than that in which Cromwell's New Model Army took Him.

When my mother informed me that Mr. Theophilus Compton had gone to his reward, I felt so much better that I asked for a poached egg and a kipper.

My father embalmed Mr. Theophilus Compton, which I suspect he always supposed was the height of his earthly mission.

And yet this man did more for me than my own father had ever done. First, he showed me the horrors of intolerance. Second, in his will he left me two thousand dollars in trust, 2 percent interest compounded annually, at which time I began to appreciate the appeal of a child's upturned bottom to an old, insecure, starved ogre who had never come to terms with the usual normal relationships between men and women and had his only pleasure, on this earth, with fantasies connected with spankings that were not spankings at all.

My majority came at eighteen, and the nine years after the death of my benefactor did not go quickly. But go they did. And on reaching the required age, on the very day, I packed a wicker suitcase, dressed in my best Sunday frock, because it was spring-time, went to the bank to take out my money, and took a steam train to Boston, where I had already arranged by correspondence a place in Mrs. Victoria Willings's boarding school for young ladies.

That day at the bank, a very improper vice-president, who appeared to be impressed with my striking appearance, told me whence the Compton money had originally come. The triangular trade. Sugarcane, rum, and African slaves. For in that time after the Portuguese and the Dutch and the English had stopped dealing in black flesh from the Ivory Coast, naturally American ship-owners had taken it up full scale.

The Comptons had been one of those. So there I was, in Mrs. Victoria Willings's boarding school for ladies, spending some of the money that had come down to me, all of it started not five blocks away on the docks of Charles River.

But regardless of how it originated, I did not hesitate to spend it thus. In fact, it rather amused me. I could now pursue the study of Greek and Latin and needlework, all of which had been on the list of mortal sins in my father's household.

As it developed, the Greek and Latin and needlework of Mrs. Victoria Willings's boarding school for young ladies soon lost all their charm. Not from any fault of the Greeks or the Romans or the colorful thread. But because I found something for which it seemed I had been waiting all my life. I met Clarissa Harlowe Barton.

Clara Barton was everything my mother had not been. She was lovely of face and with deep lights in her eyes that shone when her lips turned up in the famous smile. Her hair was gray, parted in the middle and drawn back to a plaited bun behind most delicate ears. She was hardly any taller than I, yet there was in her carriage the hint of a stubborn will and determination not to be trifled with, even by those in the offices of the mighty.

The day she came to visit her old friend Victoria Willings, she had already founded the American National Red Cross and was its president. Everyone had heard of her and the Red Cross, supplying emergency needs to persons caught in terrible disasters and going to battlefields all over the world to assist the various medical departments and chaplains in the physical and spiritual care of soldiers. Already she was nationally famous for being able to raise money simply by virtue of her quiet speeches, turning it to use in helping those unfortunates who were not being helped with taxes levied by our government.

She and Mrs. Victoria Willings had lived in Oxford, Massachusetts, together. At the close of her visit she listened attentively to my expressions of admiration for her work. And apparently seeing my intense desire to join in such an endeavor, she accepted me as one of her assistants.

As a result, I saw many wonderful and terrible things. Including Cuba.

CHAPTER 2

THE war with Spain began for Carlina Newton on the night of April 22, 1898. A Friday. In the outer lobby of the Knickerbocker Theater in the city of New York.

She and her mentor Clara Barton were making their slow way from the doors of the auditorium to the street, less encumbered than most of the ladies here were with their rather distinct bustles—these two in jackets and coats of a neutral gray with severe lines, in keeping with their calling of service to the needy. At least, that's how it was explained by Clara Barton.

Their hats were plain as well, compared to the high crowns and feathers and flowers and colors of other women's. Nor were their waists pinched to waspish dimensions so popular then, accenting a V of white lace at the neck showing off to good effect the breasts, whether prominent or only average.

The gentlemen, of course, were in monotonous black and white, with bow ties, and now were drawing high silk hats from the cloakroom and starting up large cigars, which had already begun to fill the high arched lobby with a pale blue smoke that seemed to lift like clouds and form around the heads of fake marble statues depicting Greek gods, set sturdily into their niches.

They had just seen a play called *The Bride Elect*. It was a very mediocre effort, not in the same class at all with performances some of these same theatergoers had seen when Edwin Booth was still alive. But this was a different age and had a different feeling. And on this night, when the players stood to the footlights and sang a song called "Unchain the Dogs of War" the reaction had been what it had always been since the battleship *Maine* had blown up in Havana harbor.

As though stung by a patriotic shock of electricity, the audience had stood up and cheered.

They had done that since February, when Mr. Hearst and Mr. Pulitzer in their newspapers had displayed graphic drawings illustrating exactly how the dastardly Spaniards had done the deed. Neither Mr. Hearst nor Mr. Pulitzer had explained in their columns why the Spaniards would do such a thing, Madrid having been all along scrambling about to find some way of avoiding any kind of serious shooting.

Nonetheless. *The Bride Elect* had become Broadway's most popular presentation because of that song. And so tickets were selling with no apologies to Mr. William Shakespeare's *Julius Caesar*.

And Carlina Newton had found herself caught up in the frenzy, despite her best efforts to avoid it. And had stood with all the others to cheer when the flaming faces just behind the footlights had chorused out the call to combat. Now, moving across the lobby, she was more than a little embarrassed.

But as she moved out through this glaring light with all the people, escaped from the darkness of the theater, where one can be caught up in dream-world emotions, she began to feel much better. And began to hear the scattered conversation, making her swell with pride that here she was, amongst all these wonderful people.

"There's Mr. John Jacob Astor. He's funding an entire artillery battery, my dear, including the ammunition!"

"Was it young Rothschild in that box to stage left?"

"I saw Senator Lodge tonight. I swear I saw Senator Lodge."

"Senator Lodge would not be caught dead in New York at night."

"It was Senator Lodge. I know it."

"Get me some of those peppermint candies."

"My dear, your gardenia is turning brown. Throw it off in the corner there."

"Did you hear what William Jennings Bryan said today? It was printed in the *World*."

"I do not care a damn what William Jennings Bryan says."

"Clarence, your language, please. It *was* printed, what he said."

"To hell with William Jennings Bryan!"

"Where should we go to eat? I understand Delmonico's has a divine lamb pie."

"To hell with Delmonico's, too. We're going to Ned Stokes's old place, where I can get a decent drink and some oysters."

"In April?"

"All right, then. Poached salmon."

There appeared before Clara Barton a tall, extremely handsome man, perhaps the most handsome man Carlina Newton had ever seen. He was in the uniform of an army general officer, blue with gold braid here and there at appropriate places. He bent to Miss Barton's hand and smiled, showing teeth arranged on line but somehow suggesting that behind these there were more, in column, in case they might be needed as a reserve.

"Aw, Miss Barton," he said. "I had come to New York on business and was persuaded to attend this production without ever suspecting that I might have this pleasure."

"Thank you, General," she said.

"So wonderful to see you again."

"Thank you. I suppose that now you are in high spirits because you can use some of your soldiers against a real army instead of those naked savages in the West."

"Oh yes," the general said, his smile growing even larger. "Only today, the navy has reported that they have their blockade in place, and it means war, of course."

"Of course." Clara Barton saw the direction of his glance and turned toward Carlina Newton. "Sir, may I present my assistant,

Miss Carlina Newton of Massachusetts. My dear, this is Nelson Miles, Commanding General of the United States Army."

She hardly knew what she said. She hardly knew where she was as the commanding general took her hand and bent to it.

"I am most charmed," he said. But immediately turned back to Clara Barton. "We will be needing your services, you know. I wouldn't say this to one of the newspaper reporters who are always lurking about, but there are certain areas in which we are woefully inadequate. And one of those is medical and general services."

"My dear general," Clara Barton said, patting his hand as though he were a naughty grandchild, "your army is woefully inadequate in all respects. It is my understanding that there are some eighty thousand Spanish soldiers in Cuba. And by last report, our own army numbers totally in the area of thirty thousand."

Nelson laughed. "I wish I had you on my intelligence staff."

Carlina Newton could not help but hear a lady standing nearby say, "Is that Phil Sheridan?"

"My God, Sheridan is dead. Come on. Come on, I'm hungry!"

"We will have an expeditionary force in that island within a short time," General Miles was saying. "It is no secret."

"I suppose so," Clara Barton said. Who had seen the Civil War. Who had seen the Franco-Prussian War. Who had seen many things. "But General, other than yourself and a very few others, we do not have a single officer on our rolls who has ever seen a formation any larger than a regiment. And my dear Nelson," patting his arm again. "Not many have seen even a regiment."

"I know," General Miles said, and he was no longer smiling. "But our national spirit will prevail, as it always has."

"Yes," Clara Barton said. "To whatever end."

"We will see you, then," General Miles said, and now it was he patting her arm. And he smiled and nodded.

"We will see you."

The General bowed slightly, only slightly as befitted the nation's top soldier, and smiled again.

"Miss Barton. Miss Newton," and turned and moved off through the throng, somehow quickly, somehow without pushing aside those who stared at him, somehow in a whiff of blue uniform and gold braid, and somehow completely detached from the small cheer from the theatergoers who suddenly grew and followed as they recognized him.

There was a soft spring breeze outside, coming along the canyon shafts of New York City, and it took away the smell and the violence of cigar smoke. Both women breathed deeply before moving to one of the hansom cabs waiting at the curb. In line, one horse drawing each, one cabby with his top hat driving each.

"It was so exciting," Carlina Newton said as they settled onto the leather seats of the cab.

"Yes, wasn't it," Clara Barton said and looked out at the flame of light slashing down over the people still coming from the theater. Carlina thought she looked so old in that light. And as they drew away from the curb she could hear the sound of the horse's hooves on the pavement, and still Clara Barton stared out the side of the hansom, serious, lips set.

It came to Carlina Bessaford Newton in that moment that this woman beside her was very old. It had never occurred to her before, even though she had known from the time they first met that Clara Barton, the angel of the Red Cross, was coming close to eighty.

"Are you tired?" Carlina asked, laying a hand on those delicate gloved hands of Clara Barton.

"Moderately. But much depressed."

Then she turned and smiled and took Carlina's hand in both of hers.

"Just a passing melancholy, my dear. Floods and famines and tornadoes. And now the worst of all natural disasters."

"The war?"

"Of course. Can't we call it a natural disaster? It comes so constantly."

She turned away as their cab clattered into Twenty-fourth Street and on toward their hotel.

"Now, we must continue to see to things," she said and the tone of her voice was different. "The supplies. You will find in this work, my dear, that you are constantly worried with supplies. Coffee, laudanum, bandages."

"Yes, ma'am."

"They are all terrible things." She suddenly laughed. "Well, not the coffee. Except in this use."

And then she was watching the lights along the street passing as the horse ahead beat his steel hooves on the street.

"Terrible things," Clara Barton said almost to herself. "Terrible things. You'll see. I'm afraid soon, you'll see."

It made a little chill pass up the graceful back of Carlina Bessaford Newton. Here was she, in a cab with the world renowned Clara Barton. A woman who had been to Cuba now many times, helping the poor and sick in Havana and the countryside beyond. A woman who had actually dined as the guest of Captain Charles Sigsbee on the battleship *Maine* the very night before it had exploded in flame and smoke. A woman who had only recently obtained the charter ship *State of Texas* for use by the Red Cross.

And now I, Carlina Bessaford Newton, am a part of this great enterprise, she thought. Soon powerful men like General Nelson Miles will pause to converse with me as I pass through the lobbies of grand theaters and hotels. And famous people will stare at me and say, There is Carlina Bessaford Newton, world renowned, of the Red Cross.

Dylan ap Rhys ap Llewellyn

Even now, these many years gone by, I can see the spearheads gleaming. Just as in the old battle hymn. But there was no singing in my throat then, for dry it was as last week's spit. Plus mouth and tongue besides. Watching the day's light go out as the sun disappeared beyond the barren ridges of Natal, there was barely time to catch a breath free of powder smoke, much less realize, my comrades and me, that the killing had only just begun.

A fight at night is both good and bad. Good because many brutal horrors are mercifully hid. But bad because the smell of it is there and the sudden flash of muzzle blasts that sears the black with portraits of red and blue-white figures, all to punctuate the sounds of agony and rage coming from open mouths in faces seen an instant and then gone. The young soldier always selects daylight for his fighting, and the sight of horrors be damned. But the young soldier never has his choice.

There was me, a young soldier. Fresh and proud and standing with those other men of the Second Battalion, Twenty-fourth Infantry Regiment, a Welsh formation as the record puts it. And disappointed, only a company of us, having watched the rest of the regiment cross over the Buffalo River and strike out into Zululand. And us to play housemaid to a few hospital wounded and sick and maintain a small supply depot and damned small glory in any of that. Disgusted to see our mates off into the hills east of the river, their red coats and beehive khaki helmets bobbing out of sight toward some romantic place to fight the childlike savages who carried long cowhide shields and a short stabbing lance with a blade full one meter long.

It was bitch and carp, like good soldiers do everywhere, bitch and carp and complain when they're left behind on that treeless knoll above the crossing of the Buffalo. Other companies of the regiment on to find adventure and a lark against ignorant niggers, artillery and all, and us only to collect dust in the cracks of our arses and nothing more exciting than scratching at the bites of unfamiliar bugs who took delight in chewing on our exposed European flesh.

Some lark those others had! Even with their artillery. Because hardly out of sight and the entire regiment and others slaughtered man for man at a place that was no place at all but only a long, ugly ridge called Isandhlwana.

And then we had our own fill of Zulus. Abrupt and headlong they came. Us about one hundred thirty men, rank and file and a company commander who was hard of hearing. And the black ones about four thousand, give or take a few.

Oh, in later times, to grandchildren and pub keepers and various whores, the stories we told were grand. But in that afternoon and night, there was little grand about the fear, with painted faces coming closer in their thousands and the stink of burning thatch and of human meat as well, and the roll underfoot of empty brass cartridge cases, and the constant volley fire, and the stabbing, slashing, cutting with bayonet, them close enough to smell their sweat. What a man needed now and again was a leisurely relief of bladder but most of that had to be done right in the trousers.

And the kick of those old Martini rifles so fierce that by the time the dead were stacked like mealie bags before us and the little hospital had burned down to red embers, and by the time the sun came up after the heaving, grunting night, after all of that, those old Martinis, barrels too hot to touch, had done their work on our shoulders, the butts slamming back so often and so hard that the blood ran down into our armpits as freely as it did from the gaping holes we had put in the breasts of the charging Zulus.

A long time ago it was. In South Africa. Me a boy of sixteen and serving good Queen Vic, and all these years since wondering

[33]

why, and my old father turning in his grave that a good Welsh lad would go off in the blue trousers of the goddamned English army.

But at least, I've always said, no better place to do such things than that desolate little outpost just across the river from Zululand, with seldom a tree in sight but a hell's pot full of niggers trying to stick their blades into my gut.

It was there that I learned what guts are all about. Not the real kind, slimy and gray that spill out with the proper thrust of a Zulu assegai and leave an outhouse smell, but the kind of spirit. Of courage. It was seen there all about me, and not only beneath red tunics. But beneath the naked, glistening black skins protected only by those cowhide shields as the warriors came and came and came against us, only a few with firearms, and all of them hungry to make it a close combat. Only with iron blades. But came, nonetheless, against the hail of .45-caliber lead slugs that put them down and racked them up like fence posts just sawed off and lying askew in the dawn before proper stacking.

And me there, sixteen years of age.

Well, sixteen is a time of childhood memories, is it not? Of walking into countryside with schoolmaster to collect the blooms and butterflies. Of throwing stones into the next pasture. Of good Welsh leek soup in the warm kitchen of a grandmother's cottage. Of stolen kisses and squealing rapture. Sixteen.

No, sixteen in the year 1879 was long past childish things for some of us.

And so did I come of age. My hands blistered from the heat of rifle barrel. In my nose the stench of caking blood syrup-spread across the sand. Open eyes, dead and opaque like marbles just before the muzzle of my weapon. Ears ringing from the crash of gunfire. Tongue thick with the taste of black powder.

So did I come to manhood at a place called Rorke's Drift. And have never yet recovered from it.

CHAPTER 3

IT was a long way from Swansea to Tampa. And although both were near the sea, all else about them was so different as to defy comparison. Yet there he was, Dylan Price, who had come originally from the Welsh city of copper smelting to this west Florida place that could hardly be called a city at all, having as it did in that year of 1898 one major structure of any consequence.

A multistoried resort hotel, erected upon the sand. And now each of its levels occupied by the American military hierarchy that would orchestrate the invasion of Cuba. Like ants in a layer cake preparing to assault the jelly on an adjoining plate.

At least, that was the planned program, although planning had hardly anything to do with it. Dylan Price, seeing things only from the perspective of a corporal in the Thirty-seventh Infantry Regiment of the United States Army, much like viewing the scene through the wrong end of a pair of binoculars, doubted that this army of which he was now a part could be successfully moved the short distance from Tampa down to the single wharf, much less launched across the water against a force of Spaniards he suspected were a hell of a lot better at this war business than any of the flag-waving, motto-shouting, ill-equipped Yankees gave them credit for.

And so in that sweltering spring, Dylan Price and his regular army comrades sat in the sun, picking sand fleas from their hair and wiping dust out of their new Swedish magazine rifles, and watching with absolute astonishment the comedy of newly called out National Guard and militia volunteers arriving like drunken yokels for a public hanging. Their officers apparently had learned their lessons about military sanitation by watching cows defecating at random in a field. And had learned no lesson at all in how to provide drinking water, hot food, medical attention, training, or discipline for their so-called troops.

In consequence of which the units already established on the sand around the Plant Hotel staked out their perimeters as though they were old Norman fiefs to be defended at all costs. Which was done with fists and army boot as the ill-equipped, ill-uniformed, ill-weaponed civilian soldiers began to arrive. So the mob, gurgling with enthusiasm for starting the job of killing Spaniards, who after all had blown up the battleship *Maine*, drew off to their own stinking places. Some with bloody noses, shouting insults having to do with ass kissing and such things as is common among soldiers' salutations to one another, with the regulars replying that if they come back they might just likely be met with naked bayonets.

"No mind the poor wretches," said Dylan Price to his squad of men. "If they desire to shit in their own nests, then who are we to object. But none of that we will have here on our own wee patch of sand!"

And all the soldiers of his squad agreed and grinned and hoped the newly recruited featherheads would come back again so another whack could be taken at them.

Not that many of Dylan Price's squad could understand his words completely, because they were a Swede and three Germans and a Scots Irish Presbyterian, so he claimed, and a Bulgarian. All of which had been in the United States of America only long enough to have enlisted in the army and been trained in its various drills and none of whom could be called completely conversant with the language except for the Ulster Scot, and he with a strange concept of what English words meant. But if they did not understand the words, they certainly could appreciate the meaning, and so they grinned when Dylan Price spoke to them, and hoped the featherheads would come back. For another whack.

They had, all of them, been soldiers long enough to know how to lace their leggings. Which it was obvious those intruders on their soil had not.

So the army collected about the Plant Hotel, in little plots like the breeding circles of East Africa cobs, the militia in a wild, disorganized hodgepodge, the regulars with their shelter tents laid in long lines with company guidons at the end of each row, staffs set into the sand and colors fluttering in the breeze that came always from the Gulf of Mexico so close by.

And there, too, canvas flies stretched round the latrines to allow the men to take a chance at pissing and other things, unobserved by the growing number of ladies who were appearing on the verandas of the Plant Hotel among the officers, who seemed to make preparations for the coming campaign primarily by reclining in large wicker chairs, arguing about whose commanding office ranked highest, and drinking Cuba Libre highballs, named in honor of their having come to free oppressed peoples from the yoke of Madrid and made with Jamaica rum and a mixture of kola nut juice and the squeezings of lemons or limes or anything else that came handy. Sometimes, even medical alcohol.

Each day it was a new excitement for Dylan Price and his grinning regulars, to hear the various staffs, and there must have been twenty of them and not one a real staff at all, shouting at one another about who would lead the expedition.

"Today it's Colonel Brotmorton," Private Swenson said. "He just made general."

"No," said Dylan Price. "It's already Colonel Jennings. He was promoted, too. Three minutes ahead of this other one."

Which provided some relief from the constant attack of sand fleas. And the constant attention to keeping grit out of the Swedish rifle bolts. And the constant vigil against the invasion of their territory by one of the drunken militia.

Sometimes late at night, when the surrounding camps were finally quiet and there was only the racket of merriment and the glare of light from various levels of the Plant Hotel, Dylan Price walked down toward the shore. To smell the sea air. To hear the ocean birds that seemed here always to be circling and calling, even after darkness had long fallen. Or perhaps to them, he thought, darkness has not yet fallen, with all those lighted windows stacked one on the other at the Plant Hotel and officers proclaiming their own choice for the commanding general, themselves sounding like sea birds, squalling over the remains of some dead and rotting whale washed up on the beach.

Somehow then, with the night stars above and the feel of salt air on his face, it reminded him of his father. And it made him wonder why, because he and his father had never stood beside any sea, nor heard birds calling. But somehow, the night breeze recalled to his mind a face he had almost lost to memory it had been so long since he had seen it. So long since he had heard the great baritone note that issued from the mouth along with a spray of good stout ale and gin, perhaps, and maybe a little raw leek.

Yes, Dylan Price thought at such times, this is a long way from Swansea and South Africa and Egypt and India, too. And all the other places that he'd been with the British army.

It was all the same to him, now a man of thirty-five years, tough muscled and hard boned and face brown and lined as old leather left too long in the sun, which his face had been. He was tall and long-armed and pale of hair and eye, in the usual manner of Celts from northern Wales.

But why from Swansea, if Dylan Price from northern Wales? Because of that old man. Because of Dylan Price's father, who took much of his thought now. They had come, this family, from Denbigh but somehow the old man saw his fortune to the south and so moved a few miles closer to the Bristol Channel with each birth of a new son that his wife, Helen, gave him.

And she gave him nine.

Dylan Price was the last and at birth full thirty years younger than his oldest brother. By then, by the time Dylan Price arrived and killed his mother, Helen, in the coming, they were in Swansea, all the brothers and the old man doing smelter work.

The only mothers Dylan Price had ever known were that long succession of women hired to keep him and their mud-walled hut on the edge of Swansea's rabble town, most of them Irish, their own husbands there for working in the tin and copper and hated by the Welsh because they would work for less. And many a cuff he got with hard hand about the ears and many an arm he had left the imprint of his teeth in and many a night he had heard the old man huffing and puffing in bed with the housekeeper, whom Dylan Price knew was supposed to have returned to her own shack and husband long before.

That old father, Dylan Price thought. He never thought "Da" as some Welsh did when their memories lingered over sires. That old father! Rhys ap Llewellyn. What a great boasting, whiskey soaked son of a bitch who maybe knew more Welsh history than any don at Cambridge. He'd had only a smatter of literacy. But it didn't matter. He traced his genealogy back to that Welsh hero who had won a great battle at a place called Welshpool in the eleventh century, before the Norman Conquest.

And the old man, by the by, always said the Normans were a lot better than those goddamned Lost-in-the-Soul Saxons, which is how he always referred to the English.

Not that the old man would have known a Norman or Saxon if one had fallen into his soup. That is to say, even if there was such a thing as a Norman or a Saxon by the time the old man lived in the nineteenth century. But that didn't matter, either.

Old Celtic Welsh, he claimed himself to be. And so hung onto his sons that "ap" business in the name, meaning "son of." Not son of a bitch, as he often called them to their faces. But son of the father. So his ninth son was christened in a Swansea chapel, Methodist it was, as Dylan ap Rhys ap Llewellyn. And the old man would have been happy to attach another dozen ap some-thing-or-others had he been able to recall any more good Welsh names, but at the time he could not because he was too drunk to understand where he was or what he was doing.

In his early years, Swansea was the only world Dylan Price knew. And he often wondered why people spoke of hell when they were already living right in the center of it. At least, he reckoned, nothing could be worse than this. It was a cesspool. The River Tawe was dead, a ribbon of sludge, its banks without grass or any green and no trees and no flower and no hedge. It was gray and metallic, like copper ore. And no fish swam there. And above, in the sky colored green and thick, no bird had the courage to fly through. The smokestacks of the smelters lifted their thick fingers of soot each hour of each day and at night the furnaces, throbbing red, reflected their garish color against the low, artificial clouds, and along the quays the ships stood, filling with copper and tinplate and their sailors from every point of the globe roamed the streets near the docks, drunk and puking and looking for tattoo artists and women and the women they found there were as tough and as hard and as metallic as everything else about the city. And the whole of it stinking of sulfur and other chemicals nobody could yet even identify.

And at sixteen, himself already working beside his brothers in the mills, Dylan ap Rhys ap Llewellyn broke and ran. He ran east to Cardiff and there enlisted in one of the queen's regiments of Welsh infantry, the Twenty-fourth. Into the army of his father's hated Lost-in-the-Soul Saxons. Red coat and blue trousers, and off at once to South Africa. And after that, many other trips too, expenses paid by the government of Queen Victoria, but never one anywhere that measured up to Rorke's Drift.

"Aw, this night," Dylan Price said aloud, standing in the sand and looking westward, where he knew somewhere in the dark lay the Gulf of Mexico. He could smell Yucatán, he thought. And he knew that he heard the whistle of ships and thought how lovely it would be to lie on one of those ships, in a nice metal bunk, porthole open to the wind, and feel the heave and surge of the water underneath, and sleep with no scent of land anywhere about. And with that thought suggested to himself that maybe in the long lost Welsh past his old father had neglected to mention that he had Norse blood in his veins from one of those many Viking raids just after the Romans had come.

Then he had to laugh at such a thought. His old father? Admit a drop of blood from Denmark? Not even had there been forty generations of Danes standing before the dragonhead bow of their warships and glaring down. Not that old man! Not that old man, Dylan Price thought.

"But there is a certain pull about the sea," he said aloud and turned to move back along the sand.

And a pull about other things. Like an army. By the time Dylan ap Rhys ap Llewellyn had served his queen for fifteen years, and had survived his few scuffles with the British army's system of courts-martial for various minor offenses, such as being drunk in quarters and making indecent proposals to the maiden aunt of a customs official in Cairo, it was time to run again. This time, to America.

By then, he had no idea what had ever happened to his brothers or that old man. Throughout his service, he had never once written a letter. Nor ever once received one. He was one of those called by his officers a hardcase. He asked nothing. He gave nothing. He soldiered.

He had long since changed his name, of course. Dylan ap Rhys ap Llewellyn was not a name the Lost-in-the-Soul Saxons could spell, pronounce, or understand. And the Americans sure as hell couldn't. So it had become Dylan Price. A small concession, because that Rhys of the old man was there hidden, only spelled a little differently and with at least the back end of the "son of" tacked onto the front.

On the record of immigrants kept in the place called Ellis Island in the harbor of New York, there is an entry. It states, much like an auction notation for cattle, that one Welsh male, aged thirty-one, did come and was found to have no disease or other physical defect that might prohibit him from becoming, in time, a citizen of the United States of America.

And so it is assumed that Dylan Price entered upon the nation where the streets were paved with gold.

For Dylan Price, at least, they were not paved with gold. Rather with horse dung. Because he earned his first dollar in the borough of Manhattan working with a street cleaning gang. The other sweepers were mostly half his age and all Irish. Which set not too well with Dylan Price. It lasted a month, until the foreman, also Irish, remarked on the natural Welsh deviate nature, plus the fact that all those who had served in the British army were dyed-in-the-wool sons of bitches and homosexuals besides for standing against the freedom of Ireland. The deviate business and the sons of bitches part Dylan Price could abide. But the other thing he could not and therefore broke the foreman's jaw with the leading edge of a garbage can lid. And then ran for his life up Second Avenue.

He was pursued by all the sweeping Irish children. It was not a very long race. Two of the lads caught Dylan Price at the corner of East Fourteenth Street. There were residents of Stuyvesant Square out on their daily stroll who ever afterward called that corner the Place of Irish Massacre. Although no one was actually killed.

So away again. He didn't like the city anyway, that small flat on the hell's tip of Manhattan, shared with a one-armed poet from Serbia or some such place and a deaf-mute pencil peddler who, once off the sidewalks, talked faster and louder than the prime minister of England. Dylan Price was disgusted with the whole business and so began to walk north. It took a long time just to get clear of the city of New York.

He ended at Plattsburg. Or perhaps began. For there he went back to the only thing he knew. He enlisted in the army.

The army then was not much army. A few thousand made up the whole duty roster, which suited Dylan Price because he could show his knowledge of weapons and compass and field fortifications and first aid to wounded with only a small show of what he really knew, after all those years serving Her Majesty.

But despite all his best efforts, he attained the rank of corporal squad leader in December 1896. And that's what he was a year later when the Hearst and Pulitzer newspapers and a lot of saber shaking politicians like Theodore Roosevelt started branding the Spanish colony of Cuba a boil on the ass of the Monroe Doctrine that required lancing and Mr. Roosevelt claiming that he should wield the lance.

At that time, Dylan Price said what the hell. He had seen his share of political scream and bellow and politicians lusting for cavalry charges, them at the head. But even as he was saying to himself what the hell, he was saying to his squad they had best prepare themselves to go poach some Spaniards because whether they wanted to or not, that's what they'd be doing in short order.

He'd read most of the stories in the newspapers. About the cruel Spaniards. About their stripping ladies down past their undies to search them. Dylan Price wasn't sure what it was these atrocious Spaniards were searching for, but he enjoyed the picture of that naked lady done by some artist named Remington.

Maybe Dylan Price believed all the stories. A lot of people did.

From those same newspapers, he was aware that Cuba had been of interest to a lot of politicians and do-gooders and naval officers beginning with the close of the American Civil War.

None of this, fact or fiction, interested him too much, but adding it all together surely indicated that it was only a matter of time before the Yankees would thrust themselves into the situation with battleships and Gatling guns. That single fact was all that interested Dylan Price. Because when it happened it meant he would be required to do the job for which he was being paid and clothed and fed. The Great-Scheme-of-Things reasons for his having to shoot at various people had never seemed worth a second thought. Not in Natal. Not in the Sudan. Not in India. And not now.

Insofar as causes were concerned, he viewed it all dispassionately, almost with boredom. If you were a soldier, you marched against those the powers-that-be told you to march against. Whether you went in red tunic and beehive helmet and carrying a single shot rifle to test your marksmanship against naked savages with shields and spears, or whether it was khaki jacket and felt campaign hat and carrying a repeating rifle to shoot at soldiers who carried repeating rifles, too, it was all the same.

Well, when he thought about it, which wasn't very often, there was a difference now. So far as he knew, all those former enemies of the British army he had faced had been enemies for the first time. But these Spaniards were descendants of men who had sailed the Armada against old Queen Bess, a Tudor and part Welsh by blood, by God, and had their Catholic asses blown to bits by good British gunnery.

[43]

He was aware of such things not from reading newspapers but because of that old drunken father in Wales.

Of course, there's another difference now, he thought. Twenty years ago I was in a different army. If you can call this undisciplined mob we've got here an army.

He was not unhappy with his lot. In fact, he rather gloried in it because he had always been a soldier and he was Welsh besides and he was good at being both. He knew what it meant.

Thanks to that cantankerous old man who always found time after coming home each night filthy and smelling of smelter grime to sit his youngest son down at table before the hired lady of the house set out the boiled potatoes and mutton and before any grace was said, and there in the soot-encrusted hut explain the splendor of his blood.

Of course, all of this was liberally laced with stories from the Bible, the version from King James, who, as the old man explained, was not a Welshman but had at least ascended to the throne because a good Welshwoman had said he should, she being old Queen Elizabeth. And once in that seat he had commissioned the scholars who dug into Hebrew and Greek and Latin writings to come up with a Book the common people could read in the language of the English. Whom that same old cantankerous man despised as Lost-in-the-Soul Saxons but nonetheless gave grudging credit for being able to spread their language around, even in Wales, and providing a Bible that even people like himself, a Nonconformist Methodist who knew all of the great hymns of William Williams by heart, could read. Except that the old man had never learned too much about reading.

All that part was too contradictory and confusing to figure out, and Dylan Price never did. He was just grateful that he'd had the lessons. It gave a man something to think about when the last drop of thick beer was gone from the cup and the woman of the evening was sleeping and the winter wind was howling outside the window making the black night alive with whatever voices a man might want to imagine.

Sometimes the old man's lessons came at uncomfortable times.

He would come in late, a staggering, belching Rhys ap Llewellyn, and waken his youngest son and sit on the edge of his son's bed in the darkness and spray the words out with whiskey scented breath. And tell of the English kings who had always considered Wales the mother of British infantry, an infantry so instrumental after all, in establishing and maintaining the greatest empire since the Romans.

And the lad Dylan would lie shivering, not from the cold but from the words. The words of empire and even before that, a long time before that. During the Hundred Years' War. When the English army was across the channel fighting the arrogant French, who were the terror of two continents in their armor and riding their massive, battle-trained horses. Vicious, brutal men, Norman knights who had trained from childhood for war and nothing else. And then at places called Poitiers and Agincourt, names that still made chills go up Dylan Price's back, those haughty horseback knights were defeated. By lowly men on foot.

Not just defeated. Ravaged. Arrows pinning them inside their shining armor like worms in metal cocoons. By Welsh longbow-men.

Thanks to that old man, Dylan Price knew all of this. And it was a source of fierce yet secret pride that he was latest in that long line of soldiers whose lineage could be drawn all the way back to the time when even the Roman legions avoided the mountains of Wales because it was one hell of a lot easier to ignore the forbidding mists than to face the howling, screaming, impetuous Celts who lived there.

That's why Dylan Price loved the memory of that old man, even though the father had talked and never done, had worshiped valor from afar, worshiped it as much, maybe, as he did the idea of Jesus Christ.

But maybe, Dylan Price always thought, understood and even tasted the same courage that Christ had shown, in some smaller way. Never involved in battle yet each day of his inexorable march toward his own Golgotha in the smelters of Swansea a horror he saw but could never avoid.

Maybe, thought Dylan Price, an even greater courage than facing something simple like the Zulu assegai or the Mauser rifles of the Spaniards.

And so he marveled at that old man because the battles he had fought were more complex, less ephemeral. Not flashing moments, but constant, minute by minute throughout his life.

Well, Dylan Price had never gone back, after running that first time, never gone back to tell the old man what those stories had come to mean. And assumed, after the years had gone down, that the old man was dead, and the brothers, too. Dead of the lead poisoning or the fiery accident in the mill or from too much booze in the grogshops along the Tawe. Dylan Price wasn't too proud of the fact that he didn't know, so he tried not thinking of it. He tried thinking that somehow the old man must know that he, Dylan ap Rhys ap Llewellyn, unlike his grime coated brothers, had followed in those ancient footmarks of Owain and the primitive Llewellyn and all the others who had been warriors in a time before the atmosphere in so many places had turned puke green with the modern age of coal and steel.

Standing in that Tampa sand, late at night, looking through the darkness toward the place where he knew the water was, Dylan Price felt that maybe this Cuba thing was special. Because now, after all the centuries, he would be called against the Spaniards, the same Spaniards who had tried to crush the Virgin Queen. A Tudor. A Welsh.

He rubbed his arm where the blue tattoo of a flying dove spread its wings through the stiff blond hair. A little memento of Liverpool from one of those rare instances when his regiment was on home leave in Britain, and him more than a little drunk that night. And although the artwork had been done these many years ago, it still itched from time to time.

His other tattoo never itched. It was on his backside, and he'd had it etched in New Delhi. It portrayed, in various colors, a hound chasing a rabbit into a hole. The hole being, as Dylan ap Rhys ap Llewellyn characterized it, a true Welsh butt pucker. His own!

And then turned back toward his sandy bivouac and on the

way, his boots sinking with each step into the grit, was stopped only once. By a militia sentry. Whereupon Dylan Price displayed a small portion of the lewd and base language he had learned from fifteen years in the British army, all of Anglo-Saxon origin and mostly four-letter, in telling the featherhead civilian trying to hold his rifle at high port exactly where said rifle might be placed in the sentry's quivering anatomy.

And then on to sleep for what was left of the night with the sand fleas whispering in his ears, reminding him of the breezes off the Nile and the trumpeting of elephants working in the teak and the gentle clatter of Zulu shields against the dry grass of Natal, coming always closer, closer.

Major General William R. Shafter

Many vicious, vindictive, malicious, malodorous lies are written about me. One would suppose from such rantings that I am among the despicable multitude of men who hope that a bloodless little war is an appropriate stepping stone to high public office.

Such men deserve whatever they get for two reasons. First, anyone who would trade casualties for votes is beneath contempt. Second, these fools are so ignorant they think there will not *be* any casualties. For the sweet sake of Christ, don't they know the Mausers of those Spaniards are better than any of the rifles supplied to our own troops?

Yet, many officers who have been bitten by the political bug and many who are not officers at all but simply armed civilians wearing a uniform only for this specific occasion have fared well at the hands of professional scribes.

This is patently unfair. It is, in fact, a gross load of bullshit! And a disgusting comment on the quality of writers who vilify me. For two reasons. First, everyone knows that I have never entertained any political ambition. Second, I am nothing more than a regular soldier trying to do a task set for me in an atmosphere alternating between that of the center ring of Mr. Barnum's circus and that of a public cockfight. In short, a goddamned wretched hash!

It is infuriating, especially under these conditions, to watch sensation seekers trying to make national heroes of the glory hunters. This assignment is difficult enough without having to perform it constantly enraged as I am by these scribbling bastards exalting stupid opportunists.

There are some critics among my army friends who say that I would be better off if I adopted a policy of forgive and forget, because it would help my blood pressure. To them I say, take forgive and forget and use it as an enema.

Chief among my detractors is the star in the crown of William Randolph Hearst and his abominable newspaper, the *New York Journal*. I will only identify him as R. H. D. He has published numerous distasteful items concerning me and I have information that he has confided to friends even more vile opinions reflecting on my professional competence, my personal character, and my private appreciation of good food and drink.

It is an honor to be so ruthlessly pilloried by such an obnoxious, self-centered, pompous, ill-mannered son of a bitch! It would be unbearable if such a creature as he found me admirable.

This R. H. D. is an egg sucker! He moves about in the company of men while inside his Manhattan-tailored trousers repose globes of orange marmalade which he mistakenly assumes are real gonads.

It is not his writing that irks me so much. It is having him hanging about, demanding special treatment. Because he is a Hearst man. I finally told him I did not care a damn who he was and that he would be treated like all the others in the howling pack of press hounds. It seemed to disturb him very much. It gave me great satisfaction.

How wonderful it would have been if R. H. D. had been posted to me in the 1870s on the Texas frontier, where my troops of the Twenty-fourth Infantry Regiment called me Pecos Bill and we rode our asses threadbare chasing Comanches and Lipans. There would have been no strutting in fine clothes then, no making smug remarks. No flash of manicured fingers. He would have ridden then, attached to an army mule or wild cavalry horse, eating dust and nothing else, thirsty and constantly afraid that in the very next moment a Comanche arrow shaft would drive into his belly. Afraid like the rest of us.

But we are not in west Texas now. And it is more than twenty years since I have led an Indian fighting squadron. My breathing now is sometimes labored and my knees give me great pain. And R. H. D. is a young man. Full of vinegar.

He said the War Department had to send out a special uniform made from a Sibley tent in order to clothe me.

He makes much of the fact that I once testified before a committee of the Congress to the effect that if Porfio Díaz didn't get his goddamned revolution in shape and close his border to the red hellions who used Mexico as a sanctuary, the United States should declare war on them.

And by God, we should have. But it never happened. The starched shirts in Washington never saw the atrocities.

Well, no matter, I suppose. In those young days, I led many raids into Mexico, Ord and Mackenzie and I, and we scalded a lot of hostiles and killed them on Mexican soil and, as I saw it, to hell with Porfio Díaz and his constant bellyaching that we had violated an international boundary.

Long past. Long past.

But there in Texas. My troops were magnificent. Most especially the Twenty-fourth Infantry and the Tenth Cavalry, both colored regiments. What soldiers! There are a few of them here now, but I wish I had twenty thousand of them. They were tough and disciplined and loyal and brave to the point of recklessness. With only ten battalions of those colored troops, and three weeks to explain to them what was required, I could go into Cuba and destroy the Spaniards before there was any chance of the yellow fever season catching us.

This is the kind of thing R. H. D. can never understand. I try not to think of it. I try not to think that he has said I am profane. God damn him! I try not to think of his writing that I am short-tempered. I try not to think of his remark that I am a harsh disciplinarian.

Living Jesus!

I wish I could be the kind of disciplinarian my rank and position would normally allow me to be, for if that were so, I would on this instant court-martial about forty National Guard officers for flagrant incompetence. But were I to do so, every governor in these United States would rise up indignantly against a regular army West Pointer trying to instruct their precious homegrown idiots in the arts of war.

Which is just an indication of the vast knowledge of these

governors, because I am not a West Point officer. I have risen to my present rank from a volunteer regiment during the Civil War, just like Nelson Miles. No comparisons should be drawn from this, except that neither of us is comparable to some of these goddamned volunteer so-called officers we have now.

Nelson is a good man. Of course, I have always suspected that Nelson watched Sam Grant go from soldier to White House and decided that he could do the same. There is no doubt that he is a better-looking man than Grant ever was, but he rides in this army under the stigma of having come to his first star only by virtue of Edward Ord being forced out of service to make a billet for him at the general level. Ord was my commander in Texas when we were chasing Indians into Mexico. Nelson is my commander now. They are both my friends. In the army, these kinds of things are hard to reconcile to anyone else.

Sheridan had a hand in forcing Ord's retirement, I think. Nelson was always one of Sheridan's protégés. Sheridan collected protégés like some men collect butterflies, and I think Nelson was one. George Custer was another, of course, but he didn't last too long after the Civil War. And now, Sheridan's dead. Little bastard!

But it all seems of another age. All those officers gone, retired or died or gone crazy. Pope and Augur and Grierson, Crook and Hancock and Gibbon and Mackenzie.

Good God! We could use some of that experience here. Someone who knows how to organize and supply an army.

Dear Jesus! Do you know why Alexander was great? Do you understand how Napoleon conquered? Why Lee finally failed? Logistics. Meat and goddamned potatoes and ammunition. And if someone gets it there, the soldiers will do the rest, but for sweet Jesus' sake, you've got to get it there. Soldiers will do almost anything you ask, but you've got to at least feed them. And keep ammunition in their belts, for God's sake.

Nobody around me understands that. They think we can talk the Spaniards to death. And even if that were not the goddamned case, there's nobody around who knows how to get a railroad car close to a combat unit, or even knows that it makes any difference that the damned boxcar is filled with ammunition. Nobody knows what a front is, what a base camp is, what an axis of communication is, what a main supply route is. Jesus Christ, nobody knows anything!

We could use someone at the War Department with sense in his head, too. When they called me there and promoted me to major general and said I would command the invasion force in Cuba, I awaited instructions. All I got was a hodgepodge of conflicting missions the majority of which appeared to be nothing more than supporting the goddamned navy, an organization presently led by a gaggle of white-uniformed snobs constantly arguing amongst themselves and each with a copy of Alfred Mahan's book in one hand and a Newport social register in the other.

It is my considered opinion, from having conversed with some of these Annapolis graduates, that their primary purpose is not to prosecute a successful war but rather to protect their damned ships from hostile fire.

At any rate, I was given command of Fifth Corps, a high-sounding name for a military formation that did not exist, and packed off to Tampa, an eyesore on the western coast of Florida, and here have had to contend with hordes of politicians, newspapermen, and frantic Cuban rebels, all of whom are anxious to explain to me exactly how the Spaniards could best be expelled from the Western Hemisphere.

Since then, the only orders I have received were rescinded within hours. In fact some of my instructions from Washington have been canceled before I even received them.

I feel as though I am a shuttlecock being racketed back and forth at the mindless whim of idiots. By capons who try to give the impression that they still know how to copulate, when in fact, they are sans balls. As one of my colored first sergeants in the old Twenty-fourth would say it, "They's so dumb they couldn't fuck!"

So here I have this mass of men, in regular units and from the National Guard and the volunteers. None of them have ever trained in large-scale maneuvers. Of course, the regulars know the basic military skills, like providing latrines and taking care of their weapons. But the National Guard and the volunteers don't even know this, and their officers, whom the men elect, are utterly incompetent. The Guard and volunteer units are equipped with old Springfield single shot rifles which fire black powder. Black powder sends up a great cloud of smoke which is impossible to see through and which provides any enemy a perfect aiming point for his own directed fire.

The regulars are well equipped but these others have no tents, which they wouldn't know how to put up even if they did. No canteens, no web equipment of any kind, no kitchens, and no men trained to provide food for the troops, no medical personnel or facilities, no nothing!

Of course, there is *one* volunteer unit that is well supplied with modern rifles and tropical uniforms. The cavalry regiment officially commanded by Wood, a damned doctor for Christ's sake, but whose real commander is Roosevelt. His supply system is better than mine.

This Roosevelt will be in my command. And it is abundantly clear that if I or my staff make any decision he doesn't approve, he will not hesitate to flash off letters to his powerful friends in the Senate, or perhaps to the secretary of the navy, for God's sake, or to William Randolph Hearst.

Oh yes, this Roosevelt is the center of press attention. They follow him about like docile cows and I have been thinking that I should place a bell about his neck.

Did I say my staff? What staff? Dear Jesus Christ, I have no staff. The officers I have been provided, and they are few, stand about wide-eyed waiting for me to solve their problems instead of bringing me solutions which I can act upon. They have no conception of what a staff is supposed to do.

It isn't their fault. They simply have had no staff training. There are some very intelligent young men among them.

For example that Pay gentleman. Who is always shadowed by the Indian with facial tattoos. Perhaps he can be useful.

My God. To think I got him through a letter of introduction

from Roosevelt. A lawyer, Roosevelt said, the son of an old Republican friend in Missouri. What the shit am I supposed to do with a lawyer?

Well, he seems a bright young man. Perhaps he can be useful. I am told he is not politically inclined and is in fact not even a Republican like his father.

More's the blessing if all so-called officers in this army could forget the next election.

But that damned Indian. He's so big, I think he may draw fire.

I suppose Roosevelt expected me to commission that young man on the spot. Hell, I haven't got authority to do that. So the paper I had prepared for him will have to do. "Special Staff Assistant to the Commanding General." Damned impressive. Of course, there is no such thing in any table of organization I ever saw. But none of these people around here will know that. None of these people around here even know what the hell a table of organization is.

We'll feed him, and that Osage. But I doubt they'll ever see a penny of pay. My God, I haven't got time to start a recruiting service and sign up everybody Roosevelt decides to send me.

Maybe he can even find a weapon out there in that quartermaster madhouse. Frankly, I wouldn't mind seeing a weapon in the hands of that tattooed Indian, so long as he stays on *our* side.

And what in Christ's name am I supposed to do with Clara Barton? And that filly she's hauling around with her in train? Here to go to Cuba they are. Here to service the troops they are.

I just hope that young one doesn't get serviced herself. Soldiers will always be soldiers.

Well, let the navy worry about getting them to wherever it is we're going, along with their cartons of cotton and gauze. The navy should be good at that.

The good God Almighty should strike me dead for being ungrateful. That old lady, Clara Barton, coming down here to this hellhole to help my troops. They'll need help from any direction it might come, I suspect.

Now I've got to find that goddamned adjutant. We've got to

get somebody lined out for this "reconnaissance in force" the War Department wants. If they don't change their minds. If all our telegraphs would break down then we'd be like that damned Dewey out in the Pacific. We could do what we damned well please without interference every fifteen minutes.

And we've got to line up a ship from the navy. Hell, the last I heard, they claim all their vessels are tied into keeping the Spanish navy bottled up someplace or the other.

And I need another pitcher of lemonade. It's hotter than the goddamned devil's testicles in this place.

CHAPTER 4

EBEN Pay and Joe Mountain stood near the railroad siding, not five hundred paces from the rear porches of the Plank Hotel. Their boots were ankle deep in the hot sand and the sweat ran down their cheeks in thick, salty streams. The warrant from General Shafter that Eben Pay held in his hand was limp and soggy from the humidity. The sun, even though lowering, was a scalding presence at their backs and Eben Pay wished now he'd brought one of his wide-brimmed Indian Territory hats instead of the thing he wore, a river captain's billed cap. He could feel the heat turning his neck and ears a blistering pink.

Beside him, the big Osage stood bareheaded, his hair glistening blue-black in the afternoon light and the tattoo dots on his cheek looking purple. Joe Mountain's grin seemed permanently in place, frozen in the heat, as meaningless as the sculpted open lips of some sandstone sphinx in Egypt's desert.

"Eben Pay," he said. "I never heard so many cuss words."

"It's something soldiers are noted for," Eben Pay said. "If you're after learning new ways to swear, you've come to the right place."

A line of boxcars stood on the siding, doors gaped open. Soldiers on quartermaster detail from the nearby encampment of the

Thirty-seventh Infantry moved in and out of these rectangular black caves, carrying crates and boxes and assorted tangles of equipment, shouting their oaths and obscenities. They were dressed in blue woolen shirts, khaki trousers secured at the bottom with leather puttees, army issue lace brogans. And on their heads campaign hats obviously new but already taking on a casual, sweat-soaked appearance like formless dishcloths. From headband to armpit to crotch, they were crusted with the gray-white stains of body salt.

Scattered along the siding were great, haphazard piles of boxes. Rushing about among them was a quartermaster captain, frantically screaming instructions nobody seemed to hear, waving a lined tablet in one hand.

Crates had been ripped open, their contents belched out onto the cinders and sand. There was a litter of cooking pots and lids and the soldiers moving through them kicked and thrashed, making a loud clatter. In one jumbled pile were what appeared to be hundreds of folding canvas camp chairs. In another, white enamel chamber pots. Tangles of leather harness and half-gallon tin cans and rows of wire-banded pitchforks and D-handle shovels, and incredibly, a small disc harrow. A scatter of French forage caps complete with havelocks, a pile of socket bayonets that didn't fit any rifle the army had issued since 1812, a ruptured pine case showing winter overcoats with capes, a great many sacks of flour, some of them burst open to reveal a squirming, writhing colony of black bugs, and innumerable cases of hardtack and molasses with a fading stencil on the side of each reading Product of Angus Morchuson Wholesaler, East Amboy, New Jersey, 1863.

"Joe, let's get this over with," Eben Pay said.

The quartermaster officer was Captain Ephriam Cooper, who had been a captain for twenty-eight years, having been demoted to that rank from his brevet majority during the Civil War. There was an odor of madness about him. All his frustrations were cut deeply into his face, each line seeming to point upward and inward to the bulging eyes.

"For God's sweet sake," he screamed. "I don't know where any of this fornicating tidbit shit is." He waved General Shafter's memorandum in Eben Pay's face. "I'm trying to supply an army. Don't you see that, for Christ sake? I'm trying to supply an army!"

So he turned them over to a corporal on detail from the Thirty-seventh Infantry.

"Christ," Cooper shouted. "He knows as much about it as I do. Anybody knows as much about it as I do. I'm only the god-damned quartermaster officer, but any whore in Tampa knows as much about it as I do."

The corporal they were assigned to came up slowly, eyeing them, long arms dangling, eyes slitted against the sun. And with a small smile on his square face.

"A paper," he said, taking General Shafter's memorandum from Eben Pay's hand. "Of course, everybody's got a paper, now don't they?"

He gave a great, weary sigh and sat down on an unopened pine board crate, pushed his campaign hat to the back of his head, and looked at the paper. He ruffled it, squinted, then inspected Eben Pay and Joe Mountain, looking from head to toe, coldly. Even with the little smile still on his lips.

"Have you come to this war with any good cigars, sir?"

"I'm afraid not," Eben Pay said.

"It's a terrible war indeed without good cigars," the corporal said and produced a handful of black stogies from his sweaty shirt pocket. "But the commissary has provided. And matches as well."

He handed a small cardboard box to each of them.

"Over there," the corporal said, waving his hand vaguely toward the line of boxcars, "we have discovered seventy cases of these matches. Fifty gross of matchboxes to the case, each filled with matches, too. Whoever is on the other end of this railroad expects us to *burn* bloody Cuba, wouldn't you say, sir?"

"I don't know," said Eben Pay. Joe Mountain already had a lighted cigar held between his teeth, puffing clouds of blue smoke that were whiffed away immediately in the strong coastal breeze.

"No, I suppose you wouldn't." The corporal sighed again and rose, shaking the Shafter memorandum as though trying to rid it of drops of water. "Well, sir, I am no quartermaster man. I am

[58]

an infantry soldier. Fortunes of war, Mr. Pay. Now come along with me. My name is Price. Some of these men are members of my squad. I'm reasonably sure one or the other of them has found something he doesn't want to steal that you might use."

"I'm much obliged," Eben Pay said. "And you don't have to call me sir."

"Oh but I do. When a gentleman comes with a paper signed by himself, the commanding general, then I will say 'sir.' There's no disrespect in it."

They kicked their way through the debris, which reminded Eben Pay of the leavings in the wake of an Indian Territory cyclone. A soldier staggered up with a large crate on his shoulder, stenciled Desiccated Vegetables.

"Where you want this, Corporal Price?"

"Dump it in the bloody ocean."

They moved on, Corporal Price muttering something about finding some puttees and tunics in the great pile of offal. Once he stopped and looked back at Joe Mountain and shook his head.

"There is nothing we will find that can fit onto him," he said. And then moved on. Once he stopped and picked up a quart-sized tin can and bounced it in his hand. "Do you see this, sir? It's canned beef. If ever you are unfortunate enough to have to eat it to keep from starving, be ready to swallow as soon as you cut it open. Because it will spoil in this heat before you can have a second thought."

"What happens to it in a man's stomach?" Eben Pay asked.

"It lies there and rots, sir. But better there, out of sight, than out in the open to attract maggots and other vermin."

"You're not doing much to encourage my appetite," Eben Pay said and for the first time, the corporal's smile expanded and he laughed, a deep, gurgling sound. They moved on, Corporal Price peering intently at each pile of crates, all set in a jumble like the blocks a careless child had left scattered on the floor. And talking always, almost to himself.

"Ammunition. That's what we're trying to find, sir. Me and my men and all these bloody soldiers, trying to find ammunition, a thing you would think somebody could understand that we are going to need. You cannot chastise the bloody Spaniards unless you have ammunition, sir."

Eben Pay became conscious of the flies. They seemed to swarm about his neck, biting like alligators. Off to the east, he could hear a locomotive huffing and puffing and its whistle made a sharp, distinctive mark against the muttered profanity of the soldiers.

"Well," Eben Pay said. "Maybe the ammunition's coming now. On one of those other trains."

"Of course, sir. One of those other trains. I will tell you what will be on those other bloody trains. Horseshit spreaders and fountain pens. Are you familiar with armies, sir?"

"I'm afraid not."

"Good. The less you know of them the better you will sleep, not wondering how battles are ever won. Over there beside that flatcar, there are twenty-three cases of writing ink. Over there. . . ."

He stopped and watched a tall, freckled, blond soldier prying off the lid of a crate with a wrecking bar.

"Swede!" he bellowed, making Joe Mountain start and bite the end off his cigar.

"Yah, Corporal Price," the tall soldier said, dropping his wrecking bar and coming toward them, running, dancing between the rubble. "Yah?"

"You know our special boxes?"

"Yah, Corporal Price. Behind that stack of crossties."

"Yes. Bring one of each. Here. Now. Hop, goddamnit!"

"Yah, Corporal Price." The tall soldier laughed and ran off and they stood there waiting, Joe Mountain puffing his truncated cigar, Eben Pay slapping at the flies and Corporal Price looking back and forth along the siding.

"That dear quartermaster gentleman," he said. "A fine officer with a trying task. I hope the son of a bitch isn't close by now."

Soon, Eben Pay saw why. The tall soldier returned with a large tin can in one hand, marked Peaches, and in the other a half-gallon bottle with a label proclaiming that inside was genuine, Missouri copper whiskey.

"You dumb goddamned Swede," Corporal Price said, snatching the bottle from the tall soldier and handing it to Joe Mountain. "Under your shirt with that. And these peaches, you, sir. Both little presents from the men of the Thirty-seventh United States Infantry."

"By God," Joe Mountain said.

"Back to your work now, back to your work for the love of Jesus," Corporal Price barked and the tall soldier, grinning and his freckles shining, nodded and bounded away.

"Yah, Corporal Price, yah."

★

Before it was done, they could hear bugles playing Recall in the nearby regular army encampments. The purple shadows were running off toward the line of tropical trees in the east and there were crickets starting their evening love calls and there was already a moon, coming full, lifting into the still brilliant sky. Gulls were crying somewhere to the west and there were some high enough, soaring, for the sun below the horizon to catch them in its light, making delicate white figures of their wings.

But it was still hot. And in their Plant Hotel room, Eben Pay and Joe Mountain sweated, even under the movement of air created by the ceiling fan, which rotated like an ancient horizontal windmill with little creaks and squeaks counting each revolution of the blades.

Eben Pay modeled his new assortment of military apparel. Most welcome was a wide brim campaign hat. Too big until the sweatband was stuffed with a few pages from Mr. William Randolph Hearst's *New York Journal*. The rest was not so exciting. A regulation blue army shirt. A pair of cavalry trousers, flared at the lower thighs, a scuffed brace of leather puttees.

"It looks like hell," Eben Pay said, trying to see all aspects of his wartime garb in the small mirror above the dresser.

"You look like one of them outlaws we bring in from the Nations," Joe Mountain said. He was sprawled in the room's only wicker chair, a cigar in one hand, the bottle of Missouri genuine copper whiskey in the other.

[61]

There was one bed. But on the floor was a mattress. When they had first entered the room, Joe Mountain had seen the accommodations and disappeared for twenty minutes, returning with this same mattress. Eben Pay had no intention of asking where the mattress came from, not wanting to be an accessory. Nor would he challenge it being there. Otherwise, he and the big Osage would have been sharing that one small bed.

"That was a nice man who give you all that," Joe said.

"Yes, I liked him."

"He sure knows the cuss words."

"I told you about soldiers."

Eben Pay walked over to their only window, opening to the west. The sky was deep gray and purple now, with only a long line of dim red light along the horizon. It was so straight. Like a single, quick stroke of a brush. Unusual to Eben Pay, who was accustomed to sunsets in hill country.

"He is a tough man, that corporal," Joe Mountain said.

"How do you know?"

"The look of him. When he puts his eyes on you. We seen a lot of men like that in the Nations, Eben Pay. Hard men. But that little pistol he gave you. That double action."

Joe Mountain laughed.

"I don't know why I even took it," Eben Pay said. "He didn't have any ammunition for it."

"Well, don't worry, Eben Pay," Joe Mountain said. "We ain't exactly unarmed."

When Eben Pay turned, the Osage had pulled from beneath his shirt a large Colt revolver. A .45. Single action.

"Plenty of shells, too," Joe Mountain said.

"God, Joe, here we are, right in the middle of an entire army, and you've got that thing."

"Well, Eben Pay," said Joe Mountain, "if all them army people leave some Spaniards that need to be shot, then we can do it."

"Where'd you get that damned thing?"

"I brought it from Fort Smith. Hell, Eben Pay, you seen this old pistol lots of times before. I'd rather have a good Winchester. But it's hard to hide a rifle under your shirt."

"I'll never get you out of the Indian Territory, will I Joe?"

"Hell no! I carry that place around with me." And Joe Mountain, grinning broadly, reached up and touched the line of tattooed dots on his cheek.

Olaf Swenson

My name is not Olaf Swenson. But the army thinks it is because that's what I told them. I will not say my real name because if I did the police from Milwaukee, Wisconsin, would come and get me and they would try me in a court and then hang me for murder.

Or maybe now in Wisconsin they got this new electric chair. And they would put me in that.

But whatever they got in Wisconsin, they would do it to me for murder. And I didn't do it.

I ain't ever told anybody. Except I told my squad leader, Corporal Dylan Price. And he just laughed and said don't worry about it and patted me on the head.

It was all because I loved somebody. And she loved me. I worked for her husband. He was a Polish man and he had this sausage factory. It was just a little sausage factory. Only three of us worked there and his wife, too. And they lived upstairs, him and his wife.

I won't say their names either. Because if I did, then the police at Milwaukee, Wisconsin, would know it was me and they'd come and take me off up there and try me and hang me or put me in their electric chair, whichever they got.

She was very kind to me. I just got here. In the United States of America, I mean. I won't say where it was I came from because if I did then the police in Milwaukee, Wisconsin, would know who I was and come get me. The police in Milwaukee, Wisconsin, are very smart about things like that.

Her husband was gone a lot at night. He went to these Populist meetings, making plans for big political things. I never knew anything about that. So she would call down the stairs and tell me to come up and I'd go and there would be some wurst from their supper and she'd let me eat some and she'd give me some wine and bread. And then she'd give me herself.

She sweat a lot.

Her husband was very mean to her. She told me that. She said he gave her bloody noses all the time.

She laughed a lot when I talked because she said I didn't know how to speak the Queen's English. I never knew they had a queen in the United States of America. She had the biggest tits I ever seen.

One night I was the last to leave the sausage factory. I was always last to leave because I was young and he always called me a dumb Scandinavian, so I cleaned up the sausage factory. So I was cleaning it up and I heard her start to scream. So I took this meat mallet, which is a large hammer we used to kind of break up the pork before we put it in the grinder. I ran upstairs and he was being cruel to her and her nose was bleeding.

He started yelling at me. He hit me with a chair and the meat mallet fell out of my hand. It scared the shit out of me. He was ready to jump on me and stomp me.

But she picked up the meat mallet and hit him in the head. He looked very surprised. So she hit him again and he fell down on the floor and was making all these crazy sounds and his head looked all lopsided from where she had hit him with the meat mallet.

She started screaming that I'd killed him. Hell, I hadn't even touched him. She kept yelling I'd killed him and even if I was a dumb Scandinavian, I knew things were getting very dangerous. I ran like hell.

I went down to Chicago on a freight train. It wasn't far enough. I could still hear her screaming that I'd killed him. I went to Cleveland. I think it was Cleveland. Then I went to Buffalo. It was winter and I was cold and hungry. I finally came to Plattsburg and enlisted in the army. The Thirty-seventh Infantry. I didn't know nothing about armies, but anyway, I wasn't cold and hungry no more.

[65]

That's where I first seen Corporal Price. He was this older guy. Once or twice, I done something wrong, like turning left when I was supposed to turn right, and Corporal Price took his fist and knocked me on my ass. He done that to a lot of guys. He didn't mean anything bad. He was just teaching us.

We learned fast that way. He taught us how to shoot and how to use a bayonet and how to look at stars at night and know where we was at and how to read a map.

And how to wrap up a wound so a guy wouldn't bleed to death before the medical soldiers got there, and how to move around at night, listening to things. And how to look at the ground and see where you could hunker down and not get hit by some guy who was shooting at you.

Corporal Price was the best man I ever knew. He'd say, "Swede, when I tell you to jump, you do it. Because someday," he'd say, "when I say jump and you stand there and ask why, while you're standing there, you'll get your ass shot off."

Hell, it wasn't just me. It was all our guys. Corporal Price, he knew all the soldier stuff. He'd been doing it all his life.

Once, at Plattsburg Barracks, I seen into his locker. There was this little ribbon, red and purple I think it was, with a fat medal cross hung onto it. I didn't say nothing.

But a couple nights later we was in the canteen, drunker than hell on that black Plattsburg beer. It was payday. And soldiers always get drunker than hell on payday.

So I asked Corporal Price about that little ribbon I seen, and he was real drunk, but he said a strange word. Rorke's Drift. I said where the hell's that. And he said a long way off.

That's all he said.

I forgot it. Then a while later, I was in the company dayroom one Sunday afternoon. And the company commander had bought a new book for our library there, where we could come and write letters and play pool and read. It was a nice book, all about military decorations and awards.

It was a book with a lot of writing, and I didn't pay much attention to that. But there were these pictures, all in color, on slick paper. I liked those. And I was just looking at them and I seen it. That same ribbon and medal that was in Corporal Price's locker.

It was a nice-looking thing and I was happy Corporal Price had one. Down at the bottom of the page, it said what it was. It said it was the Victoria Cross.

CHAPTER 5

IT was raining. The double file of men moved along the railroad tracks, stumbling into one another, swearing softly. The lights of the Plant Hotel were now lost somewhere behind them in the night and the few lanterns carried by half a dozen sergeants seemed only to deepen the texture of darkness as though the soldiers were only bulky clots of lampblack flowing unsteadily forward in a sea of ink.

There was no lightning or thunder, only the persistent fall of water. Straight down, without wind slanting it.

It was nine miles from their Tampa bivouac to the shore at Tampa Bay. It seemed much farther because this was no normal march but one interrupted always with halts and starts and halts and starts and the men standing in the rain wondering what kind of idiot was up ahead. And besides all that, the going had been rough because railroad ties do not make for good footing on marches.

They had started just after dark. And now, as they felt the splintered wooden planking of the dock beneath their feet, it was almost dawn. It was a dock that jutted out into the Bay of Tampa, which did not impress them in any way. All they knew was that here they stood, bowed under the rain.

Well, they knew a little more than that. They knew this was a secret mission and that there was still time to board their ship in darkness. Still time before the dawn caught them, exposed them. With the rain and the low clouds, early light would come late today. And so they could carry out this operation that was said to be very, very secret.

They all knew. They were to deliver a large shipment of arms and ammunition to the rebels on Cuba. To the insurgents, standing against the cruel Spaniards.

"It's a covert movement," had said Captain John Stoval, their company commander. "We will slip into Cuba unobserved and quickly, and then out again, and deposit the arms with our friends down there. Our own Cubans serving with this army know the exact beaches where we can go to supply their comrades."

And so they started it. There were elements of two companies, E and F. About one hundred men. Some of them were enthusiastic. Some of them, the old soldiers, thought as they always did, Wait and see.

Now, not knowing what was ahead, they could hear shouting. They assumed these were officers' voices, and stood in the rain, heads bowed, the brims of their campaign hats dripping, their rifles muzzle down, carried at sling arms.

They were not wearing raincoats. They had been issued rain gear, including ponchos, but none of them wore the clinging, rubberized covers. Because after days of intense heat, the falling water offered the best relief from heat.

But now, after almost seven hours, it was beginning to get uncomfortable. The water on the shoulders was nice, but in the crotch after walking so long, it had begun to be galling. They cursed the Spaniards. They cursed the people who had ordered this march. They cursed the rain.

At first, the rain had smelled refreshing. But as they neared the Bay, which they could not see, it began to smell more and more like dead fish.

"Keep closed up, keep closed up," the sergeants kept saying urgently, furiously.

Then they were at the dock. And they stood in the rain.

Maurice Barry, the E Company first sergeant, moved along the line of men, carrying a lantern. Its light was dim, pale blue in the rain, as though shining from behind a thick glass lens. But no matter. Every man recognized the massive bulk carrying the light.

This was a longtime regular. He had been on the Indian frontier through most of his adult life, from the time his family arrived out of Limerick in 1873 and he had enlisted. Barry had been in the American army so long that he knew no other home. And in that time had lost most of his Irish brogue.

He was a good first sergeant. Resourceful, profane, tough. With his own fists, he could thrash any man in the company who might require it. But new men assigned learned quickly Barry's capabilities, and seldom challenged him.

Of all the men in his company, he called only one by his first name. Dylan Price.

Because they were both soldiers. Old soldiers. Not that Dylan Price was as old in age, but because he was as old in service.

There was a mutual respect. But an antagonism, too. Hidden, and controlled.

Barry dreaded no challenge from the younger men of his company. But sometimes he lay awake at night and hoped somehow that Dylan Price would ask him to take off his chevrons and walk behind the barracks to do fists.

Because Barry was an Irishman and a tough first sergeant, and both of those loved combat, and he knew, each night as he thought of it yet guessed it would never happen, that if he and Dylan Price should square off, it would be the most glorious, bloody, longtime contest he would ever be able to talk about in his retirement.

"Gimme a count," First Sergeant Barry repeated as he walked down the column of troops.

Dylan Price ran his roll call as always, by nationality. He was very sensitive to nationality, even though he knew that the members of his squad, like himself, were American citizens now, their naturalization having been facilitated somewhat by their enlisting in the army.

But there was another reason. If he went by nationality, he was sure not to forget anyone. And usually when he took a roster count his mind was elsewhere. As now, recalling in his thinking the preparations for coming action. Did we issue forty extra rounds for the rifles? Yes. Did we issue salt? Yes. Are machetes sheathed and properly hung on web belts and are canteens full? Yes. Does each man have ten hardtack crackers? Yes.

My God, those crackers, hard as the good solid slate shingles mined in Wales, and just as tasteless. Sure to have been manufactured as far in the past as the Civil War.

First, the Germans.

"Telner."

"Here."

"Mittelberg."

"Here."

"Ulrich."

"Here."

Then the Scot.

"Reed."

"Here."

Then the Bulgarian.

"Vanic."

"Here."

Then Swenson.

"Yah."

There was a long pause and Price could hear some of his men snickering, a sound almost like the rain falling on his hat.

"For the sweet love of Jesus, man, haven't I told you enough how to answer roll call you dumb bastard?"

"Yah. Here."

And although he could see nothing of Swenson's face, only the dark hulk crowned with drooping hat brim, Price added softly, "And stop grinning at me like a bloody jackal."

"Yah."

Up ahead troops were boarding their ship on a number of gangways, lighted by the dim hand-held lanterns. The line moved forward, halted, moved forward again.

Somebody along the line swore loudly, "Stop shovin' into me you son of a bitch."

"Be at ease," Price said.

They could see almost nothing. As they clomped up their gangway and onto the deck there were a few lights above them, trying with little success to shine down from the ship's superstructure.

Their place was on a covered deck, so for the first time in hours they were out of the rain. On the deck above them they could hear the heavy stomping of boots. Find a place then, settle down on the deck, gouging one another with rifle muzzles, and canteens and machetes rattling as their butts were lowered into standing puddles of water. Captain Stoval was moving among them, speaking softly, encouragingly. They could not see him, except as a passing black shape, but they all knew his voice. They all liked Captain Stoval, small and fiery, with fifteen years' service, out of West Point. He always looked after his men.

Sitting there in the dark, Dylan Price thought about his squad. None of them had ever served in combat together. In fact, except for Price, none of them knew what combat was, at least beyond what he had explained to them. But he had a sense of confidence in them. They were not short-timers. Two of the Germans and the Bulgarian were serving their second enlistment. Their second "hitch." The others were likely to be soldiers all their lives because they could likely find nothing better outside.

None of them were drunk. Not because they had anything against being drunk at a time like this but because no high spirits had been available for two days.

And they were well trained. Dylan Price knew because he had trained them. But how would they react when suddenly they realized somebody they could not see, did not know, had no quarrel with, was trying to kill them?

He felt confident in that, too, because these men were the stuff of good regular soldiers. Not stupid, but rather with a native intelligence and toughness, none too well educated in the formal sense. And, he thought, the worst kind of common soldier is the one who has a fancy book education. Asks too bloody many questions. Has to have high-sounding reasons for everything, from digging latrines to shooting at other human beings.

[72]

No, he thought, they'll do. They don't know why we're here. I don't either. And nobody cares. This is our job. And we'll stand and fight for one another. For nothing else.

He'd seen enough of armies surely to have learned this and so he was confident. They'd stand and fight for one another because comradeship was stronger than fear.

Price leaned against a bulkhead, his rifle held with butt on the deck, barrel alongside his cheek. It was a reassuring sensation, the cold metal of a weapon. No need to worry about weapons, he thought. You learn their assets and liabilities quickly, he thought, and these are constant.

Some of them slept. But not many. There was too much excitement. They were off to Cuba, across the Gulf of Mexico, on a secret mission. And some of them didn't sleep because the Cubans on board were making too much noise. High-pitched, exuberant Spanish conversation, all meaningless to the men of the Thirty-seventh Infantry Regiment.

"Sounds like a convention of goddamned red-assed apes," Private Reed grumbled.

"Our allies they are," said Price softly. "Speak with respect."

But there was a lilt of scorn in his voice and from the darkness he could hear the low laughter of the men in his squad.

As the dawn came, gray but with the rain slackening and the clouds beginning to break up, they saw for the first time this vessel that would take them to a hostile shore.

She was a side-wheel paddle steamer. A riverboat. And the impression was not enhanced by the name inscribed across the pilothouse in scaling black paint. *Gussie.*

"God help us," muttered Dylan Price.

"What was that you said, Corporal Price?" Vanic asked.

"I said she is a fine ship to transport us to Armageddon."

"Is that in Cuba?" Private Ulrich asked.

"Of course. Haven't you ever read the Bible, you blockheaded bratwurst?"

"I never read that part."

"All right now, lads, dry off those rifles and have your fine breakfast of shingles and no more idle talk from you."

They expected to be off quickly, on this secret mission. They had expected to be off before dawn. But they sat at dockside, the old river steamer huffing and puffing and sending up noxious clouds of black smoke from her two stacks just behind the pilot-house. There was a low swell and the boat reared up and down against the hawsers, her hull grinding against the side of the pier.

And as the morning wore on, the skies clearing and the sun coming out to boil all the night's moisture out of the air, groups of people began to appear along the half-mile wharf. Civilians and officers and ladies in flowered bonnets and holding parasols gaily colored in orange and red and green. They were laughing, pointing at the *Gussie*, waving little American flags.

In addition to the pier where the *Gussie* was tied up, there was another alongside, also with railroad tracks laid along its half-mile length, creating a narrow strait of water between the two. The crowds of people were coming along both piers. Waving their flags. Well-wishers, flooding close to the ship of conquest, a dilapidated old river steamer.

"God help us," muttered Dylan Price. "God bloody help us."

The Cubans on board the *Gussie* were lining the rails, shouting unintelligible salutations to the gathering throng.

Toward shore, a locomotive whistled, then came into view, pulling three flatcars crowded with excursionists, some with wicker baskets filled with sandwiches from the kitchen of the Plant Hotel, some waving wine bottles, all coming joyfully to watch the dispatch of the secret mission.

Soon, on the dock, there was observed a famous artist making a sketch of the historic event. From one of the flatcars, a small covey of newspapermen scrambled down and across the dock and up a gangway onto the *Gussie*, pads in hand, tan worsted coats flying out behind them, pencils in their pockets.

Out in the blue bay, until only a short time before invisible in the darkness, there were two navy gunboats, small steam craft, each with an unimposing cannon mounted near the bow. They began to make themselves known with short blasts of their whistles.

Some of the people on the piers were waving Florida newspapers. On the front pages of which was the glorious story of the United States beginning its campaign against the dastardly Spaniards this very date, about to bring arms to the oppressed. The Cubans on the *Gussie* were hysterically excited and one even fell overboard and had to be hauled back dripping by the *Gussie*'s crew.

Then, with some of the people onshore singing a disjointed version of "The Battle Hymn of the Republic," the *Gussie*'s crew cast off the ropes and the side-wheel paddles began to churn and lift a salty spray and the people along the docks cheered and waved handkerchiefs and bottles. Easing back along the narrow channel between the wharves, the river steamer was finally clear of land and turning out into the Gulf. Nearby the navy gunboats were sending up spouts of white steam as their whistles marked the great event, the beginning of the secret mission.

It was high noon as *Gussie* cleared the Tampa Bay piers and chugged off southward, the navy gunboats falling in behind, and the people on the ends of the long piers still waving and shouting and singing.

Behind the little flotilla, a great cloud of seabirds followed along, white in the sunlight, etched hard against a sky now of emerald blue.

"God bloody help us," said Dylan Price, listening to the Cubans on board still shouting and waving far beyond the point where anyone onshore could hear them.

Captain John Stoval

I have worn this uniform all of my life, either in fact or in spirit. My grandfather, Gladius Stoval, graduated from the United States Military Academy and fought in the Seminole War. My father was an instructor at West Point when I was born. He was later wounded and lost his right leg at Cedar Mountain when his Union cavalry regiment attempted to charge a Rebel infantry brigade. My mother's brother, also a man from West Point, opted for the South and was killed in the charge of Powell Hill's Light Division at Antietam. He would have called it Sharpsburg.

Myself, I graduated from the Academy in 1875 and spent the next few years in the Department of the Missouri on the Indian frontier, and was then posted to the Thirty-seventh Infantry Regiment in New York State. I advanced in rank because I worked hard at it. And also, I suspect, because of my mother's second brother, who survived the war and was a member of Sheridan's staff and won the Medal of Honor at Yellow Tavern. He was my mentor and then became a United States senator from Maryland and through it all was a close friend to Sheridan. In the matter of advancement in the army, Sheridan was not a bad friend to have, even though he was not actually my friend but that of my uncle.

I make no apologies.

It is therefore distasteful, after having made a life of the army, to describe the excursion of the *Gussie*, because in all the annals of military history in our country, this expedition is one which could best be forgotten. In fact, by revealing its true nature, I feel I may be breaking my oath of allegiance.

And for that, I make profound apologies.

However, the truth must be served, as someone once said. Painful as it may be.

At the outset, I will state that my soldiers are good men. I will not have them maligned. In this war, they have consistently done the best they could while being innocent victims of somebody else's incompetence.

As an example of that incompetence, and putting the halter on exactly the right horse, we received instructions that the Fifth Corps would stage in Key West and the Dry Tortugas, leaving there for our invasion of Cuba. There is not enough drinking water in those places to provide for a company, much less tens of thousands of men. It can only be assumed that the people in Washington who made such a suggestion do not realize that soldiers, like everyone else, must have drinking water. Once this fact was pointed out, the instructions were rescinded.

Let me make it clear that I admire President McKinley. I voted for him. But he is no soldier and apparently he has no soldiers to advise him. And no geographers, either. In the instance cited, one would think the name of Dry Tortugas alone would have provided some clue so that investigation could be made before the War Department went off half cocked and started issuing absurd instructions.

My trepidation when informed that I would command a foray onto the coast of Cuba in order to deliver arms and ammunition to the insurgents there was considerable. This feeling changed to one of almost total anguish when I first laid eyes on the dilapidated old river paddle-wheeler *Gussie* and then watched the fantastic public knowledge of what was supposed to be a covert operation.

Officials and members of the press apparently felt that they could trumpet the news worldwide while the Spaniards on Cuba would politely turn their eyes and ears aside.

At any rate, we were off and the spirit of the troops was good. Certainly better than mine. It did not help my disposition any to learn, before we were hardly out of sight of the piers at Tampa Bay, that the Cubans on board the *Gussie* were suspected of stealing raincoats and other gear from my sleeping soldiers.

But under the circumstances, I thought it best not to press the issue at the moment.

A river steamer is not made for passage across the open sea.

And soon the tossing and heaving of the vessel produced widespread seasickness among the troops. The Cubans on board seemed to be especially hard struck, which I took as a blessing because in that state perhaps they would be less inclined toward expropriating United States property.

I was particularly grateful to two of the noncommissioned officers of my own company at this time. First Sergeant Barry and Corporal Price, who went about the decks making rough jokes and shaming the seasick soldiers into putting a good face on a bad situation.

We were scheduled to land our cargo at Mariel, just west of Havana harbor. The Cubans had said their compatriots would be waiting there. But as we approached the beach those same Cubans frantically began to explain that we could not land. It became quickly obvious why. Gunfire was coming out to greet us. It all fell short, but obviously the Spaniards were at Mariel in force.

So we simply sailed westward along the coast. Astonishingly, a troop of Spanish cavalry appeared on the beach and pursued us along the shore, firing small arms at us.

"They knew we coming, they knew we coming," the Cubans on *Gussie* kept screaming. For God's sake!

Pounding like an old butter churn, the *Gussie* soon outdistanced the horse troop of Spanish soldiers.

We came to a place called Cabañas. Our Cubans said we could get our cargo ashore and that their insurgent friends would be waiting. We hove to about a hundred yards offshore. The navy gunboats hovered just behind us, all hands watching.

The landing site did not please me. There was a very heavy swell and some breakers going onto the sand. However, I dispatched three boats. A small one with some of our Cubans and two larger ones with about forty of my men to go ashore and establish a foothold before I sent in other boats with the weapons.

Somehow, despite my specific orders to the contrary, one of the newspaper reporters on *Gussie* accompanied the men in one of the larger boats. I think he represented a San Francisco newspaper.

Approaching shore, the Cuban boat capsized in the surf and

the Cubans swam like drowning rats and disappeared into the jungle. We never saw them again.

By now, the naval blockading squadron was arriving. God only knows if they had news that we were coming. If they didn't, they were the only ones in the Western Hemisphere who had been left in the dark. A whole flotilla began to collect behind us.

My own men, in the two larger boats, were rowing in and a sudden, vicious rain squall developed, making it hard to see anything. But through it came two small steam vessels, rails crowded with waving, shouting men in mufti. They were steaming straight up alongside my rowing troopers.

I knew what this was—two of the vessels hired by various powerful newspaper interests and called Mr. Hearst's Navy. My God, those newspaper people had better communications than we did, and I could only assume they had news that had to be imparted to my men going into that beach.

We tried to signal the newspaper ships so they would know that the command apparatus of the expedition was still aboard the *Gussie*. They continued to steam through the rain toward my rowing men, shouting and waving. Then suddenly, they turned back to take their place among all the other spectator ships. My two boats continued their slow progress to the shore.

It was only later that I learned the purpose of the dash of the newsmen. They were shouting to my soldiers, getting the names of men in the bows of the boats so they could write stories about the first Americans to set foot on Cuban soil.

My God!

Now, above the sounds of falling rain, we could hear the sharp reports of Mauser rifles from the jungle. And in the water swimming toward the shore were half a dozen horses, a Cuban handler clinging to each tail. We had brought these horses for some of the Cubans in case we needed them to contact their friends on the island, and someone had pushed the horses off the *Gussie*'s deck and they were nearing the beach. As they came out of the water, the Cubans came with them, scrambling, mounted them and rode off into the jungle. We never saw them again, either.

My boats were going in. I saw Corporal Price and his squad, running, firing into the jungle. They were soon lost in the heavy foliage but we continued to hear firing, the sharp reports of the Mausers diminishing, finally stopping, and only the deeper sound of our own Swedish rifles. Then, as the rain stopped, so did the firing.

We waited for Cuban insurgents to appear and my men on *Gussie* had other boats loaded with weapons and ammunition, ready to shove them off and onto the island. But all we saw was our own men, coming back out of the jungle. And into their boats. And back slowly to the *Gussie*.

With the two boats coming near beside the *Gussie*, the navy decided to enter the fight. Although by then there was nothing to be seen onshore except the wall of green jungle. A few of the smaller steam gunboats moved almost even with *Gussie* and began to shell the shore. The sounds of their guns came across the water to us. Onshore, there was no indication of the strike of their rounds except for an occasional lazy lift of white smoke above the jungle's green canopy.

My boats were alongside. I have never seen soldiers so profoundly furious and disgusted. Corporal Price had one man by the scruff of the coat collar and was heaving him onto the deck, but he was not a soldier. He was a civilian and there was a slight smear of red on one sleeve of his coat. It was the newspaper correspondent. I could see Corporal Price berating him. That was the only casualty we had.

Now it began to rain again and the navy stopped firing. We secured our boats. The language of those men who had gone ashore was dreadfully obscene. In my own mind, it was equally so.

As suddenly as it had begun, the rain was gone once more and the sun was out, brilliant bright. We still had a few Cubans on board. They stood about looking glum, saying nothing. It was just as well. Had they opened their mouths, I am afraid some of my soldiers who had been in those two boats would have stuck bayonets into them.

For two more days, shadowed by the newspaper tugs and the

navy, we swam the *Gussie* up and down Cuba's coast west of Havana, looking for Cuban insurgents so that we might deliver weapons and ammunition to them. All we saw was an occasional Spaniard. A number of times we drew fire, but it was always short.

Our Cubans stayed in a tight little group, clustered just behind the pilothouse. I saw my own soldiers eyeing them from the lower decks. The Cubans were intelligent enough not to go down among my men.

Finally, I decided the whole thing was absurd and we headed back to Tampa Bay. It was disgusting. We were all in a black snit.

On arrival, as I stepped onto the pier, a courier from General Shafter greeted me with a sealed envelope. I was sure it was an order for my court-martial. Instead, it was an order for my promotion, jumping me one grade, to lieutenant colonel.

My God!

CHAPTER 6

IN the vulgarly ornate grand
hall and dining room and lobby of the Plant Hotel, it continued
as it had before. The staff of the Fifth Corps and the various division commanders, at least one of them a Confederate veteran, and
the smaller unit commanders and the military hangers-on, and the
newspaper correspondents and the wives and children and the politicians and the businessmen and a few discreet and very expensive whores sipped their lemonade and their iced tea and their
Cuba Libres and ate their meals of fresh fish and chatted and
strolled and read the newspapers and discussed the fine appearance of the recent assistant secretary of the navy, Mr. Roosevelt,
who had just arrived and was now the nominal commander of his
already famous Rough Riders. People nibbled popcorn and peeled
fresh fruit, like oranges and bananas, in keeping with the spirit
of the tropics, and deplored, many of them, the lack of lamb
chops and oxtail soup and complained about the transportation
system, that single line constructed to this dismal place by Mr.
Morton F. Plant.

And Mr. Plant himself moved about through the lower floors
of his hotel, crowded for the first time, hoping the Cuban venture
would last at least forever because the cashboxes were bulging
and prominent people with whom he could converse were at every

table and on the round, plush couches beneath the wildly Greek statues illuminated by clusters of clear glass electric light bulbs set in towers and spires of metal flowers or else in minarets in imitation of Moslem shrines in the land of infidels. The string quartet, abetted by a cornet and a slide trombone, played in the great rotunda their own unrecognizable version of a Rachmaninoff tone poem, which Plant thought was as pagan and therefore as spicy as the statues and light fixtures.

Most of which was lost on the patrons, many of whom knew the light bulbs came from that man Edison in his New Jersey laboratory, and knew the music was being produced by Cubans because they were not expensive to hire, working for a few dollars a day plus one meal of beef stew and potatoes, like all the other hired help ate, and none of the pompano. And therefore the music was not only nonpagan but decidedly in contrast to the prevailing mood, which called for repeated choruses of such things as "When Johnny Comes Marching Home Again, Hurrah, Hurrah" instead of Russian tone poems.

But Mr. Plant was oblivious to such nice distinctions, and so allowed his underpaid Cuban musicians to honk and sweat but with the admonition that when guests broke spontaneously into renditions of "The Battle Hymn of the Republic" or "Dixie," they should lay down their instruments and wait until the wave of patriotism spent itself. Which the Cuban musicians enjoyed doing because it gave them the opportunity to sit back and do nothing but smoke marijuana cigarettes.

On that spring day those who knew about the *Gussie*, and few did, were cloistered in a suite on the third floor, standing about the reclining commanding general as he lay sweating on his bed in his undershirt, waving a rattan fan before his face, wondering why in hell he had been picked for this assignment and why in hell he didn't have some real staff officers and why in hell the people in Washington were such a flock of idiots who visited on him all the trials of Job and then some. He sipped his glass of lemonade and wished that he could sit at a table groaning with good British roast beef and potatoes. And noodles. And apple pie. And a gallon of good brandy.

Downstairs, very few of the people were even aware of what had happened on Captain Stoval's mission. They knew only what they could read in newspapers, which explained that everything had been just swimmingly good except that, of course, the weapons and ammunition could not be given into the hands of the insurgents because of the bastard Spaniards. Shots had been exchanged and good American soliders had shown their courage. And nobody had been killed or wounded, which was exactly what everyone expected in this little war. Nobody died. Nobody bled.

In her usual place at one corner of the dining room that evening was Clara Barton, with her young, attractive consort. Well, can a young woman be a consort? they asked, and laughed.

And with them was the same young man who had been there almost every evening, that young man from Arkansas with the savage servant who was not allowed in the dining room but spent his meals in the kitchen with the Cuban hired help.

Eben Pay had some considerable sense of history. Which Clara Barton did not because she had always lived by the moment in her long life. But Eben Pay had known and worked for Judge Isaac Parker and now he knew he sat again in the presence of one who would be remarked upon and remembered by writers in the future.

Unlike so many of his contemporaries, Eben Pay did not leech off the mighty. Instead, he had an appreciation for them and was willing to stand nearby just to watch. And, of course, he always got caught up and became involved.

And so Eben Pay enjoyed the evening suppers with Clara Barton, and they spoke of many things. Of her service in other wars, of his learning of the law, of her concern for natural disasters, of his study of Indian tribes.

"Yes," Clara Barton said. "I've seen that very large Cherokee who is your servant."

Eben Pay laughed and shook his head, looking into the candle shine on the center of the table.

"He's no servant," he said. "He's my friend. And he's not a Cherokee. He's an Osage."

"There is some distinction, I suppose."

"Very much," Eben Pay said, and laughed again. "If Joe Mountain thought someone had called him a Cherokee, I don't think I could ensure the safety of any white man in Florida."

"Then tell me the difference," Clara Barton said. And Eben Pay knew the gray lady was only promoting conversation. Perhaps, he thought, because she had Miss Newton's interest at heart and it had been obvious from the start that Miss Newton's interest was in Eben Pay.

It was not an unwelcome or an unpleasant thing to have such a worldly, to him, and attractive, to everybody, woman watching his lips as though to catch each word. To taste it. There was that quality about her, he thought. That she was tasting everything around her because she had never had the opportunity to sample such flavors before.

On the night after the *Gussie* returned, Eben Pay moved through the great lobby of the Plant Hotel without feeling any distress, even though he had been present in the room where General Shafter had heard all the horrid details from Captain Stoval. Nothing of great value was lost, he thought, except some considerable face. But this sort of thing would be quickly overcome by the still wildly enthusiastic popular feeling for the war, the certain knowledge that corrupt Spaniards would collapse before the righteous might of the United States. So if not now, tomorrow, and everyone could continue to enjoy this little carnival ball in Florida for just a moment longer. And he, too, was caught up in it, moving that night to his usual table in the corner of the dining room and Mr. Plant himself bowing and smiling and knowing full well what everyone knew now, that Eben Pay was one of Shafter's men and besides that a friend of Mr. Roosevelt.

Well, what the hell, he had thought when these tidings came to him through idle gossip and casual talk along the bar. Mr. Roosevelt would likely not even know me now, he thought, but in fact I did come here with his letter in hand, from San Antonio.

And it amused Eben Pay that even Joe Mountain, who most certainly was not allowed to promenade through the great halls of the Plant, was considered one of Shafter's men. Sent here by Mr. Roosevelt, too. And because of that sat in the kitchen and ate his large fill of oysters and fish and no doubt wondered why the hell there wasn't more red meat and corn. But in any event, no one challenged his being there, not simply because he was an awesome presence due to his size, but because he was one of Shafter's men.

Shafter, of course, didn't know any of this. But there were high ranking officers in this hotel who knew that the tattooed Osage was more often in Shafter's rooms than they were, because wherever Eben Pay went, the Osage went.

And because of that, far away from the rooms of the commanding general, the lowly came forward to Eben Pay and offered drinks and smiles and condescension.

So in the places of this hotel where electric lights cast silver unreality across the overstuffed circular settees and the wicker rocking chairs and the red shining glasses of wine in stemmed glasses, Eben Pay had become a man well recognized.

He had not come here ignorant of power. He had served in the court of Isaac Parker, and among men who were deputy marshals of that court, all of whom held ultimate power in their hands. By the gavel or the pistol. And although he had never held it in his hand himself, he had been close to it. And knew how it felt.

And he knew he was in the same position now. No matter how all the rest sneered and snickered at Shafter, he was indeed the commanding general of this Fifth Corps, and so long as he was, the sneering and snickering had to be done out of sight. And Eben Pay was one of his men, and Eben Pay knew it as well as anyone else in all of Florida.

And because of loyalty or maybe because of ambition or perhaps because any ability to change it was beyond his grasp, he embraced it.

All of which was a little intoxicating. Particularly when he saw the light in the eyes of Carlina Bessaford Newton while he was speaking to Clara Barton.

During the dinner hour on the night after the *Gussie* expedition Clara Barton said, "I have always been uneasy about the way we have treated our Indians."

"As was Judge Parker," Eben Pay said.

"My impression of him has always been that he was rather bloodthirsty."

So Eben Pay went into a long discourse about the trials of his old mentor, a friend to his father as was Mr. Roosevelt. Not only the trials in his courtroom but those in his conscience as well, having been left on a lawless frontier with minimal instructions from Congress and a ruthless catalogue of punishments for crimes that should have been brought before state circuit courts.

These stories spinning from Eben Pay's mouth enthralled Carlina Bessaford Newton as nothing else ever had, and part of the attraction was that same power this young man held and knew he held. Although in her short association with Clara Barton, Carlina had seen plenty of people worthy of public respect, nothing in that experience and certainly not in her Puritan upbringing had prepared her for this sudden familiarity with men who were involved in the deadly business called war.

And Eben Pay seemed to her a man gentle and above such games, and yet she knew he was neither a shy man nor a stranger to violence or to men who were anything but gentle. Her fascination with him was partly due to the apparent contradiction and it made her heart beat a little faster when he touched her hand across the table, because she did not know if she was afraid of him or if there was some other sentiment growing. Whatever it was, it made her feel sinful, but delightfully so.

Clara Barton, on this evening, as she had done before, soon retired with the excuse of old age and her need of sleep, although Eben Pay observed that her eyes were as bright and wakeful as anyone's in the room, and went to the elevator. Eben Pay and Carlina Bessaford Newton rose and watched her go and then, as they had been doing for a number of nights, went to the veranda for a stroll, his arm held out for her and her hand inside his elbow, her fingers lightly on his sleeve but somehow, he thought, with a rather possessive grip.

The first-floor veranda of the Plant Hotel was much like those verandas found on southern mansions, wide enough to accommodate chairs and settees and swings well back from the porch railing, leaving more than adequate room for those who wanted to promenade without having to step over stretched legs or angle around cocktail tables. As usual, there were a great many officers and newspaper reporters and assorted women in the chairs, talking softly and smoking and drinking afterdinner iced tea or cups of chocolate or sometimes stronger stuff and munching the pineapple-mint candy wafers that were the specialty of the house.

The couple walked slowly, looking down across the sands, where they could see distant fires of soldier encampments and hear an occasional bugle call in the regulars' bivouacs. After a late afternoon shower, the skies had cleared and there was the moon, turning all the sloping landscape around the hotel to an icy-looking counterpane although the day's heat yet lingered and caused the sweat to pop out around the collar after only a little exertion.

Eben Pay talked about the difference in these skies, in this southern clime, from that in the center of the continent, where he had spent many nights in the Indian Territory with nothing between him and the dark sky but a thin blanket.

"Even with full moonlight there, the sky seems darker," he said. "Here, it's almost like milk."

"You sound like a poet," she said. And he laughed.

"Well, my mother always told me I should have been a writer."

They rounded the first corner of this square building and continued to walk, and here, away from the main entrance, there were not so many loungers in the wicker chairs. They walked on and round the corner to the back of the hotel and here there was no wicker furniture at all, and ahead they could see the loading ramp behind the kitchen doors, where each evening wagons arrived to deliver the produce and the fish and the fruit that would feed them all the next day. On this night, the wagons had already arrived and there were stacks of crates, waiting, their contents to be carried into the kitchen in the wee hours of morning by the kitchen crew, who would prepare breakfast.

They paused and Eben Pay turned to her and both her hands were on his arms and he moved his face close to hers and kissed her on the lips, a rather light brush, like the stroke of a butterfly wing, and started to kiss her again, more strongly. But then there was movement among the crates of produce and a figure rose dark in the moonlight shadow of the veranda roof, looking strangely tall yet somehow heavy and solid, like an oak stump.

Eben Pay drew back from Carlina and she caught her breath and moved behind him. The man standing in the shadows among the crates held two bottles of milk in one hand and in the other a burlap sack bulging with fruit obviously taken from an opened crate of oranges at his feet.

Eben Pay felt a sudden surge of tension, looking at this dark figure with a hat brim turned low over his face and yet not concealing a glint of eyes. And then a glint of teeth as well as the man smiled, or at least parted his lips.

"Good evening to you, sir," he said. "Good evening to you, ma'am."

It was then that Eben Pay recognized him.

"Who is that?" he said. "Price?"

"Ah, yes, sir. On a small forage for my men. You see, if you'll pardon me, ma'am, we've bloody nothing to eat except hardtack and rancid bacon the last week, and I supposed your good highnesses would hardly miss a little fruit and milk."

He turned and moved to the edge of the porch and the moon caught him full face as he turned and grinned.

"Sorry, sir, I haven't any more of those cigars for you and that savage of yours this time. Maybe next."

And then he was down into the sand and quickly off in the moonlight and even as they watched, gone, disappeared into the brilliant night like a fox, gone before their eyes.

"Stealing food?" she whispered.

"Yes, it seems so," Eben Pay said. "Come on. It's time I take you to your room."

They moved back along the veranda quickly and she was trembling and he held her arms now, and then put his hand along her back. As they moved away, Joe Mountain came out of the shadows and stared down through the night where Dylan Price had disappeared.

"A dangerous man," Joe Mountain said aloud, and his fingers caressed the cold metal of the big revolver in his waistband under his coat. "But maybe a good one, too."

He turned back to where all the crates were stacked and bent over the one Dylan Price had pried open and took out a half dozen oranges and slipped them inside his shirt and, grinning, went along the veranda toward the front entrance of the hotel and then to the rear stairway and upward to the room that he shared with Eben Pay.

Carlina Bessaford Newton

One does not spring into the real world from a rigid Puritan up-bringing full grown as Aphrodite from the sea.

And were my father to suspect that I had ever made such an analogy, he would clasp his strong hand about all that represented me and fling it into the flames to purify his household of such blasphemy. And could he get the same hand on me, he would cast me in as well, a kind of warning suggestion concerning the eternal hellfire deserved in cases like mine.

From time to time, since I departed Fitchburg for Boston, I have sent a short letter to my mother in order that she might know I have not been consumed by the wicked world. I have never received a reply. I doubt she ever saw a single one of those notes, my father being postmaster in his own house and deciding the fitness of each word sent to every addressee.

So I have been cut off. I do not know if they live. And in some perverse way, it doesn't matter. It is, rather, a kind of glorious seal on my independence. On my rebellion.

Perhaps rebellion is the better of the two words. Because I am rebelling against a creed that refuses the pleasures of living and against the tyranny of men. First, my father, who embodied both, and now my young gentleman friend, who can be accused only of being a man.

My young gentleman. From the glances we get I know that's how he is regarded. I am sure he does not himself consider that he is somewhat like a puppy dog on a leash, to me or anyone else. In fact, he is a man who somehow gently implies that he is the one who holds the leash, even the leash on the savage red Indian he has with him who follows him around and who terri-fies me.

It is fascinating beyond description, his stories of that land from whence he comes, so cruel and barbaric and untamed. It sounds, as he tells of it, so different from Mr. Cooper's novels of frontier lands, such as *The Deerslayer*. And yet a well-educated man, a man of law, a man who never has dirt under his fingernails.

My young gentleman. And he is that. A gentleman, for he has never pressed himself upon me in words or deeds. Yet, I have come instinctively to know from his eye and manner there is a desire within him that is managed only by good breeding and self-control.

He has kissed me, a most pleasant experience. He has touched me in ways I have never been touched since childhood when the Reverend Compton had me over his knees for punishment due to my wicked ways.

The temptations have been most overpowering. This new freedom seems to challenge me to test it and yet thus far I have successfully saved my virtue from almost certain rout.

It isn't that I do not respect my young gentleman. Or that I do not find him strangely attractive. It is simply a case of applying some new power to have my own will, other than someone else's, particularly a man's.

Much of this I owe only to myself. But much as well to Clara Barton, who has shown me what a woman can be. Not just a doe-eyed whim for a strong man.

Before we arrived in Florida, Clara Barton was aware of my upbringing. She is a person of such compassion that one cannot be long in her presence without revealing hidden things. And she knew that in all my life at home I had never had a moment when I could go into my room and close my door.

So she said that due to her old age, she needed her own room alone. She said that she did snore a great deal and that she did not wish to disturb my sleep with it. She said all these and other things and even in this beehive of people, because she is Clara Barton, managed to find accommodations for both of us, rooms alone. Of course, mine is not much larger than an ironing board, yet it is my own.

So in this dreadful heat, in late afternoon, I can come and

bathe myself and lie for a while in only my chemise with the breeze coming through my window. And at night sleep without fearful dreams.

What a delightful life I have discovered! Myself and Clara Barton, superior to all other women that we see here, all subjects of their rulers either permanently, in marriage, or in more sordid arrangements.

Clara Barton has told me of her meeting with President McKinley on the subject of aid to the Cuban mission. He laughed. He asked her how women of the Red Cross could know what was expected in Cuba. She replied that she and her women knew a great deal. The president said, still laughing, that they should all go home and ask their husbands what was required.

But through the force of her will, she had overcome even that kind of male arrogance.

And now what a thrill to know that I am capable of making the decision which may bind or release me, that my fate and future can be in these hands of mine and not in those of anyone who importunes me, no matter how tenderly or suggestive the entreaties, no matter how outspoken the demand, no matter if on the spur of the moment I am swayed to a kiss, yet have the strength to cast the deciding vote.

Good heavens. It sounds like a political convention. It is not. It is even more wonderful in that, were my young man despised, the decision each time would be elementary. But he is not despised. He is much treasured. Yet with all that, it is not he who determines the course of our relationship. It is myself.

Astonishing! Here in this place, there is the opportunity for what I have read is love. But refusing it is more exciting. Denying it is an exhibition of strength I have never known before. It makes me light-headed.

There is one note of disappointment. Clara Barton has gone off to take command of her "troops," as everyone calls them, aboard the ship *State of Texas* and will soon return to Cuba, where certainly the insurgents will welcome her, knowing her good works from her previous visits to that troubled island.

Meanwhile, she has left behind one of her most trusted assistants, Miss Marian Winchel, with a small party to go later on another ship with more supplies. I am of that party and I can only hope that we will be away from here before everything is finished in Cuba.

The ways of the military become a mystery. Regardless of the supposed good offices of General Nelson Miles, the United States Army does not desire the assistance of the Red Cross in this campaign. Which has not daunted Clara Barton. And it will not daunt me. We will go to Cuba and assist anyone we find in need.

Now, after a hard day of work with all these obstinate porters and army people, trying to arrange for our supplies to be loaded on the small contract vessel which will take us from here, the great adventure is ahead. Perhaps even tomorrow.

And the breeze comes into my open window. It is not cool, but at least it brings the smell of sea. And I am so completely content.

Who was it that wrote what I read when I was just a child? Who was it? Who was it? Henderson? No. Henley?

I am the master of my fate.

I am the captain of my soul.

Not my young gentleman. Not any of these powerful men who plan the invasion of Cuba. Not even Clara Barton. But myself. It is intoxication beyond any earthly pleasure.

And perhaps tomorrow we go. Perhaps tomorrow we go to that imprisoned isle. On this glorious crusade, to free the downtrodden.

It is almost unbearable.

CHAPTER 7

IT was June 6, 1898.

In every small community across the United States of America, mayors and aldermen and ministers of the gospel and freckled urchins were already joyfully preparing celebrations for the Fourth of July, especially significant this year because the Great Republic would by then have liberated another people of the Western Hemisphere from European tyranny.

Firecrackers and red-white-and-blue bunting would be everywhere and choice phrases delivered amid delightful odors of roasting pig and cinnamon pie, which were being set aside now to be protected until the proper time like the precious jewels of some mad Moslem prince.

In the more sophisticated urban centers, the mood was much the same although the excitement, perhaps, was more over the expansion of commerce that of personal freedom.

Even so, there were as many per capita showings of Old Glory along the canyons of Sixth Avenue in Manhattan, New York, as there were along Main Street of Manhattan, Kansas. Give or take a few.

It was, in all respects, a wonderful year. The Civil War was so long past that many of the veterans in old blue or gray who had cluttered up the sidewalks showing their truncated legs and

[95]

arms and slashed faces, were dead now, so people had forgotten what happens to flesh when exposed to flying metal.

This was a year when a man named Ronald Ross discovered the bacteria that caused malaria. Nobody paid much attention to him. It was the year an unknown Japanese researcher explained the causes of dysentery. Nobody paid any attention to him at all.

It was the year that thousands of men would be sent into an area where malaria and dysentery were a way of life, even among those who had lived there all their days.

This was the year after Queen Victoria's Diamond Jubilee, an extremely good omen for the war, some said, because after all it had been a British queen who destroyed Spain's world domination almost three centuries before.

It was noted in intellectual circles that Bismarck and Gladstone had just died. End of an era. And now, with the help of God, and a full appreciation of Alfred Mahan's book about naval power, it was America's Turn.

"Joe?" Eben Pay asked. "Have you ever heard of a man named Bismarck?"

"Sure. Judge Parker hanged him back in 1890, the year you came to Fort Smith. He was a little weasel-faced son of a bitch who done murder over in Okmulgee."

"No, that's not the same Bismarck."

In the White House, William McKinley grew more and more inured to the vicious blasts of Grover Cleveland and William Jennings Bryan. Yet the deep purple patches under his eyes grew more pronounced, like ripening Concord grapes, and there was a haunted glinting of the eyes as though he could foresee that soon an assassin's bullet would find him.

And what a magnificent time, too, because the nation was being bound up in the web of railroads and telegraph wires. Now good news could be carried quickly to all places, and once there spread widely through the wonderful highspeed rotary presses.

"Why look here," shouted William Randolph Hearst. "Our circulation today is well over half a million."

"I will match that," shouted Joseph Pulitzer. "I will *surpass* that."

"Give me bigger headlines," the publisher of the *New York Journal* snapped. "Give me illustrations of Spanish cruelty."

"Give me secret reports," said the publisher of the *New York World*. "Give me *patriotism*."

In Manhattan, New York, and Manhattan, Kansas, the people were living on headlines and patriotism, on Spanish cruelty and America's destiny to change the world, with the help of God and a solid Republican administration.

Of course, in both these places, far removed from smoke and noise and hostile bullets, everyone was squirming with eagerness to go liberate some oppressed peoples. And why not do such holy work against a weak enemy?

But those expected to smell the smoke and hear the noise and feel the bite of bullets in their flesh, sometimes, though not always, had a different perspective.

As with Dylan Price, who told his troops, "Look to your weapons, lads, and depend on the soldier next to you. Your rifle and your comrade, the only friends you'll have on a fire swept field."

So the crusade to avenge the *Maine* and drive the wicked Spaniard from the Western Hemisphere began. At least, it appeared to begin. On the morning of June 6, 1898. A Monday. A good day, everyone said, to start a week's work. And, they said, this will only take about a week.

Everybody didn't say that. General Shafter didn't say it because he remembered such expectations regarding suppression of Comanches in west Texas. Dylan Price didn't say it because he remembered Isandhlwana. Clara Barton didn't say it because she had seen too many wildly optimistic civilians who had no notion of how hard it could be to subdue an armed adversary.

But the pundits working for Mr. Hearst and Mr. Pulitzer said it. Old generals of the Civil War said it, because they had forgotten, and mortal conflict was, in their minds, a hazy glow. Ministers from their pulpits said it because they didn't know what they were talking about. Businessmen in the canyons of lower Manhattan, New York, said it because they were already looking forward to expanding markets. Barbers in Manhattan, Kansas, said it because they had read it on the front pages of their newspapers.

So on this Monday morning of optimism, three of the regular regiments, most of Shafter's staff, and some of the artillery loaded onto flatcars in the dawning and moved to the piers. Actually, they moved very little. Mostly they stood and waited, the locomotives at the head of each line of cars immobile through most of the morning. They stood like greasy elephants, puffing black clouds of smoke up to be caught by the sea wind and dispersed in a sulfur scented mist back along the line of impatient troops.

Ahead, alongside the ships, there were already strings of boxcars, their varied contents being carried onto the waiting vessels, all coastal steamers contracted by the War Department. Some had loading booms. Some did not. Some looked seaworthy, some did not. What most had in common were scaling paint and rust.

Behind, there were more trains, coughing, waiting, all lined up to use a single set of rails to the shore. The train in front had to unload and then back out before the next serial could puff forward.

Lieutenant Colonel John Stoval, in a locomotive cab at the head of eight flatcars where the men of his regiment sprawled about in the sweltering sun, explained to the engineer. "This is a goddamned masterpiece of inefficiency!"

On his own flatcar, Private Reed had similar thoughts.

"Christ's sweet sake, Corporal Price," he said. "Why don't we get off and walk?"

"Never walk when you can ride," Price said.

He was lying back against a case of ammunition, his hat pulled low over his eyes, now and then swiping a hand at the flies that were coming thick and biting.

"Not much ride, huh? By Gott," said Mittelberg.

"Yah, and when we get down on the water we gonna get that old paddle-wheeler again I bet." Swenson laughed, brushing sweat from his face with the flats of both hands.

"Talk of drink and women," Price said from under his hat. "But not military operations, you sweet muttonheads. Your time will come. Sooner than you want."

First Sergeant Maurice Barry was moving along the flatcars, stepping over his reclining troops, like a great beer barrel with arms and short legs, carrying his rifle like a straw in his right fist. He squatted beside Dylan Price. His seamed face was etched in deep lines.

"A load of mule shit, all this," he said.

"Indeed it is, first soldier, indeed it is."

"Your lads seem up to it," Barry said, glancing back along the flatcar.

"We'll see," said Price.

"Yeah, we'll see," Barry said. "And right now, I'd trade a year of life for a thimble of good whiskey, huh Dylan?"

"At least a year."

It took all day to get the leading elements of the invasion forced onto the ships. Locomotive engineers, leaning from their cabs and staring incredulously from beneath their long-billed rail-roader caps, and ships' masters and crews leaning over their rail-ings, were astonished to witness the kind of chaos and confusion that only an unorganized army can create.

Eben Pay and Joe Mountain were in place early, having arrived with much of the rest of Shafter's staff and taking their position on board the command ship *Seguranca*. This was a small steam vessel that was to be the Fifth Corps headquarters ship until the army was placed ashore. It was a two-stacker with completely inadequate billet space for those who were supposed to debark in her, but at least there was a canvas canopy over the back deck. It gave her the appearance of an excursion ship, which she was, and there Eben Pay and Joe Mountain took their position early in the day to watch the unending disorder on the dock below.

It was quickly apparent that this ship did not have enough facilities for answering the myriad calls of nature.

"I guess we just have to do it right over the side," said Joe Mountain.

"It looks that way," said Eben Pay.

"Well, how about the other thing? How about a shit? Where do you do that?"

"Joe, we'll work something out."

Even with all the tumult, Eben Pay felt a part of some great movement, a man among many who was off on a splendid undertaking. He was well enough read in history to know that most of Mr. Hearst's and Mr. Pulitzer's bombast against the Spaniards was self-serving nationalism. But he was caught up, swept along with being at the eye of this hurricane, at the very basic human vortex of something inexorable. Something, therefore, that was grand.

Later that night, when some more of General Shafter's staff arrived on board, looking harried and gaunt and exhausted and terrified, he was somewhat disillusioned. As a captain passed him coming on deck, he looked at Eben Pay and said, "For God's sake, when the Old Man gets on board don't go near him. He's burning every ball in sight."

And Eben Pay learned why from these same staff officers. All day, the navy had been sending urgent messages to Washington urging that an invasion must be mounted at once because they had the Spanish navy bottled up in Santiago harbor. The War Department sent these pleas on to Shafter at Tampa, disregarding all his previous reports about the sad state of his army and their lack of training and supply. Finally, directly from the White House, came the order. Go! Now!

Shafter may have been fat and sweating, but he was under no illusions about the condition of transport from the Plant Hotel to the docks. And thus he issued his most famous order.

It was sent as an action copy to all units. It said, in effect, "We sail for Cuba tomorrow with the dawn. Anybody who gets to the ships, goes. Anybody who does not, doesn't."

It set off perhaps the ultimate military stampede of all time.

The Plant Hotel exploded. Marian Winchel said later she would not have been surprised to have seen officers leaping through the screen windows. Carlina Bessaford Newton was terrified, caught in a maelstrom of rushing officers, some of them sober. Marian Winchel was unperturbed.

Mr. Roosevelt and his men stole a locomotive. One regiment took the wagon train of another. Fistfights broke out. A terrified mule broke from its artillery harness and ran onto the front veranda of the Plant Hotel, squealing and kicking aside the wicker chairs.

Catching the excitement, locomotive engineers pulled their

whistle lanyards. A newspaperman recovering from the latest round of conviviality was seen running down the sands toward the beach, nine miles away, waving a pencil in one hand, a magnum of champagne in the other, and shouting, "Wait, wait!" Soldiers scrambled aboard flatcars just returning from the docks, holding others at bay with fixed bayonets. A Cuban musician ran from the hotel and down the front veranda steps carrying a bass violin, stumbled and fell, shattering the instrument and becoming entangled in the strings.

It was at this time that General Shafter and what remained of his staff at the hotel took to horse with what dignity they could muster and rode toward the piers, passing along the railroad tracks, where utter bedlam was the mood, his large bay horse grunting with protest at the massive weight that pressed down in the saddle.

Two soldiers, going into the hotel to deliver messages to their commanding officers, passed through the kitchen. Observing the disorder among employees and the platters of entrées hot and just ready for service to the tables, they sat down and ate what Mr. Plant later estimated to have been seventeen pounds of red snapper and beef Wellington. Along the tracks, another soldier ran to a flatcar, carrying a squealing pig he had just liberated from a Tampa pen. As he threw the pig up and then scrambled aboard, he discovered too late that these men were not of his unit. They kept the pig but threw him off into the sand as the train pulled away toward the shore.

An unidentified civilian rushed out into the moonlight firing a pistol into the air, shouting, "Cuba libre, Cuba libre!" An army chaplain, left completely behind, not knowing how to get to the ships nor even where they were, fell to his knees on the kitchen loading dock and prayed. A number of Mr. Plant's Cuban employees joined him, many of them smoking marijuana cigarettes. "Hey, padre, you want some hemp?"

As a number of officers' ladies collected on the front veranda of the hotel to hold hands and peer off into the milky night toward the west, where they knew their husbands were boarding ships to take them to combat, a small garlic-smelling man passed among them with a brass musical instrument. "Only three dollars," he kept saying. "A very fine cornet, only three dollars." Until one of the largest and most imposing of the ladies adjusted her umbrella-sized hat and shouted, "Transport your ass out of here, boy!"

And at the other end of this ribbon of madness, the scramble continued through the entire night, Eben Pay watching with the sense that he was seeing history being made.

"I never thought a white man's war was like this," Joe Mountain said.

"I didn't, either."

One regiment had commandeered a ship and its soldiers were on the gangways keeping everyone else off with drawn pistols. A colonel with a squad of armed infantry took a small steam launch out into the darkness of the bay, and pirated a steamer still lying off the docks, claiming it for his regiment.

Three mules fell into the water. Twice that many soldiers did and were fished out by Cuban stevedores, crawling dripping onto the pier with their packs and rifles gone. The mules swam off into the darkness. Trains were bumping back and forth like the cars in a carnival ride for children, their head lamps yellow puffs of light in the night, the locomotive bells clanging. Now and again a ship's master, for no apparent reason, blew a steamy blast on his foghorn.

Eben Pay saw the quartermaster captain he had first seen on the day of his arrival, among the boxcars, now rushing up and down the dock, screaming and waving sheaths of papers. Nobody paid any attention to him.

The electric lights at the top of the metal poles set at fifty-foot intervals along the docks cast a vague, pale light across all that went on below. The great commotion had roused sleeping birds and they flew about with harsh squawkings and dipped into the faint glow above the piers. With a dull thud a confused sea gull slammed into the wheelhouse of the *Seguranca*, shattering glass.

"Throw the poor ruddy son of a bitch overboard," Eben Pay heard someone shout.

By dawn, his eyes were grainy. He tried to rub out the sting.

Behind him, on the deck, Joe Mountain was stretched on his back, mouth open, sleeping.

"God, I wish I could do that."

But the excitement was too intense. Even now. After a full night of it, they still streamed down to the dock, the men and the mules and the trainloads of unopened boxes, the contents of which nobody knew.

Eben Pay leaned against the ship's railing, unable to stop watching the mad scene on the pier below. He felt the hot Florida sun rising at his back and soon the sweat was running through his hair and down his neck.

Joe Mountain woke and began to roam along the deck, grumbling about the lack of anything to eat. As the hours passed, each was marked by the ringing of a bell on the bridge.

And then, in midafternoon, having shown himself in various places along the line and the pier, General Shafter arrived at the *Seguranca*. Some modicum of sanity descended. A few last mules and horses were loaded. The massive general walked up the main gangway. Eben Pay was there, with others, to meet him.

Shafter stared at Eben Pay a moment, his eyes bloodshot, the sweat streaming down along his great jowls.

"Well, Mr. Pay," said General Shafter, "how is everything going?"

"It's going very well, sir," said Eben Pay.

"The hell it is," Shafter said. "But at least, by God, we've got most of it aboard."

He turned to his adjutant and nodded as though they were seeing one another for the first time that day.

"We've got it mostly aboard, haven't we Malcomb?"

"Yes sir," Captain Malcomb said, nodding. "Most of it."

"Oh Christ!" Shafter said, turning toward his stateroom, if any cell on this ship could be called that. "All right, let's get these goddamned ships to sea!"

Half a dozen officers of the staff turned toward the wheelhouse, where a telegraph line had been linked from the shore to serve while they were tied to the dock. But Shafter stopped them in midstride with a great roar, sweat spraying off his upper lip as he shouted.

"And for God's sweet sake, keep that bunch of punta holed sons of bitch newspapermen off me for a little while, most especially Richard Harding Davis. I don't want to start this damned campaign by committing murder."

Shafter turned back to his stateroom, but first looked at Eben Pay and Joe Mountain and allowed himself a small grin.

"This is one helluva way to make a man earn his pay," he said. "Come on in, I want to hear how it went here on the dock today."

They followed him in and the general collapsed with a great, moist sigh onto a bunk not nearly half as large as it should have been.

Looking at this great hulk, Eben Pay could not help but be impressed. Not with the size of the man, nor with his purple language, which was indeed impressive. But with the mere fact that he had known his soldiers well enough to have issued that mad order that sent everyone scrambling for a space on the invasion fleet. Known them well enough to understand that detailed orders not being possible, it was best only to point them in the right direction and allow initiative and enthusiasm to get them on board those ships.

A little later, looking out from the chart room of this command vessel, Eben Pay saw just how effective it had been. There was now afloat in Tampa Bay an army of seventeen thousand men, rank and file. Two infantry divisions, each with about a half dozen regiments, a separate infantry brigade, four batteries of artillery, including one of Gatling guns, and a division of cavalry.

Of course, the cavalry was dismounted. The only animals aboard were some mules and horses for staff members and artillery units. The effort to get even those few down to the docks and onto ships had amazed Eben Pay.

"I never seen anybody handle livestock as bad as them army men," Joe Mountain said. "Me and my brother Blue Foot coulda did better than that when we was still waitin' to be weaned."

"Joe, don't talk bad about soldiers when we're right in the middle of so many of them. And find us a place to sleep."

"I already have," the Osage said. "Right over yonder on the ass end of this boat under that tent they got stretched over everything back there."

"All right, Joe. Gimme one of those oranges you stole."

"I never stole nothin'," Joe Mountain said, pulling an orange from his shirt and handing it to Eben Pay. "I got some of them little cans of corned beef, too. You want one?"

It took a while for the ships to clear the docks. But before the first afternoon rain squall drenched everyone on deck, giving a welcome relief from the scalding heat, most of them were out into Tampa Bay, bows pointed in the direction of the open sea.

Eben Pay was standing at the rail just outside the commanding general's stateroom. Inside, Shafter had taken off his blouse and shirt and lay on his bunk in underwear only, fanning himself with a folded copy of the *New York World*, trying to start a small nap after almost forty hours of work without sleep.

Watching the movement of the ships over the surface of the placid bay, Eben Pay could not help but think of a flock of chickens arranging themselves in proper pecking order. Flags were up, whistles were blowing, decks were crowded with troops waving to one another. There was a smell of salt and fish and far places, and above it all a dome of clear blue sky interrupted here and there with billowing cloud, white as virtue, thick as cotton batting, pregnant with water.

And while he was breathing deeply of the Gulf breeze, Captain Malcomb came running along the deck, a yellow sheet of paper in hand. Before going into the commanding general's stateroom he paused, eyes hollow and uncomprehending, and showed Eben Pay the dispatch.

"Christ, he'll explode," Malcomb said.

"What is it?" Eben Pay asked and then read the words on the flimsy paper.

"Wait until further orders before sailing," it stated. Sent by the secretary of war.

"Because the navy says," Captain Malcomb said, "that maybe all the Spanish fleet *isn't* bottled up and we can't go until they are."

"Oh shit," Eben Pay said and turned and moved back toward the fantail quickly, not wanting to be near when Shafter read that message.

Joe Mountain was there, sitting with his legs dangling over the stern. He had his boots off and his great toes were wiggling in the sunlight.

"This is pretty good, Eben Pay," he said. "Some of these men who run this ship come back here and said I couldn't do this, but I said they was wrong. So they went back to whatever they got to do someplace else. C'mon. Take off your shoes."

"What the hell," Eben Pay said and he sat down beside Joe Mountain and took off his shoes.

Dylan ap Rhys ap Llewellyn

'Tis a bloody pucker.

And my apology to dear old father for speaking as though I learned all my swearing from the damned Midland English.

But a redcoat long I was, and like Irish or Scot or other Welsh, the words rub off and we begin after a time to talk like any London Saxon.

Little matter the words, I suppose. That good Queen Vic I served so long and faithful and everybody knows she talks with her loving consort in German. Well, not now, her loving consort dead and in the ground.

My God, Albert dead and in the ground before my first service to Her Majesty. So why do I still think of her as a young girl, a young queen, when by the time I even knew what a queen was and shipped off to Africa, her already an old and doddering lady fat and leading her little dog about.

But no matter when or how. Queen she was. And still is, and leading another little dog around I suppose.

I have never heard of President McKinley leading a little dog around. I have never seen President McKinley come out on a blustery day to review the troops, riding regal in an open carriage as each regiment one by one presents arms as he passes.

In fact, I have never seen the president at all. I saw the queen once. The regiment was in great bib and tucker just after some bloody little shot in the Sudan. I think it was, I'm never sure anymore. All red and blue and the colors in front waving in the breeze and the battle streamers going out and the queen prancing by. Well, her not prancing. Her matched bays prancing at the lead of her coach, and all the lads standing proud and sober.

That day she had riding beside her one of her grandsons, or

some such thing, all plumes and silver helmet and a sword long as my pecker and twice as hard, the one, you know, they call Willie and they say will be next to run the show in Germany. At least I'll say this for him. He knows how to grow a mustache that catches the eye.

It's a different army here. Tan and dirt color and a little blue. The food's about the same. Terrible it is. The noncommissioned officers are all the same, I think in all armies. Tough. We've got a first sergeant that one of these days I will scald. Not because he is bad, or not because I don't enjoy his company, but just because he's there waiting for me.

Someday, I will scald him.

And high command in all armies is the same, too. Stupid. Here we have been in these mucking ships for days, sitting on the bay in view of where we cast off, sweating and waiting, waiting and sweating.

Drinking water is rationed. One canteen cup a day. No bathing off sweat at all. And the longer we sit in this sun, the more slimy the water becomes. By now, the fourth day, each sip tastes like frog piss.

'Tis a bloody pucker.

What little plunder we carried aboard in our shirts is now gone. So it's commissary. Rancid bacon and hardtack. And that tinned bully beef. Our cooks do the best they can.

There is a National Guard outfit on this boat. They have no cooks at all. They are ready now to eat the paint off the sides of this ship. I feel sorry for them. Why they are here I will never know. And all they talk about is getting their teeth into some Spaniard.

They may get a tooth broke off, with that bite.

I remember old veterans in the redcoat army, talking about the Crimea and how bloody mucked up it was and how the only thing that saved them was that the Russians were more mucked up than they were. And that their allies the Turks were most mucked up of all.

So now we've got these Cubans. There are about thirty of them on board. Our allies. Stealing everything they can lay hand to. And my men can't forget the *Gussie* and we went onto that beach against fire and found no single Cuban to take the arms we had. So I just tell my men to keep away from the bastards.

Keep your sights set at three hundred yards, I say. And don't worry about anything else, I say.

God, the only relief lying here in this goddamed bay, is the afternoon rain. It comes in gray and slanting from the west, right off the Gulf, a downpour, a blue, cooling downpour. And we all get out on deck and turn our faces up against it.

Then it's gone and the sky is suddenly blue again and the sun is laughing down on these goddamned ships lying at anchor in this bay.

My three Germans are seasick. Sweet Jesus, we haven't even left the shore yet.

And the rumor goes round. We'd best get to Cuba quick and out again before the yellow-fever season beats us to it.

No fear, I tell my troopers. I've seen typhus and cholera and dysentery and all the plagues of lung and asshole and those, too, of frequent use of uninspected whorehouses. Just eat your bully beef, so long as you can stomach it, and keep your sights set at three hundred yards.

What I don't tell 'em is that for every one the enemy puts down, the sickness will put down five.

CHAPTER 8

 T was a strange harmony, the relationship that had developed between privates Reed and Vanic. Nor was it lost on Dylan Price, who almost instinctively sensed the quality of soldiers, much as his native countrymen almost instinctively sensed the quality of chords in an old Welsh hymn.

Strange because these were two of the most disparate men imaginable. In fact, it seemed they could hardly speak to one another. Although on his second hitch in the American army, Vanic had never made much effort to learn the fine points of English except as they applied to commands given during close order drill. And whatever he had learned he kept locked behind the flat, expressionless face, as though the words to him were like unruly sheep that he was reluctant to let out of their pen.

And Reed, a naturally taciturn Scot, gave the impression that he would not waste his words on anyone he did not trust, and that included just about everybody except Corporal Price.

Yet, these two were inseparable. The squat, stolid Slav with the pale eyes set in a bullet-shaped head attached to his shoulders by almost no neck at all, and the lank, slightly stooped, copper-haired Ulster Presbyterian whose glance was always half ice, half fire.

Dylan Price remarked all of this to himself. But he did so

without prejudgment, because of all the things he might be, Price was foremost a philosopher of soldiering.

He would not have put it that way. He would not have put it any way at all. He simply observed and without definitions or mental masturbation classified some men as magnets, others as iron filings. And the patterns of response were as inevitable and predictable to him as anything could be. As sure as the solid click of metal when the bolt of a rifle was seated, locking a round in the chamber, ready for firing.

In this case, Reed was the magnet, Vanic the iron filings. Some men are leaders, Price knew. Some followers. Maybe with Reed and Vanic there was more.

Well, Price thought, a man's love life is his own business so long as he doesn't make it mine or it doesn't muck up the bloody squad. And for Reed and Vanic, perhaps love, or whatever passed for it, had no part to play. Maybe it only looked that way. All three of the Germans in the squad thought it looked that way. If Swenson had been aware that such things existed, he might have thought so, too.

Certainly if there was some actual proof, or even some hint that fairyland, as Price put it, was involved, it would be straight to First Sergeant Barry with the two of them, and thence to Lieutenant Beaster, their new company commander, and then to Lieutenant Colonel Stoval, the regimental commander now, and from there straight into a general court-martial. And on conviction, a long stint in some army stockade prison, such places coming as close to a full manifestation of hell on earth as anyone had yet come up with.

Dylan Price knew there could be appearance without substance. Not that he was naïve enough to reject the substance out of hand, but he knew how soldiers bonded together.

There was that unspoken, always unspoken, camaraderie that worked such chemistry and held men close during the trials of training and boredom and combat, in carousing and offending decent women, in late-night, after lights-out Taps had been played on the bugle, and two men, dark figures on either end of a foot locker, sitting, smoking, talking in low tones and exposing the colors at the very depth of the soul. Neither really aware of how much they were revealing. Until the full measure of it came years later, after retirement, in the twilight of a life spent learning the technology of violence but now involved with growing tomatoes or petunias, scratching old wounds and recalling to uncaring spouse or uncaring children or maybe only to themselves what it was like in the Old Army.

Dylan Price knew enough about all this to understand that even the conquerors of the known western world three centuries before Christ, the ones who had served in the phalanxes of Alexander the Great, finally went home to Macedonia and bitched about the new army and how it was better under Philip, and in their bitching remembered the words of dead comrades and appreciated them for the first time.

And hoped that somewhere there were other veterans scratching at the same kinds of wounds and memories and recalling words they had themselves spoken. Because each of them knew that there was no closer kinship than that of old campaigners. No wife or father or brother or child could ever take the place of hallowed comrades-in-arms.

Not short-timers, of course. But regulars. Old soldiers.

At least that's how Dylan Price perceived it. But at the same time recognized that his view might be somewhat biased because he had had many comrades-in-arms but never a wife and hardly what could be called father or brothers in the normal sense and certainly no children.

Well, anyway, no children he was willing to claim.

So Reed and Vanic were men he could measure and lose no sleep over. They did their job. They didn't cause any trouble, like Swenson did, always falling into imbroglios due to his dumb innocence, bringing punishment from the company commander. Price didn't like that. He didn't like his squad members standing in front of the company commander and getting two weeks' extra duty. He didn't like the names of his people appearing in the company punishment book.

But Price failed to recognize that sometimes if a man stays

out of minor trouble, when trouble finally comes it is very large indeed.

The trouble finally came to Reed and Vanic on the sixth night the Fifth Corps flotilla lay in Tampa Bay, sweltering in the heat, impatient to be off to Cuba.

The Thirty-seventh Infantry was on board the *Salvador*, a two-stack coastal streamer whose superstructure looked like an asparagus patch gone to seed, booms and masts going up and out in various directions. She was a produce boat, until recently, plying the waters of the Gulf primarily between Panama and Colombia and Mobile and New Orleans.

The *Salvador* was manned by a polyglot deck crew of Colombians and Brazilians, and an engine room crew of Cubans. She was scaly gray in color and smelled of rotten bananas and fermented sugarcane. Except when they pumped the bilges, at which time she took on the aroma of dead rats.

Like the other ships of Shafter's invasion force, she had sat these long, hot days in the bay, a rusting gull resting on the water. On her decks, the men of the Thirty-seventh Infantry had done the best they could, which was not very good at all, mostly hungry and caked with sweat salt and bored. The National Guard troops on board had done no better.

There was little hard money among the regulars, it having been some time since the bugles sounded pay call. But the Guardsmen had a little and soon this was circulating back and forth over games of dice, the usual system of cash flow among soldiers.

"The good soldier," said Price to his squad, "loves women, hard spirits, and gambling. In that order. You may find all three at one place in heaven. But in your present bloody life you damn well take whichever is at hand. And lucky to get it."

So the dice games had become as constant on the decks as the seasickness was at the rails, even though they were not yet technically at sea.

Observing his three Germans, Price said to them, "It is a bloody fine thing, as much as you people puke, that Frederick the Great marched his troops to victory over solid land and could avoid the prospect of water. Otherwise, your motherland that you talk so much about would still be ruled by some Austrian duke."

On this particular day, Private Vanic, E Company, Thirty-seventh Infantry, had won a total of thirty-seven dollars and eighty-four cents. It was a rather grand haul. And after this game, as the sun disappeared among the sweeping gulls and the black thundercloud bank to the west, he and Private Reed, E Company, Thirty-seventh Infantry, sat on the main deck in their usual place, eating their ration of raw bacon and hardtack, leaning against a bulkhead, thinking about the glorious ways thirty-seven dollars and eighty-four cents could be spent if only they had been in Chattanooga or Albany or almost anywhere else but on the deck of this foul tub in the center of Tampa Bay.

They didn't say much. They chewed their meat and crackers and stared out across the placid water, watching the deck lights on all the other ships beginning to reflect in the bay now that it was turning dark, seeing the shore of Florida, their shoulders touching, both hoping the cloud bank in the west would roll in with a soft shower of rain to wash some of the heat from the air.

And still without saying much, as it grew totally night, they slid down onto the deck, using campaign hats as pillows, and went to sleep. Once, when the moon was past zenith, Vanic rose and went to the rail and relieved himself. All along the deck in either direction were the motionless forms of other men from E company.

Vanic knew, as he resumed his position beside Reed, that Corporal Price was sleeping close by. Vanic always assured himself about the exact location of Corporal Price, just in case. Just in case of what, he wasn't sure. But it made sleep easier with the knowledge that the squad leader was near.

It was close to dawn when the Cuban came. The rain had fallen already but there had only been a little and the men of E Company were dry because there was the overhang of an upper deck. The moon was down and the only light was the feeble glimmer of other ships' lanterns reflecting on the water and a dim hurricane lamp on the *Salvador* back toward the stern.

The Cuban moved slowly along the rail, but surely, as though he had measured out the exact spot. He paused, looking along the deck. Nothing moved. Silently, on bare feet, he approached the sleeping forms and bent to Vanic and began to explore with quick fingers for the wallet.

The Cuban didn't see Reed's arms coming up but he gave a sudden, choking grunt as the Scot's hands closed on his throat.

It may have been the thump of the Cuban's head against the deck that woke Dylan Price, sleeping only a few paces away. Whatever it was, Price sat up and saw in the dim reflected light a kicking, thrashing, struggling shadow, and, still half asleep, he was up and moving quickly along the deck.

They were a tangle of arms and legs, Reed and Vanic and the Cuban, and Price saw bare feet thrusting against the deck. The Cuban was pinned under Reed's long form and he was making a wheezing sound that abruptly ceased. Everything had gone still except for a few final quivers in the Cuban's legs and Vanic was pushing himself away and back along the deck on all fours, panting.

"I never done nothin'," he whimpered.

"Shut your mouth," Price whispered, harshly because he was awake now and realized the possibility that there was something happening here better kept quiet.

Reed's hands were still tight around the Cuban's neck as Price reached down. Reed looked up only when Price's hands touched his, and his eyes glinted, like a cat's eyes caught in lantern shine.

Reed whispered, "I think I broke the bastard's neck."

"Let him go, man."

Reed pulled away, almost reluctantly, and the Cuban's head lolled sideways against the deck. Price could see his eyes, open, shining almost like Reed's. And he could smell the thing that gave proof to Reed's whisper. The Cuban's bowels had emptied in his trousers.

"Move back," Price said softly. "Move back away, man."

Reed, on hands and knees like Vanic, crawled back. Vanic was gasping, his face almost on the deck.

"He was try to rob me," he whimpered.

"Shut your mouth," Price said.

He ran a hand inside the Cuban's damp shirt and felt for a heartbeat. There was none. It was a very small and bony chest.

"Christ's bloody sake," Price said to himself and straightened. He looked back and forth along the deck and there was no movement. The long lines of sleeping soldiers were still as they had been, motionless. Someone was snoring. The bilge pumps were working, sending a soft throb through the ship. From somewhere across the bay a bell rang once, then again. The lights from the other vessels were the same and on the shore, Price could see the lights of Florida, twinkling like stars from far away.

Price remembered the *Gussie*. He remembered the sortie ashore, expecting friendly Cubans and finding only hostile Spaniards. And their own Cubans running off into the jungle, leaving him and his soldiers alone. And the rage he'd felt that day against those men rose again now, like hot bile in his throat.

And there beside me, he thought, crouched like a bloody dog on his haunches is the best soldier I've got, waiting to be crucified for killing this Cuban pig.

Vanic was sobbing silently, his face in his hands now, and he reminded Price of some fanatic pilgrim praying before a flaming idol, on his knees. Reed was still watching Price, eyes shining.

"Reed."

"Yes, Corporal?"

"Get your ass over here."

Reed crawled over the Cuban, whose naked toes now looked obscenely grotesque, pointing toward the deck above.

"Get this body over the side."

Reed waited a long moment then slowly rose, his face coming level with Price's and his breathing hard and deep. They stared into each other's faces.

"Now," Price hissed.

Reed did it quickly, quietly. There was only the small dragging whisper of the Cuban's naked heels across the deck. And then a splash of water, hardly any different from the splash of bilge water being emptied.

Then Reed was back, standing before Price and Price's finger stabbed out against the Scot's chest.

"A bad dream is all it is," Price said. "A thing that never happened. Into your head, get that. And make no more of it. For if you do make more of it—" and Price was jabbing hard with his finger now, "if you make any single whisper of it, so God is my bloody witness, I'll be dumping you into that same soup!"

"Yes, Corporal Price."

Price turned, then stopped and looked back at Vanic, still cowering on the deck.

"He'll be all right, Corporal," Reed said. "I promise it."

"He'd goddamned better be."

Taking one last look along the deck before the first light of dawn began to turn everything to milky gray, Dylan Price swore, went back to his place, and tried to sleep.

It wasn't easy. The last thought he had before he slept again was, We have to keep the young soldier free of sin, is it, until we can turn him loose on our bloody ememies.

The morning staff meeting for the commanding general aboard *Seguranca* included a statement by Captain Malcomb that a dead Cuban had been found floating in the bay. It was the third time such a thing had happened since they'd left the docks.

Nobody paid much attention to it. As General Shafter said, What with all that crazy shit they smoke, it's a God's wonder more of them don't fall overboard and drown. Besides, there were bigger things to think about.

When Eben Pay came out from the general's briefing and found Joe Mountain waiting, leaning against the rail, he clinched both fists and pounded them together.

"Joe, the message just came in from Washington. Today, we're on our way to Cuba!"

II.
CUBA LIBRE

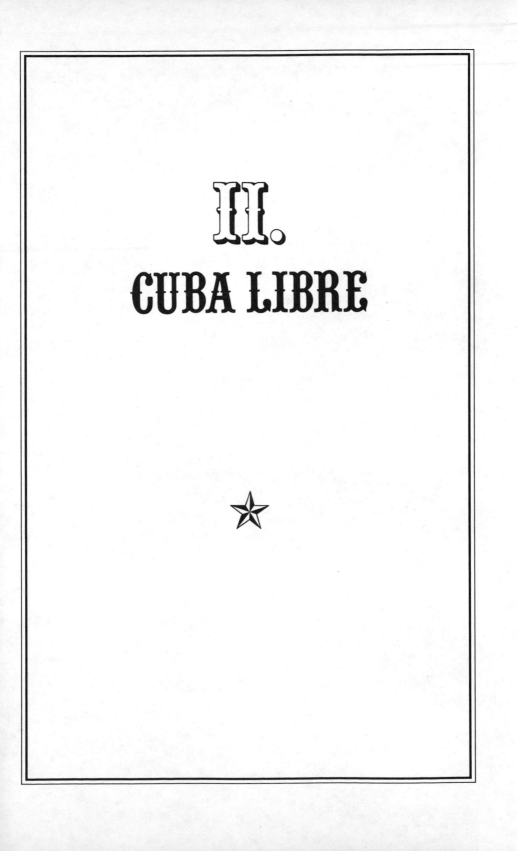

Major General William R. Shafter

So first the navy raised such a storm over our failure to rush off to Cuba. Then, when we had our people loaded, they started screaming that we must not venture into a dangerous sea against the possibility there were Spanish warships loose. Now, finally, they have given benediction. Washington, bowing and scraping before all the white uniformed baboons, allows us to go, but only after festering for a week on these wretched, stinking ships in Tampa Bay. A time we could have damn well used to load properly.

Blood of God, nobody knows where anything is stowed in these vessels. All of it thrown in during that frenzy to be under way prompted by the stupid, mandatory order to sail at once, and now I am sure we've got ammunition loaded in holds where it is covered with tons of tenting and harness and medical supplies, so deep beneath cases of typing paper and ink bottles that nothing we really need in our first hours on the island will be available until we've spent a week taking off everything right down to the bilge water.

Harness? Hell, yes, and there's not a single cavalry mount in this flotilla. Only a few artillery horses. And medical supplies? It makes me retch. There have not been enough doctors assigned to this expedition to service a reinforced regiment, much less an army of seventeen thousand men!

Most likely the first ammunition we uncover in this shambles will be black powder issue for the single shot rifles of the National Guard units we've brought along. And my God, all the artillery ammunition is black powder. I can see the clouds of smoke rising now, like a beacon to enemy gunners. We might as well send them our dispositions and save a lot of time. Every major country in Europe has been using smokeless powder for years, and here we have this ancient shit because those Washington nits, general staff officers and congressmen, have all the foresight of a new-hatched duck.

We did the best we could, the ships lying in that sweltering stewpot of Tampa Bay, reorganizing the cargo in the holds as we waited. But shifting tons of matériel lying off dockside is not easy. The best time, obviously, is during loading, when there is no shifting at all but simply putting in first what comes off last and putting in last what must come off first at the assault beaches. Now, we can only wait and see.

Each moment is precious. I've had the Yellow Jack. I know what it does. If we don't get this job done in four, at most five weeks, my army is going to be flat on its butt with the fever. If not the Jack, then malaria.

And the goddamned navy is carping about the coming hurricane season. Hell's eternal bells, they can just steam off to covered inlets. They've already proudly informed me that their marines have taken this big harbor at Guantánamo, where they can service and protect the whole fleet.

Taken it? For Christ's sweet sake, there was no resistance. The Spaniards are at Santiago!

Well, my fine nautical friends, there is no safe haven for soldiers. When I get thousands of men ashore and they start dropping from yellow fever, there will be no protected harbor for them. You don't just pluck that many people out of battle with two hours' notice of danger from approaching black clouds.

Nor does it help my disposition to contemplate the history of invasions of this island over the past two hundred years. They have all been disasters. The officers of foreign armies who are here to observe this war have been more than generous in supplying me with the details of each such fiasco. Especially that little French major, a toy soldier bastard if I ever saw one.

Well, perhaps he is an expert on disasters. He was in the French army in 1870 at Sudan when the Germans came.

But I must control my temper. And modify my language. If for no other reason than to show Mr. Richard Harding Davis of the Hearst newspaper that what he writes about me being profane and irascible is an unadulterated load of horseshit!

So now I've identified him, by name and not only by initials. A thorn in my liver, that son of a bitch!

Newspaper people are nothing more than dog-pecker gnats. My concerns are with greater things. Like these damned ships we're sailing in. The War Department, in all its splendid wisdom, drew contracts with their owners which allow individual captains to retain authority and command over these floating junkyards. They carry my troops, but the ships' captains are not responsible to me. They are responsible to their owners, expected to look out for the vested interest of men lying around in Mobile and New Orleans whorehouses smoking their cigars and sipping their Cuba Libres.

Free Cuba, indeed! Such scoundrels are willing to free anybody or anything so long as it does not involve having their own asses peppered with canister and so long as it involves making a profit. I would take such people out and line them up against a wall and shoot them!

So now we have these ships wandering about all over the ocean. Since we rounded Key West and started along the Saint Nicholas Channel, the navy gunboats are on twenty-four-hour service rushing about driving these ships back into the convoy where they belong. It is like a flock of insane hens pursued by a randy rooster. If it were not so serious, it would be hilarious.

Only today it was reported to me a tugboat, very important to our getting troops ashore in Cuba, simply sailed off toward the west and has not been seen since. The son of a bitch just steamed off, no matter his role in all this. The master of that ship should be arrested if ever he sets foot in a port of the United States and carted off to life imprisonment! The goddamned infamy!

But I have to control my temper. There's work to be done.

Be calm with my staff and my subordinate commanders. Most especially that former Confederate general who now commands one of my divisions. Calm. That's the order of the day.

The navy has the Spanish fleet blockaded in the harbor of Santiago. And now, it would appear, they have made their case to Washington, and Washington has agreed. My troops will land and move to storm Santiago, therefore neutralizing the Spanish harbor so the navy can move in without being shot at by the shore batteries.

For the love of Christ! I'm supposed to spend the blood of my soldiers while those goddamned white-shoe bastards are taking pictures with their Kodak cameras, standing on their quarterdecks and out of harm's way until my men make it possible for them to steam in without having to receive hostile fire from shore cannons.

Why, those stupid, unfeeling jackasses! I will damned well not do any such thing. I will damned well invest the city and demand surrender. But I will not have my troops slaughtered just so the goddamned holy vessels of the navy sons of bitches can steam in blowing their whistles.

The navy may be willing to accept long army casualty lists like those we had in the Civil War. But the American public is not so inclined. For the sake of God's blood!

I must control my temper. This is a joint effort. Us and our sister service. The clean-underwear sons of bitches who never have to sleep in the mud.

Where the hell is Malcomb? Every time I need my adjutant he's out on deck with one of these newspapermen or else some goddamned Cuban who claims to be a general and rattles around the decks with pistols showing under his coat.

Where the hell is my lemonade? The racket of these typewriters in my compartment is driving me mad. There is no place to go and think. The ship is stuffed with all sorts of people. If I could only be with the troops, lying on the deck, feeling the breeze. My goddamned teeth hurt. The heat is unbearable. I'd give one of my stars now for a tub of ice.

CHAPTER 9

THEY had come to expect almost daily showers but now, well out into the Nicholas Channel north of Cuba, there was very little of the rain that usually developed in short afternoon bursts along the west coast of Florida. Here, out of sight of land, the sky was a perpetual blue, deep and endless, the ocean emerald green, and the rain always somewhere else, far off, a slanting gray against the sky dropping to the sea like a veil across the face of a delicate widow.

It was calm, mostly, with only an occasional white fluff of salt foam running along the crests of low waves. And there was always a fresh breeze, a westerly coming off the Gulf of Mexico. The soldiers were less inclined to seasickness than they had been while sweating in Tampa Bay.

And there was something to do now other than contemplate distant lights along a shore where there might be whores and bad whiskey. The troops stood along the rails of their ships, all thirty-two ships, and watched the flying fish and the leaping dolphins and the transparent domes of Portuguese men-of-war bobbing serene but deadly in the swells and troughs of the blue-green, surging water.

Nor did they miss the mad comedy of ships wandering about, all the way to the horizon sometimes, chased frantically by the naval gunboats trying to herd them back to where they belonged. And sometimes, they were themselves on one of those wayward ships and wondered, What the hell are we doing out here on this ocean going away from all those other sons of bitches?

On *Salvador*, Dylan Price consoled his men. "So every one of these bloody ships' captains takes his own route to Cuba," he said. "But luck it is, boys, because look at us."

And it was true. The vessel on which the Thirty-seventh Infantry sailed had a master more inclined to discipline than most of the others and so stayed close abeam of the command ship *Seguranca*. So close, in fact, that now and again they could see the massive form of General Shafter taking the air on the flying bridge, topped by pith helmet, and each time they saw him, Dylan Price made his point.

"You see that? No whale it is. But our own Old Man, and we follow him to Cuba or to Hell or anywhere else he takes us."

"I like him," said Swenson.

"You'd not know him if he fell on you. But feel the pinch of weight," said Price. "And follow him you will, you ironheaded regular soldier, you misbegotten."

"Yah," Swenson laughed. "Follow him I will."

"Jesus," Price whispered. And then louder, so all the squad could hear. "You'll damn well follow me. And no worry about the commanding general himself. Just me."

The smell of open sea was so penetrating that it overpowered the odor of the ships, so long as men stayed topside. Which they did both day and night.

Sometimes along the horizon to the south there was the dim blue outline of mountains and the soldiers looked at them and at least for a few moments were silent, knowing this was the island they had come to assault. Knowing this was Cuba. A faint rib of land under the shining sky. So far away, and without any real substance.

"It's Cuba," they said, quietly.

As they sailed along for hours, seeing it, knowing it was seven, ten miles away, staying north of it, they realized it was so much bigger than they had ever imagined it. Big and full of mystery, perhaps dangerous, too. Because it was unknown. And because of the Spaniards, who were unknown as well.

By now, the warnings of a few old soldiers not to take lightly anyone armed with Mauser rifles had begun to penetrate patriotic euphoria.

But then the course of the convoy would take them out of sight of land and they'd go back to watching the flying fish and the glassy bubbles of the Portuguese men-of-war. And marvel, many of these men never having seen the ocean before, at the vast, endless extent of it, a whole, entire world of water.

"Eben Pay," said Joe Mountain aboard the command ship, both men standing as they so often did at the fantail, "I never thought I'd see so much of this stuff that you can't even take a drink of."

In the shade beneath the canvas canopy running from superstructure to stern, they were out of sunlight, but the wind was strong and whipped Joe Mountain's hair across his face like a raven-black silk scarf. Beneath them was the crackling white phosphorescence of the ship's wake, the gulls dipping low toward it.

"I know, Joe," Eben said.

There had been so many things to occupy his mind that Eben Pay had not until that moment thought of it. But now, watching the big Osage's face, the flat water horizon reflected in the black eyes, Eben was strangely startled that his friend had never in his life seen more water than flowed between the banks of the Arkansas River at Fort Smith.

Then he thought, And neither have I.

He reached up and placed a hand on Joe Mountain's shoulder, he had no notion why, and said it again.

"I know, Joe."

Then dropped his hand quickly, embarrassed at the gesture. And Joe Mountain turned his face and the great shining grin was there, the hair blowing across the black eyes. And the Osage laughed.

"You ain't gonna see anything like this in Muskogee, are you?"

"No," Eben said. "No, not in Muskogee."

There was some new, disquieting movement in how Eben

Pay felt about this big Osage. An old superiority until now suppressed, the ascendancy of educated white man over savage, apparent only as it crumbled. In Fort Smith, Eben Pay had come into Joe Mountain's world, a wildly strange and vicious world, and he had tried to understand it. All the while, the Indian meeting him with open hand and mind.

Now, Joe Mountain had come into his, Eben's world, and there were still the long, easy strides of confidence as though they were walking Garrison Avenue two blocks from Judge Parker's court, where everybody knew Joe Mountain and respected him. Or at least they were afraid of him.

He comes at everything head-on, Eben thought. Without reservations. Honest. No deceit. And he thought that maybe study from all the books in the world could not teach a man such things. And that maybe Joe Mountain knew instinctively much that could not be learned at places like the University of Illinois law school. Had learned, in fact, in the same place that a cat learns to walk at night. It made the chills dance up Eben Pay's back.

This is just a man. This is just a man, like me. My God, this traveling on the ocean, he thought, puts strange things in an idle mind. But there was some good cause.

For one thing there was the popularity of the Osage. Back at the Plant Hotel Joe Mountain had been confined to the back places. But now, afloat, he could not be ignored. No more ignored, Eben thought, than an elephant in the drawing room.

Joe Mountain was especially a celebrity among the newspapermen and the foreign officers who were attached to General Shafter's staff as observers. For various and obvious reasons. None of them had ever seen a real, live, flesh and blood barbarian red Indian. Eben Pay was sure he would be rushing to the defense of this poor, uneducated primitive man, and stood about expectantly as all these curious people asked questions.

At first, Joe Mountain leaned against the ship's railing and answered their questions with nods and grunts. But then, as he had done with Eben Pay a long time ago in Fort Smith, he began to tell stories. He began to tell about his time with Parker's court and about times before that, when there was no court at Fort Smith and when there was not even a Fort Smith. And along with all the rest, the newspapermen and the foreign officers, Eben Pay listened, listened to the tales of when the Osage fought the Cherokees coming in from the east and when the Osage went to the west of their country and hunted buffalo and made a little war now and then with the Kiowas.

"My little brother Blue Foot," Joe Mountain said. "He ought to be here telling you stories. My little brother Blue Foot, he's an old-line Osage. He could show you how to roach hair."

And that same night, sleeping on the fantail in their usual place, flat on the deck in the cool breeze, the third day out of Tampa Bay, Joe Mountain said, "Eben Pay, them white men sure ask crazy questions."

And Eben Pay thought, Sure, as crazy as some of the questions I asked a long time ago. But he said only, "Go to sleep, Joe."

Before he slept, he recalled some of those questions asked on board this ship.

"Tell me, sir," said Mr. Richard Harding Davis of the *New York Journal*, "do you people still scalp your dead enemies?"

Joe Mountain was grinning, but there came now a hard, metallic glint in his eyes as he looked down on the reporter.

"My people never scalped too much," he said. "Me, I worked for Judge Parker. But my people, back in the old days, they'd cut off an ear now and then. Or sometimes a finger, like them blanket-ass Cheyenne Cap'n Roosevelt probably likes. Just to take a little trophy. But if an enemy was really brave, we wouldn't scalp him. We'd cut off his whole head. Like my daddy said they done once when they attacked this Kiowa camp, out in buffalo country, and they left the heads in these copper kettles the Kiowas had in their camp."

Mr. Richard Harding Davis turned and walked away along the deck.

Then a captain from the British army. "Sir, what could possibly bring you here?"

"Oh, me and Eben Pay come down here to see the ocean."

And another.

"Mr. Mountain, I understand you were an officer in the court of the Hanging Judge."

"Oh we never called him that," said Joe Mountain. "We just called him Judge Parker because that was his name. He was a good man. There was a lot of people hanged on that gallows in Fort Smith. But it wasn't Judge Parker's gallows. He didn't build it. The white man's government built it. Judge Parker, he just put bad people on it."

And still again.

"How many of your people are here in this army to drive the Spaniards out of Cuba?"

"Hell, I don't know. I'm maybe the only one. My people don't cotton much to folks being drove out of any place. We know a lot about folks being drove out of places."

No, Eben Pay thought, don't worry too much about Joe Mountain. Besides, there were other things playing on Eben's mind.

He tried to find a time and place where he could write it all down in a letter to his father. The *Seguranca* was not the easiest of environments in which to perform such a task. Sometimes he managed with a lead pencil and a lined tablet, sitting on the fantail with Joe Mountain looking over his shoulder. Sometimes, late at night, he filched a few moments on one of the headquarter's typewriters in the chart room. It came in spurts and jolting stops because he wasn't sure exactly what he wanted to say. Exactly what was in his thinking.

There was much talk among the officers and newspapermen about Admiral Dewey's accomplishments in the Philippines and how a colonial government would be established there, Eben Pay wrote. "So," these people said, "why not in Hawaii? Why not in Puerto Rico? And in fact," they said, "these Cubans we're liberating don't look ready for self-government yet, so why not a colonial government there as well?"

"Take a place in the sun alongside Britain," they said, finally making clear what they were really thinking. "Let the sun never set on the Stars and Stripes."

All this imperial talk disturbed Eben Pay in ways he could not explain. Not to himself and least of all to others, even his father. He listened as he heard men say, "Hail, Columbia, and let's absorb a few of the inept of the world while there are still a few left over from the British and the French and the Germans and the Belgians, showing the delights of real civilization to these backward children who need a little force-feeding about superior ways of life."

And in fact, "let's take a few away from somebody like Spain, where the Roman church and the bullfight are the only visible structures of human existence."

Here we are, Eben Pay thought, going along the same route as the old conquistadores and in the same part of the world, the only real distinction being that they spoke Spanish and we English.

And when he looked at Joe Mountain, the whole thing seemed even closer to hand than the sixteenth century. It is one thing, he thought, to move out across one's own country, one's own continental land, and absorb people there. But yet another to take ship for other shores. He always brought himself up short with that thought because when the white men came to the place that eventually became Fort Smith, Arkansas, it hadn't been their own country at all.

It had been Joe Mountain's.

He tried to console himself with the thought that Joe Mountain's people had likely taken it away from somebody else. He tried to console himself with the idea that there was a long history of tribes in North America taking things from weaker neighbors. Just like Europeans or Africans or Asians. Long before the white man came.

It didn't help much. It didn't console much, this whole business of the powerful taking from the weak from the beginning, back through time. Because he had somehow thought such things were in the past, even in the recent past, the grasping, vicious self-interest of past peoples, past tribes, past nations, past empires.

But finally he knew it wasn't in the past. It was now. The flame of empire. And not Macedonians or Romans or Normans, those ancients. But Hail Columbia. That's who it was now.

It didn't set too well. And after three days of trying to write it down in a letter to his father, he stood on deck in the tropic breeze and wadded the papers in his hand and threw the crinkled ball into the sea and Joe Mountain watched him do it but saw from Eben Pay's expression that it was not a thing to ask about.

So Eben Pay took his mind off it, as best he could, and concentrated on watching this wild flotilla going across the blue-green waters north of Cuba.

It didn't go very fast. They steamed slowly through the Saint Nicholas and Bahama channels. White winged gulls followed every ship, seeming to lie motionless above the wakes, as though the passage of the metal things through water had created a gravity free vacuum. The sea was unchanging. It was only in the chart room that one could watch their progress toward the eastern end of the island. Their average speed was four knots.

When the sun had set, while the troops could still look south and see the rising blue spine of Cuba, they inched along with all lights blazing. Like a floating city that never slept. And the regimental bands broke out their instruments and martial airs and ragtime music floated across the low waves.

"Jesus Christ!" said Lieutenant Colonel John Stoval aboard the *Salvador*. "I hope the Spaniards haven't got any gunboats on the north side of that island because this thing we've got here is the biggest, brightest target I've ever seen!"

But no Spanish gunboats came. And many of the men on these vessels refused to believe that there was any danger in all of this, and they danced on the decks of their transports as the regimental bands blared away.

General Shafter, sweating on his bunk, gave no order for lights out. He knew he probably couldn't enforce such a directive anyway. So he lay sipping lemonade and fanning himself and hoping his ragtag staff could somehow dig out enough ammunition from the ships' hold to sustain the expedition once it was put ashore.

The days passed, and slowly they rounded Cuba's eastern

finger, past Cape Maysí, into the Windward Passage, then steered back to the west along the island's southern shore, passing Guantánamo and Daiquirí and finally to the mouth of Santiago Bay, the city lying out of sight some miles inside the vast inlet. But then steamed back to Daiquirí and hove to off the shore where they would force a landing.

They had begun their voyage from Tampa Bay a week before. Now it was Monday, June 20, 1898. And as they collected themselves like an undisciplined gaggle of geese, the gray hulks of the blockading naval vessels moved close among them, large and menacing, not gunboats these but ships with big guns. And there before them was the white line of breakers on the beach and behind that the lifting, brooding, steaming green jungle ridges rising rank on rank to the Sierra Maestra. The dancing had stopped now. Each of them, for the first time close enough to Cuba to see the trunks of the royal palms and the color of the bougainvillea, knew that somewhere there on the land brilliant in the sunlight an enemy waited.

Lieutenant Colonel John Stoval

There are disadvantages to being jumped in grade. A captain yesterday, commanding about a hundred men. And today, a lieutenant colonel perhaps commanding almost ten times that many.

In my own instance, there was no perhaps about it. The third day of my new rank, and assigned to continue duty with my old outfit, the Thirty-seventh Infantry, the colonel of the regiment was sent off on some War Department detail elsewhere leaving me in command of the unit of which my old company was only a small part. God, how I loved to see the familiar faces of my E Company men amongst all that sea of strangers.

This practice of sending regimental commanders away from their formations is one of the more assinine proclivities of the War Department—ordering a colonel off to sit on some never ending board of inquiry or court-martial, or to wander about obscure military installations on inspection tours, or to act with others of his kind and rank in drawing up new regulations, and leaving the lieutenant colonel in command.

Naturally, it provides the younger officer an excellent opportunity, which is generally appreciated by all concerned, perhaps with the exception of the soldiers in the unit.

Subsequent to advising my wife, Earline, in Plattsburg of my surprising good fortune, she sent no less than three flowery telegraph messages of congratulations, which I had in hand prior to departure from Tampa Bay. Earline, like most of the people in the country, seems to have taken the Cuban adventure as a great lark with no danger involved, a short walk in the tropic sun, as it were, with glory and prestige and honor for all. Directly proportionate to rank, of course.

She pointed out to me in her last message that she was bursting with pride, her John now being a lieutenant colonel just like Mr. Roosevelt.

Yea gods!

For myself, I cannot help but recall the most infamous of these incidents, when a certain Colonel Smith was detached on errands for the War Department, leaving his lieutenant colonel in command just previous to a field operation. This campaign was in Montana Territory, the regiment was the Seventh Cavalry, and at least for the lieutenant colonel and many of his men, it ended abruptly and fatally on the banks of the Little Big Horn River.

Having been commissioned only three years before and serving on the frontier at the time of the Custer debacle, the Little Big Horn left a lasting impression. Being no more or less superstitious than any soldier, I nonetheless try not to think of my following in those wretched footsteps. It has not helped to recall as an evil omen the *Gussie* expedition.

But happily, I found our civilian ship's master aboard the *Salvador* a good and brave sailor, much superior to any of the other merchantmen captains I observed. He held his position throughout the voyage and once arrived off Daiquirí he anchored less than two miles off the coast even though the Thirty-seventh Infantry was not scheduled to disembark until late in the operation. Some of the ships carrying troops who were to be first ashore were far on the seaward side of *Salvador* because their masters refused to come any closer.

The navy had agreed to assume responsibility for getting the army ashore because for one reason or another the army did not have enough civilian contract craft to do the job. The navy would do this by using small steam cutters each towing three or four boats behind them, into which the troops would load. So there were these strings of vessels going out toward the sea, looking for the ships with soldiers to be taken off and carried to the beach.

On board the *Salvador*, the sailors and many of my own soldiers watched all of this, pointing, laughing, and making pointedly obscene remarks about the game of marine tag taking place incredibly before their eyes. Confusion close inshore was bad enough but many of the troopships were far out to sea, and a few seemingly headed for the southern horizon with the navy cutters and their strings of boats in hot pursuit.

It was the most absurd thing I ever saw. I could imagine the language of our commanding general as he observed the same fantastic scene.

If our own men had not been aboard those outlying contract vessels, I think the navy men-of-war would have opened fire on them. And they damned well would have deserved every salvo.

At least a bad situation was made less appalling than it could have been. Because at first, the navy had refused to use their vessels to get us ashore, saying it would fatigue their sailors, who needed to retain their vigor in case the Spanish ships came out of Santiago harbor. But after General Shafter explained the breakdown and desertion of the tugboats we had hired for the job of beaching our men, the navy relented.

We thought it was damned magnanimous of them what with the both of us supposedly in a war against a common enemy.

The mad scramble started early in the morning, and much of the day toward noon was wasted before the navy had all the troops in the assault boats. The troops I observed through my field glasses were literally jumping up and down with impatience to depart the prison hulks, which is what they all called the contract troop carriers. So when the navy cutters steamed alongside a ship with soldiers scheduled for the initial landing, the troops bounded and scrambled into the waiting boats in their eagerness and many fell into the water and were fished out with grappling hooks having lost hats or packs or blanket rolls or rifles. And, I would suppose, a lot of enthusiasm for amphibious operations.

It is heartrending for a professional officer to watch enlisted men put to such lengths of discomfort and even into danger through no fault of their own but because of the bungling and even cowardice of those who are supposed to be supporting them. And the staff at the War Department level must bear the onus for such things because it is their decisions and orders that create the situation in which these fiascoes can occur. But they are so far away, in time and place, and they have forgotten, if indeed they ever knew, how their directives can absolutely ensure suffering at the cutting edge of the operation.

Perhaps there were landing sites on the south coast of Cuba that were worse than the one at Daiquirí, but such a thing was hard to imagine. There was little indentation of the shoreline there, which meant that nothing broke up the turbulence of ocean waves.

In the town, which was only a scattering of shacks with sheet metal roofs, there was a mining operation of some sort, and there were narrow-gage railroad tracks running down from the hills and through the jungle and onto the beach. Two piers jutted out into the surf, one a rickety wooden one that looked useless, the other of steel but very high above the water.

When our troops were finally into their boats, they had to wait while the navy delivered a bombardment of the shore. The boats bobbed up and down violently in the waves and many of the soldiers in boats near enough for me to see were becoming obviously seasick.

The naval shells going in threw up a great deal of earth, and tin roofs flew off houses and a few of them caught fire. At one end of the beach was a blockhouse with embrasures looking down on the place where our troops would land, but I saw none of the gunfire directed at it. Needless to say, everyone had been watching that blockhouse since dawn. Nobody had seen any movement there, which didn't mean it was not occupied by Spaniards ready to devastate the beach when the landing came.

It might have been better had we seen some Spaniards. But in the entire area, there was nothing visible. No movement, no sign of resistance. It was nerve-racking.

Finally, the shelling stopped and the assault waves headed for the shore. Troops still on board the transports, like my own men of the Thirty-seventh, waved their hats and cheered. I watched through my field glasses, holding my breath, waiting for the holocaust. But it never came, thank God, and the first of our men were onshore.

Later, I learned that our only casualties were two colored soldiers of the Tenth Cavalry who had tried to leave their boat and mount the higher of the two piers, fell in the water, and were drowned.

CHAPTER 10

THE troops stood along the railings of the *Salvadore* like delighted children watching their first circus parade. It was an excellent day for watching parades. The night before had been glorious. After a hard rain the sky had cleared, with stars and a fresh westerly breeze.

There had been great excitement sitting there dead in the water looking at the land they had come to attack, even though earlier in the evening Lieutenant Colonel Stoval had come down from officers' country and walked among them and told them they would not be going in until after the initial assault.

"We'll need to get off this bucket soon, sir," said First Sergeant Barry. "The water's so low in the tanks now these men are drinking more paint chips than water when they try it."

Stoval had reassured them, promising only one more night of the stale slime they'd been drinking since Tampa Bay.

"Maybe this time tomorrow night, you'll have a sip of coconut milk," he said.

"Coconut?" Vanic asked.

"Those tall trees onshore are coconut palms."

After Stoval had passed on to other companies, Price pushed his face close to Vanic's. And hissed.

"You clabber-headed bohunk son of a bitch, don't you *ever* talk to the colonel until he talks to you first."

Vanic had been about to protest when Reed took a fistful of Vanic's shirt and pulled him away across the deck, the Germans snickering behind them.

"But Reed, that Barry talk to him!"

"And you can, too, when you're a first sergeant."

They'd stayed up late, watching, though there was little to see. The beach, two miles away, was a pencil line of white foam and above that the mountains were clearly outlined against the bright sky, a jagged silhouette pointing at the stars. All about them, the ships were lighted as they had been since they left Florida, but tonight there were no regimental bands playing.

Just before Dylan Price went to sleep in his usual place on deck, he had heard Private Telner sharpening his bayonet.

And now it was parade time, bright sunlight making the water sparkle and dance. At dawn, they had seen a flight of flamingos going west along the shoreline, the early sun touching their black-tipped wings.

"Look at them pink geese."

"No, Swede, flamingos, they are." Price was the only one of them who had ever seen flamingos.

Some of the ships carrying assault troops were far offshore, beyond the *Salvador*. As the navy cutters towed them in, they passed close alongside and the soldiers of the Seventeenth hooted and jeered.

"Hey, you in that canoe, did you think Cuba was out there in the ocean someplace?"

"You landlubbers look puke green to me."

"You gonna be sorry you ever left your mama!"

"We'll come join you boys after you stomp all the snakes in that jungle."

"Hey, you save coconuts for us, huh?"

"Give the Spaniards a kiss from me, boys."

Some of the noncommissioned officers were in a little group

together, smoking cigars that First Sergeant Barry had produced from some unknown source.

"Jesus," Price muttered as the troops continued to razz the nervous, silent occupants in the boats. "All alike, they are."

"All who?" Barry asked.

"Soldiers. Jabbing their little jokes at the ones off to spank the heathen."

"Heathen? I've heard the Spaniards are all good Catholics."

"Never mind," Price snapped. He'd been thinking of another time, him left behind at Rorke's Drift while he watched the bulk of his regiment march off into Zululand. And he thought, I hope to God it doesn't happen to those lads now, what happened to my dear old comrades at Isandhlwana.

The naval bombardment didn't make much impression on them. The sounds of the cannons seemed to be soaked up by the vast surface of the water, even though they were close enough to some of the men-of-war to smell the powder smoke as it drifted to them on the continuing westerly breeze. They could see debris flying on the shore, but there was little noise to that either, being two miles away.

They could hear officers on the flying bridge above them exclaiming about the deadliness of the shell fire. But Dylan Price suspected correctly that none of these officers had ever observed the effects of naval fire before.

When the first soldiers went ashore it was like watching ants, tiny specks rushing up the beaches, disappearing into the streets of the village, where buildings were still burning, and some into the jungle, swallowed immediately in the green curtain. They tried to see signs of enemy fire, or hear it, but with no success. It made them laugh, trying to break the tension, looking at one another to reassure themselves with confidence. Trying to convince themselves that this was just a big, tropic picnic.

It began to get a little boring. Most of them drifted away from the railing. About midafternoon, they heard cheering from the ships closer to shore. Soon Lieutenant Colonel Stoval called down to them. Colonel Roosevelt's Rough Riders, dismounted of course, had taken the blockhouse, found no oppositon, and had raised the Stars and Stripes above the little rock and adobe structure where the embrasures had looked down silently on the entire landing.

Sure enough, as they rushed back to the railings, they could see a tiny fleck of color fluttering against the green jungle background. They cheered along with all the rest.

"They ain't gonna leave us anything to do," Reed said.

"Don't bet your pay on that," said Price.

Word somehow passed through the flotilla that when Colonel Roosevelt's men stormed into the empty blockhouse, they'd found a number of wine bottles only half empty.

"Shit," First Sergeant Barry said. "When soldiers leave wine bottles half empty, you know damned well they were in a mighty hurry to get out."

As more and more information came to them, passed down from the flying bridge by Stoval, they knew that it was true. The Spaniards had been there. Maybe right up to the time the navy started shelling the place. Maybe even later, as the assault was going in. But somehow, they refused to resist.

"They could've butchered us," Barry said.

"Don't question good fortune," said Price.

"Dylan, you're beginning to stick in my craw," Barry said, but Price turned and walked away, shrugging.

The sun was finally settling toward the horizon in the west, but still the troops hung on the railings, perhaps expecting Colonel Roosevelt to pull off another exciting victory. Trying to squeeze the last ounce of excitement out of a memorable day before darkness came.

Dylan Price was ready to make his evening meal of the raw bacon and hardtack already issued and now making a moist greasy spot in one of his trouser pockets. Then Olaf Swenson began tugging at his sleeve.

"Corporal Price," Swenson said. He was staring wild-eyed at a nearby transport just inshore from the *Salvador*. There, a cargo door had been opened and they were shoving horses out into the ocean, the horses squealing, legs thrashing, bodies twisting, striking the water with great awkward splashes.

"What're they doin' there? What're they doin' to them horses?"

"No lighters to get them ashore," Price said.

"Lighters?"

"Boats. No boats to get them ashore. So they let them swim in."

Once in the water, the horses began to swim, only their heads above the waves.

"God!" Swenson cried. "Some swimmin' out, Corporal Price, some swimmin' out!"

The horses were swimming in all directions, having no sense of where land might be, and at least two of them, glassy-eyed, struggled directly beneath the bow of the *Salvador* and on toward the southern horizon.

"God, Corporal Price, they swimmin' out to the ocean!"

Swenson was crying. Tears ran down his cheeks and were whipped off his chin by the freshening wind. He leaned far out over the railing and waved his hat wildly.

"Other way, other way," he screamed. "Swim other way, horses!"

More soldiers were watching the horses now, some laughing. First Sergeant Barry walked past, chewing a mouthful of bacon.

"Dumb brutes," he said. "Shark bait now."

Olaf Swenson leaped toward Barry's back but Price already had the Swede in both his hands, yanking him about, shaking him, but when he spoke, he spoke softly.

"All right, Swede, come on now," and he shoved Swenson against a bulkhead.

"That son of a bitch sayin' that and them poor horses. They ain't done nothin' to nobody."

"Come on with me," Price said, voice still gentle but his hands gripping Swenson's arm hard. "Let's go over to the port side and eat this lovely bacon, is it?"

He guided the still sobbing Swede across the deck and forced him down against a ladder away from the railing. Then settled beside him.

"Now, I'll tell you about good Queen Vic walking her little dog," Price said and launched into a few of his most polished lies about having actually seen Victoria walking in her flower gardens at Kensington Palace with a tiny dog on a diamond studded leash.

Olaf Swenson was staring up into the darkening sky, tears still running down into the collar of his open shirt, and Dylan Price knew the Swede was not listening. He was still seeing those horses, swimming out to sea.

Joe Mountain

We had to watch all those soldiers riding the little boats in to the land so they could see if there was any Spanish army around. Me and Eben Pay didn't get to go because this big fat man, Cap'n Shafter, who is the chief of this whole shebang, likes Eben Pay and wanted him to stay on the ship with all these other army men who had field glasses.

Cap'n Shafter even give Eben Pay field glasses, too. But he didn't give me any. He likes me all right, though. He don't care if I call him Cap'n. It don't make him mad like it did that Roosevelt fellow in San Antonio. Cap'n Shafter talked to me a couple of times while we were sailing out here. He liked to talk about the time he was chasing Comanches in Texas.

Cap'n Shafter asked me if I'd ever chased any Comanches. I said I hadn't but my father had chased a lot of Kiowas, or sometimes they chased him, and Cap'n Shafter said he'd chased a few Kiowas, too.

He was so fat, he reminded me of that old Comanche everbody had heard of out in the Territory. This old Comanche was so big he couldn't find a pony strong enough to hold him. So they had to drag him around on a travois. But he was famous for another reason, too. When he died, he owned more than a thousand horses. My father told me that one old Comanche owned more horses than the whole Pawnee tribe. I forget his name. I never had much truck with Comanches but when I saw how fat Cap'n Shafter was, I remembered that story my father told.

But I don't think Cap'n Shafter owns no thousand horses. If he does, he sure didn't bring 'em with him to Cuba.

I reckoned that Cap'n Shafter didn't have enough field glasses to go around so it didn't make me mad when I didn't get any.

Ever now and then, Eben Pay would come out of that little room on this ship where they got all these windows and where all the army men and Cap'n Shafter were looking at what was happening and talking loud and writing stuff down on little pieces of paper, and when Eben Pay came out, he let me see through his field glasses.

Eben Pay said that me and him would get on land later, maybe when Cap'n Shafter did. Then he said we'd get a couple of mules from some Cubans who were fighting the Spaniards, too, and me and him would ride around looking at things and letting Cap'n Shafter know what his army was doing. Eben Pay said that's what staff officers do in a white man's army.

Of course, Eben Pay wasn't any officer in the army. He was just a civilian like me, but we were there to help Cap'n Shafter however we could.

Eben Pay had been acting like he had a bellyache. But now, with everything going on, he was all perked up and feeling good. He said the invasion was moving right along. It looked like hell to me. All those soldiers running up and down on the beach and some of them falling in the water even before their boats got to land and that village on fire like it was an old-time Kiowa raid on one of our Osage hunting camps when all the warriors were out looking for bufffalo and nobody was home except the old men and the women and children. Kiowas were always wild and messy as hell when they raided one of our hunting camps.

But us staying with what Eben Pay called the command group just proved what I always thought from the first when Cap'n Shafter was always yelling and cussing at everybody else but was always sweet as frost-bit persimmons with Eben Pay. The only time I ever saw Cap'n Shafter smile was when he was talking to Eben Pay.

Hell, it wasn't any surprise to me. Everybody liked Eben Pay. Well, maybe a few of them men he helped hang in Fort Smith didn't care too much for him. But even some of them men liked him.

Like old Smoker Chubee. He was a mean, mean man, sent

to Judge Parker's gallows for murder. He killed a deputy marshal over in Okmulgee and he killed a few others besides. He was part Seminole and no telling what all the other parts were.

Anyway, old Smoker was a man who hired out to kill people over in the Indian Nations. He wasn't one of these popheads they got over there, crazy and shiftless. He was good at what he done. Always sober. Strickly business.

Smoker had this Colt single action revolver, as pretty a weapon as anybody ever saw. So on the night before they took him out to Judge Parker's gallows and put the rope around his neck, he asked to see Eben Pay. And he said he wanted Eben Pay to have that pistol. After they had old Smoker in the ground, Judge Parker said it was all right so Eben Pay ended up with Smoker's big .45.

Hell, Eben Pay didn't care nothin' about guns. So he just treated it like junk, throwing it around here and there and never cleaning it.

So when we were getting ready to leave Fort Smith for the war, I was over there at Eben Pay's house and I saw that gun in a kitchen cabinet and I just took it. And brought it along with me because I knew Eben Pay would leave it in Fort Smith anyway.

When I finally showed it to Eben Pay in our room at Tampa, he never even recognized it. It was just another pistol to him.

But it was really old Smoker's Colt all right.

Just to show how Eben Pay never paid any heed to firearms, the double action he got from that Corporal Price, he didn't even try to get ammunition for it. Hell, I always reckoned carrying an empty pistol was like having a water bucket without no bottom, so I talked one of the army men on our ship out of a dozen cartridges for it.

Eben Pay didn't get too excited when I showed him the shells. So I just took his little pistol and swung the cylinder out and loaded it and gave Eben Pay the six extra cartridges and told him to put 'em in his pocket. He just laughed.

"If it makes you happy, Joe," he said.

It wasn't to make me happy, I told him, but if a man's going out on a war party he ought to go armed. I also told him that little

.38 popgun wouldn't stand much chance of hurting anybody but at least it was better than nothing and maybe he could find a snake to shoot.

Eben Pay shook his head and laughed some more but after that he started carrying the gun in the hip holster that hooked onto the web belt he'd got from Corporal Price that day in the railyard at Tampa.

Anyway, standing on that ship and watching all the boats and the soldiers and the navy shooting big guns was all right, I guess. It was something to do. But when I looked through Eben Pay's field glasses, the thing I saw that I liked best was the timber on the land. I never saw timber like that around Fort Smith. It was a deeper green. And vines and bushes and this one plant that had long leaves sticking up from the ground and they had sharp points. Eben Pay told me that was called Spanish bayonet.

And those palm trees with the little skinny trunks that looked like somebody had cut rings around them and the leaves at the top all fanned out like a star and the dark lumps just under the leaves. Eben Pay told me those were coconuts.

I wish my brother Blue Foot could see one of those coconut trees. He'll never believe me when I tell him I saw nuts on a tree big as a half-grown watermelon. I'll tell Blue Foot all about those coconuts and he'll just look at me and then say I've been back into the white man's whiskey again.

But those woods bothered me, too. A lot of dangerous men could hide in there with high velocity rifles like everbody said the Spaniards had and they could blow your head off without you ever seeing 'em. Going after dangerous men in a woods is touchy business, especially if you don't know the woods too well. My father always told me the worst place to run down a mean Kiowa was in a patch of timber. And I knew it was true about some of those men we'd hunted for Judge Parker in the Territory.

Well, it turned out there wasn't anybody hiding in the woods we were looking at that day. But if they weren't there, I knew they'd be someplace else, waiting for us. And we'd have to go find them. Hell, that's what we come all the way down here to Cuba for, isn't it?

I didn't say anything to Eben Pay about this because he looked like he was having such a good time now and I didn't want to spoil it for him. But once we got on land and into some of that timber, I knew I'd better remember all I'd learned from my father about traveling through country the Cherokees thought belonged to them, and all I'd learned about going into some Arkansas River bottom thicket after a man we were trying to convince to come into Fort Smith so Judge Parker could hang him.

CHAPTER 11

FOR the soldiers watching from the decks of the transports, those who would ultimately survive, the day the Yankee invaded Cuba became a memory they called out and replayed for wide-eyed grandsons well into the twentieth century. At least until those same grandsons had seen a few invasions of their own.

Like the stories of all old soldiers, it was glorious in the extreme, growing more so with each telling. Finally taking on colors and odors and tastes of which they were only casually aware as they stood offshore that bright afternoon looking toward Daiquirí. Some things would loom gigantic. Like the foul taste of water on their troopships. Other things would be discreetly overlooked. Like the almost universal grousing with having been so long away from any opportunity to contract a little venereal disease.

It had been exciting. At least in spurts. It had been hauntingly exotic, everything happening across the backdrop of those brooding green jungles, the lifting mountains beyond, the towering, dazzling white thunderheads in a sky of breathtaking blue. It had been thrilling occasionally, as when the navy guns began to shoot, or when the boats passed by going toward shore and the hedge of bayonets glinted like deadly silver in the merciless sunlight.

But as with most such experiences for line troops, the titillation of the moment had indeed been momentary, to gain its passion and meaning only with the march of years, like good sour mash whiskey aging in a charcoal barrel. On that day, it was just another scene in a drama that overall was about 90 percent waiting for something to happen and 10 percent trying to understand the action once it had commenced.

As they grew older, the vague images would become more pronounced but the precise details would blur along with the chronology, for they, like their counterpart common soldiers through all of history, seldom had the slightest notion of what was going on across the wider stage. They saw only the surface of it, as they saw the sea, and had no appreciation for its depth or meaning.

Not so on the bridge of *Seguranca*, where the command group was very nearly hysterical with astonishment, a jubilation that grew as the operation progressed through afternoon and evening.

For it was impossible of belief. It was beyond most cherished dreams. After the hectic bedlam of loading out the ships, after the griddle-hot week lying like bloated whales in Tampa Bay, after the haphazard meandering cruise across Cuba's northern shore, after the initial comic snarl of heading troops toward the beach of Daiquirí, after all of that, everything had begun to work with steam engine precision, perfectly in accord with the plans and orders Eben Pay had seen emanate from General Shafter's chart room.

The progeny of efficiency is more of the same, Eben Pay thought, especially in a military process. General Shafter's staff began to act like a real staff that perhaps even a German officer would have recognized. Making notations on the margins of inadequate maps. Sending instructions to subordinate units, logging reports, concerning themselves with matters appropriate to a corps rather than fretting that five men from one regiment had reported to sick call with a sweat rash, making recommendations to the commanding general instead of asking him questions.

Subordinate commanders began to act like subordinate commanders, sending back from the shore their semaphore flag messages to apprise Shafter of their whereabouts and status.

The contract shipmasters, now confident that the dastardly

Spaniards were not going to shoot a lot of holes in their rust buckets, moved in closer to the command ship and sent lantern blinker messages that they awaited instructions.

The white uniformed United States navy liaison officers on the corps flagship assured the commanding general of their ability to provide boats and signalmen and stood about with their hands behind their backs, smiling, or else watched the beaches through binoculars, muttering, "Good, good, good."

The foreign officer observers had stopped smirking and explaining to Shafter all the various ways his expedition was about to be blown square to hell.

The newspaper correspondents were subdued. Mr. Richard Harding Davis, the Hearst man, was not present, having slipped away, nobody knew how, to assault the beaches with Colonel Roosevelt. Proving that he knew where the news was.

Mr. Clement Eggmont, among others, was on the bridge.

Mr. Clement Eggmont, of a San Francisco newspaper, was notable for two reasons. First, he was the man who had been wounded on the *Gussie* expedition and second, he had become more repugnant to the commanding general than even Mr. Richard Harding Davis. An awesome distinction!

The staff had taken to calling him Eggie. He was very young, and everyone figured that if he worked hard at his craft for at least forty years, he might attain some small bit of the status enjoyed by Mr. Davis. Provided, of course, that someone like General Shafter didn't in the meantime shoot him in the head.

But even Eggie, during this momentous occasion, managed to restrain his enthusiastic obnoxiousness by standing along a rear bulkhead and taking little notes in his little book with a little lead pencil.

Perhaps most impressive of all, the Cuban officers in the chart room had fallen almost silent, whispering their Spanish phrases only to one another in tones more modulated then had been heard from them since William McKinley was elected to the presidency of the United States.

Eben Pay and the Osage were on the edge of this collection

of people who were packed into the space from port flying bridge to starboard and the wheelhouse in between.

"Joe," Eben Pay said, his face showing clearly that all the uncomfortable philosophical mists concerning this operation had been burned away by witness to action, "this thing is working!"

"It's about time something did," Joe Mountain said. "When're we gonna get off this damned boat? I need to feel some dirt under my feet."

"Later, Joe, later," Eben Pay said, holding his field glasses up and squinting through the glare of late sun on water toward the smoldering village ashore.

"Well, shit," Joe Mountain said and turned and walked back along the deck to the fantail, which was deserted now, everyone on board being up front watching Daiquirí. He leaned against the railing. He spat into the water. He leaned far out and did it again, watching the spittle fall like a tiny, silver raindrop, then be blown under the stern by the westerly breeze so he couldn't see it strike the water. "Well, shit."

Then he saw, just beneath the surface, a long, gray, sleek form, gliding through the emerald green.

Hell of a big fish, Joe Mountain thought. Blue Foot ain't never gonna believe the size of the fish they got down here in this ocean.

Soon, there were others, swimming deeper than the first, but Joe Mountain could see them. He counted more than a dozen, sliding without effort through water that seemed as nonresistant to the swings of their great scimitar tails as air to the movement of a rattan fan.

Them look like big catfish, Joe Mountain thought. If I had me some line and some big hooks and some hog liver, I could catch enough fish to feed everybody on this boat.

And while the Osage watched the sharks the men around General Shafter standing on the bridge watched Cuba.

"By the holy blood of Christ," Shafter shouted, the sweat running down beneath his pith helmet in salty streams to spray from his many chins and wet his woollen uniform coat. "That Henry Lawton is a good man, a good man!"

Well, Eben Pay thought, having by now edged himself back into the chart room, after all he's been faced with, what a wonderful thing that he can see the whole business coming together.

And somehow, perhaps seeing the young civilian's sentiment in his eyes, Shafter almost laughed.

"Now you see, Mr. Eben Pay, the old army can do the job."

"I never doubted it, sir." And as he said it, there was a little tickle of rising hair along the back of his neck when others on the bridge glanced at him sharply as if to say, "We damned sure doubted it!"

It had been a simple plan. Elements of the Second Infantry Division, Brigadier General Henry W. Lawton commanding, would assault Daiquirí on the left, then wheel regiments in column toward the west and cross the jungle-choked high ground between Daiquirí and Siboney, driving off any Spaniards before them, and secure the beaches at Siboney, which were much more extensive than those at Daiquirí.

This done, the flotilla would steam to Siboney inlet and disembark the units of the Fifth Corps still afloat under the direct supervision of General Shafter. The navy would provide a beachmaster and crew to ensure the movement of men and matériel across the landing areas.

Meanwhile, elements of the Cavalry Division, dismounted, Major General Joseph Wheeler commanding, would land on the right and after securing Daiquirí would also swing to the west and follow Lawton. And would stay behind Lawton's division until the remaining units of the Second Infantry Division and the Cavalry Division and Brigadier General Jacob F. Kent's First Infantry Division were ashore, at which time the entire force would march on Santiago, in column.

The Cubans had informed General Shafter that there were probably as many as twelve thousand Spaniards defending the Santiago area.

"Good," said General Shafter. "With our entire army ashore, we will attack them and those we don't kill we will drive back into Santiago and force their surrender!"

Of course, along with the infantry formations, artillery would be put ashore, including a battery of four Gatling guns. And a medical detachment. And supply wagons, which would be taken in dismantled and reassembled on the beach. And somewhere in all this was a signal section with a hot-air observation balloon.

Everything proceeded apace. Everyone on *Seguranca* watched for Lawton's signals, as his action was pivotal. They were not disappointed. The signals came, almost too rapidly for the staff officers to write them down in their logbooks. When the beach operation succeeded, the flags spelled it out. Lawton's leading units were crossing the timbered high ground west of Daiquirí. His leading units were investing Siboney, a scatter of shacks. His leading elements had received hostile fire and returned it in volume and the few white-uniformed Spaniards resisting had fled along the road that led to Santiago. No casualties.

Somewhat disquieting was a signal to the effect that the road from Siboney to Santiago, which appeared on all the maps, was not really a road at all, but something that looked like a pig trail with jungle close in all about. But no matter.

By this time, the signals were coming via lantern blinker, a device operated by men of the signal section, who had laid down their flags as dusk came on, and with assistance from a few navy personnel who understood how to keep the obstinate things burning.

By this time, too, preparations were already under way for sailing the short distance down the coast to Siboney inlet, where the disembarkation would proceed. Some of the transports had already been gently moved in that direction, the navy vessels among the contract ships like shepherd dogs in a flock of sheep. The gunboats moved back and forth in the flotilla, coal smoke from their stacks spreading layers of sulfur scented thread among the transports like an odorous spider web. All across the waters before Daiquirí, the blue-white blinker lights flashed on and off, augmented now and again by the sharp hoot of steam whistles or the clanging of brass bells.

And then the last flickering signal came from the high ridge jungle south of the Daiquirí beach. The landing area, it said, had been secured at Siboney.

"By Christ's holy beard," Shafter shouted.

His staff officers muttered their approval and the French army major extended his congratulations and the Cubans began to shout again.

After wiping his face with a handkerchief, Shafter remembered something. He turned to Captain Malcomb, who had stood all afternoon and evening a little apart with his field glasses.

"Malcomb!"

"Sir!"

"What from Wheeler and the Cavalry Division?"

"He signaled his troops onshore. Early on."

"Hell's fire, we could see that! Eight hours ago. What else?"

"Sir, it's the only signal I've had from the Cavalry Division."

Suddenly Shafter seemed to smell the human odor in this confined space, the pungent reminder that nobody had bathed in over two weeks, and in blistering heat. His upper lip curled. A deep crease appeared between his eyebrows and he yanked off his great pith helmet and swiped a hand across the top of his head, sending a shower of salty moisture across the bridge.

"Well," he said, trying to hold his temper. "Where in God's name is the Cavalry Division? Where is Wheeler?"

"I don't know, sir."

Eben Pay perceived two things. First, that the very worst words a staff officer can say to a question from a commanding general is "I don't know." And second, that somewhere in all this steam engine precision there was a sudden, unwelcome squeak.

General Shafter began to swell, like a hog about to emit some horrendous squeal. Eben Pay pushed his way quickly off the bridge and moved along the deck toward the fantail, but even as he walked quickly away he could hear the roar behind him and was aware that others, like himself, were escaping. He felt a great compassionate pity for Captain Malcomb.

Joe Mountain was a silent, reassuring dark form at the very tip end of this ship.

"Well, I seen some big fish back here," Joe Mountain said.

"That's good, Joe."

"I wish I had some line and bait," the Osage said. "I ain't ever been a big fish eater, but right now, it might be good."

"Yeah, it'd be good." Eben Pay leaned against the rail and then was aware that Joe Mountain was smoking a cigar. "Where'd you get that cigar?"

"One of them little men in a fancy uniform give it to me," Joe Mountain said. "He had some snuff, too, but I told him I ain't much for dippin'."

"Probably the Frenchman," Eben said.

"What's all that yellin' up there?"

"They're just making arrangements."

"Damned noisy arrangements," Joe Mountain said. "Listen, I'll tell you about those fish I seen."

And so Eben Pay and Joe Mountain stayed on the fantail away from the shouting in the chart room and even after the ship had begun to turn into the flow of vessels moving west. And after a long time, the great bulging form of General Shafter moved toward them, tentatively coming along the deck, his eyes trying to adjust to the darkness after the lights of the bridge.

"Mr. Pay?"

"I'm here, General," Eben said.

"Good." Shafter moved close to them and after one swipe at his head with a palm, after taking off his helmet, he sighed. "I want to talk to you."

He slapped the helmet back on his head and Eben wondered why the hell he wore the thing now, in pitch-darkness, the only light from the various lamps of ships. In fact, Eben wondered, why the hell does he wear that wool uniform coat? But there was no time to speculate on it because the general had begun to speak.

"When we arrive off Siboney, Captain Malcomb will be taking a boat ashore to set up my advanced command post somewhere near Lawton," he said. "You and your Choctaw friend will accompany him."

"Osage," Eben said.

"Whatever," General Shafter said and Eben could see Joe Mountain's eyes shining. Then Shafter spoke with a rush of words, almost in a whisper, as though he wanted it out in a hurry yet only for the ears of these two before him. "You can drop your truck there, whatever you have—I expect a change of clothes—with my advanced headquarters group. And then I want you to find General Wheeler. I'm sending a Cuban officer with you and two of his men and I hope the bastards can find you a mule from one of their insurgent friends."

"Two mules, sir."

"Whatever. I want you to find Wheeler and the head of his column. If it still *is* a column. And get the information back to me. Use the Cubans. Use anything you can. But get the information back to me. I've got to know where that son of a bitch is. Are you familiar with his background?"

"Only a little of it, sir."

"Listen. Wheeler was a cavalry leader during the Civil War. A damned good one. For the Confederacy. He has been given his commission in the United States Army for this war, a kind of concession to brotherhood or some goddamned such thing.

"As I say. He is a fine soldier. But very volatile. I am sending you because you know what *tact* means. And we must be tactful with General Wheeler. I cannot afford any more competition and hateful rivalry than already exists in this army."

"I understand, sir."

"I hope to God you do," Shafter said. "Don't intrude on him. Be circumspect. Just find out what the hell he's doing and where his troops are and keep me informed. It will be a great service to this expedition."

"I hope I can justify your confidence, General."

"Aw," Shafter said and he slapped Eben on one shoulder with a great, meaty hand. "I'm sure you can, I'm sure you can."

The general started to turn away. Then paused, taking his pith helmet off once more and running a hand across his head, a gesture Eben had come to associate with command frustration. Shafter looked out across the dark sea where there were lights of vessels going toward Siboney. They could hear the swift, crinkling swirl of their own ship through the water, the wake just under the stern beneath them making a gentle popcorn whisper.

"Two other things," Shafter said. And Eben Pay knew these were not afterthoughts but the most important words the general had to say. "As I'm sure you are aware, having been privy to our plans and order of battle, Wheeler has in his division five regular regiments of cavalry. And one regiment of volunteers. Who are a unique bunch, along with their commander."

"Colonel Wood's regiment?"

"No," Shafter shouted and Eben could hear the irritation snapping in his voice. "You know as well as I do that Leonard Wood doesn't command that outfit."

"Roosevelt?"

"Yes. Him. He and his wild bunch and Wheeler are a quantity unknown. I don't think I can control them, but at least I need to know what the hell they're doing."

Shafter sighed and started to leave once more, then stopped and spoke, urgently.

"But most of all, most of all, remember that Confederate business. There are many southern soldiers in this army. But Wheeler ranks next to me in the whole corps and there are a great many citizens, north and south, who take him as a symbol. Of exactly what, I'm not sure. Reconciliation, perhaps. But no matter. He is a symbol. And we do not ruffle the feathers of a god-damned symbol."

And he was gone, abruptly, lumbering across the dark deck toward the bridge, a great, stooped figure gasping for breath and muttering profane and obscene curses into the hot westerly wind.

"Now we gonna get off this boat?" Joe Mountain asked.

"Yes. And go looking for a symbol."

"We used to have a lot of symbols with my people," Joe Mountain said and Eben Pay knew he was being hazed. "We had all these symbols and we'd tattoo 'em on our skins."

"We won't tattoo this one on our skins," Eben Pay said. "Let's get our gear together."

His voice had gone hard now because it was something he didn't want to be hazed about and the Osage knew it and made a gentle laugh and said, "Hell, Eben Pay, all I want is to get off this damned boat, then I'll help you find any symbol you want."

For a reason he couldn't explain, Eben suddenly thought of the Newton woman. And of Clara Barton. But mostly of the Newton woman. He couldn't remember her first name. He could remember her face, but he couldn't remember her first name. From his time spent in General Shafter's chart room, he knew the Red Cross operation would be coming to Cuba later. So it wasn't as though he didn't know where she was or what was in store for her. But it was a little shock that now, with so much else in his head, he should think of her. And not even remember her name.

Missy Bishop had been in his mind a great deal. He could not prevent himself from thinking, as he saw for the first time something like the flying fish or the distant gray mountains of Cuba as they went through the Windward Passage, I wish she could be here to see it. It was so powerfully painful. Yet somehow gratifying, to think of Missy Bishop.

Now, there was no pain or gratification or anything else as he thought of the Newton woman. Just amazement that he thought of her at all. So he pushed it all out of his head and turned his complete attention to Joe Mountain's descriptions of sharks, while they prepared to go ashore in search of a former Confederate hero, hidden somewhere in the dark jungle.

Olaf Swenson

There was this one time in Plattsburg Barracks when I got me a pass for the weekend right after a payday. I could put on civilian clothes and go anywhere I wanted.

Well, I couldn't really do that. It said right on the pass that I wasn't supposed to go any farther than fifty miles from the post. But when I got back from the orderly room with that pass, Corporal Price was waiting for me and he said what the hell, why didn't I just go on down to New York City.

Because, he said, in New York City I could really have a good time and forget all about being a soldier for a little while.

Corporal Price, he's the one who got me the pass in the first place. From First Sergeant Barry. Because Corporal Price said he was getting damned sick and tired of me getting into trouble at the post canteen and ending up on the company punishment book every month, and mucking up everything when they were trying to get the morning report done for the regimental personnel sergeant major.

Listen, the regimental personnel sergeant major was a six-striper. And even the company commander didn't want to get him upset. Hell, there's only two six-stripers in the whole damned regiment! The other one was the regimental sergeant major. And when him and the regimental personnel sergeant major walked down the street together, old soldiers said there's two master sergeants and there ain't but seventeen of them bastards in the whole damned army!

I don't usually talk like that, but it's the way noncommissioned officers talked when they saw twelve stripes all walking along together. My God! Twelve stripes!

Listen, Corporal Price told me. There's lots of things you can get away with in the army. But you never want to get crosswise with a sergeant major. It's better to double up your fist and hit the regimental commander in the mouth. Because then, Corporal Price said, you just get a nice little court-martial and off you go for thirty years' confinement at hard labor. You muck around with sergeants major, he said, you get the same treatment but a lot of bloody head and busted balls along the way.

I don't know if any of this is true.

But Corporal Price said he didn't want some goddamned six-striper always looking down his nose when an E Company soldier walked past. Because, Corporal Price said, E Company soldiers are the best soldiers in the world. And he wanted it to show without him having to stomp the hell out of anybody who thought different.

Listen, I never have really understood these army guys.

But that's why I got the pass. It was the only one I ever had. And I got it because Corporal Price was sick and tired of me coming into the orderly room after payday and causing a lot of problems when everybody was trying to get the morning report off to the personnel sergeant major.

Anyway, Corporal Price said I ought to go down to New York City on the train and let those policemen there worry about cleaning up my puke in their guardroom and maybe that way I would stay off the company punishment book at least until next month.

So he asked me how much money I had. And I told him four dollars because even though it was just after pay call I owed a lot to guys who had loaned me a dollar here and there at 100 pecent interest and I'd have to pay these guys or else get my nose busted out behind the latrine or anywhere else they could catch me.

He really called me some bad things then and cuffed my ears and gave me fifteen dollars. And told me that I'd better be back in reveille formation Monday morning or he'd report me for desertion and come after me himself and if the army didn't do it, shoot me.

Hell, I knew he was just joshing. I think he was just joshing. Well, you never know about Corporal Price.

New York City was bigger than any town I ever saw. It was

bigger than Milwaukee where I worked for that sausage guy. They had these steam trains that run on steel bridges up above the streets, throwing hot cinders down on everybody. They had these brown houses made out of rock that were six or even seven floors high. They had these guys on the sidewalk with pushcarts with big umbrellas over them and they were selling hot knockwurst and a lot of Jewish food and sauerkraut and strawberry ice.

They had a lot of whores in New York City but I didn't have enough money for those. I never heard of whores who charged so much. One told me she wouldn't do nothin' for less than two dollars. And she was ugly as hell, too.

New York City smelled like coal smoke and horse manure. The streets were full of the horseshit. They had these guys with brooms and shovels trying to keep it cleaned, but they were always behind because there were so many horses going up and down.

They had all these places where you pay to go in and see stuff. I went into one called the Barnum Museum. It cost a dime. They had all these stuffed animals that were freaks. They had a calf with two heads. For another dime, you could go in back and see a lady who had tattoos all over her body. And another one who was half man, half woman. The two headed calf was enough for me so I saved that second dime.

I went into this theater. A lot of the people in the seats were eating hot baloney wrapped up in newspapers. The place smelled like garlic.

Anyway, it was a show about this guy who shot Jesse James. They claimed it was the real, actual guy who done it. I didn't know who Jesse James was but he must have been a dyed-in-the-wool son of a bitch the way he was about to throw this pretty little girl right out of her home into the snow. That's when this other guy came in with a silver pistol and told Jesse James what a dyed-in-the-wool son of a bitch he was and then shot him. Everybody put down their baloney and clapped.

The thing about it was, that theater where me and those other people sat was all dark but they had these bright lights up there on the stage when the guy shot Jesse James. When we came into Siboney, it was the same thing. The whole ocean where we un-

[163]

loaded was dark but the whole beach was lit up with these navy searchlights. The beach just curved around and had white sand on it and these guys on the navy ships turned their searchlights on it and made it bright like a stage and that's where we were going into Cuba.

It was like walking out of a deep cave and right into bright sunlight, going onto that beach.

They threw these cargo nets down over the side of the ship. So we'd just climb down those nets like they was ladders and get in the boats alongside. The big ships we were getting off of just set there in the water but the little boats we had to get into were going up and down in the swell. So one minute they were right under your boots and the next they'd dropped twenty feet and would be banging against the side of the big ship.

It was scary as hell.

Corporal Price and First Sergeant Barry went down first and got in the small boat and held the bottom of the cargo net. Then the rest of the soldiers went down. And when we'd get to the bottom, Corporal Price would wait until the boat lifted on a swell and then he'd yell, "Now!" And we'd just turn loose of the cargo net and drop our asses into the boat. Then Corporal Price and First Sergeant Barry would kick us out of the way so there would be a place for the next soldiers coming down to land in the boat.

Our German guys were always good at doing stuff like that but I wasn't. Corporal Price said I was clumsy as a pregnant moose.

We all got into the boat and nobody fell in the ocean or got caught between the big ship and the boat when they were banging against one another. That happened to some guy in F Company. I guess he didn't have somebody like Corporal Price hold the cargo net and he missed the boat and fell in the water and got caught between the ship and the boat and it broke both his legs. We could hear him screaming. It was scary as hell.

They had some navy sailors in the boat who rowed us into the beach. Some of us had to help with the oars. It took quite a while to get in and the navy guys kept cussing at us because we didn't know how to use the oars.

We finally got ashore and those navy searchlights were so bright you couldn't look right at them or it would hurt your eyes. We got in the sand and started up toward all the trees and we passed right by this bunch of soldiers who had started big bonfires with the planks from packing cases and they were naked and dancing around their fires like heathen savages of some kind, drunker than hell.

Listen, Corporal Price and First Sergeant Barry and the new company commander Lieutenant Beaster were mad as hell about it and they kicked our asses right past all them drunk guys, naked and their balls and tallywhackers bouncing up and down while they danced around their fires.

One of them naked soldiers run over to our column and that was a mistake. First Sergeant Barry just stepped out and hit this guy one whack on the jaw, I never saw such a hard lick before, and this guy fell down in the sand and was thrashing around like a chicken with a wrung neck and we just marched right on past him toward this palm grove.

"Close it up, close it up," Corporal Price kept saying, which meant he wanted us to move quick into that palm grove where there were a lot of tents. We went right on through that place and there were soldiers there getting ready to bed down and we could see little groups of officers and noncommissioned officers watching everything. We went right on into the edge of the jungle. We got lined out in something like company formation in the jungle and pretty soon Corporal Price got a detail of men together and went back down to the beach and when he come back they had some tentage.

It didn't amount to much, that tentage. Just a little strip of canvas for each man, but Corporal Price and the other noncommissioned officers told us how to put it together. First Sergeant Barry called these things dog tents. And he was cussing pretty fierce because he said this stuff was old Civil War issue.

Two soldiers laced their pieces of canvas together and then put it up with little poles and ropes and there was a tent big enough for two men to crawl into and sleep. I ended up with Telner and after we were inside our tent laying there, there was enough light coming from the beach for us to look up at the canvas and see that all the filler was gone and only the threads were there, and it looked like cheesecloth.

Corporal Price came around checking everybody.

"Swede?"

"Yah."

"Where's your weapon?"

"Right beside of me."

"Where's your ammunition?"

"Right beside of me."

I heard him go all down the line asking guys where their weapon and ammunition was. We could still hear those drunk soldiers on the beach, singing. And I heard First Sergeant Barry say the tents wasn't worth a shit.

It rained like hell that night. The water come right through those tents. Me and Telner got wet as drowned rats. I never heard so much cussing in German before.

Then after it stopped raining Telner let out this bellow and threw something over against me. I had this little tin with matches in it and I took one out and struck it and there I seen what Telner had thrown out of his blanket roll. It was the biggest, ugliest, hairiest spider I ever saw.

I hit that spider with the butt of my rifle and it made a squishing pop, like I'd just busted a big goose egg. But that little dog tent wasn't big enough to be jerking around with a rifle and so it got all tangled up in the canvas and before it was over the dog tent was down and Telner was still cussing and we didn't have no tent left.

It wasn't worth a shit anyway.

CHAPTER 12

THEY had come onto this is-
land from Iowa and Georgia and Wyoming and New Hampshire
and other ordinary places, and on their first night in hostile terrain
there was not yet any thought of danger from the enemy. It was
not Spanish rifle or artillery fire that concerned them but rather
the absolutely strangling foreign feel and smell and touch and
sight of the place itself. The kind of suffocating pressure that
made even a can of bully beef with English words written on it
an old friend to be held close against the breast and stroked.

This was an alien slice of soil, with dark and quietly violent
whispers that nobody understood.

Plaintain, frogs, insects, and God only knew what else made
night noises in the jungle, chirps and clatters and buzzings and
whines and coughs, and more than one soldier, without any knowledge of the source of these sounds, fully expected a jaguar or
whatever vicious predator they had in Cuba, to spring out of the
dark foliage, fangs bared.

Mosquitoes began to feast on all the newly exposed flesh, but
such tiny nibbles didn't bother them like the thought of bigger
wildlife crawling into the blanket rolls, things they had already
seen in the beach lights, slithering and bounding and scurrying
away among the fallen palm fronds. Tarantulas and juicy pink

scorpions and shiny centipedes six inches long. Some had observed the hissing iguana and noncommissioned officers had to be forceful to prevent startled soldiers from opening with rifle fire on the monsters. Or anything else that moved.

"Them's just big lizards. They ain't gonna hurt you."

"Do them som-bitches bite, Sarge?"

And later in the night, the chilly rustle of land crabs moved through the camps. A few men realized by noon the next day that the last thing a civilized man wanted was to kill one of these grotesque little crustaceans and leave it to rot in the sun because the resulting odor was absolutely overpowering.

The only familiar thing in all of this wilderness of green was the pine tree. They recognized pine trees well enough but everything else was a stranger. The red and purple bougainvillea, the kapok and mahogany and granadillo ebony trees. Even the palms that they'd seen from the ships were somehow different, now that they were directly under them, graceful and coolly aloof, with the constant threat of dropping coconuts on their heads.

There was one thing that allowed a few of the more discerning listeners to realize they were still on the same planet from which they'd started. The mockingbirds. All along the edges of the palm groves, enthusiastic singers gave voice to the night, sending out their welcome to these latest visitors, and if one could filter out all the other tropic noises, it sounded surprisingly like an east Texas pecan grove on a lazy summer evening.

When Eben Pay and Joe Mountain came ashore, they had little time for observing Cuba's flora and fauna. There were three Cubans with them. A Captain Juan Carlos Smith, of all things, and two others, both responding to "Garcia."

"Are all these hablar people named Garcia?" Joe Mountain wanted to know.

They left Garcia Number One to guard their rolls and packs where they dropped them at the site Captain Malcomb had selected for General Shafter's advanced headquarters. It was a place well back from the confusion of the beach, with patches of moonlight coming down through the young coconut palms that somebody had been cultivating here.

Then they set off looking for General Lawton. And soon learned that a recently invested beach is not an easy place to find someone.

There were pine board packing crates everywhere. Some had been emptied. Some were still waiting to be opened. Others were being ripped apart by details of soldiers with wrecking bars and claw hammers. And considerable swearing and sweating. They passed a surgeon, a major, who was frantically running up and down the beach with a lantern in one hand although the search-lights made the place light as high noon, shouting that somebody had misplaced all his medical kits.

Columns of soldiers were coming up from the shoreline, rifles slung over one shoulder, blanket rolls over the other, faces serious under the brims of campaign hats, noncommissioned officers marching alongside keeping them moving smartly to assigned areas.

Near the beachmaster's tent, a crew of men stripped to the waist were hammering together wagons that had been lightered in disassembled. There was a string of braying, wall-eyed mules along a picket line, animals that swam in at Daiquirí and been led over the intervening high ground by the troops advancing on Siboney.

There were ordnance details opening cases of .30-caliber am-munition, discarding about half of it because it didn't fit any of the weapons Fifth Corps had, taking the rest and reloading it in cases and the cases stacked in well-defined lots to be picked up by regimental carrying parties later.

Sitting alone as though they had been forgotten were a pair of 3.2-inch breech-loading artillery pieces, looking like gate decor at the main entrance to a Civil War battle park, their gaping muzzles pointed out to the dark sea, their trails buried in the sand. And near those, a caisson and limber, hatches open showing empty ammunition bins.

At one point, a number of noncommissioned officers were trying with limited success to get a group of naked soldiers back into their uniforms as two huge bonfires blazed nearby.

Joe Mountain, taking in all the sights, was grinning and he waved to the naked soldiers and some of them waved back and shouted obscenities. Then the big Osage remembered something important he had forgotten to say and he moved up to walk beside Eben Pay, Captain Juan Carlos Smith just ahead of them.

"I don't like leavin' our truck back there with that Garcia man," Joe Mountain said. "I don't trust these hablar people ever since that kid in Austin sold us that cornmeal mush and called it tamales."

"That was a Mexican kid. These are Cubans."

"Yeah? Well, they all sound alike to me when they start that hablar lingo."

Lawton was well away from the beaches in a palm grove and it was past midnight when they found him. Eben Pay had seen him once on General Shafter's command ship and noted him as a solid, quiet, efficient regular who knew his job and followed orders.

Yes, Lawton told them, he'd seen Wheeler. In fact, Wheeler had been here to the beaches less than an hour before with a whole convoy of people and then he'd gone back to his column. When Eben asked where that was, Lawton shrugged and waved a hand vaguely toward the dark jungle behind the beachhead.

"General Wheeler is the ranking man ashore right now," he said. "And he apparently doesn't consider it necessary to tell anyone where he is or what he's doing. I've got my own opinion from what he said to me, but it's not something you'd want to file a report on. Let's just say he's off the leash."

So Eben Pay and Joe Mountain and Captain Juan Carlos Smith and Garcia Number Two picked their way through encampments of troops preparing to bed down or already in the rolls and on into the jungle, Captain Smith leading. It started to rain about then and rained for about an hour and then the moon was out once more, giving them some sense of direction.

"Keep it in mind where the beach is, Joe."

"Hell, Eben Pay, you ain't gonna lose me in this timber. I just hope nobody starts shootin' at us."

"That's a pleasant goddamned thought."

"I just wish I had a Winchester. I'll tell you, this is the last war I ever go to without a Winchester."

Captain Juan Carlos Smith led them through thickets and heavy stands of tall trees, finding paths in the moonlight that were more apparent than real. It was about three in the morning when they found General Wheeler.

It was a glade that opened before them in the jungle, a place that had been cut and burned for farming, and now there were only a few Spanish bayonet and kapok trees to interrupt the grassy open space. At the center was a small fire, an orange eye in the silver moonlight face of the clearing. There were men around the fire and there they found the general and Colonel Wood and Lieutenant Colonel Roosevelt and some other lesser officers.

Eben presented his written credentials but General Wheeler waved them away.

"I don't need that," he said. "I remember you on Shafter's ship."

"Well, Mr. Pay," Lieutenant Colonel Roosevelt boomed, coming over and shaking Eben's hand vigorously. "We're a hell of a long way from the Menger Hotel, aren't we, sir."

"Yes sir, we are."

Eben noticed a few saddled horses at one edge of the clearing and behind that a dark formation of troops. A lot of troops.

"Glad to see you again," Roosevelt said, his teeth and glasses shining in the moonlight. "Bully!"

In later years, Eben could not ever recall Colonel Roosevelt using that word except for this one night in the jungle behind Siboney.

"I see you've still got your big friend with you," Roosevelt said, looking back beyond Eben to where Joe Mountain and the two Cubans were standing apart.

"Yes sir, he's an asset."

"I suppppose he would be."

Eben had the sense that Wheeler was extremely impatient. They had a few casual remarks to make and mostly it was Eben telling them the progress on the beach. They want my ass out of here, Eben Pay thought. I've interrupted something.

He kept glancing back to the jungle beyond the horses. There were a lot of troops there. They were not making any preparations for bedding down. They were standing, weapons in hand. Colonel Wood kept watching him with what Eben thought were beady little eyes, saying nothing. General Wheeler was brusque, anything but cordial. Eben thought, he'd as soon General Shafter sent his liaison people to Lawton and Kent and let it go at that.

And suddenly Eben Pay knew who those troops were. They were the Rough Riders. They were Roosevelt's men. And they were ready to move. Not a forward detachment, but the whole damned regiment.

He brought to focus in his mind the principle operations map in Shafter's chart room, with all the units of the army penciled in, their positions and lines of march. And he superimposed the beach behind him, and even though Captain Juan Carlos Smith had taken some turns and twistings, he knew that where they were standing now was not behind Lawton, where Wheeler was supposed to be. Where they were standing now was well ahead of Lawton on the route to Santiago. Wheeler was moving ahead of Lawton to get first whack at the Spaniards!

And with that realization, Eben Pay had the overpowering urge to do something, anything, to avoid confusion of General Shafter's plan and in his eagerness to help that great, sweating, inefficient man, he forgot what Shafter himself had said about how to treat Wheeler. And the moment he heard his own words issue from his mouth, was dreadfully sorry he had spoken them.

"General, I think perhaps as a member of the commanding general's staff I might review for you the plan of operation."

Wheeler was facing Eben, his back to the fire, his face in the moonlight beneath a narrow-brimmed hat. And in that moment, in that instant that he spoke, Eben knew he was staring into the blackest, most resentful fire he had ever seen in a man's eyes. When Wheeler spoke, it was with great restraint.

"Young man, I do not care a bucket of boll weevil spit who you are and I do not need some wet eared civilian coming out here to tell me my business. Would you please return from whence you came and give my compliments to General Shafter and tell him that I am moving against the Spaniards."

And that was all. Wheeler and his entire entourage were pulled by one quick movement away from the fire and Eben Pay was left watching their backs going toward the horses and those waiting troops.

"Christ!" Eben Pay muttered. "Why did I do that?"

Joe Mountain moved up beside him.

"That's a cranky old son of a bitch, ain't he?"

"He's right, Joe," Eben said. And thought, Of all the pompous, presumptuous idiots on earth, I must be in first place, talking to that general like that. "Let's get back to the beach. In a hurry."

They dove back into the jungle, Captain Juan Carlos Smith leading once more. Eben thought perhaps he could send Garcia Number Two running ahead with his message about the whereabouts of the Cavalry Divison and Wheeler's intention and then decided against it. Then saw that there were only three of them moving along the shadowed paths.

"Where's Garcia?" he said.

Ahead of him, going forward quickly, Captain Juan Carlos Smith shrugged and said, "Quién sabe?"

It seemed farther going back. Because now Eben Pay was in a hurry. He didn't know what difference it would make, but he wanted to send a message to Shafter. He could imagine how the commanding general would react.

Soon, they could see the gleaming of the navy searchlights through the trees ahead and there Captain Juan Carlos Smith stopped and bowed and said he would go now to find those horses señor the general had requested for Eben and Joe Mountain.

"But how are you going to find us . . . ?" He stopped. Captain Juan Carlos Smith had disappeared into the jungle, soundlessly.

"By God, Joe, I'm getting pretty tired of people turning and walking away from me!"

"Yeah, well, I'll tell you what would be good. If that hablar son of a bitch stole Wheeler's horse for you."

Eben stared at the Osage and saw the flash of teeth and started laughing. He couldn't stop laughing. He turned and staggered on toward the shine of the searchlights on the beach, tears running down his face.

"And Eben Pay, maybe he could steal Captain Roosevelt's horse for me."

"God damn, Joe," Eben gasped. "This is serious."

"Not near as serious as if somebody stole Wheeler's horse."

By the time they had reached the advanced headquarters of the corps, Eben had his laughter under control. It had been a near thing to hysteria for a while, listening to that damned Osage.

Captain Malcomb was there and when he heard what Eben had to say, he swore. And said they'd best compose a written message and have it taken out to *Seguranca* by steam launch.

"These damned blinker lights are all right," he said, "but none of our people are worth a damn reading them and most of the navy people have been pulled back into the fleet."

So they wrote it on a piece of yellow message form, and it stated, "Wheeler has bypassed Lawton on the north through the jungle and now appears to be advancing toward Santiago with the First Volunteer Cavalry Regiment leading. It is assumed that the entire cavalry division will follow."

It was almost dawn. Eben Pay was suddenly very, very tired. But when they went to the base of the palm tree where they had dropped their rolls and packs, nothing was there. Not even Garcia Number One.

"I tried to tell you about these hablar sons a bitches."

"Joe, I'm in no mood for your goddamned analysis of the characters of Spanish speaking people," Eben snapped. "Lay down in the sand and get some sleep."

"Well, I don't know what all that you just said means, but I'm hungry as hell and I'm going to mosey down along this beach and find us something to eat. They gonna find out that these hablar sons a bitches are not the only ones around here who can steal stuff."

But two hours later, it wasn't anything stolen that they ate. It was iguana tail, roasted over a small fire at the base of their palm tree, and when Eben Pay woke and sat up, smelling the meat cooking and rubbing the sand from eyes swollen with mosquito bites, Joe Mountain was squatting there, turning the meat and grinning.

"I ain't never been much for lizard," Joe Mountain said. "But these big bastards were about as easy to catch as a Caddo squaw and twice as easy to skin."

It was delicious. Like chicken breast, and Joe Mountain even had some salt.

"Joe," Eben Pay said, his mouth full. "You never really skinned a Caddo squaw did you?"

"No. But there was one I knew over at a McAlester whorehouse that sure deserved it."

Lieutenant Colonel John Stoval

The twenty-seventh day of June, Anno Domini 1898. It was then that our troops discovered to their dismay that the politicians and newspapers had played them false. For many, it was the very last thing they learned in this mortal life.

Oh yes, my good wife, Earline, has accused me many times of preaching. And it's true. Some things need saying. And if some of it is preaching, then so be it!

On that day it became clear that the Spaniards on Cuba were not craven beasts as they had been portrayed. They were soldiers brave and well trained, with fine weapons, and they knew how to use them.

The knowledge of that deception no matter how innocently it had been made was universally hurtful. The stings of Spanish bullets or artillery fire was bad enough, but for all those even untouched by metal, there was the question: "How have I been used?"

Well, maybe not everyone. The old regular noncommissioned officers had some idea of what armed combat was all about. They anticipated high velocity rifle fire. They expected those vicious round steel ball pellets of shrapnel. And they were not disappointed because the Spaniards had both. Oh yes, they knew from the start that Cuba would be no cakewalk. They were too cynical to accept such a notion. They had long since learned not to take large gulps of the pap placed before them.

Well. Since that time in Cuba, I have seen a full life with my wife, Earline. I have seen my only son into a good banking career. I have seen his children on my knee and felt their moist kisses against my cheek. I have seen a great and terrible war in France.

Yet, of all my memories, none is more bright and shining than the gallantry and courage of those American soldiers in Cuba who were ill managed and hardly paid at all, who saw themselves in later years congratulated for their little war, when all the while they knew that there is no such thing as a "little war" for the man who in the moment confronts the ultimate doorway.

Yes, Earline, I preach! I preach!

It is, you see, a devastating moment, when you see the eyes of a man blown out and his brains splattered, and even as it happens know that in your own home country almost nobody gives a damn. Because this is a cakewalk. So sing another song!

Yes, Earline!

My regiment came across the beach at Siboney in good order. More than I can say for some of the others, especially the National Guard outfit that somehow, inexplicably, was included in the corps.

Politics, I supposed. Those poor men. Terribly equipped, terribly trained. Just wear a uniform and wave a flag and this makes one capable of going into combat against professionals. My God, the vicissitudes brought on by elected officials and their constituents where pride and ignorance together decree that all required in war is a grand parade down Main Street with flags waving.

Yes, Earline!

But that day on Siboney's beach there was little time to worry about the problems of others. Each of us had enough of his own.

The Thirty-seventh Infantry Regiment moved close to General Lawton's headquarters in a large coconut grove well before midnight and bedded down. The troops were restive and understandably sensitive to all of this that was so new and exotic. Somewhere, it sounded as though a rifle fired. But it was in another regiment. As the night went on, the call of wild things from the jungle was disconcerting and even frightening. And for hours, incongruously, a dog was barking somewhere far to the west.

I moved among my soldiers in the darkness, once while it was raining furiously, speaking words of encouragement. I suspect my presence was of little account. The noncommissioned officers did the duty they were expected to do.

My old Company E seemed well ordered. Perhaps, I thought, more than all the rest. And at one time, there was First Sergeant Maurice Barry, standing in the rain before a line of tents and barking.

"And for the first dog robber amongst ye who comes out and wanders 'round, there will be me to deal with, you water-soaked, red-eyed, starvin' sons of bitches! An' if you don't sleep with them goddamned rifles, I will take each one I find and shove them into your Holy Moses!"

By God, you win wars with men like that!

All of Lawton's regiments were ashore by dawn, having come in throughout the night in that silver glare of navy searchlights. Had the Spaniards wanted to attack against the beachhead, I shudder to think of the results. But as at Daiquirí, the Spanish army refused to take advantage of our weaknesses. It was as though they had little stomach for any kind of fight until pressed into a corner.

When the sun rose, promising another blistering day, Lawton's regimental commanders gathered at his headquarters, which was marked by two small wall tents, a kitchen fly, a picket line of three horses, and a number of folding canvas chairs set half buried in the sand and fallen palm fronds. The whole area smelled of rotting vegetation, somewhat like an old greenhouse.

But in reference to smells, there was no breakfast but the coffee Lawton's two colored cooks boiled in some one-gallon tins which originally had held saltine wafers. I have never experienced a brew that had such an outrageously delicious odor and tasted so deplorably bad. And worst of all, here we were in Cuba, and there was no sugar for the coffee.

No one had had any sleep. We were a scarlet-eyed group. General Lawton was explaining in some detail his plan for the advance of his division once General Shafter had determined that he had enough ashore to support an advance. But he seemed preoccupied. I had served with Lawton before and held him in some considerable esteem. Certainly not a brilliant officer, but a steady one. Now, he was less than astute. I attributed it to lack of sleep. Until I heard him pass a remark, made almost as though to himself.

"Wheeler is loose on the road to Santiago."

It was indicative of what I had suspected all along. That there was a counterproductive, fierce competition. Not just between regiments, which can sometimes be healthy. But between officers. Between regulars and volunteers, between West Pointers and other commissions, between army and navy. And now, between old Confederates and Yankees.

As we sat in these ridiculous little canvas folding chairs under the royal palms, our heels sunk in the soil of Cuba, I had a sense of the absurd. Of grown men racing to be first in punishing the hated enemy, like boys running after the greased pig at a county fair. And just as frivolous. Cheered on by a multitude of newspapermen.

But all this was soon forgotten. We began to hear rifle fire from the west. It began as a scatter of shots, like hunters out for upland birds, but quickly increased to a serious volume, a rattle of sound that crackled through the green foliage.

Lawton rose slowly from his chair and looked off into the jungle beyond the palm grove. There, the early sun was making brilliant green patches interrupted by purple shadows. There were a number of cuckoos there, long tails striped with gray and white, and they had begun to fly about frantically as the sounds of firing increased.

Lawton turned his head and looked at me. There was in his eyes a kind of fierce light, a kind of smoldering fire.

"Stoval," he said quietly. "Have your regiment stand to arms."

The officers and men of the Thirty-seventh had heard the firing and when I moved toward them they were already up and weapons in hand. All back through the palm grove I could see the regiments moving into columns, looking expectantly toward me, who commanded here the leading unit. Thank God for regulars.

I turned back once more to General Lawton and informed him that we were ready when he chose. At that point, a junior officer on his staff said, "Somebody up there is engaged."

Lawton looked at this unfortunate officer as though he were an idiot.

It was at about this time, the exact sequence failing in my memory due to the excitement of being committed to battle, that one of General Shafter's staff advisers came running into the grove, this rather handsome, tall civilian young man we all knew who went about with the most enormous red Indian anyone had ever seen always following him. He went directly to General Lawton and began to speak as I returned to the group of officers.

This young man was well known in our army, at least by sight, because from the time we gathered at the Plant Hotel in Tampa he had been associated with Shafter's staff. Rumor had it that he was sent by Colonel Roosevelt. As a result, everyone assumed he was Roosevelt's man on the staff of the commanding general, a circumstance not conducive to making him popular with the regular officers in the corps.

Now, this Mr. Pay had appeared and placed in General Lawton's hand what we called a flimsy, a thin yellow paper which our signal people used for messages. We assumed it was something from General Shafter, still afloat off Siboney. When Lawton read it, he laughed harshly.

"Well, gentlemen," he shouted. "It seems that General Shafter has ordered General Wheeler to remain in place. But from the sound of things up ahead there, it appears to have come a bit late, wouldn't you say?"

"I need to get to General Wheeler and give him this message," Mr. Pay said.

"Not now, young man, not now," Lawton said. "It's too late for messages such as this. Tell me, did you find General Wheeler last night after you left me?"

"Yes sir, I did," the young man said. He seemed taken somewhat aback.

"Did you see troops then?"

"Only the head of the column of the First Volunteer Cavalry Regiment. That's all I saw."

"Roosevelt's men."

"Well, Colonel Wood was there."

"We can dispense with all this charade, Mr. Pay," Lawton said. "We all know whose regiment that is. You should know most of all. And when you were with me last night, why is it that you failed to inform me of their intentions?"

The young man stiffened and grew red faced and I will admit that, Roosevelt's man or not, I had to admire his sharp retort and the manner in which he bent forward and glared into General Lawton's face.

"I had no idea of their intentions, General. I discovered it only after I had found General Wheeler!"

"I see," Lawton said.

"It was my own message to General Shafter that first informed him of it after I had found General Wheeler, whose whereabouts, I might say, you did nothing to assist me with."

There was a long and embarrassed silence. The staff officers standing about were somewhat open-mouthed that anyone would speak in such a way to the division commander. And in that moment, the Indian walked up behind Mr. Pay and spoke in this great, low voice that carried across the palm grove like the beat of a drum, not loud, but somehow insistent.

"Tell this cap'n about that cranky little son of a bitch Wheeler, Eben Pay."

The young man waved a hand impatiently, as though he were trying to shoo off an overeager dog. The large Indian did not shoo. But none of this was lost on General Lawton, and when he spoke again there was a softer tone to his voice.

"Mr. Pay. Do you have any notion of who might be involved in that fight up there?"

"No sir," the young man said. And by now he had his own temper under control. "All I saw was the head of Colonel Wood's column. I assumed some of the regular regiments were close by."

"A valid assumption," General Lawton said, and he nodded and perhaps even smiled a little. "Thank you, Mr. Pay. But please, sir, I must ask you to remain with us a moment, for your own safety."

Mr. Pay was highly agitated. He paced back and forth, kicking at the dead palm fronds on the ground. His large Indian friend turned and, because I was nearest him, spoke to me.

"That Wheeler man, he's a cranky little son of a bitch."

I could hardly have agreed more.

And then the first casualty came out of the jungle. It was a civilian packer, one of the many contract people hired by this army to handle mules and supplies. What few mules there were. But the man was in a bad way, staggering along and holding a hand to his neck and blood running from between his fingers and down across his cotton shirt.

"It's an ambush, it's an ambush," he gasped. "They're all butchered, all butchered."

Lawton's medical people had hardly taken the wounded packer in hand when two Cubans appeared dragging a makeshift litter. On the litter was a newspaper correspondent shot through the spine and singing a dance hall song, his trousers and boots soaked with blood.

"Stoval," General Lawton said. "Move your regiment up. I'll be in support with the whole division."

My old steady E Company was in the lead and all it required was a move of my hand and they started forward, going into the trail that led to Santiago.

"And take this young man with you," General Lawton shouted, and Mr. Pay and his Indian friend fell in beside me as we plunged into the shadows of the trees, behind us the sounds of troops coming on, the whisper of their boots in the sand a steady, crunching rhythm.

By God, we were into it!

CHAPTER 13

O call it a road was the abso-
lute height of optimism. The surface was spongy even under the
weight of a man, boots mushing into the moist, sandy soil and
the thick accumulation of years of fallen and rotted foliage from
jungle close on either side. What would happen to it when artillery
and heavy ammunition wagons came through required little imagination.

But the Thirty-seventh Infantry Regiment gave such things
little thought that morning as they marched along this road in-
tending to rescue Joe Wheeler. In any case there was little they
could do about it. It was the only road that passed through the
green tangle toward the sound of battle and thence on to Santiago.

Lieutenant Colonel John Stoval hurried ahead, taking with
him two enlisted men as runners and accompanied by the commanding general's courier, Eben Pay. And of course, Joe Mountain, whose perpetual grin seemed to have taken harsher contours
and whose eyes seemed to grow bleaker the nearer they came to
the racket of firing.

Eben Pay, sweating as he trotted along behind the colonel,
had time to note a thing he had seen before in the Indian Territory
when out on posse with the Osage. The rather disconcerting
impression that Joe Mountain's eye teeth, startling prominent

even in calm times, grew longer and sharper as danger approached. Eben Pay knew it was absurd. Yet the notion persisted, and it was not particularly comforting because at such times this big Indian whom he trusted and considered as dear a friend as he'd ever had took on the appearance of a very hostile creature indeed. Like a normally genial tail-wagging dog who suddenly threatens to bite off every hand reaching out to pet him.

They were soon far ahead of the regiment. And by design, for Stoval did not believe in bringing a unit onto line without himself having first seen the ground where they would be committed. Worse still, to his thinking, was having soldiers arrive for action dispersed helter-skelter like pins on a woman's clothesline.

So behind them, as they came close enough to whatever was ahead to hear the slap of high velocity slugs through the trees overhead, they knew the Thirty-seventh was coming on. Methodically. Inexorably. The officers and noncommissioned ranks keeping the unit tight, almost at lockstep, in column of twos along the jungle trace, like a single block of striking power pushed along without loss of integrity. The noncoms using those same words that every American foot soldier had heard going to the sound of the guns from Princeton to Queenston to Matamoros to Antietam.

As they passed through that tunnel of green only occasionally splashed with brilliant little incursions of sunlight, Eben Pay thought of it, thought of those men back there, coming on. And it made the chills go up his back. He had some considerable appreciation of history as recorded on the printed page but none until now of the sights and sounds and smells of it where real flesh and bone and blood and staring eyes confronted him, everything mixed and stirred with the odor of his own sweat.

And moving along that dismal road in southern Cuba, Eben Pay for the first time came to the realization that in times of imminent peril, a man's mind could dash off hither and yon into strange places, just when concentration should be on naked survival.

He had no idea what was ahead. But there was some assurance of what was happening behind. The regiment was coming on. And looking at John Stoval's hard-set features and squinting eyes, he knew at once the heart-pounding, breath-stopping trepidation of facing unknown hazard. Yet by God the regiment was back there and coming on!

Stoval knew a great deal more. Not of the fight they were approaching. But in his head, whether or not he was aware of it consciously, he could hear those saw-toothed shouts of his non-commissioned officers.

"Close it up, close it up, goddamnit, suck in that interval behind the first platoon, move, move, move, close it up you dog-robbin' sons a bitches, you're slowin' up this parade, close it up!"

On their right the jungle began to clear. There were longer and longer vistas of cleared ground, going down to a small stream-line. They began to pass wounded men lying beside the trail, which had widened now and could almost be called a road. There were a few dead, lying in that limp and completely boneless posture impossible to achieve so long as any life moved through the blood vessels.

Down the slope to the north, to their right, they could see men in blue shirts and suspenders, taking what cover they could, and firing their rifles. It was a scattered and undisciplined fire and directed toward a far ridge along the road to the west, clear of all vegetation and with entrenchments along the crest. There, Eben Pay saw his first Spaniard, at that range only little flicks of white shirt and brown straw hat as the sharpshooters moved from position to position to deliver fire against the halted line of American troops.

And there, in the widening road, they found General Wheeler, bristling like a tiny boar hog in heat, eyes snapping black and furious, but with a vacant, lost expression that gave Eben Pay one brief moment of triumph because it was obvious that Fighting Joe had not been prepared, after his excellent service in the Civil War, to face rapid-fire small arms putting his men down at long range with copper-jacketed bullets.

Within ten paces of him, lying in a ditch, was a man whose jaw was mostly shot away, the front of his shirt a gummy purple-red, making horrible sounds as he bled to death. The slugs of the Spaniards were making hard, whining ricochets off the ground near Wheeler's feet, and Eben Pay had to concede that the former Confederate might be a son of a bitch, but none of that had anything to do with courage.

There was a chorus of yelling for water from the wounded, some of it very weak, and south of them, in the jungle, which was still dense there, were sounds of heavy fire and shouting. And punctuating all of that, the twitting, sharp cries of the cuckoo birds, long tails like narrow fans, who darted about in the edge of the jungle with irritation at all the racket.

Wheeler and one of his officers, looking terribly frightened, stood there in the center of the road, in full view of the Spanish soldiers on the far ridge. As though the little cavalryman were disdainful of enemy fire or else thought he was still on some battlefield of 1863 where rifles from almost a third of a mile away could be ignored. The dead and wounded around him should have cleared up that misconception. Eben Pay had to give him grudging admiration for pluck if little credit for discretion.

As Stoval moved up quickly to the general, Eben Pay had another of those quick little mental detours from the subject at hand, thinking, My God, I've seen Stoval a number of times and came with him along this road, but until now never realized he is a tall man, as tall as I am!

"Support?" Wheeler was shouting. "Why hell's own fire, sir, we need no support! Down there—" and he pointed along the slope toward the small streamline, "I've got elements of two regular regiments. And back there—" and with his other hand swept in the direction of the jungle to the south, "is Wood and Roosevelt with the entire First Volunteer Cavalry Regiment. And, I might add, sir, every goddamned newspaper correspondent on this expedition!"

"Sir?" Stoval shouted, leaning over Wheeler. "Where is the rest of your division?"

"Division? Why hell's own fire, sir, there someplace—" and he waved back in the direction of Siboney. "We had no time to wait for them. But they'll be up!"

"Sir!" Stoval shouted again over a fresh burst of Spanish fire, and bending over Wheeler and glowering, said, "I have a full infantry regiment just behind and it is General Lawton's desire that I support you."

"Good, good, put them in. We'll charge those damned Yankees," Wheeler bellowed, forgetting which war he was fighting.

Stoval was finished with the general and wheeled about and dispatched his two runners back to the regiment and himself ran over to the north sloping hill and looked down along the ragged line of troops. Wheeler glared about, and seemed for the first time to see Eben Pay and the great, towering form of the Osage just behind him.

"Oh, well, you again, young man."

When Eben Pay offered him the flimsy paper, the general jerked it from his hand, read it quickly, and threw it aside.

"Stay in place?" Wheeler asked. "Stay in place?"

A Spanish bullet whined off one of the nearby hardwoods and Wheeler looked up at the sky and sighed, a long, painful sigh.

"I am fighting the enemy," he said. And without further comment calmly walked to the side of the road and shouted toward his soldiers down along the slope, more in exhortation than anything like instructions. Then turned and over his shoulder shouted, "I've got twenty wounded and I don't know how many dead. Why in Christ's holy name doesn't the corps give me some support?"

It was a statement, not a question, and Eben Pay was about to point out, regardless of Shafter's warning to be circumspect, that had not Wheeler jumped the gun there might be all kinds of corps support. But Wheeler had dismissed him. And standing there in that road, exposed to Spanish fire, and grinding his teeth in frustration, Eben Pay suddenly felt himself yanked backward and into a low ditch where water was flowing. Joe Mountain had the back of his shirt in one hand, and was holding him down in the small cover provided by the ditch. Eben Pay could feel the water wetting his crotch.

"Damnit, Joe, you're getting my ass wet in this water!"

The Osage gave no indication that he had heard and said nothing himself, but squatted there behind Eben Pay, his hand still holding the back of Eben Pay's shirt.

"Damnit, Joe . . ." But then he fell abruptly silent because the head of the Thirty-seventh Infantry column was coming out of the jungle, trotting now, rifles held at high port, Stoval's runners leading them on, and Stoval himself just down the slope across the road waving them into position.

First, there were a half dozen regimental officers and enlisted men and then directly behind them was E Company, led by Dylan Price. And as he passed the dead man with no jaw, Olaf Swenson was greener than seasick, and Dylan Price was shouting.

"A dead soldier it is, man. Move on Swede, and no more sightseeing with you."

They were peeling off the road, coming on line behind Wheeler's men, and as Price stood in the road slapping the butts of his passing soldiers he turned for a moment and saw Eben Pay and Joe Mountain squatting in the ditch and he laughed. There was a glint of exhilaration in his eyes and Eben Pay thought, My God, there are men who actually enjoy this!

"Well, sir," Dylan Price shouted. "Right to the battle is it? I took you for a rooster the first time I clapped eyes on you!"

Then he was off down the slope with his men, oblivious to the Spanish fire, which had increased again.

"Keep those pieces locked, and find your position and fire when I tell you," Price was yelling. Swenson kept looking back toward the dead man in the road's ditch. "Swede, goddamnit, I will puke you, I will puke you now, get along with it."

And then all the firing stopped. There were no more snarls of Mauser bullets through the foliage. There were no more rasping ricochets. Wheeler's men had stopped firing, too, and there was only the grunting sound of the Thirty-seventh soldiers running down the slope into position.

"They've gone," Joe Mountain said and released Eben Pay's shirt.

The far ridge was empty. There were no more straw hats, no more flashes of white shirt. There was only the cuckoo's rhythmic chant, repeating its name, "kuh, kuh," taking its natural place once more in the noise of the jungle. Even the wounded had stopped calling for water.

"They're gone," Joe Mountain said again.

Now, with the Thirty-seventh still going into position, General Wheeler began screaming his men forward. They leaped up, shouting, and for the first time Eben Pay saw that some of them were the black soldiers of the Tenth Cavalry and behind him, in the jungle, he could hear a great shout from the Rough Riders. Everyone moved forward now, against no opposition.

"Come on, Joe," Eben Pay said and he leaped up and ran too, the excitement making him forget his sweat and the swarm of gnats around his face and the crawling itch in his crotch where the water of the ditch had soaked his underwear. And as he ran down into the streambed and up the following slope behind Wheeler's men, he could hear the big Osage, running with him, breathing easily, like a laughing, friendly dog once more.

The troops of the Thirty-seventh were all in position, but now left behind. Stoval was cursing. He was not alone.

"I'll be double goddamned," shouted First Sergeant Barry.

"The bloody bastard's mucked out on us," said Price.

"You can't trust a goddamned Spaniard," bellowed Barry. "Shoot and run, shoot and run. No spirit to stand and give a man his fight."

"But good Catholics, First Sergeant," Price said and he was standing now and opening his pants to relieve himself.

"Good Catholics in a pig's pink ass," Barry shouted. "Worse than red Indians, shoot and run."

"Well, a fine time to make some water," Price said. "Better when nobody's shooting at you, right First Sergeant?"

"Aw, go to hell, you Welsh cretin. Hey you, there, keep the muzzle of that rifle out of the sand, you dumb, mule eared mud sucker!"

Price was laughing, but without much mirth in it. "You are a man for the ages, Sergeant Barry. Someday I will teach you some good British discipline."

Barry turned on him, his eyes pointed like fire.

"Now, Dylan?"

"No. But later. I promise it," Price said, and he was no longer laughing.

And Wheeler's men ran up the deserted ridge cheering, leaping into the trenches where the empty brass cartridge cases of the Spanish rifles lay thick, like golden roller bearings underfoot. There were some blackish splotches of moist earth along the revetments, the blood that showed some of the American fire had gone home. There was a single straw hat, discarded metal canteens, empty canvas bandoleers, and a frayed copy of last week's *New York Sun* newspaper. And already the men who had occupied this position had disappeared to the west.

In Manhattan, New York. In Manhattan, Kansas. It was hailed as a great victory. The Battle of Las Guásimas. Nobody knew how to pronounce it, but small matter. It proved the invincibility of good American arms. It proved the rightness of the Cause.

And the grand hero was naturally Colonel Roosevelt. All the newspapermen had been with him. He was played in the gray columns of print all across the land. Oh yes, the stories said, Colonel Leonard Wood was really the commander of the Rough Riders. It said this in about the seventeenth paragraph of the stories. But there was no doubt about the courage and verve of the former assistant secretary of the navy. He had gone forward shouting, his teeth and glasses blazing. No one ever afterward denied it. He was brave. He could lead men. All who had actually seen him agreed to this.

It was a vision to be kept bright. Colonel Roosevelt the first victor. Colonel Roosevelt the first to draw an enemy's blood since Five Forks, or whatever that fight was they had just before Appomattox, they said.

Well, wait a minute, they said. His superior in this thing was a former Confederate. So maybe it would be better to say, first blood since Cerro Gordo, or one of those battles back when Van Buren was president. Wasn't that a battle then? Wasn't Van Buren president then? they asked. Or Polk? No matter. It's Teddy now, and the Rough Riders.

There were some quotes from the hero himself. Right in the newspapers. That business of the commanding general of the entire expedition being on board a ship out in some harbor while the boys with Teddy were winning the victory. Why look at this, they said, why don't we make Teddy a brigadier general?

Mr. Hearst and Mr. Pulitzer were beside themselves with delight. Their newspapers detailed step by step the fantastic feat of arms. They were not alone. Even hidebound Democratic journals gave way to the valor of the Republican leader of the Rough Riders.

Mr. McKinley was more reserved. He had heard a great deal of sour grapes from his commanding general in Cuba. Which had begun to irritate him. And with a public announcement and a few private communications through his secretary of war, he insured that Shafter commended General Wheeler for the initiative of the former Confederate cavalry leader. In fact, for Wheeler's *courageous* initiative in action against the enemy.

And after that, perhaps the president allowed himself to partake in some small way of the celebration and general euphoria that was running up and down the streets of the nation's capital like quicksilver.

But not everyone was ecstatic. General Nelson Miles, who was already planning his invasion of Puerto Rico, knew that this "great battle" would not even have been mentioned as a skirmish in any real war. It had cost sixteen men killed and fifty-two wounded. Miles, as well as anyone, knew that to those men it deserved to be called a battle, or something important. And those who had been there would someday be able to tell their grandchildren that they had helped make a president. And to Miles, this was a galling thought because it was not he whom they had thus started on the way to the White House with a little run up to some deserted trenches.

So it cost the Fifth Corps in Cuba a few lives. Nobody knew what it had cost the Spaniards. They were faced with revolution at home and financial collapse and didn't have much will to stay and fight anywhere. And were certainly not interested in making presidents, their own or anybody else's. But at least they were still soldiers to the extent that when they left that ridge, they took their wounded and dead with them.

"Just like the goddamned red Indians," said First Sergeant Barry.

There, in Cuba, those few men, the advance guard of the Fifth Corps who came onto the ridge in sweltering heat and with the wind of the Caribbean blistering their faces, looked out over a long valley with jungle below where a stream flowed, and on beyond to a naked ridge that ran for two miles north and south, and the Cubans with them pointed to it and said, "Sí. San Juan Hill." They could see the entrenchments on the crest.

And beyond that, there were the flat, low roofs of Santiago de Cuba.

III.
SAN JUAN HILL

Carlina Bessaford Newton

I felt like the ship's figurehead. It was hardly a proud ship. Rather a dirty little brown and gray coastal steamer whose master was as dirty brown and gray as his vessel, obviously addicted to rum and constantly chewing cocoa leaves which he carried about in a small canvas bag at his belt. His munching gave his teeth the same rust color that streaked the bulkheads wherever one looked.

But standing near the bow, as we finally labored out of Tampa Bay and onto the real sea at last, the wind in my face and the superstructure of the steamer at my back so I could ignore its ugliness, I felt like a figurehead. Delicately carved by an ancient craftsman, in my native New England. With chin held high and pointed toward some exotic destination far below the distant blue horizon.

A rather large bit of romantic balderdash of course, but easy enough bringing myself back to earth simply by remembering that I had been set on my course initially by money from that wicked old mortuary mogul who acquired his fortune from the slave trade of ancestors. I wondered if slave ships had figureheads.

Nontheless, it was such a blessed relief to be free of Tampa and on our way. I will always remember Tampa as a cauldron of heat and humidity, and that was only in the month of June.

After the military expedition embarked, we had watched the Plant Hotel shrink back into what we assumed was its usual pre-summer lassitude. A gigantic, ornate barn with all the livestock out to pasture.

Once the great army circus rolled itself down the railroad to the beach and was away, no one remained to partake of Mr. Plant's hospitality except the wives of departed officers and the casual ladies who were in abundant supply so long as the soldiers were there. The latter disappeared immediately after the men did, and the wives left over the next two days, Cuban porters and hack drivers struggling with an inordinate amount of baggage to see them successfully onto northbound trains at the Tampa depot.

Most of the hotel hired help was dismissed. There was no longer an orchestra playing in the great ballroom and even some of the electric chandeliers were extinquished. It became a dark, uninviting hall, echoing our footsteps as we walked through it to the dining room.

There were perhaps half a dozen people still eating their evening meals there. Only two surly waiters remained on duty to take our orders. Marian Winchel and I assumed that most of the kitchen staff had been let go as well because the food was badly prepared, as though thrown quickly together like slops for the hog trough, and delivered mostly cold. Ice for our tea and lemonade had already melted before our glasses were set before us.

There was a small party of army men still in Tampa overseeing the loading of supplies for General Shafter's expedition. They spent their waking hours along the railroad sidings, coming into the hotel only at the last moment each night, their uniforms soaked with perspiration, obviously not bothering to bathe before they ate. There were three of them, all junior officers and they looked haggard and worn as I supposed soldiers must look who have sustained a long period of hardship in battle. They always wolfed down their food with hardly a glance at it and then were up and off again to their duties. We never saw any of the enlisted soldiers, but from time to time we could hear them. What terrible language!

In our party were the two other ladies, Miss Nettie Gowan and Miss Gertrude Slosen, each almost as old as Clara Barton herself, and maidens. It gave me a sharp twinge of sympathy each time I saw them, their lives spent in service to others and now in their twilight with no children, no family. Except for Clara Barton herself.

It was a shock to wonder if they, like myself, had come to

this work long ago without the slightest notion that they would grow old in it, barren and alone at the end of their lives. But such thoughts were quickly pushed aside because my energy and anticipation hardly seemed to fit their natures even as I visualized them forty years ago.

At least Miss Nettie and Miss Gertie, as Marian Winchel called them, had each other. They went about like two little timid mice, looking askance at the world and whispering to one another. It was very pathetic.

And then there was our general handyman, Jenkins Oberhorst, who was overseeing the loading of our supplies on the ship that would take us to Cuba. Our supplies were pitifully few. A small field kitchen that Marian Winchel had designed herself from her experience in the field, which included a tiny stove with pots and inserts for making coffee and soup and a supply of tin plates and cups and spoons. And our two medical cabinets for bandages, and some surgical scissors and bottles of disinfectant.

Marian Winchel insisted that we keep our supply of laudanum in our rooms until departure, saying that were it allowed to be carried along to the ship with the iodine and zinc oxide, it certainly would never reach Cuba.

It was difficult to understand that there were men who actually sought out this vile liquid. Miss Marian had me taste it once to ensure that I could recognize it if the need arose. It was perfectly wretched. She explained that it was an opium resin mixed with alcohol. We would use it to ease pain for wounded soldiers, in the event there were any.

Jenkins Oberhorst made my skin crawl each time he was nearby. He was about forty with a burn scar across one side of his face and a slack-lip smile that revealed three large teeth in his upper gums and none in the lower. He reminded me of derelicts I'd seen on wagon trucks in Boston. He always wore a woollen stocking cap, as though his head were perpetually cold.

As for Miss Marian Winchel, I had come to love her as much as I loved Clara Barton herself. She was not as old as Clara Barton but had been with the Queen, as Clara Barton's friends called her, for so long that she had taken on many of the habits and idiosyncrasies of the great lady. Most charming to me was her constant misplacing of her eyeglasses.

But she was a firm, strong-willed lady, demanding respect. We were confident in her ability.

And now at last, the United States Army had reluctantly agreed to Red Cross assistance in their military hospital in Cuba. Miss Marian showed me the message from Clara Barton. And so the Marian Group, as we styled ourselves, would be serving American boys after all.

We were at the mercy of the army's supply plans. Our little ship had been contracted to carry canned rations and animal fodder to the war zone and we had been allotted some small corner of it. I am sure at the orders of General Nelson Miles. It was nice to know we had friends in high places, though even General Miles could do nothing about the snail's pace of loading.

But at last the day came and Miss Marian and Miss Nettie and Miss Gertie and I donned our ankle-length white dusters and our own version of the broad-brimmed campaign hat, only with a small cup crown, and went down to our ship, Mr. Oberhorst tagging along behind with what was left of our personal baggage and grinning and staring at me as though he had never seen a young woman before.

And so off to Cuba. To a place called Siboney, where we would offer our services to chaplains and surgeons of the army. I had never seen a military hospital, even in peacetime. I was so anxious to be there to serve in one if brave men needed help. Although from rumors I'd heard, there was little likelihood there would be any serious need for nurses in Cuba. So there was the happy thought that it all would end as a wonderful tropical vacation.

CHAPTER 14

THE rains came in earnest now. Almost every afternoon the forward troops were drenched. Like all soldiers on the march, they had discarded along the way equipment they considered good only for adding weight to their already overburdened shoulders. So such things as ponchos and raincoats and blanket rolls had been thrown aside. And as quickly picked up and carried off into the jungle by the Cubans.

Each afternoon they were soaked to the skin and each night they shivered with cold.

Even so, spirits remained high. Contributing to this was the dark humor always found along battle fronts, encouraged or even initiated by the noncommissioned officers, who understood the value of laughter in a bad situation.

His squad collected around him one night in their own little patch of dripping jungle, Corporal Dylan Price held what he termed discourse on the ways of armies.

"The high mucking brass on staff, sitting cozy before a warm fire, make the decisions. One will say, 'Well, look here, our chaps may come to a cliff fifty feet high which will impede their march.' And another one will say, 'Then by God, each soldier will carry sixty feet of rope.' "

"Did they have good chow in that warm place?"

"Of course, Swede. A lovely roast of beef with Yorkshire pudding, a cup of custard, brandy and cigars."

"Jesus!"

"Then this first mucker will say, 'Well, look here, our chaps may find horses on the battlefield who have lost a shoe.' And the second one will say, 'Then by God, each soldier will carry a horseshoe.' And the first will say, 'Perhaps two horseshoes and nails besides.' "

"This Yorkshire pudding. Is that like rice pudding with raisins in it?"

"No, Swede, it is thick biscuit made with the drippings of the beef. Now, for the sake of this story, close your goddamned mouth!"

"Jesus!"

"So after all this mucking staff work on what might happen, the soldier goes into battle carrying everything except Aunt Maudie's chastity belt, and they'd carry that as well if the brass thought they might need it. And the good soldier, using what little brains he has, chucks this shit aside.

"But then one day the high brass muckers say, 'Well now, maybe it will rain on our chaps and perhaps it will be cold at night.' And the other one says, 'Then by God, each soldier will carry rain gear and blanket.'

"But the poor bleeding soldier is too dumb to know that *all* the shit he carries should not be chucked aside.

"So here you be, wet and freezing in the jungle. Now, pleasant dreams, and if you happen to find any dry wood build the fire close to your lovely corporal so he may feel the warmth of it."

And Dylan Price wrapped himself in his poncho and went to sleep.

"Telner," Olaf Swenson said. "What's a chastity belt?"

"It's a gag to keep fools from asking so many questions," Telner said and all the squad laughed, shivering in the dark. And Olaf Swenson thought about roasted beef and Yorkshire pudding.

After Wheeler's triumph Eben Pay had returned to the corps advanced headquarters at the beach. There he had seen that there were other kinds of discomfort, more painful than being wet and cold.

"Good God," the harassed Captain Malcomb said. "Did you see all those stores stacked along the shore? Canned rations and bacon and bread boxes? Half the damned stupid division commissary officers never sent carrying parties for their outfits. So now those troops forward are hungry. Did you see that road I'm supposed to use to get wagons up?"

"We just came off it," Eben Pay said. "Not much more than a one-way trace and a little muddy."

"A little muddy?" Malcomb shouted. "My God in heaven, we haven't got enough mules here to pull wagons along Pennsylvania Avenue in Washington City and we're trying to supply an army with them and we've got a single trail that has developed bottomless pits with this goddamned rain every day."

"I can understand it might be a problem."

"Might be? Might be? And what makes it all worse is that some of those units up there raid the trains we do get through. That bunch of Roosevelt's is like a pack of Mexican bandits. They ambush supplies while these worthless civilian teamsters we've hired are trying to disengage wagons from the infernal soil of Cuba. Half those troops up there are hungry tonight and the other half are likely eating like hogs making ready for the slaughter."

Eben Pay laughed. "Well, it may be an apt metaphor but I hope the slaughter part of it isn't accurate."

There was another even greater embarrassment. Nobody had wanted to talk about it, especially after General Shafter and the remainder of his staff finally came ashore and were making preparations for the attack on San Juan Hill.

Eben Pay began to perceive it when new rolls of charts, some merely rough maps, were spread out on the folding table in Captain Malcomb's operations center.

After the Rough Riders and the fragments of the two regular regiments had secured the high ground past Las Guásimas, the rest of Wheeler's division came on line, generally north of the

Santiago road. They were somewhat scattered because the fiery little ex-Confederate did not want to billet them in the dense jungle. As a result, they were in patches of blade grass and Spanish bayonet wherever such places could be found in the mahogany and kapok and ebony forest. But at least they were on line.

Lawton's division was not far behind, in what might be considered a reserve position. To Wheeler's left, on the far side of the Santiago road, was the First Division of Brigadier General Kent, which after debarkation had moved immediately to the anticipated battle area.

As the reports came in from Kent's regiments, detailing their locations, each was plotted on one of Malcomb's charts. But after about half the division was accounted for, the reports ceased. Runners were sent off. They returned to say that they could not find the rest of the division. "Where the hell is the rest of that division?" staff officers asked.

"Where the hell is General Kent?"

"Did they all wander off into the jungle?"

Joe Mountain, who had been watching this over Eben Pay's shoulder, perhaps did not understand all of what he saw. But he understood about things missing.

"Maybe some of these Cubans stole it," he said.

Everyone glared at him. Particularly the Cuban officers with corps headquarters. Except for Eben Pay, who could hardly suppress his laughter.

"Well, Eben Pay, I think it's time for me to go find us another one of those big lizards," Joe Mountain said, grinning. "But they're gettin' scarce. These soldiers have decided they'd as soon eat lizard as starve."

General Shafter was like the rest, asking, "Where the hell is Kent and the rest of his division?" Finally, the suggestion was made that perhaps Kent was still conducting a feint to confuse the Spaniards.

That was when the embarrassment set in and the staff officers found it hard to look one another in the eye. Because only then was it remembered that during the Siboney landings, Kent and about half his division had been sent on their ships to make what everyone hoped the Spaniards would think was a major landing at Cabañas.

So the lost commander and his lost troops had been sitting for three days off the coast some miles west of Santiago inlet, sweating and swearing and drinking sour, rationed water, eating raw bacon and wondering what the hell was going on. And from observing activities onshore they knew they had not fooled anybody.

They had, in fact, been forgotten. And now, with the rest of the army on line, they were still in their rusty convoy lying off the coast miles to the west.

For some perverse reason, Eben Pay found the whole situation hilarious and had great difficulty keeping a straight face as he watched the flurry of messages sent off by steam launch to retrieve the lost battalions. Yet, he could not help but feel compassion for the great, sweating, puffing commanding general, who after all, was finally responsible for the whole mess.

Joe Mountain didn't find his lizard that day, so in the evening he and Eben Pay shared a concoction from the headquarters cook tent, composed of boiled corn beef and desiccated vegetables that tasted as though they had been dried at about the time of First Bull Run. Eben told the Osage about the lost battalions, having some difficulty with it from laughing. But Joe Mountain didn't see much about it that was funny.

"Well, Eben Pay," he said. "It was better than if the hablars really had stole it because now at least we know where it's at."

General Kent and his troops crossed the beach at Siboney, muttering curses about the incompetence of the corps staff, and struggled along the congested road to their position with the rest of the First Division. And there suffered the usual taunts and gibes of their comrades from the other regiments.

"Hey, where'd you peckerwoods think they was holdin' this war? Out in the ocean?"

"Too bad you couldn't stay hid 'til after the real dance begins."

"You catch any fish out there?"

"Your mama's gonna be sorry she sent you out here with the men!"

But one way and another, alternating curses and laughter, the army moved into position to carry out General Shafter's design to invest Santiago. Of course, the navy was still bellowing about an assault on the harbor guns so they could steam in and do the same thing to the Spanish fleet there that Dewey had done to one in Manila Bay.

The artillery, what little there was of it, finally got their light guns pulled up near high ground the Cubans called El Pozo, which overlooked San Juan Hill about a mile away. Shafter moved his headquarters up close behind them, Eben Pay and Joe Mountain there as well to watch in astonishment the confusion and frustration and the clogged trail along which the entire army was trying to move.

"That damned road is a quagmire worse than the quicksand little Powell Hill's men had to traverse at Beaver Dam Creek at the Battle of Mechanicsville!" This comment was naturally made by General Wheeler, who seemed constantly now to recall various Rebel misfortunes.

But there was no question about it. The army was massing to attack. The trenches on San Juan were clearly visible, and heavily manned by the white shirt, straw hat soldiers of Spain. And now from El Pozo they could also see Spanish artillery. That news didn't take long to filter back through the entire army, and when Corporal Dylan Price heard it he snorted.

"Krupp guns, you kraut head bastards," he yelled at his squad men who had been born in Germany. "Likely made in Essen by your uncles to create havoc among the good soldiers of the queen." It appeared that General Wheeler was not alone in occasionally forgetting which war and which army was his present concern.

But Dylan Price was quickly contrite and he gently kicked his German soldiers in the butt and reassured Telner and Ulrich and Mittelberg, explaining that German-made artillery would be forgiven them if they each killed at least half a dozen Spaniards before the yellow fever stilled their trigger fingers.

"Yellow fever?" Olaf Swenson asked, for it was the first time Price had mentioned it and now he was sorry that he had.

"A slip of the tongue is all, Swede," said Price. "For a quick moment there I imagined myself back in Natal."

"Where's Natal at?"

"A long way south of Plattsburg, Swede. Now get back to the lubrication of that rifle. Or I will have you eating that bloody oilcan."

Olaf Swenson laughed.

"Yah, they ain't must else to eat, is they Corporal Price?"

With inadequate staff work, terrible terrain, and no roads worthy of the name, it was amazing to Eben Pay that the army was actually oozing out of the Siboney beachhead and into battle formation. Even the medical department people, so insignificant in number and equipment, had somehow managed to establish what could be called a forward aid station behind El Pozo, and at Siboney an installation they grandly called a base hospital.

This base hospital consisted of two Sibley tents, a squad tent that would accommodate about twenty patients on folding canvas cots that were yet to arrive from shipboard, and a wall tent, which was the morgue. Of course, they had no one who had been trained for field mortuary work.

The entire medical establishment would have appalled one of General Wheeler's Civil War generals in 1864 even though their facilities then had been extremely primitive.

The Cubans had their own hospital tucked into a corner of the Siboney palm grove area. Cuban insurgents were expected to screen the flanks and rear of the American Fifth Corps, and to create whatever hazard they could to the movement of Spanish reserves. General Calixto Garcia, the tough old insurgent commander, had had a lot of experience at war, and to any impartial observer, his medical facilities were better than General Shafter's.

The rumor was about among rear area troops that the Red Cross would soon arrive, which meant Clara Barton and other ladies. It meant something else as well, which the noncommissioned officers were quick to point out: "You pissant short-time fornicators are gonna have to clean up your goddamned language around here!"

The operations tent had been moved forward to the reverse slope of El Pozo, and under its fly, where the chart tables were set up, Eben Pay could see how the assault was taking shape on

Malcomb's maps, symbolized by little squares and arrows drawn with blue pencil. Two divisions abreast would attack San Juan Hill. To the north, on the far right flank and slightly in rear, was another Spanish strongpoint called El Caney. Lawton's division would reduce that and then join the main attack.

El Caney was like San Juan Hill, one meager road approaching each through very heavy jungle. Then within small arms range of the blockhouses and trenches, all vegetation simply disappeared and it was a long sweep uphill with no intervening cove or concealment. And before each position there was barbed wire.

Someone, after seeing those Spanish positions, sent a message back to Shafter's headquarters to the effect that the nippers, which certainly had been loaded on ship at Tampa Bay, were nowhere among the forward units and would somebody please go back out to the transports still lying off Siboney and see if they could be found because wire cutters seemed essential for the attack.

But on the day that the hands of First Corps troops first closed on the Spanish wire, the nippers were still somewhere in the holds of the cargo ships.

Major General William R. Shafter

We are trying to get an army into position to end this war before the Yellow Jack comes and I start getting those damned priority messages from the secretary of war, the Right Honorable Russell A. Alger, that require time and energy better spent on other things.

In Sam Grant's administration, there was a Hamilton Fish, his secretary of state, a big New York society man with a great deal of money, who for twenty years busted his arse to keep us out of Cuba. Which he succeeded in doing. Now his grandson is recruited by Teddy Roosevelt and made a sergeant in the so-called Rough Riders, and in their first real fight takes a Mauser bullet square through the heart.

The Fish family can walk into the office of the secretary of war, or into the White House, for that matter, much more easily than I could, and make demands known. Their demands at this critical point in our campaign are about young Hamilton, dead in battle.

So I get a message, personally addressed to me from the secretary, saying that the Fish family wants to know if young Hamilton's body has been embalmed. Further, they want the body shipped back home to New York. And the secretary asks how best to get a heavy casket in here so the remains can be properly cared for and sent back.

Dear holy blood of God, I don't know if any of those men killed in Wheeler's skirmish were embalmed. I suspect that due to heat and humidity they were quickly put in the ground, which any rational commander would have insisted upon under the circumstances, but now I have to detail a staff officer I can ill afford to look into the matter and I suppose have a detail of troops go out there and dig young Hamilton up and put him in this big box, which I have no doubt is already on the way, although Jesus only knows how we are going to get it up over that damned miserable road along which we are trying to supply this army.

Now, this is going to do a lot for the morale of my soldiers, having to go exhume men dead for a week in this climate. Have we got a man in the whole First Corps who knows how to embalm somebody?

Well, I am in great sympathy for the bereaved. But in God's name, when a young man enlists for war, such things must be expected. Especially if that enlistment is in a group who think of nothing but running out in front of everyone else so they can have the honor of being shot at first. Wheeler is the one who should be saddled with this onerous task. It was that little Rebel son of a bitch who disobeyed orders and pushed his command out there where he had no business. And by God, I had to give him a public commendation! He should be the one using the shovel to dig up what's now left of young Hamilton Fish.

Perhaps it isn't so bad as I think. Perhaps they have those bodies back there in Siboney in that miserable little medical facility. But if I were a poker playing man, I would rather bet on drawing to an inside straight.

Then of course, there is the press. They are on to this dead bodies being sent home business. Not my beloved Richard Harding Davis. He is out there somewhere in the jungle with Teddy Roosevelt, of course. But there's this nit Clement Eggmont of San Francisco. For some obscure reason, he has attached himself to my staff and hangs about worse than one of these blood sucking mosquitoes. Asking stupid questions and getting in the way. If he could only fall down and break his goddamned leg, we could carry him back to our medical facilities and he could see at first hand what problems we have there.

Which gives me pause. My personnel staff man has reported that the first soldiers have begun to come on sick list with all the early symptoms of dysentery. I hold my breath, waiting for the first to complain of fever.

Dear beard of God, I wish I was back in Texas chasing wild

Indians. Except there are few wild Indians left in Texas. Or anywhere else.

And Lord, the heat. If Tampa was hot and muggy, it was indeed an icebox compared to this forlorn goddamned place.

At least there are some compensations. Early on I berated Captain Malcomb something dreadful but he was to become a most trusted staff officer.

And this civilian, Mr. Pay, with his big Cherokee. A man devoted to duty. I wish I had a dozen like him. I like him. I like him very much.

But damn this heat! And damn the navy! I don't even want to think about the navy now. Still insisting that I assault the Morro Castle guns to clear the entrance to the Santiago bay so they can sail in and get at the Spaniard in his ships. And least of all, I do not want to think about that damned Clement Eggmont, the little son of a bitch!

CHAPTER 15

BEFORE the attack, General Shafter dispatched Eben Pay back to Siboney with a number of messages to be sent over the Signal Corps network of telegraph lines and cables that had been established and would ensure the text of Shafter's dispatches on the desk of the secretary of war within hours. Eben Pay had no notion of what might be in those messages and Shafter didn't volunteer the information.

The general was becoming more obviously ill with each passing hour, spending much of his time lying down and making no noticeable effort to get out among his troops, even though many of them were nearby and even though the Cubans had supplied him with a gigantic gray mule which they claimed was stouthearted. The Cubans did not say whether it was still stouthearted after it saw Shafter and realized what it would be like carrying him if the general ever decided to journey forth from his headquarters.

Shafter's only instructions to Eben Pay, given in a wheezing, bubbling grumble, was to get the messages to the Signal Corps post on the beach at Siboney and return quickly to Wheeler's division north of the Santiago road.

"And keep me advised," were his last words.

It was not an inspiring scene. The general had been in his tent, the walls rolled up, lying on a wooden door his staff officers had found somewhere and propped up with ammunition cases so Shafter could recline at about a forty-five-degree angle and look at visitors without the difficulty of lifting his head. To Eben Pay, it was a pitiful sight, the corps staff assembling for various instructions around a commanding general in his underwear lying on an inclined plane, like a great steer on the slaughterhouse chute that would send him sliding down to the man waiting with the hammer.

Eben Pay, and Joe Mountain certainly, were happy with any opportunity to get clear of the command post and out with one of the units. But first, to Siboney.

It was not a pleasant walk. They had to thrash through the jungle much of the way alongside the road, which was crowded with troops and wagons and mule trains going in the opposite direction. It was late afternoon by the time they arrrived at the old beachmaster's station on the Siboney shore and there passed over their package of messages to a Signal Corps captain who appeared to Eben Pay to be about sixty years old.

"Somebody over there been waiting for you," the captain said, pointing to a small, beaming Cuban in a large straw hat, wearing duck trousers and jacket and a belt hung with machete and two large pistol holsters and a canteen twice as large as his head. It was Captain Juan Carlos Smith.

"I didn't fin' no horses for you," he said. "But I come back to guide you in the jungles. And I bring these."

Juan Carlos Smith had a large canvas bag with coconuts and plantains. Anxious to avoid wherever possible the Fifth Corps version of army field cooking, Eben Pay and Joe Mountain were more than glad to accompany the Cuban back into one of the Siboney palm groves and have their dinner.

The afternoon rain had come and gone and now the sun was out, sending strong light into the trees. Juan Carlos Smith expertly opened the coconuts with his machete, spilling only a small amount of milk with each whack. They drank them dry, then ate the white, firm, crisp meat and finished with the course-fibered plantains. Joe Mountain asserted that he enjoyed these big tough bananas better than the normal ones.

Juan Carlos Smith then produced from his bag a fistful of fine cigars and a large jug filled with rum. At least partially filled. He had long since been at work on it and was now a little more than slightly drunk. Joe Mountain was happy to assist him in attacking what rum was left.

They leaned back against the trunks of the palms, leisurely puffing their stogies, the chocolate-colored Havanas, which sent wisps of sweet smelling smoke in lacy gray-blue tendrils around their faces until the Caribbean breeze whipped them away. In the lowering sun, the ships standing off the beach looked golden and clean and they watched the small boats going back and forth and heard the bells and the whistles.

Now, between sips at his jug, Juan Carlos Smith began to talk.

Yes, he had been with the Cuban rebels when they attacked the Spanish positions from the rear at Daiquirí, forcing their quick retreat during the American landing. As he told it, gesturing and smiling, his face gleaming with sweat and the color of the cigar he held daintily between thumb and forefinger, Eben Pay thought him a rather handsome little man. He had a smile as engaging and sincere as a silver dollar.

And the way he described the rebel part of the initial landings, it sounded like something as decisive and magnificent as the repulse of Pickett at Gettysburg.

Yes, he had been fighting Spaniards as long as he could remember. He had killed many of them. Mucho!

Yes, his grandmother had been a slave, brought as a child from the Ivory Coast of Africa during the time the British had many ships in the area trying to catch slavers. But the vessel on which his grandmother had come eluded them all because the master was good at such things and had been doing it for a long time.

His grandmother had been a child of much beauty, Juan Carlos Smith said with pride, so she was bought and taken into the house of a captain in the Spanish army occupying Cuba. Whose wife,

Juan Carlos Smith explained, had just returned to her home in Guadalajara because of the fever, and so by the time Juan Carlos Smith's grandmother had matured, she had become the mistress of the Spanish officer. The issue of this couple had been many, but one most important. A baby girl in the year the Yankees were fighting the Mexicans.

This little baby girl grew to have more beauty even than her mother, said Juan Carlos Smith. And after the Civil War in the north, an Anglo man had come, one who had fought with the South and who brought with him only the clothes on his back and a brace of silver-inlaid dueling pistols. He became a very important man, an overseer in the cane fields. And he fell in love with the little mulatto girl who was now no longer just a girl but a young woman.

He would have married her, too, but this was the time when the Yankee politicos were making much noise about coming into Cuba and the Anglo had great apprehension about Yankees hanging him for fighting against them and so he took a ship one night for Colombia. And a few months after he was gone, the beautiful young mulatto woman gave birth to a little baby boy.

"It was me, amigos," shouted Juan Carlos Smith. "And my mother gave me the names of her father from Spain and of my father from the United States of America."

So that's where the Smith came from, thought Eben Pay. And if that man was really a fugitive with more to account for than fighting for the Confederacy, the chances of his real name being Smith were about as slim as chances can get.

But obviously Juan Carlos Smith was very proud of it nonetheless.

By the time this genealogical recitation was completed, it was full dark and Joe Mountain was asleep. The early parts, about the slaves working the cane fields, had kept him awake despite the many sips of rum because he could remember his own grandfather talking about catching slaves for the French to send to this very part of the world. But after that, it grew boring for him.

Even Pay as well began to yawn, feeling the heavy weariness brought on by all that thrashing through the undergrowth beside the road on his mission to Siboney. Juan Carlos Smith, although by now very drunk, understood and stopped talking. And began to sing. But in a soft voice.

The last thing Eben Pay heard before sleep took him were the liquid sounds of Juan Carlos Smith's Cuban love song, accompanied by the usual sympathy of jungle noises and the trills and whistles of the mockingbirds. And Joe Mountain snoring.

In the morning's bright sun, Captain Juan Carlos Smith had lost all his exhilaration. He was surly, with eyes puffed and red, and his mustache seemed to droop with his early sweat. Joe Mountain produced two cans of sardines form the pocket of his jacket but would give no hint of where he might have appropriated them.

Captain Juan Carlos Smith managed to gag down one small fish.

"It's like in the Nations, isn't it, Joe," Eben Pay said, recalling the times he and the Osage had been in the Indian Territory on posse and subsisted almost solely on sardines.

"Yes," Joe Mountain said, lifting one of the sardine cans to drink the oil. "But it still don't taste as good as beefsteak and quail eggs."

Eben Pay laughed. "I remember that morning in Eufaula when you ate twenty-six quail eggs. I counted."

"Yeah, well, quail eggs ain't so very big," said Joe Mountain and the Cuban gagged again.

Then it was time to go to Wheeler and Eben Pay saw that Captain Juan Carlos Smith was going to insist on guiding them. He tried to explain to the little Cuban that he knew where the cavalry division was in position, but Juan Carlos Smith waved it all aside.

"I have this shortchop."

"A shortcut?"

Juan Carlos Smith's bloodshot eyes widened and he looked offended.

"Sí. That's what I said. You just follow behind me, amigos."

They were out of the palm groves behind Siboney at once and deep in the jungle undergrowth, Juan Carlos Smith darting here and there along his forest trails, which were virtually invisible until he plunged into them. Eben Pay found himself wondering if this really was a shortcut to the forward positions near San Juan Hill, but by all his reckonings they were at least going generally west.

There were fine, flashing parrots or some kind of tropical bird, red and yellow and green and with long purple tail feathers, making a shrieking uproar from their orange colored breaks, which were shaped like fat little garden trowels. There were festoons of bougainvillea, red and violet. And orchidlike plants, white and yellow. It is so completely foreign to war and violence, Eben Pay thought, this whole island like an emerald set in the blue sea. And was immediately embarrassed that he allowed his fancy to run wild, let his mind go to the poetry he had read at the University of Illinois in the only course he had taken in any kind of literature.

He was sorry now he hadn't taken more. Of course, the requirements in Latin and the laws of torts and criminal procedure and legal history and precedent required for a degree in law forbade any great amount of frivolous undertakings such as poetry, and at that moment he was envious of the Osage who came behind him, because he knew that poetry to Joe Mountain's people was a part of singing and chanting in everyday life, all of which they found not at all unusual.

These strange wool-gathering thoughts were brought abruptly and rudely to a halt when the rain started. It came earlier that day than it had before. At first, the sun was blotted out by black clouds, and then they heard the rain against the jungle canopy above, like the roar of surf on a resisting shore. They'd gone almost a quarter mile before the water percolated through the leaves and began to reach them, not an unwelcome new wetness to wash out some of the sweat salt in their shirts and jackets.

Behind him, Eben Pay could hear Joe Mountain grumbling about the aftertaste of sardines and when he looked back the rain was running off Joe Mountain's bare head, streaming along his cheeks and making the tattoo marks stand out like ink-black bullet holes. Ahead, Captain Juan Carlos Smith was plunging forward, using his machete to hack away creepers that had invaded the trail since his last passage.

They came to a widening of the path, almost a clearing in the jungle, and here they hurried along. Eben Pay almost laughed at the low, hunched figure of the Cuban so intently forging ahead and he started to call out that there was no need for this much haste and why not pause a moment and have a sip of water. They were nearing the far side of the cleared space where the jungle closed in again, a solid wall of green.

And Eben Pay saw the sudden balloon of white smoke as though it were something separate and apart from the crashing explosion that came with it.

Juan Carlos Smith stopped, straightening, his back rigid, throwing up the hand in which the machete was clasped, and he uttered one surprised, startled word before the smoke blossomed again and with it the roar of a volley.

"Qué?"

Eben Pay saw the little Cuban jerk violently and then fold like a moist dishrag and he felt Joe Mountain's fist in the fabric at the back of his shirt, yanking him down into the saw grass, smelling the black powder fumes in the rain as the clouds of smoke from the line of trees floated lazily across the clearing like dirty cotton. And he heard someone shouting from the jungle and then, belly down and held there by the pressure of Joe Mountain's hand, shook with the earsplitting reports of Joe Mountain's pistol. He struggled to free his own revolver from it's holster, finally managed it, and got off one shot, which he knew had gone toward the treetops.

Suddenly, it was still, the only sound the Osage hulling empty shells from his single action Colt and pushing in new rounds and when Eben Pay squirmed about and looked up, he could see the Indian's eyes, deadly black, looking at the trees, and the perpetual smile, and now the eyeteeth looking very long. He caught a quick glimpse of the cartridges Joe Mountain was pushing into the chambers, the huge, greasy gray slugs at the end looking like some kind of deadly grubs.

"Stay down," Joe Mountain said, squatting, his pistol up again, ready. It was still raining hard and when Eben Pay twisted on the ground and looked, he could see the figure of Captain Juan Carlos Smith, a rumpled fluff of duck trousers and jacket, one arm grotesquely extended and in that hand, the machete still held firmly.

"Hey!" It was a high-pitched voice from the timber. "Who are you?"

"The son of a bitch speaks English," Joe Mountain said.

"Wait, Joe," Eben Pay said and he lifted himself to his hands and knees. "Members of General Shafter's staff. On the way to General Wheeler's division."

There was a long pause. In the driving sound of rain, they could finally hear voices in the jungle.

"I'll give 'em a couple more," Joe Mountain said, and Eben Pay did not recognize his voice.

"No, wait," he said.

"Don't shoot anymore," the same high voice called. "We're Americans. We're coming out."

"Stay down, Eben Pay," Joe Mountain said and once more his hand was on Eben Pay's back.

They began to appear slowly from the trees. Blue shirts. Suspenders. Campaign hats. And Springfield single shot rifles and from that Eben Pay knew they were volunteers or National Guard. A few paces in front was a frail-looking man, almost a boy, with a pale face and a small well-trimmed mustache and a snow white cork helmet, as though he were an English lord out to shoot leopards in British East Africa.

"My God," Eben Pay gasped and shook off Joe Mountain's hand and came to his feet and ran to Juan Carlos Smith. He could hear the Osage just behind.

There were three jagged holes in the middle of the back of Juan Carlos Smith's jacket. Eben Pay knew they were exit wounds. But in the driving rain, the blood that came up was quickly washed away and so they seemed hardly like wounds at all.

"Goddamn," Eben Pay breathed.

The soldiers moved closer, finally making a semicircle around the tiny figure of Juan Carlos Smith, their lieutenant staring with eyes wild and bright under the nose of his helmet. Joe Mountain slipped his pistol back underneath his jacket and bent to the fallen Cuban and placed one hand on the neck, just behind the left ear. It didn't take him long.

"He's dead," Joe Mountain said, rising and looking at the line of soldiers, none of whom would meet his gaze.

"We thought you were Spaniards," the lieutenant said. His eyes darted around the wall of jungle, as though trying to find a place to hide. "We were out patrolling from the beach. We came in yesterday, to secure the shore installations."

"There haven't been any Spaniards in this area for over a week," Eben Pay said and he was panting, and amazed at the harsh vehemence of his voice.

"Sir," the lieutenant said, and he appeared about to cry. "We saw the straw hat and they told us the Spaniards wore staw hats."

The soldiers stood woodenly, staring at the body of Juan Carlos Smith, holding their rifles in front of them.

"You dumb, stupid . . ." Eben Pay started but couldn't find anything else to say. He could only look down at the body. Its clothing now soaked in a rust-colored liquid.

"Was he one of ours?" the lieutenant asked, voice quavering.

Everyone waited for a long time but Eben Pay couldn't speak. Finally Joe Mountain did.

"He was one of ours. And his grandmama was a slave from Africa and you sons a bitches has got yourself in more trouble than you ever saw before."

"Well," the lieutenant shouted, "you killed one of ours, too."

As if, Eben Pay thought, this was a game of Turn About Fair Play.

"I'll go look," Joe Mountain said. He brushed through the line of soldiers and they made an effort to avoid being touched by him. Everyone stood there in the rain, listening to it, smelling it. After only a little while, Joe Mountain was back.

"One slug in the throat," he said. His face was returning to normal again. "I just aimed at the smoke. Too bad I never killed a couple more you bushwhackers."

He glared around at the soldiers but still none would meet his eyes.

"You wanta come look at him, Eben Pay?"

"No."

"You want me to turn this hablar over on his back so you can see his face?"

"No."

Eben Pay took a deep breath and turned to the necessities. The administrative details, he thought they were called. Get this officer's name and outfit and commanding officer. Give him our names and mission. Making sure the lieutenant would take disposition of bodies. Make necessary reports. Eben Pay wasn't sure exactly where he stood in all this, being a civilian.

"We've got to move along," he finally said. He'd been writing on a small pad with a lead pencil and now he tore out some of the wet pages and gave them to the young officer and put the rest in his own shirt pocket. "I want your assurance that proper arrangements will be made for this man you've killed."

"Oh yes sir, yes sir, we'll get him back to the beach and our own too and—" He stopped. Overwhelmed with what was going to happen to him when he came in from patrol and had to report to his commanding officer that he'd killed a Cuban ally and lost one of his own men. "Oh God," he whispered.

Suddenly, Eben Pay had to be away from here, no matter the military necessities. He looked down one last time at Captain Juan Carlos Smith. He is so small, he thought. And that's the end of the line, of the Ivory Coast slave and that beautiful mulatto girl and that Spanish officer and that southern renegade. The end of it all. Unless maybe he had some children somewhere. He didn't say in all that proud, drunken speech he'd made last night. And if there were children someplace, it made Eben Pay feel even worse.

"Come on, Joe," he said and they abruptly pushed their way past the still silent, bloodless, wooden soldiers standing there in the rain with their rifles and dove into the jungle.

But they went only a little way. Eben Pay had begun to tremble. He stopped. He sat down, the rain still filtering from the canopy, but less now. Even so, the drip of it on his hat brim was like a slow, gentle drumbeat.

"God, Joe. We killed one of our own men," Eben Pay said, his head sinking down between his knees.

"No, we never," Joe Mountain said, softly and looking back toward the clearing where Juan Carlos Smith lay. "I did. I killed him. And he ain't one of *my* own. He was tryin' to kill us, him and all his friends. I still wish I'd got a couple more of the sons a bitches."

Eben Pay retched and the Osage looked down at him.

"Well, like I always tell you, I never seen a man who puked so much, Eben Pay," Joe Mountain said.

The rain had stopped but the trees still dripped. As always with these Cuban rains, the last drop had hardly fallen before the sun was blazing again and now sending tiny shafts of yellow light through ragged holes in the canopy to touch the undergrowth below.

Joe Mountain looked at Eben Pay as a doctor might look at a recovering patient.

"You ain't gonna cry, too, are you?"

"No. Not now, I guess. I came close."

"Well, pukin' now and again is all right, but don't take in to cryin' on me Eben Pay. If I have to go home and tell my brother Blue Foot that you taken in to cryin' on me, he ain't gonna believe a thing I tell about any of this, not about them big nuts or the big fish or the big lizards or anything."

"All right, Joe, I won't cry on you." Eben Pay wiped his nose with his sleeve and Joe Mountain held a massive hand for him to hold and lift himself. "Joe? Was that a young soldier we killed back there?"

Joe Mountain snorted.

"Hell, I dunno. Throat shots make a man's face get all squeezed up. I didn't look too close. He was old enough to shoot at us. I know that. But he wasn't no old man. Most soldiers I ever saw wasn't no old men, except for some of these captains. You worry about the damnedest things, Eben Pay."

Eben Pay wiped his nose again, on the other sleeve, and Joe Mountain was frowning.

"And I told you. *We* didn't kill him. I did. That shot you got off, maybe you killed a bird in the top of a tree. That's all."

Eben Pay smiled. He shook his head.

"You noticed that?"

"God, Eben Pay, I hope everybody who ever shoots at me from here on in ain't any better at it than you are. I—"

Joe Mountain stopped and turned his head, tilted it. Then Eben Pay heard it. A far, tiny clatter of rifle fire. Then almost at once, a heavy booming, a thumping sound. Artillery.

They looked at each other for only a brief second and then Joe Mountain was off into the jungle, Eben Pay behind.

It's north of here, north of here, Eben Pay thought, and tried to reconstruct in his mind the charts on Captain Malcomb's table. El Caney. The ball had opened at El Caney.

Now no longer any worry about some National Guardsman dead in the jungle, now no more concern about Cuban love songs, now no more repugnance at death by friendly fire, now no more nausea. And thrashing along behind Joe Mountain through that Cuban jungle, Eben Pay understood yet another thing about soldiers. Memories of the last killings can be impermanent as smoke when there is the sound of new battle just ahead.

Olaf Swenson

Getting into a battle where a lot of men are shooting can make a man so scared he wets himself. Back at Plattsburg, I heard old soldiers talk about it and laugh. I was afraid I'd wet myself the first time on that beach where we got off the *Gussie* and went to find some Cubans to give them guns and ammunition. Well, my pants got good and wet and all right but it was because we jumped out of the boat when it was still in the water and had to wade to the shore. It wasn't me that done it.

But that had been just a little fizzle of a fight. That's what Corporal Price called it. Not really any fight at all. So it didn't count as a real battle would. But when we started to El Caney, I got to worrying again about how scared I'd get.

We went along this little jungle road. They got the worst roads in this place I ever seen. And while we was marching these gnats and other bugs was flying in our eyes, after our sweat I guess, and there was plenty of that, and they got in our mouths and up our noses. Private Ulrich said if he had all the bugs that got in his nose that day he could fry them and have more meat than the army'd give us in the past week.

When it got dark, we wasn't there yet. So we tried to bed down but I couldn't sleep much, thinking about how I'd probably wet myself the next day and all the guys would laugh at me. I got to thinking that maybe I should have stayed in Milwaukee and just told the police that it wasn't me who killed that Polish guy. But I knew such a thing was crazy. They'd never believe me with the woman yelling and screaming and flopping herself around. Anyway, I was right there, in Cuba, and a big battle the next day and I knew I'd embarrass myself in front of all the other men in the squad.

It wasn't even dawn yet when they kicked us up and we had a breakfast of hard crackers. They'd almost break a tooth. But we went on toward El Caney and I was still worrying. Corporal Price was keeping us closed up but he acted happy and I knew he'd laugh harder than anybody if I got scared and wet myself.

We come to the edge of the jungle on that damned narrow road and Corporal Price told us to lock and load our rifles and he wasn't laughing now. It had got real serious because it was time. Then we went into line formation and started coming out of the trees and there it was. El Caney. Jesus, it was ugly. Just looking at it I thought I might ruin my underwear. And the Spaniards were already taking shots at us and we could hear those bullets making a "ping" right around us like the biggest wasps you ever saw.

This El Caney was high ground. From the edge of the trees, where we was, it was a long slope uphill with nothing there but some grass. Like somebody had cut it a long time ago and it grew out a little. Along the ridge were trenches and these little block-houses like forts and Spaniards with their big straw hats and white shirts were everywhere. Like they knew we'd been coming and they were ready for us. And in front of all this, down the slope a ways from the ridgelines, was barbed wire. God, they had barbed wire strung all over that hill.

Corporal Price got us down in the grass and started directing our fire, just like in training. Shoot low, pick a target, take your time. Things like that. So we lay there shooting at the Spaniards and they were shooting at us. And right then I knew I wouldn't wet myself. I was so damned scared my old talleywhacker wouldn't work at all.

But by golly, it was more than that. It was a queer thing. I got into this kind of trance. In a kind of dream. Maybe it was like that Polish guy in Milwaukee when his wife hit him the first time with the meat mallet. He just got dazed and glassy-eyed and he could hear everything and see everything but he didn't really give a shit what happened. Of course, he never had much time to think about it before his wife hit him the second lick with that mallet.

But it turned out battle was like that for me. I never would have thought. As long as the other guys in the squad were around me and I could see them and hear them, I'd just do what Corporal Price said. Like I was watching somebody else do it. Like it wasn't even me. And I could be scared as hell but not doing anything embarrassing.

I remember once Corporal Price said a good soldier don't like to embarrass himself in front of the other guys, especially in a battle. And he was right. He said it was what made a soldier keep going in bad times, not wanting to embarrass himself in front of the other men who depended on him. I found out in Cuba that all of that was right.

Our outfits were coming up on line. The whole damned regiment. The whole damned division, I guess. We'd shoot at the Spaniards and move out a little way into the grass and shoot some more. But we didn't move out too far. And after a while, there was all these soldiers along the base of that hill at El Caney. Laying there. Shooting.

They had this battery of light field artillery with us and from someplace back in rear they'd found some high ground and they started shooting, too. It made a hell of a racket. Some of the smoke drifted down through the jungle and out into the grass where we was laying. It smelled like rotten eggs to me, that smoke. Corporal Price was cussing about bloody black powder. And no matter about that artillery shooting, it didn't make any difference to the Spaniards. They just kept pumping shots into us.

And a lot of them were hitting, too. We could hear guys up and down the line, yelling when they got popped by one of them Mauser bullets. And I figured for every one we heard yelling, there was likely some who wasn't able to yell.

Corporal Price started cussing about us just laying there. I heard First Sergeant Barry complaining about it, too. And even Colonel Stoval was prancing up and down behind our lines fuming about not charging.

Somebody said the division commander wanted to just lay there and shoot at the Spaniards. God, we did it a long time, and the sun going up the sky and it getting hotter and hotter, and we still just lay there. And Corporal Price was screaming that you had to go in there and gouge those bastards out, you couldn't just shoot at them because they'd be there forever if you did.

A lot more of our guys were getting hit and we were just wasting ammunition. I don't guess the division commander heard Corporal Price, but he finally decided he had to go up that hill. The hardest thing I ever done in my life was stand up from laying there in that grass and start up the hill at El Caney. Everything sucked right up into me like my butt was trying to eat my trousers. But when Corporal Price got up and went, I got up and went.

The bullets was flying around and it was dusty and hot and guys were yelling and I started seeing some blood. It looked bright red and slick in the sun and it made me a little sick so I tried not to look. It was hard.

Our squad was heading right square at this little blockhouse with trenches all around it. We could see those Spanish straw hats. Corporal Price was right with us, keeping us spread out and making sure none of us was right behind the other because those Mauser high velocity bullets would go through two guys if they was lined up just right. Maybe even three. But none of our squad got hit and Corporal Price was right there, yelling at us like he always done, and it got so we figured none of us was going to be wounded or anything. Like those Spanish bullets couldn't hit us at all.

We were coming closer to the blockhouse and we could see faces in the embrasure and those Spaniards shooting at us and the racket was so terrible it made a man's ears hurt. Then we came to the barbed wire. God, those big steel thorns strung all across there made it look like we'd never go no farther.

Vanic was out front, kind of a point, and when he come to the wire, Corporal Price was yelling, "Machete, machete." Because we didn't have no wire cutters. So while the rest of us went belly-down and started shooting at the Spanish position, that damned Vanic pulled out his machete and he was on his knees right at the wire and he started hacking at it. Like a wild man he was hacking at it. God, he looked strong as a bull, and he'd swing that machete and when that wire came apart it made a sound like "twang." Like somebody busted a string on a big guitar.

I don't know if I heard the shot that done it. When it happened, I didn't even know what it was. But all of a sudden Vanic just sort of looked around at me and Corporal Price, and his hat had just flew off, and he had this funny look on his face, and then he sort of fell right into the wire he'd been whacking at, like he was awful tired.

Reed was up there close to Vanic. And when Vanic fell into that wire, Reed went crazy. I never seen a man go that crazy. He jumped up and was yelling and shooting and he ran right through the wire where Vanic had cut the hole and went right straight at that blockhouse. Corporal Price was shouting something I didn't know what and he jumped up and I went with him, right with him, and we were shooting while we ran and there was Reed up there going crazy, running straight at that embrasure in the blockhouse.

Jesus, then I saw the three Germans in our squad. Hell, they was even in front of me and Corporal Price, right through the wire, charging, shooting and yelling and the goddamned Spaniards were getting out of their trenches and running like hell and I saw two of them flop down and knew they'd been hit and I started yelling, too.

But the Spaniards in the blockhouse were still shooting and Reed was running at them. By now, me and Corporal Price wasn't far behind and we seen Reed run up there and it was like he was just diving through the embrasure to get at the Spaniards but he got only a little ways and stuck, just hung there in that hole like he couldn't dive no farther and there was blood all over his back and running down his legs and one of his suspender straps had been cut in two by bullets.

When I run through that wire, though, a barb shagged my leg and tore my trousers and ripped open some meat on my left leg and I was running but looked down and I seen Vanic's face laying there against the ground and his eyes were open like he was looking back to see where Corporal Price was at and his eyes were just like real, live eyes. But he never had no back to his head. There was just like raspberry jelly. And it almost made me sick.

But hell, nobody had any time to stop and think about that kind of stuff.

Me and Corporal Price was running right at them Spaniards, too, and went past the blockhouse where Reed was stuck in the embrasure. We was after all those Spaniards running back off the hill.

But the Spaniards in the blockhouse never got out. Because while they was trying to stop Reed, Telner and Ulrich come in their back door and they went right in there shooting and with bayonets and later we found five dead Spaniards in there.

But me and Corporal Price and Mittelberg were beside the blockhouse, shooting at those Spaniards running down off the back of the hill. We damn sure hit some, too, but a lot of them got away.

Listen, them Spaniards in the blockhouse didn't get away.

Telner came out of the blockhouse and he'd lost his hat and there was blood all over him. But Corporal Price saw right away it wasn't Telner's blood. And Telner had this crazy light in his eye, like he was maybe someplace else. Then Ulrich came out of the blockhouse and he looked like he was on parade, neat as Lottie's pin, and he was reloading his rifle. I never seen nothing like it!

All of a sudden, the shooting stopped. It made my ears hurt. Like now just air was rushing in without all that racket. And Corporal Price was shoving us around in the Spanish trenches, getting us where he wanted us so in case the Spaniards came back we could kill the bastards real good. Everybody was just fine, except Telner was panting a little. Like a dog that had run a long time. He was looking down at the blood all over his shirt and trousers.

God, I was thirsty. I never been so thirsty. And my canteen was empty but I couldn't remember taking a single drink. All the others were dry, too, but Corporal Price had carried along an extra canteen and now he passed it around so we could all have a sip. He was yelling at us about how dumb we was, not having any water left, but hell, I didn't care. That was the best tasting drink of water I ever had.

First Sergeant Barry was coming along the ridge. Checking casualties and ammunition. Corporal Price got out of the trench to meet him. That's when Telner started laughing.

"By God," he said. "I wet myself!"

We all laughed. But we wasn't making fun of Telner. The way he'd gone into that blockhouse, you don't make fun of a guy like that. Jesus, a little later I looked inside that blockhouse. It was like a slaughterhouse in Milwaukee where I worked for that Polish guy. Right after we'd butchered a half dozen big hogs. It made me a little sick to my stomach.

But I was glad it was Telner that wet himself and not me. Hell, he just set there in that trench and laughed and nobody thought it was embarrassing and he just set there, cleaning his bayonet.

God, I never thought there was so many things in a war that could make a man sick to his stomach.

CHAPTER 16

THEY were standing at the blockhouse embrasure where the body of Reed was still hanging, his head and arms thrust inside, only his bloody back and limp legs visible to them. His rifle was lying on the ground beside his turned-in toes and Corporal Dylan Price bent and picked it up and opened the bolt. It was empty.

"This man took a lot of metal before he died," First Sergeant Maurice Barry said. "I'm surprised he got this far, coming straight at it, you said."

"Yes. Straight at it. A good soldier, that Scot."

"And you got one more?"

"Down at the wire. A head shot."

When they looked, they could see Vanic's body below them on the hill, somehow a part of the landscape now.

"You got a couple more up there in the trenches." Barry looked around the corner of the blockhouse toward the crest of the ridge.

"No. A barbed wire scratch. He's getting it bandaged now. The other one. That's Spanish blood."

"The hell you say! Well, his shirt looks like hell. He'll need to give that a good scrubbing, first chance."

Price had loosened the sling on Reed's rifle and now slung it over his shoulder along with his own.

"Ammunition?" Barry asked.

"Low, First Sergeant. All that mucking business at the foot of the hill. Lying there popping away for hours."

Barry swore hotly, violently. "Goddamned stupid business! We should have come up here as soon as we saw it, no lolly-gagging."

"We may have twenty rounds a man," Price said. "No more."

"Get the ammunition from your dead."

"I'm counting that."

"I don't know when there'll be any more."

"I know. But the water's more the worry. We're not low. We're out. Half a canteen I've got left for the whole bloody squad."

Barry laughed harshly. "Well, you've got two less now to worry over, Dylan," he said.

Price bristled and started to retort, feeling the heat rising in his neck. But then they heard someone down the slope, shouting. It was Lieutenant Beaster, the company commander.

"Get your dead buried," he yelled. "We'll be off from here on the quick. Back to the south to come in with the First Division in their fight."

Perhaps because their ears were still ringing from close-in firing, it was only now that they became aware of sounds far to the south that could be battle, faint but unmistakable.

"Jesus," Barry said. He looked up at the sky where the light of setting sun was making gold and red and orange lace around the clouds that hung above them. "We've got a goddamned night march on our hands, Dylan."

The first sergeant wheeled and started away then paused, looking back at Reed hanging in the embrasure.

"Well," he said quietly, "you heard the man. Get 'em in the ground. And get your bunch in walking trim."

It was the worst possible duty. Burying their own dead. They had no shovels so they did it with bare hands and bayonets. Quickly, with the whole earth turned brilliant around them in the sun's final salute before dying until dawn. Other companies around them were doing the same. But Dylan Price said the graveside service for his own men. Hat in hand, two rifles slung on his shoulders.

"Rock of ages, cleft for me."

That was all. And it was hardly said before Beaster and Barry began to assemble the company below the wire. By then, the clouds behind the mountains to the north had turned dark purple and to the west only the highest fleece caught any of the remaining sun, long since dipped below the western horizon. And seeing it, the troops grumbled, tongues thick with thirst. "No damned rain tonight."

"Keep down the chatter. Get them slings up on your god-damned shoulders. Tighten up them laces on them goddamned leggings. This ain't no Methodist picnic stroll we're gonna make."

"Yeah, Sarge, just get us some water, Sarge, hey, Sarge, they any girls at the end of this march?"

And so the usual litany.

It was full dark before the regiment was organized and started south, not so many now as had come to El Caney. And Dylan Price thought, I pray to sweet Jesus that somebody at the head of this column can read a bloody compass. It startled him a little that praying had come to mind.

He turned back for a last look just before the company was away and there was lightning in the mountains to the north, out-lining El Caney, that ugly little ridge with all the blockhouses and barbed wire, and Dylan Price thought for a moment of Vanic and Reed and hoped to God that this wretched hillside in Cuba had been worth its cost. And knew damned well it wasn't.

They struck out straight for San Juan Hill, moving easily at first. Then there were the sounds of shots from the head of the column and everything stopped. Word passed down the files.

"Spanish pickets."

Darkness and strangeness and men bumping into one another and confusion and some fear and some saying, "Shoot the buggers and let's get on to water."

But General Lawton didn't want to risk a night fight in un-known country. So the whole column about-faced and marched back to the foot of the hill at El Caney. And there found the pitiful road they'd used to come up in the first place, and started along it to the south.

"Good God," they wailed. "How many times we gotta stomp this son of a bitch down?"

Straggling became very bad. Troops were dropping off into the night, many not seen by the noncommissioned officers who brought up the tail of each serial of the column. As with all night marches, there was the accordian effect, stretch out and hurry, slow down and bump into the man ahead. If they hadn't been so tired and thirsty, there would have been many fistfights. But as it was, there were only sullen curses.

Each stream they crossed was a place to dip hands and bring a palmful of water to the mouth. Drag open canteens through it. Gain a few sips. Gain a little lead on dysentery although none of them knew that. And a few were feeling hot but suddenly couldn't sweat. And there was some nausea. They didn't understand what that was, either. So they blundered on, all night. Until they came to the road from Siboney to Santiago, where they had started for El Caney in the first place. And were given two hours' rest.

It had been forty-eight hours since they'd had anything of substance to eat. It had been that long since they'd had enough water in this sweating climate. In that time, they'd had about four hours' fitful sleep. In that time, they'd fought an all-day battle against a prepared Spanish position. In that time, they'd seen the first of their friends shot down and then buried.

But when dawn came, they were up, going west now, the noncommissioned officers pushing them.

"Close it up. Close it up."

And finally they came onto the right flank of General Kent's First Division.

Dylan Price knew it had been one hell of a fine march. He was so proud of his men that he didn't trust himself to speak to them. But they arrived too late. The battle of San Juan Hill was over.

And when he realized that, very nearly within sight of Santiago, Dylan Price released the most glorious, purple, blasphemous, obscene, outraged diatribe perhaps ever heard in the Western Hemisphere, coming as it did not only from his frustration but from his years as a soldier in the British and American armies. But this time, his squad members did not cringe before him, did not try to find places to hide, did not stand rigidly to attention. All of them, lying on their rifles, were dead asleep, dead asleep almost before they had stopped marching.

Seeing it, Dylan Price began to laugh as he sank back into the old Spanish trench among his men and that's where First Sergeant Barry found him and stared at him a long moment.

"Have you gone daft, Dylan?" Barry asked.

"No, no, no," Price said, lying back, his head against the hot soil of Cuba. "I am just passing information that I will now sleep until September."

"The hell you say."

Dylan Price opened only one eye and looked at the first sergeant.

"Well, now, only once in that time will I rise. To have you, First Sergeant."

A slow, wicked grin spread across Maurice Barry's face.

"I'll be here, Dylan Darlin'. I'll be here. In the meantime, sleep well. A water wagon's on the way to this lovely regiment."

"Blest be the tie that binds, you Irish son of a bitch," Price said, pulling his hat brim down over his face.

And Barry laughed again, joyously.

"I'll be here, my Dylan. I'll be here!"

Joe Mountain

It seemed like Eben Pay had took a shine to this outfit called the Thirty-seventh Infantry. It didn't surprise me. Eben Pay was the kind of man who patted dogs on the head when they come past him on the sidewalks at Fort Smith. Even the mangy ones.

This Thirty-seventh Infantry was the bunch who came behind us the day when Wheeler got out front of everybody, where he didn't belong, and run into some Spaniards.

Mostly, I think Eben Pay was thinking about that corporal we seen first in Tampa who give us all our equipment. Price, he said his name was. We saw him again the day me and Eben Pay was in that ditch behind Wheeler's troops and the Thirty-seventh came up and this Price was leading the whole shebang.

Eben Pay was always asking somebody where the Thirty-seventh was and I think he sort of liked the looks of that Price man. Like Price was one of those books Eben Pay told me about reading at the University of Illinois, so he could find out all these things. Price seemed pretty tough to me. Like one of those mangy dogs on the sidewalks at Fort Smith. But Eben Pay was like that.

He was always getting interested in some killer we'd run down. He'd want to find out about his family and where he come from and how he'd got to be a killer. Maybe that was it with Price. Eben Pay wondered how he'd got to be a soldier, a real full-time soldier. And if I ever saw a real full-time soldier, Price sure as hell was him. So maybe Eben Pay was as curious about how a man got to be a professional soldier as he was about how a man got to be a professional criminal. Maybe he figured the road they took to get to either place was pretty much the same.

Well, after Juan Carlos Smith got himself killed trying to guide us through the woods, me and Eben Pay came right on up to the cavalry division, where Cap'n Shafter said he wanted us to be. Hell, I didn't need no damned Cuban to show me where we was going. But that Juan Carlos Smith did have fine cigars. His rum was just so-so.

Anyway, the first thing Eben Pay did when we got to some staff officers was ask where the Thirty-seventh Infantry was at and this staff officer said they was up on the right flank fighting at El Caney. So the way it turned out was that in the biggest battle of the war, Eben Pay was a long way from his favorite outfit. They came up later and what they missed was some of the damnedest stuff I ever saw.

Part of it was all about a child's toy. Or what I'd always thought was a child's toy. A white man's child's toy.

In Fort Smith when there was a big celebration, like the Fourth of July or the elections for Sebastian County sheriff or when we were hanging the Rufus Buck gang or somebody, a lot of people came to town. Not just white people, either, but Choctaws and Cherokees and a few Creeks. All along Rogers Avenue close to the federal compound where Judge Parker had his court and where the gallows was at, the merchants brought stuff out onto the sidewalks to sell. Gingerbread and apple turnovers and pig knuckles and chicken pies.

And there was always a lot of things for the children. Little wooden monkeys on a stick and doll furniture like cast-iron cookstoves no bigger than a man's fist and balloons. All color of balloons, red and yellow and blue.

They'd get these tanks from the gasworks and fill the balloons with the gas and tie a string on the balloon, and they'd float up in the air. You could see the children all up and down Rogers Avenue and around the federal courthouse and the gallows with these balloons floating above their heads.

I never thought much about it. Those balloons were just something the white children liked. Maybe the Choctaw and Cherokee and Creek children liked them, too. I don't know. Because except for official duty, I never bellied up too close to any of them Civilized Tribe people out of respect for my grandfather, who hated all of them. I could understand some of how my grandfather felt about it, the white man calling them Civilized Tribes because they rode in spring wagons and built rock fences around their fields and cut their hair. It never bothered me much, what the white man called those people. But a man's got to respect his grandfather.

Anyway, nobody that I ever heard of said there was anything dangerous about those balloons. They were just little balls that floated in the air on a string.

But in Cuba, I found out balloons can be dangerous as hell. It's one of the things about a white man's war. Stuff that was never dangerous before can get pretty bad when somebody figures out how to use it in a fight.

Hell, I guess my old grandfather would have used balloons to fight the Kiowas and Cherokees. Or anything else. But I don't think he knew what a balloon was. He understood hatchets and clubs and arrowheads, but I don't think he was too good on stuff like balloons.

Eben Pay said it would have been better if Shafter and all those other big white chiefs hadn't known anything about balloons either. Because a balloon got a lot of our people killed or cut up with Spanish artillery fire.

After Juan Carlos Smith, me and Eben Pay got with the Cavalry Division again. We found out that Wheeler was sick and it didn't make me too unhappy. We found Cap'n Roosevelt and he acted like he was glad to see Eben Pay and he slapped Eben Pay on the shoulders and yelled at him and laughed. He didn't slap me on the shoulders but he saw me, all right. He looked at me through those little eyeglasses he wore and I just waved my hand at him but I didn't call him Cap'n again because Eben Pay told me not to. Well, it was all fine with me.

Cap'n Roosevelt had this little red bandana around his neck, one like I saw once around the neck of a man we chased in the Indian Nations. His name was Wallace Snake Walker. We arrested him and brought him in to Judge Parker on a charge of stealing horses and Judge Parker gave him five years in the federal pen at Detroit. But I knew Cap'n Roosevelt had never stole any horses.

Cap'n Roosevelt was always making a lot of noise and waving

his hat around and things like that. But all those crazy men me and Eben Pay seen first in the Menger Hotel in San Antonio really liked him and he sure as hell wasn't afraid of anything.

When we got up there, we could see this long ridge and there were Spaniards crawling all over it. They said that was San Juan Hill. Off down to the south, on the other side of the Santiago road, they said Kent's division was coming up on line to attack. And then the Cavalry Division would attack on the north side of the road. Hell, it sounded all right to me.

Except there was a lot of bare ground the soldiers would have to cross. I figured the Spaniards were about to have one hell of a good day for target practice.

To the south there was a lot of jungle, all the way up to where those men down there were supposed to attack. Nobody knew exactly where our soldiers were because the timber hid them. But they were coming up, everybody said. That's when the balloon got into it.

This was one hell of a big balloon. It wasn't like one of those things the children carried along Rogers Avenue in Fort Smith. It was big enough to have a basket underneath it and a man riding in the basket with a pair of field glasses and a telephone and a line down to the ground. This thing come up out of the jungle like a big moon and there were four ropes from it down to the ground, where soldiers held on to keep it from floating off across the ocean or someplace.

Everything had been pretty quiet until then. But when that thing went up, all hell busted out. Because the Spaniards figured the balloon was likely coming along right in front of the troops below, and they was right, so they opened with every rifle and artillery piece they had. Right into the woods below that balloon!

Eben Pay was fit to be tied. Anything they can see from the damned balloon, he said, we can already see from El Pozo or someplace, and there the thing is just telling the Spaniards where our leading elements are so they can shoot hell out of them. It was the damnedest thing anybody ever saw. Here we were, giving the Spanish guns something to shoot at. Then after a while the Spanish guns busted up the balloon so they shit in their own nest for a change. Why would they want to bust the balloon, I asked Eben Pay, when the balloon is telling them where the front end of our army is at?

Hell, Eben Pay didn't know.

My little brother Blue Foot ain't ever going to believe how white men fight a war. And after all that balloon business, I don't think Eben Pay believed it either, and he was right there looking at it.

CHAPTER 17

IN later years, Eben Pay would read accounts of the Battle of San Juan Hill and marvel at the clarity of it. The precise detail. The almost mathematical exactness of position and movement to the final conclusion. And like soldiers down the centuries, seeing the total design of a great enterprise in which they had been involved laid out before them by someone who had not been there, exclaim, "My God! Is *that* what happened?"

Eben Pay had experienced what he'd heard called the fog of battle. On that sweltering hot July day in 1898 on the southern slopes of Cuba, there had been no clarity, no precision, no exact position or movement. And San Juan Hill had certainly been no climactic conclusion. Because almost before the last shot was fired there, everyone in Fifth Corps already knew the truth.

The army had been butchered, straggling was appalling, the Spaniards knew how to fight, and fever and dysentery were beginning to make inroads on the present-for-duty of morning reports. And still ahead of them were the most formidable field fortifications they'd yet encountered, manned by confident troops of Spain. And these positions would have to be reduced by storm before Yankee feet could tread the streets of Santiago.

Also, the commanding general was almost prostrate with the fever.

Eben Pay had read much history. Battle history. Waterloo. Gettysburg. Sedan. Those writers were so marvelous, laying out on a clean canvas cause and effect. Everything as though ordered. Regularity, with minor disruptions quickly seen and corrected by brilliant leaders. A fantastic, surging completeness, leading to victory or defeat.

My God, Eben Pay thought on the end of that day in Cuba.

This had all been little bits and pieces of confusion, agony, killing, cowardice, heroism, irresolution, determination. A violent mosaic, the pieces of which seldom fit together, a kaleidoscope of more than colors, of smells and sounds and visual images never seen anywhere except on a field of battle where men are trying to kill one another.

Eben Pay had experienced his own small slice of it. As any man does on that field. But because of his position on the corps staff, or at least with his access to it, he was able to appreciate a larger portion of it than any common soldier. And was later astonished that anything could have been accomplished at all under such conditions. And astonished even more that he had been a part of it.

Shafter's pitifully inadequate artillery went into action on the left flank of the line. The light guns brought up to El Pozo roared their Yankee defiance, and in doing so put up a cloud of smoke from their outdated black powder rounds, which provided the Spanish gunners a wonderful aiming point. And so the Spaniards responded with their Krupp guns and the duel was short and decisive. The Yankee crews, knowing well the cliché of discretion being the better part of valor, stopped firing and retired to the reverse slope of their hill and played no further part in the battle.

Well, no part for a while, anyway.

Now the wonderful Signal Corps balloon made its ascent. The veterans of that part of the battle would give the army one of its enduring colorful phrases. Stripped of its obscenities, it was "when the balloon goes up," meaning, "when the bloodletting has begun."

Soldiers of Kent's First Division had supposed that nothing

could be worse than trying to come on line for an assault using that one, miserable, muck flooded jungle road. But that was before the balloon gave the Spanish gunners another lovely aiming point and they began to shred the woods beneath the great floating ball with shrapnel. Kent's soldiers quickly learned how men looked when they died violently. Each wagon that struggled up loaded with ammunition struggled back loaded with moaning, screaming wounded.

Finally they were in some sort of attack formation, facing the long slope. Now they felt the sting of Mauser bullets and saw to their front tangles of barbed wire strung between tree stumps. It was then that a monumental indecision set in, and so they lay taking fire.

North of the Santiago road, the Cavalry Division was in no less confusion, although not taking the fire Kent's men were receiving. The units had become hopelessly mixed, tangled with one another beyond immediate recall. By now, Eben Pay and Joe Mountain had found Colonel Roosevelt and were moving with him, along with a platoon of newspaper writers. Eben Pay was amazed to see around Roosevelt as many black troopers of the Ninth and Tenth Cavalry as there were white men of the Rough Riders.

There seemed to be some consternation about objectives. Forward of San Juan Hill, which most of them assumed they would be attacking, was a pesky knoll the Cubans called Kettle Hill. It was heavily defended by Spanish infantry.

"We ain't goin' 'round that pumpknot," one trooper of the Tenth Cavalry said. "We gone haft take it, too."

Colonel Roosevelt was of the same mind. Shouting somewhat profane encouragement, he whipped off his hat and waved it and taking with him his calico outfit, part black, part white, Eben Pay and Joe Mountain and the newspaper writers, he charged across the intervening cleared ground and on up the hill.

In later newspaper accounts, Colonel Roosevelt seemed to have been the only officer on the entire front. At least, none other was mentioned. Observing his verve and confidence, Eben Pay thought it was almost as though Roosevelt *felt* he was the only officer there. And so the newspaper writers established the one shining glory of the Spanish War: Teddy and the Rough Riders charging San Juan Hill. Of course, it was not San Juan Hill and half his troops could hardly have been mistaken for Rough Riders, dark complexioned as they were.

Eben Pay had no appreciation of his place in history, close by the man who generations of school urchins would be taught was the hero of Cuba. At the moment, Eben Pay was puffing, sweating, and frightened near to the point of stopping and lying down in the tall grass except that behind him was Joe Mountain, one of his huge hands flat against the small of Eben Pay's back.

Men around them were being hit. The muzzle crack of Mauser rifles seemed very near and the blood and dust and yelling was dreamlike, and perhaps most dreamlike of all was Colonel Roosevelt, his eyeglasses flashing in the sun like a rallying banner. They made a terrible sight. Apparently the Spaniards were of the same mind because before Roosevelt's men could close with them, they began to vacate their trenches and run back toward the main positions on San Juan Hill. And in that run took more casualties than they'd taken all day.

Near the crest of Kettle Hill, Eben Pay discovered something else about deadly combat. A young Spanish soldier rose from the trench, tossed his rifle aside, and threw up his hands. And half a dozen American soldiers coming up the slope shot him down. To Eben Pay, it was ghastly, savage. Later, he mentioned the incident to a black sergeant in the Tenth Cavalry.

"Mr. Pay, you looka here," the sergeant said. "A man there in his hole, an' he's killin' my sojurs when they comin' up the hill. That's fine. That's what he supposed to do.

"But then after long time, he still in his hole, an' he kill some of my sojurs. Then he see he may be in danger, jus' like my sojurs been all along. So he says, 'Well I jus' quit fightin' now an' nobody gonna kill me, like I done to them sojurs comin' up the hill. I jus' gonna stop fightin' 'fore I gets hurt.'

"Mr. Pay, my sojurs that man kill, they had no such selection. They gotta go up that hill, 'cause that's what *they* supposed to do, an' all the time that man tryin' to kill 'em. Then my sojurs gets close, an' he says, 'All right now, man, I gonna quit. I through fightin' now.'

"You think my sojurs he been tryin' to kill gone let that man jus' up an' quit? You think my sojurs who see friends this man kill jus' let him play his side of the game an' then stop? In a blind mule's ass, Mr. Pay. Beggin' your pardon, sir."

There was some kind of pristine, brutal beauty in this, but Eben Pay could not reconcile it. At least he had some glimmer of understanding. At Kettle Hill, Eben Pay learned two important things about battle. In a close fight, it was always very dangerous to turn one's back and try to escape. And it was near impossible to surrender.

"You gonna puke again, Eben Pay?" Joe Mountain asked.

"No. But nearly so."

Meanwhile, south of the Santiago road, the battery of Gatling artillery appeared. They took heavy casualties but they wheeled at least three of their four guns up and went into action. For the first time, the Spaniards were introduced to .45-caliber machine gun fire and it was viciously effective. With this encouragement the infantry of Kent's division leaped up and stormed the ridge, whether or not with orders no one was sure, but the men were damned well tired of lying there taking casualties.

They would have gone all the way, too, except that now their own artillery decided it was time to enter the fight again. They started to shell San Juan Hill, wounding a number of Kent's men and effectively stopping the rest. Finally, someone managed to get a cease-fire order to the billowing, booming light field guns, and then the infantry went on into the Spanish trenches without opposition.

On that day, the infantrymen of Kent's First Division expressed some very colorful sentiments regarding artillery and the Signal Corps, especially regarding black powder guns and balloons. None of these remarks appear in any of the newspaper accounts of the Battle of San Juan Hill because they were mostly unprintable. Besides, all the newspaper writers were north of the road with Colonel Roosevelt and his Rough Riders.

In fact, the men of Kent's division might as well have been

fighting on another planet for all the recognition they received from Mr. Pulitzer and Mr. Hearst. Both of whom, along with their writers, were placed in the same category as gunners and balloonists by Kent's men.

But to the north, Eben Pay was yet unaware of this and went on with Roosevelt to San Juan Hill. There, they found the trenches empty save for a number of black soldiers from the Ninth and Tenth Cavalry regiments who had got there first. Nothing on the record of the newspaper writers reveals Colonel Roosevelt's reaction to having been second on San Juan Hill.

Eben Pay found it the one incident of the whole bloody day that he could smile about, especially after Joe Mountain said, "You know, Eben Pay, I'd bet that when Cap'n Roosevelt got onto San Juan and found nothing but our own soldiers, he must have thought, Where the hell did all these black men come from?"

As the day ended they stood with the other soldiers, in the old Spanish trenches, looking down on the fortifications between them and Santiago. The blockhouses and the barbed wire and the lacework of entrenchments squirming with enemy soldiers. Beyond that was the city, amazingly flat, and even more incredible, with streetlights cutting little diamond halos in the gathering dusk. And beyond that still, the silver mirror outlines of the bay, where they knew the Spanish fleet lay protected from the American men-of-war just outside the inlet. And beyond that the jagged sawtooth mountains, black now with setting sun, lying along the coast to the west of the city.

It might have been a beautiful memory of Cuban sunset. But it wasn't. It was dismal because they were tired and thirsty and hungry and they had seen friends die. And they knew it wasn't finished with San Juan Hill. It might be just beginning. The army gave a great, collective sigh, and the soldiers along the ridges kept looking back at those fortifications that still stood between them and the city, unlike the far mountains and the bay, standing out in harsh relief under the last afterglow of the sun.

"Joe," Eben Pay said. "Let's get out of here."

Without reporting his intentions to Roosevelt or Wood or any of the other officers whom newspaper writers would not acknowledge were there, they started back across the day's battlefield under the growing light of a rising full moon. It was like all battlefields the first night after action. A garbage dump of equipment thrown aside, the lumpy black forms of the dead who had yet to be recovered, here and there a dead horse appearing grotesquely large in the shadows. But mostly the sounds. The cries of wounded men, some incoherent, some begging for water. And some who would not be found for three days. The shouts of litter parties frantically searching out the fallen. A bobbing lantern here and there. And off to the east, the mockingbirds. And through the tall grass, the whisper of evening wind off the sea. And with that, the smell of salt.

They had to pick their way through some of the Spanish barbed wire, but Joe Mountain went unerringly to corps headquarters at the base of El Pozo. It seemed to Eben Pay what a madhouse must be like after a tornado had struck. Officers were rushing about in lantern shine, horses on picket ropes were whistling with excitement, teamsters just arrived with mule trains and ammunition were shouting questions.

It was almost midnight when they came into the command post complex, and when Eben Pay saw Captain Malcomb, he hardly recognized him. Malcomb had his hat off and his hair was streaming down across his forehead in a sea of sweat and there were dark circles under his eyes.

"Where the hell have you been?" he asked.

"With Roosevelt."

"Oh God," Malcomb said and turned into his operations tent, then abruptly stopped, glaring at Joe Mountain. "For God's sake don't knock down my tent. Bend down when you come in."

Joe Mountain grinned. "You got anything to eat?" he asked.

Malcomb handed Eben Pay a copy of the message the commanding general had sent to Washington. All gushing with victory.

"The general's changed his mind," Malcomb said. "Now he's afraid to tell them what really happened. We had about ten percent casualties and God only knows how many we've lost to straggling. And we've got reports from the medical people that there are men coming in with fever. Jesus!"

Malcomb took a large plug of chewing tobacco from his trousers pocket and gnawed off a chunk and began to chew.

"And," he said around the cud, "the navy still refuses to try and force the harbor."

"Which means?" Eben Pay asked.

"I don't know what it means. Except that the only way we can wind this thing up is for the troops to take those harbor guns."

"Has anybody around here seen the Spanish positions at Santiago?"

"We know about those, hell, we know about those," Malcomb said. "Why do you think everybody around here's acting like it was a funeral?"

Two junior officers rushed in, sweat-soaked. Malcomb handed them pieces of paper and they wheeled and rushed away into the night. I wonder who the hell they were, Eben Pay thought. The lantern over Captain Malcomb's chart table sputtered and fried the incautious bugs that flew against it. There were a great many others that did not die and were buzzing about in the tent.

"They finally took El Caney," Malcomb said. "Some outfits got chewed up. The general has ordered them down here, forced march."

"The Thirty-seventh?" Eben Pay asked.

"I don't know. Hell, I don't know what's happening ten feet from this tent."

He spat off to one side, an amber spray.

"Well, I know this," and he suddenly smiled, such an incongruous expression on a tortured face. "The Red Cross has arrived. The whole business is back at base camp, at Siboney."

"The what?" Eben Pay asked, completely baffled.

"The Red Cross, man. And that young woman you paid so much attention to in the Plant Hotel."

In all this, Eben Pay could not think of what Malcomb meant, and then the name came to his mind, Carlina Bessaford Newton. It was all so unreal, this lantern shine tent, this sweating staff officer, this day of killing and blood and thirst, and there it was suddenly. Carlina Bessaford Newton.

"My God."

"Say, Cap'n Malcomb, you got anything to eat around here?" Joe Mountain asked again.

"Rations have finally come up. Finally come up," Malcomb said and he was no longer smiling. "Bully beef and bacon and . . . hell, I don't know what all."

"That sounds like the same shit you been givin' us all along."

"I've got to get some sleep," Eben said.

Malcomb ignored Joe Mountain's complaint. "Those Red Cross people will be at the advanced hospital by noon tomorrow. God, we need people there, all these wounded, the hospital's a nightmare. Pay? Pay? Where's he going?"

"Cap'n, did they bring up some sardines?"

There was no blanket, even though in the night it grew cold, sleeping on the soggy and evil smelling ground. Eben Pay tried to put away all the vicious images of the day and let sleep come gently. It helped that next to him he heard rather than saw the Osage settling on the mud with subdued curses.

Eben Pay's sleep was filled with Missy Bishop. And twice he woke, and knew how long he'd slept because at first the moon was well down toward the west, and the second time gone completely and the only thing that held him to this earth then was the sound of Joe Mountain snoring. And he reached out to touch the Osage lightly on the shoulder, just to be sure that he was there, and then was quickly asleep again.

IV.
FEVER

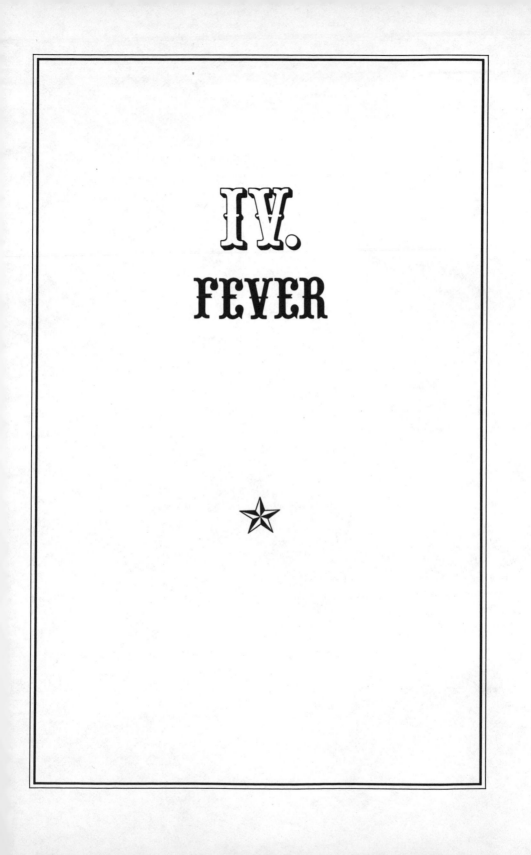

Carlina Bessaford Newton

Nothing in my experience or reading had prepared me for it. I had never supposed that anything could be as hideous. The field hospital in Cuba, near General Shafter's headquarters, was so frightfully disgusting, so evilly pervasive to spirit and sound and smell that no single part of my numbed senses was left for sympathy.

It is only now that I can even manage some recall of it without retching.

The first impression in the morning's brightness was of color. All shades and textures of red. Blood splattered on the clothing of the few army medical personnel in attendance, blood on the uniforms cut from wounded men and left discarded in sodden heaps, blood on naked skin, in hair, in eyes, in ears. Running from noses, oozing from horrid little wounds. Exposed male genitals bathed in blood. Truncated limbs with crude bandages where hands and feet were supposed to be, seeping blood. A sickening pile of those same severed hands and feet, pale blue, still bloody. Bright red blood on open lips, dark red blood on punctures below the navel, blood turned purple and black, caked like tar on a city street, lying beneath the bodies of soldiers dead or dying, their life's juice paving the sandy soil on which they lay.

And sounds. Flies worked in swarms, great buzzing clouds, black bellied, monstrous eyed, crawling, sucking, blanketing wounds with a squirming, hissing, needlepoint pattern, shining like burnished brass in the sun. The cries of the men, the sobs, the wails, the begging for water, like little children, all dignity gone. The shouts of doctors, half crazed. Glassy-eyed.

The odors of ether, open flesh, feces. Oh so much of that, as though the bowels of every soldier on the island had opened just to welcome me.

They called this place "hospital." But it was nothing more than a clearing in the jungle, a slaughterhouse, blistering hot, with a pitifully small scatter of tents, walls rolled up. A hospital! Surgeons treating men on small wooden folding tables or else on the ground. No proper bedding. Not a sheet. Not a blanket. Only a few canvas cots. Blood soaked, each new occupant sticking to the gummy gore of the last unfortunate soldier who had lain there. Most patients on the ground, too weak to brush the flies from their eyes and gaping mouths.

And even as I watched, more wounded were being brought to this place. The men carrying the litters were hollow-eyed, slobbering, crying out with thirst. Water was so scarce that only cupfuls were given for drink and none at all to wash away filth.

I saw only three surgeons. There may have been more somewhere in the madhouse. But these were haggard, defiled with blood and excrement, their arms and hands sticky from fingertips to elbow, their smocks saturated with sweat. Their eyes had the vacant shine of lunatics in an insane asylum. And I saw more than one of those lift bottles to their lips, bottles of something other than water.

It was a foul, noxious, squalid offal heap! I could not help but remember the impeccable Nelson Miles in that New York theater lobby, my first impression of the military. Clean, shining, proper, scented with expensive bay rum.

And now this. A disgrace and an abomination for which surely those same well-bathed, sweet-scented men were responsible.

A repugnance overwhelmed me. And not the least of it were the sounds of soldiers in this place, swearing. Blasphemous, obscene swearing, all of it in very sight of me and our ladies. Making sounds of hell, they were, even here in this place where there were many of them facing their Maker. Such gross and unmanly language! Even in the last moment of their extremity.

Is there no purity? Is there no regard for humanity? In that butcher shop, it suddenly came to me that redemption must surely be sealed off by the foulness that comes from the mouth.

In that Cuban jungle, soldiers leapt up before my eyes and I saw them as what they are, as vulgar, inhuman beasts. No, there was no shred of sympathy. Only abhorrence for them all. Why did they come here to be thus decimated in soul? Who but mindless creatures lost to God would be part of such beastly barbarism?

Since that time, I will not walk on the same street where a soldier walks.

CHAPTER 18

BY midmorning, General Shafter was at the field hospital again. He had been there twice during the night, watching with growing apprehension the parade of wounded men being brought back from San Juan Hill and El Caney. And perhaps most disturbing was the fact that some men were coming in without having been wounded at all but were not fit for duty because of nausea, chills, and fever. And bowels out of control.

Just past midnight he had sent a second telegraph message to Washington.

"I fear I have underestimated today's casualties!"

And even now, with the light of a new morning, yesterday's casualties still coming in, he could hear the sounds of firing from San Juan Hill, and knew from commanders' and staff reports that the Spaniards were defiantly putting rifle and artillery fire against the whole American line there before Santiago.

The measure of Shafter's concern was that he had moved from his headquarters at all, sick as he was, riding the great gray mule provided by the Cubans. And accompanied by a Cuban who led the mule and whose hat was always being knocked off in his efforts to assist the general in mounting and dismounting.

It was observed by some cavalrymen that when General Shafter rode his Cuban mule, he never did so with feet in the stirrup.

But these things were of little concern. The general was obviously suffering from intense fever. His sweating was now only in great, gushing spurts. Otherwise, his skin was pallid and dry, his eyes were puffed and bloodshot, and his lips were cracked. He constantly placed a moistened handkerchief to his mouth. But he pushed aside any effort of his medical people to assist him, telling them to get on with ministering to the wounded.

Now, standing in the midst of medical bedlam, his face was a reflection of what his staff and commanders had told him. San Juan Hill and El Caney may not have been such a glorious victory after all.

It had been a long time since he had seen these kinds of casualties. Not on the Texas frontier, where half a dozen wounded was unusual. Not since the Civil War had he seen this kind of butcher's pen. It made him cringe to think of the reaction in Washington and across the country when it was learned that Spanish soldiers were capable of killing and maiming American heroes. And that his army was now hanging on by its fingernails. Because there wasn't anything left. Every major unit had been committed and blooded. There was no reserve of fresh troops. There was no effective artillery. There was nothing except a few National Guard regiments armed with those old Springfield rifles, and committing them against Spanish regulars would be disastrous.

Besides, there were not enough of those regiments to make any difference.

So Shafter was in no mood to welcome Marian Winchel and her crew, even though he appreciated the contribution they could make to his army's pitiful medical effort. When she arrived in the hospital area, with her three ladies in neat white dusters, her handyman, and three pack mules, Shafter was just ready to depart, back to his headquarters where he could collapse for a few moments of respite.

He greeted her with gruff civility, informing that she was most needed, that she could ration with the corps headquarters company, could put up her installation on the edge of the hospital area, and if there was anything she needed, please be free to speak with Captain Edward Malcomb, a member of his staff.

And then touching his British East Africa helmet, turned and allowed himself to be hoisted onto the Cuban mule by the Cuban retainer, with much grunting and sweating, and rode off to his place and left Marian Winchel to hers. Which she understood perfectly and was happy to be rid of him, for she had already seen at first glance that two things were essential. That her main purpose would be to get some hot soup into these harried surgeons, who appeared not to have eaten in days, and while she and Jenkins Oberhorst went about that task, the girls must pitch in immediately with the doctors.

This was no ragtag, inefficient operation. Marian Winchel's troops knew what needed doing and they plowed into it. Jenkins Oberhorst was already unloading their three pack mules, then he and Marian Winchel herself put up the small kitchen fly, got the stove in trim, got a fire started with fallen wood from jungle trees along with help from kerosene they had brought in a half-gallon tin, and carefully filled the largest of the pots from the water cans brought on the mules.

Misses Nettie Gowan and Gertie Slosen, so mouselike and timid until now, were immediately into the very center of the hospital bloodbath, their long dusters becoming splattered with red almost as though it were applied by the brush of some mad painter careless with his strokes.

Bent over a folding table where a young surgeon was sewing a lacerated thigh, Miss Nettie said, "Doctor, I can suture that wound."

He gave a start, seeing her for the first time, and then barked what was supposed to be a laugh.

"Dear God, I am glad to see you." Then right to the business at hand, recognizing another professional. "We've got mostly puncture wounds. Rifle bullets or shrapnel pellets. With the bullets, they usually pass through so you can expect an exit wound. Not always so with the shrapnel. And those we have to cut out because although some are steel, we've found a few that are lead."

"I understand," said Miss Nettie, her hands already gummy as she worked on the leg. "We have laudanum."

"Laudanum? My God. You are an angel, ma'am."

Nearby was Miss Gertie, kneeling beside a soldier lying on the sandy soil in a pool of crusted blood. She was cutting away his shirt with a pair of scissors that gleamed silver in the hot sun, exposing a blue wound in his upper chest the size of a lead pencil, which bubbled blood each time he breathed.

"You'll be fine now, young man," Miss Gertie said, compressing the wound to keep air from escaping. "One of the doctors will be here in a moment. Lie quietly."

"Water, can I have water," he gasped.

"Yes, I'll bring it."

Carlina Bessaford Newton stood in the midst of all this as though transfixed. Slack-jawed, staring at the bloody scene with shock etching her features. Her unmoving white-clad figure in the roil of activity was as starkly conspicuous as a white tombstone set in the center of a meat market.

Miss Nettie Gowan moved past her, going for bandages and ointments in the little supply and sleeping tent that Jenkins Oberhorst already had staked down. She paused for only an instant, looking at Carlina's drawn, pale face.

"What's the matter, girl? Are you ill?"

Carlina said nothing. She was incapable of speaking. Her throat was contracted and there was a knot in her stomach and her knees trembled. Hurrying on, Miss Nettie said, "What did you expect, girl? Now get over there and help Miss Gertie!"

Carlina Bessaford Newton did not move.

Marian Winchel, her soup already gurgling with canned ham and vegetables, moved to stand beside the young woman, placed her hand on Carlina's shoulder, and smiled. She had seen this initial reaction before. The best remedy was action. So in a moment she was back, placing in Carlina's hands towels and scissors and a large bottle of alcohol.

"Over there," Miss Marian said. "Those soldiers lying in the shade of that small tree. They need cleaning. You do that, dear. Go now, and do that now, dear."

Carlina, hardly realizing she held anything in her hands, moved slowly, tentatively to the line of soldiers lying on their backs. There were four of them. Faces pale. Mouths open. Flies crawling over them. She moved to stand above them, and then smelled it. The overpowering odor of feces.

Clean them? Clean them? As she stood above them, their eyes on her now, she knew what it meant. Cutting off trousers and scrubbing the foulness away from their most private parts!

"Lady, could we have some water?" one of them asked.

Clean them? Even as she stood there, the sun was gone behind the afternoon clouds and within minutes it began to rain. Large drops at first, slowly pecking the ground and foliage, then driving down in sheets, no individual drops visible at all. She watched fascinated as the soldiers lying there opened their mouths, trying to catch some of the moisture.

In the cooling downpour, Carlina Bessaford Newton could only think of one word: diarrhea. These men have diarrhea. Grown men, and I'm supposed to clean them?

She dropped the towels and the scissors and the bottle of medical alcohol. She was crying, yet without crying, her expression in no way changing as the tears ran down her cheeks along with the raindrops. They were just tears, coming without her even being conscious of them. She turned and walked slowly to the Red Cross sleeping tent, which Jenkins Oberhorst had finished setting up, turning his attention now to the kitchen fly. She walked inside with her back straight and her head up, the tears running down her cheeks with the rain that slanted under the brim of her stylish campaign bonnet.

"Miss Newton, where are you going?" Marian Winchel called.

Carlina Bessaford Newton did not hear. She found her small, brown leather valise among the pile of personal baggage and bent to it, somehow the tie string on her campaign hat loose now and the hat fell to the ground. She straightened, holding her suitcase, unaware that she had lost her hat, and moved out of the tent, walking with steady stride toward the road, down the gentle slope.

Behind her, Marian Winchel was urgently telling Jenkins Oberhorst to set out pots under the drip of tent fly to catch the precious water, and then when he was done, Carlina Bessaford Newton already lost in the jungle toward the road, said sharply, "Go with her!"

"Yes, ma'am."

Carlina was at the road and started along it, eastward, ankle deep in mud. She seemed heedless of the pack mules and a number of them bumped against her. Contract civilian teamsters stared at her for only a moment in passing because they knew that now Red Cross women were in the area. One great snorting mule knocked the valise from her hand but she walked on, insensible to everything around her. A teamster pulled her bag from the mud and held it up, dripping, calling to her, but she continued on.

A column of mule-drawn ammunition wagons struggled along the trace. The loud and profane language of the teamsters was the first penetrating impression Carlina Bessaford Newton seemed to have had of the real world since standing over the soldiers with the early symptoms of dysentery. She shuddered and pushed off the road into a kapok grove, thrashing through the blade grass until she could no longer distinguish the foul words behind her, then collapsed on her back, arms out, feeling Christlike, on the cross, almost feeling nails biting into her wrists.

The rain had almost stopped. What little still came down peppered her face and she lay, eyes closed, welcoming the coolness of the water.

"Oh Papa," she murmured, "how could you let me be here?"

It wasn't a sound. It was nothing she saw, because her eyes were closed. But there was a presence she could feel and she sat up in the wet blade grass and opened her eyes and saw them. Two soldiers, filthy and unshaven, stragglers from the fighting, and they were coming toward her tentatively, like cats stalking a dangerous rat.

"Well, little missy," one of them said, grinning, and they came on faster and Carlina Bessaford Newton felt the rush of all her senses back into focus and tried to rise but they were on her. Hands tearing at the now less-than-white duster, clawing at her thighs, ripping at her shirtwaist.

One of them hit her with his fist, a blow to her temple, and she saw the trees around her spinning and saw the faces of Theophilus Compton and her mother and Nelson Miles and Clara Barton and the shipmaster with a cheek full of coca leaves, a mad whirl of images as she began to scream. And all those bloody army men, and all that foul language, washing over her, even as she felt hot breathing against her face.

She twisted and turned onto her stomach, strength coming with frenzy, heard the grunting, felt the hands. And then a voice, far away, shouting, "Run, Miss Carlina, run, run!"

The pressure on her body was gone and she scrambled off into the grass, crablike, hearing behind the wheezing, snarling, obscene voices and looking back only once saw Jenkins Oberhorst swinging the claw hammer he used to drive in stakes for Red Cross tents and still shouting, "Run, Miss Carlina, run!"

She ran. Back through the tangle and bursting into the road as yet another mule train moved along it toward El Pozo, and now she was screaming only silently, her mouth open, her eyes glazed. It was then that the mud sucked off her shoes. She didn't know it. It didn't matter. She went on, not even aware that the rain had stopped and the sun was out, riddling the dark road with patches of brilliant light as it shone down through the ragged jungle canopy.

Teamsters stopped in their monumental efforts to move their burdened animals along, watching her, some laughing.

"What the hell was that?" they asked one another. "A crazy woman." "Some Cuban whore." "Din't look like no Cuban to me." "How the hell you know what a Cuban looks like, you crazy peckerwood, you ain't ever been out of Valdosta, Georgia." "I have, too. I went to Savannah onct." "Get the damned mules movin' again." "That crazy woman done spooked 'em."

As she fled along that road shock allowed only one pained picture in Carlina Bessaford Newton's mind. There was no conception of a personal assault. Rather, the two stragglers and Jenkins Oberhorst as well represented only one thing. An effort to get her back to that charnel house, a planned program to recapture escapees. Jenkins Oberhorst led the effort to pursue her, to return her to the cesspool of blood and agony. Back to that horror. Just another fragment of the whole design, all of it coming to her like the flashing, red-colored, terrifying hallucinations that explode on the mind in delirium.

From Shafter's headquarters to Siboney it was six miles. Carlina covered the distance in under three hours. And only just behind her was Jenkins Oberhorst, claw hammer still in one hand, the recovered valise in the other, his face scratched, missing one more of his infrequent teeth and the blood from the gum running out of the corners of his mouth and coloring the stubble on his chin.

Jenkins Oberhorst. He would be all the rest of that afternoon and deep into the night getting back to his proper place in the forward hospital, and then have his face cleaned with alcohol by Miss Marian Winchel herself, and then a bowl of the soup and a cup of the coffee, with lots of sugar.

"Well, then?" she asked, but only after the cleaning and the administration of food and drink.

"Oh, Miss Marian. It is a mad world."

"Tell me."

"Men on a Siboney sentry post caught her coming in."

"Soldiers?"

"Yes, ma'am. Men of the National Guard regiment there securing the beach. And I came up, and she saw me and started to scream."

"Tell about the soldiers."

"They took her along, very kindly. Their colonel came and took Miss Carlina in hand. Very kind. Officers from everywhere were coming up. Miss Carlina was very excited and she kept taking this purse from her duster pocket and opening it and saying that she had money."

"Money?"

"Yes. To buy passage home. And at first, they thought I had been one of those who attacked her. But the good colonel remembered me from when we came across the beach and I told him what had happened and he believed me and sent a patrol of soldiers to find those stragglers. But they never did."

"And Miss Carlina?"

"She kept saying she had to get home to Massachusetts. And all the officers were saying the ships were contracted for the army. All but that one. The one we came on. The master was on the beach, overseeing the discharge of his cargo. Chewing coca leaves, he was. And he said he'd take her on board when he sailed in the evening.

"And did she go?"

"Oh yes, Miss Marian. I watched her go out on a small steam launch. She had her valise that I'd brought and the colonel gave to her. She acted like she'd never seen it at all. But she went out to that ship. To sail by now."

"Where bound?"

"Mobile."

Marian Winchel leaned back and sighed.

"I should have prepared her more for this," and she waved a hand around the general area of the army's medical facility, dark now except for lanterns at some of the surgical tents. The lines of wounded had slowed to only a trickle but there were still a few coming in, mostly beyond help now.

"It wasn't your fault, Miss Marian."

"No, but I dread the temper of the Queen when she hears of it," said Marian Winchel. "Have you ever seen Clara Barton angry?"

He laughed. "Yes, ma'am."

"And she'd lost her shoes?"

"Yes, ma'am."

"Poor thing."

"Maybe she had another pair in the valise."

"To Mobile, then?"

"Yes, ma'am. They were very good to her, those men on the beach. Miss Marian, it was like she'd lost her mind complete."

"Well, you did a splendid job, Jenkins," she said and patted his shoulder. "Now get some sleep. Tomorrow will be difficult and I expect the Queen to be here. Lost her shoes. Poor thing."

"It's not your fault, Miss Marian. It's just the war."

"Yes. This little war. But it will never be little to Carlina."

"No, ma'am."

From the west, all sounds of firing had ceased. And Marian Winchel knew that some of the men brought in only recently had not been wounded at all by bullets or shrapnel but were wounded inside. The beginnings of fever and dysentery. She knew the symptoms. The moon was out, obscured only now and again by passing cloud formations. The mockingbirds were calling from the trees around the hospital camp. All the jungle sounds were in full voice. There were still the groans of the dying. Still cries for water. To the south, she could hear a ship's whistle.

Out there, on the sparkling surface of the sea, the small coastal freighter was moving out into the Caribbean to get well clear of Cuba before turning north and west to Alabama. Its captain was at the helm, chewing, sipping rum from a chipped china coffee cup, thinking about the woman who was down the passage behind his chart room, in the same small cabin she had used with three others on the voyage from Tampa Bay. The purser had three times tried to bring her hot tea and food, and each time been refused. Well, not so much refused as ignored. And he chewed and shook his head and thought of modern times when young ladies were allowed to roam about the world's oceans barefooted.

In her cabin, Carlina Bessaford Newton sat on one of the hard mattresses laid across the steel bunk. Her toes barely touched the deck, which throbbed now with the pulse of the two-cylinder engine deep below. There was the strong odor of oil, a familiar smell to which she had become accustomed on the trip out of Tampa Bay, when she had thought herself to be a figurehead.

I must go home, now, she thought. I must go home to Papa.

The lamp in the cabin cast a dim light. And across one bulkhead above the door she saw the name of the ship, a thing she had never noticed before.

S.S. Renown.

She began to laugh, soundlessly, her shoulders shaking. She

lay back on her bunk, still shaking with the laughter. Her feet were cold now and it helped her to keep from losing all control, from becoming completely hysterical.

Finally, she slept, still wearing her soiled duster, her hair in sweat-soaked ringlets about her face. And she dreamed of black-crusted sand with flies crawling over it.

Major General William R. Shafter

The army is in disarray. The Spaniards and now this goddamned climate with its usual pestilence has inflicted grievous losses on us. And there is no opportunity for taking Santiago except by frontal assault on very strong positions. Yet, time is critical. The hurricanes will come soon. The fever already has.

It is a terrible thing for a proud man to humble himself before boneheads. Of all the things the news writers have said of me, that I am ill-tempered, profane, and harsh on subordinates, they have always ignored the keystone of my character. Pride.

I am proud of my record. By God! I am proud of maintaining command here, of this staff and army badly trained. Proud most of all of my troops, who have seemed to understand above all others the urgency in moving quickly to invest the Spanish forces in Santiago. Lord love them, having been sent here without proper training in large-scale unit operations, yet suffering through by valor and initiative.

It has been said that pride goes before the fall. By damn, I am not fallen! By the living blood of God, I am not fallen.

But I did have to humble myself before boneheads. I had no choice. I sent the navy a message. One could say I begged. I would say the same. I had no choice. For the brave men in this army, I will beg. Not for the high and mighty in Washington. Not for political favor. But for these men. So I sent the navy a message. As follows:

"Admiral William T. Sampson. Commanding, United States Naval Forces off Cuba. Sir: Terrible fight. I urge you to make effort to force the entrance to the Santiago harbor to avoid further losses among my men, which already is heavy. You can now operate with less loss of life than I can."

Good God, that had been true from the beginning, hadn't it? But now I must point to the obvious. And beg.

Their reply? Like a note from a scolding teacher to a pupil who has forgotten his goddamned lesson. They brusquely reminded me that it was not possible to force the entrance until mines had been cleared and this could be done only after land forces had taken the Spanish forts overlooking the channel!

And their coup de grace, their finishing stroke? If they tried to force the harbor they could *lose a ship*! Dear loving thorns of Christ, what did they think we would lose if we had to attack those forts? I had always supposed that the term warship meant a vessel that made war. But apparently our white suited brethren feel their goddamned ships are too precious to risk in battle. What about the blood of my troops? Is that not precious? My God, we suffered fifteen hundred casualties yesterday. At latest count. I don't know how many more are lying out there in the saw grass.

It is difficult not to lose one's temper under such circumstances. It is enough that I have to contend with an expeditionary force so dismally provided with artillery that in effect we have no artillery. It is enough that I have to employ an entire cavalry division that has no single horse except for a few for the ranking officers. It is enough to be assigned a full colonel, a full goddamned colonel no less, of the Quartermaster Corps who thinks men can carry all the water they need for a day's battle on their belts!

But all of this aside, why can't warships be used for war instead of for lying about like rich men's yachts in the tropic sea breeze?

Well, the navy is not my only cross to bear. Now Clara Barton herself has come forward from her work with the Cubans. Come to join that small team she sent ahead. One of whom bolted and went home once she saw the problem of our forward hospital.

I don't blame her. I only wish that some of those navy bastards could be privy to what real blood looks and smells like.

Well, Clara Barton. God love her. I am overwhelmed with gratitude for what her people do. They have supplied much help that Washington failed to do regardless of my entreaties to them when this expedition was being formed. But in this campaign, there is always a large thorn in the rosebush.

Clara Barton is almost as popular with the newspaper writers as is the recent assistant secretary of navy and his so-called Rough Riders. And she is not reluctant to tell them the truth about our hospital facilities. That they are a disgrace! And those words from her, appearing in the nation's newspapers, will reflect badly on this army, not upon those men in Washington who are really responsible for sending off a force one half less prepared than a ten-year-old Comanche boy on his first war party!

My God, I rue the day I accepted command of this army!

I must proceed as best I can. These magnificent soldiers deserve a good commander and I will try to give them one. But by the pulsating blood of Jehovah, it is trying!

My illness is dreadful. More and more of the troops can appreciate this because they are being brought into hospital in increasing numbers with chills and fever.

I have asked Clara Barton to establish a fever hospital in the Siboney area and she has graciously agreed. Good Lord, she has more medical equipment and more doctors than I have.

There is only insult to be added to injury here. For with all my other problems, that idiot Clement Eggmont of San Francisco informs his newspaper that Buffalo Bill Cody has sent messages to the First Volunteer Cavalry Regiment advising that the Old Scout will hire on any Rough Rider who desires work after the war.

By God, is that something short of inspirational? I can see the banners now: Buffalo Bill's Wild West Show and Congress of Rough Riders.

Dear breath of Christ, the initiative of scorpions to make a profit on war defies imagination.

CHAPTER 19

THE nation was preparing to celebrate the one hundred twenty-second birthday of independence. In May, the prospects for gladness and glory had been propitious. The year of Cuba Libre. The year the Western Hemisphere would be rid of Spanish tyranny. The year in which a crusade to lift the oppressed to freedom would illustrate to the world once more the famous Yankee resolve and dedication to liberty, all of this reinforced by the milk of human kindness.

By July 3, the resolve and dedication were sorely tried and perhaps even the milk had gone a little sour.

In the barbershops along Main Street in Manhattan, Kansas, they were saying, "Who do them Spain guys think they are?" And in the brokerage houses in lower Manhattan, New York, they were saying, "What's going to happen to sugar on tomorrow's market?" Everywhere in between, they were saying, "I thought we sent an army and a navy down there!"

And some were saying, "Where the hell is this Cuba, anyway?"

And William Jennings Bryan was saying, "You see now what happens when godless Republicans start running things." Thus, and in other ways, assuring himself a candidacy for high office at least one more time. Maybe two.

The most reliable and consistent volume of information that came out of Cuba was via the Associated Press. In fact, at one point the secretary of war instructed General Shafter that he should interrupt the AP stream of news from time to time to send his own messages to Washington through the press system of communications.

The fact that such a procedure would mean publication of said communiqués by the AP before the information could be released officially, and in fact sometimes even before the secretary himself had seen the message, seemed to escape the secretary of war. He appeared happy to read official reports from his subordinate in the columns of the *New York World*, along with two million other people including Spanish agents, because in that way he might have some idea of what was going on in Cuba. Otherwise, he didn't.

Nor did Shafter help him, with or without the help of AP. He simply didn't send any messages at all. Well, not very many.

Unlike Shafter, perhaps the secretary of war and President McKinley considered the press a part of the expedition. After all, the commanding general in Cuba had received one message to the effect that the *New York Journal*, the newspaper of Mr. Hearst and Richard Harding Davis, was doing a fine job. Which undoubtedly made Shafter grind away most of the enamel on his jaw teeth.

Besides which, Secretary Alger said later, Mr. Hearst was there on the scene in his own ship, right there in Cuban waters, on the best of terms with Admiral Sampson and the rest of the navy. Which certainly caused General Shafter to grind away once more.

Seeing the exchange of all these messages in Captain Malcomb's operations tent, Eben Pay could hardly suppress his laughter once more. It was so absurdly ludicrous. He had begun to feel considerable guilt about being roundly amused in a situation that was at bottom deadly serious. Yet, try as he would, he was unable to suppress the feeling that so much of this was comparable to a group of quarrelsome children in a school yard bickering over who should bat the ball.

Captain Malcomb took him aside and spoke softly. "Listen, if the general catches you giggling over these messages, there is going to be hell to pay. No pun intended," Malcomb said.

"I know."

"Do you know the temper that man's got? Dear God, he might have you shot!"

"I can't help it. But the William Randolph Hearst navy out there tonight, patrolling our shores!"

Malcomb lay his head on Eben Pay's shoulder and shook with laughter and they both giggled and snorted and wiped their noses as Joe Mountain, standing well back out of the lantern light, shook his head.

"Now goddamnit, you gotta stop that," Malcomb said, brushing tears from his eyes and moving back to one of his folding tables with the charts and the bugs crawling over it. "You hear? You gotta stop that."

"I know."

In the United States of America, nobody found any of it funny. Just two days after the news dispatches elevated TR at San Juan Hill to the status of G. Washington at Trenton, all the air went out of the euphoria with the increasingly dire reports of casualties and tropic fevers. Finished now with flag waving and writing only the bright side, the newspaper correspondents began to concentrate on inefficiency and the dark side.

And Shafter was taking a pounding.

In the White House, William McKinley developed an even deeper purple blaze below each eye in a face grown suddenly a shade whiter. At first there had been the message of glorious victory. Then one warning of great casualties. Then one suggesting that maybe the army would be pulled back from Santiago, say about five miles, into better defensive positions. Then nothing.

And there was an unofficial dispatch to Senator Henry Cabot Lodge from his good friend the former assistant secretary of the navy that said, among other things, that somebody had better send a hell of a lot of artillery and well-trained infantry to Cuba or else the United States would be within measurable distance of a military disaster.

"His exact words?" asked the president.

"His most exact words, Mr. President," said the senator.

One of the aides to the secretary of war asked, "Where in God's good name are we going to get artillery and well-trained infantry? Nelson Miles has got all the rest of it for Puerto Rico!"

Another said, to make a dark joke, "Well, we could go ahead and support William Jennings Bryan in raising a regiment like Teddy did."

Nobody laughed. In McKinley's office someone was heard to say, "My God! Military disaster! This is a political disaster! It's a goddamned Republican war!"

Perhaps this truism was expressed by the president himself. But whether or not he said it, he knew it. And with an election coming up soon.

Besides, the embarrassment. Queen Victoria's government and all those other people in Europe watching while a second-rate, moribund Spain made the United States of America look like a third-rate bungler! Great men sat for long hours that night in various rooms of the nation's capital, chins in hands, waiting for some word from Cuba. It did not come.

But something was happening. In fact, a great deal was happening.

One of the messages that General Shafter did not get through, whether by design or forgetfulness or press of other duties, had to do with the ultimatum.

Under flag of truce a group of officers rode down from San Juan Hill to the outer limits of the Santiago defenses and there met with Spaniards who came out to greet them. Eben Pay was with them, perhaps partly by force of will, his persistent desire to see what was going on, but partly because of the confusion among Shafter's staff, trying to decide who should go. In any case there he was on a horse with all the other officers, seeing the enemy close at hand. There were a great many horses on the island now, plenty for field and general officers at least, though the Cavalry Division was still afoot.

Eben Pay was much impressed with the Spaniards. They were neat and clean and soft-spoken, speaking impeccable English, gentlemen in all respects. Real caballeros. Horsemen, which in Spanish was the word for gentlemen. They politely declined General Shafter's demand that they surrender. Well then, Shafter's representatives said, the city will be bombarded, and Eben Pay had to struggle once more to keep from laughing.

Bombarded? With what? Those completely ineffective light field pieces that had only black powder charges? The only real artillery Shafter had was still somewhere in ships or at Tampa or at Tennessee. And even if it was at Siboney, there was no possible way to get it up. Not this month. Not this year.

"Joe," Eben Pay said later, "this thing has become a comic opera."

"What's a comic opera?"

"I'll explain later."

"Yeah. Well, there's one thing I don't like, Eben Pay. You went off down there on that horse with all those other men, and I'd as soon you didn't do that without you take me along."

"I just slipped into it, Joe."

"Well, don't do it no more. I ain't fixin' to go back to Fort Smith and tell my brother Blue Foot that I come down here and let you get yourself killed by somebody he don't even know."

Later that same day, Eben Pay visited the forward hospital, not to see for himself how bad it was but to talk with Carlina Bessaford Newton. Clara Barton had just departed for the Siboney beach area to establish that fever hospital for General Shafter, so it fell to the lot of Marian Winchel to tell Eben that Miss Newton had gone home.

"Gone home?"

"Yes," said Marian Winchel. "I think there was a requirement for her to go home."

He felt no disapointment, which in itself was somehow disappointing to him. But there was almost nothing about it that stirred him, almost as though Carlina Bessaford Newton was like one of those Saint Louis girls he'd known in his early youth, a quick kiss in the hallway and nothing more, and within a short time name and even image of the face gone forever.

"Well, I'll have to drop her a letter," he said and knew as he walked away that Marian Winchel knew he never would. "Joe, you've never been married, have you?"

"No," said the Osage, just behind him.

"Have you ever loved a woman?"

"Sometimes. For just a little while. But it never took on no permanent arrangement."

Am I that transparent? Eben Pay thought. He knows I'm thinking of Missy Bishop. And he could see *her* face in his mind and he began to feel despondent. But as they came into the headquarters area, Captain Malcomb ran out of his operations tent waving a handful of flimsies.

"God, after he snubbed the general on that proposal for the ships to force the Santiago harbor, Admiral Sampson wants a meeting."

"A meeting?"

"The navy wants to talk!"

"When?"

"Now. We've already sent a party on horseback to Siboney to meet Admiral Sampson and escort him up here into the hills."

"You're going to bring him up that damned road?"

"Hell no, one of these other trails we've found."

Malcomb was jumping around like a child just before his birthday party.

"It's a nice little glade, back off the reverse slope of El Pozo. We've already got a regiment back there setting up security all around."

"I'm going," Eben Pay said.

"Me, too," said Joe Mountain.

"Look, Joe," Eben started and then saw Joe Mountain's hardset face and shrugged. "All right, Malcomb, have you got a couple of saddle horses?"

"Saddle horses? Hell, man, I know you've been spoiled by that ride on the surrender mission but we're not ass deep in horses, you know. In fact, my getting you that plug has made a colonel of artillery so damned furious I hope I never have to serve under him anyplace."

"All right. We'll walk. How far is it?"

"Two miles from where you're standing. Here, I'll show you on the chart."

And so they started, but before he left, Eben Pay asked, "What regiment on security?"

"The Thirty-seventh."

Eben Pay laughed and looked at Joe Mountain. "It feels like good luck for a change."

Then they were off, down through the kapok and Spanish bayonet and the wild palms here on the hill slopes far above the coast. But suddenly, after they'd cleared the headquarters area and there were no other signs of military units around, Eben Pay remembered Juan Carlos Smith. He stopped. He stood for a long time, looking at the tangle of trees. Then back to Joe Mountain.

"Have you still got that pistol?"

The Osage stared as though Eben Pay might have lost his mind and the black tattoo marks on his cheek were livid, his expression incredulous.

"Eben Pay, sometimes, you ask me things that only a crazy man would ask."

"All right, all right," Eben Pay said and waved his hand to dismiss the subject and hurried on ahead. And all the way to the meeting place, all of the two miles in the sweltering heat, and finally passing through the sentinels of the Thirty-seventh Infantry, he could hear behind him the Osage muttering.

"Nobody except my little brother Blue Foot ever asked questions like you do. Blue Foot is an old-line Osage and I can understand how he'd ask crazy questions sometimes. I don't know if you're an old-line white man or an old-line anything else. But even Blue Foot never asked me a question like that one. It was the worst question I ever been asked. If you was back in old Judge Parker's court and asked a dumb question like that, old Judge Parker would have sent you to the Detroit pen along with Belle Starr just for askin' such a damned fool criminal question.

"But now that you asked it, I'll tell you. Yes, I got old Smoker Chubee's Colt right here, and you may remember we hanged him in Fort Smith for murder, and I'll tell you before you ask, yes, it's loaded. And if—"

"Joe," Eben Pay interrupted. "For God's sake, shut up!"

"Well, I just thought you'd like to know all of it, being a big-assed lawyer like you are!"

Lieutenant Colonel John Stoval

It was a great honor for my regiment to secure the area where General Shafter and Admiral Sampson and General Garcia would parley. There was little doubt in the minds of anyone involved that this could be a historic moment.

As fate would decree, it was, but not for the reasons supposed.

Most of us have seen Admiral Sampson at one time or another in this Cuban campaign. A little gamecock of a man, perhaps actually larger than he appears, always attired neatly in his short-jacket white uniform with a little pillbox cap having enough gold-braid scrambled eggs on the bill to feed a company of infantry, I have heard my men say. He is trim and rather pompous, often standing with hands on hips, his head thrust forward, his fringe of gray beard giving a somewhat satanic appearance to his somber face. One gets the impression that he never allows himself to sweat.

Always nearby is his aide, a young officer who wears a havelock on his hat, much in the style of the French Foreign Legion. My troops regard such things as the height of affectation, saying, "Listen, he can always wipe his ass with a part of his hat."

Incorrigible, my troops!

To say that Admiral Sampson is not liked or admired in the Fifth Army Corps would be putting it gently. No secret has ever been made in General Shafter's headquarters of the navy's desire for our troops to storm the trenches and forts of Santiago before their ships would dare enter the harbor to destroy the Spanish fleet. My old regulars have sensitive ears and have heard such things. And they have seen those fortifications!

To make those defenses even more formidable, General Garcia, commander of the insurgents, sent word his men have been unable to prevent a large body of Spanish troops from reinforcing the already considerable garrison in Santiago de Cuba. Rumor places the number as high as five thousand!

So the old regulars are not in love with General Garcia any more than they are with Admiral Sampson. I have never heard any of my men refer to Admiral Sampson or General Garcia by name. They say of one, "That little saltwater son of a bitch." They say of the other, "That old greaser son of a bitch."

The lexicon of soldiers is appalling to civilians but the lewd and profane words fall from their lips gently and casually, having been worn smooth by so much usage. It is claimed by the old-line noncommissioned officers that a man must be in the army for at least ten years before he begins to speak like a real soldier.

Well, this meeting could have changed the admiral's ruthless insistence that we hurl our troops against the wire and the Krupp guns and the trenches. There was a feeling of well-being and anticipation among the troops that I could sense and that had not been apparent since the actions at El Caney and San Juan Hill.

But the meeting never took place. Even as we waited, even before General Shafter arrived, there came the distant boom of heavy guns. Somewhere to the west and south. Everyone looked at one another. What could it mean?

Leaving my second-in-command with the regiment, I mounted the horse provided me only that same day and rode up through the groves and jungles to Fifth Corps headquarters. There, they knew little more than I did. But there was some information from Cuban spies who had arrived out of breath from the area around Morro Castle which sits overlooking the entrance to Santiago Bay.

General Shafter was on his feet, and in full uniform, gazing with an expression of amazed incredulity toward the southwest. As I went in to present myself, he turned and as usual swore a mighty oath. And then said, "Jack, the Lord God Almighty is looking over our shoulder this day. The Spanish fleet has left Santiago and are making a run for it on the open sea. That racket you hear is our own navy engaging them, I hope."

"What does it mean, General?" I asked, already knowing the answer.

"Mean? It means, Jack, that a lot of your men who would have died if Washington forced me to assault those Santiago defenses will get out of this hellhole in one piece."

He suddenly laughed. I suspect it was the first time he had laughed in many days.

"It means, Jack, that with their navy gone, those Spaniards left behind are going to be much more inclined to talk about surrender.

"And something else that is beautiful!"

Now he laughed again, his whole great bulk shaking with it.

"Damned beautiful! Because if Captain Malcomb's timetable is correct, Sampson is well on his way to our meeting, well on his way to Siboney. Which means, by God, Jack, that in the first naval action of this war since Dewey at Manila, that little saltwater son of a bitch isn't even with his fleet to command the action!"

And we laughed together, the commanding general and I. It was all better than any meeting could have been. And the monumental irony of it was brass in my throat and comes down to me today and will to my last hour—that when he decided to come out, that Spanish admiral, without knowing it, did more to save our troops from brutal slaughter than anything our own admiral had ever done!

CHAPTER 20

FIRST Sergeant Maurice Barry
saw them, Eben Pay and Joe Mountain, sitting on a fallen ebony
log resting after their brisk and fruitless walk.

"Good day to you sir," Barry said, walking up with his beer
barrel body rolling side to side. He was smiling broadly, looking
back with each step toward the far sounds of firing beyond the
green fringed hills. "The colonel, he'll be back in a few shakes
with news of that. But I can tell you, those are naval guns. Meanwhile, a little rest in the shade. Can I call up one of the other
officers?"

"No, thank you, Sergeant," said Eben Pay. "I suspect we're
all of us here for nothing."

"Never anything for nothing, sir."

Eben Pay looked around the small clearing. There were scattered groups of soldiers, rifles at sling arms, very casual, paying
no attention to the war, it seemed.

"Aw, those troops," First Sergeant Barry laughed. "Once they
know we won't be off to the sounds of guns, they lose all interest
and begin to bring out the playing cards once more and tell the
stories about women."

"Are there a lot of stories about women, Sergeant?"

"Aw, sir, enough to curl your fingernails," Barry said.

Joe Mountain had risen when Barry came near, moving back and standing behind Eben Pay as though shaking free of any conversation with a man of the Thirty-seventh Infantry. But now he watched with intent, black gaze, his lips open in the usual fixed grin without humor.

Barry glanced at the Osage from time to time, quickly, then looked away as quickly, as though there were some danger here that he had no intention of igniting.

"Where's Corporal Price?" Eben Pay asked.

"Oh, Dylan Darlin'," said Barry and slapped his belly. "God, sir, he does hate it when I call him that. But you see, sir, it's sergeant now. Oh yes, good Dylan a sergeant running his platoon. His old three-striper platoon sergeant and the ranking corporal besides taking bad shots at El Caney. The platoon sergeant right here!"

And Barry jammed one finger into his left eye. Then he turned and faced a near line of trees and bellowed, making Eben Pay jump with the violence of it.

"Dylan Darlin', post front and center on the double, man. A high ranker to see you!"

Barry, still laughing, turned and walked away from them with one last look at Joe Mountain, off through the glade, avoiding the Spanish bayonet, rolling his great body and muttering "Dylan Darlin', Dylan Darlin'."

Joe Mountain saw him before Eben Pay did. A tall form appearing at the edge of a near line of trees, raw and hard as the trunks of mahogany around him. He walked down slowly, Dylan Price, deliberate, a bayoneted rifle slung over his shoulder, the brim of his campaign hat slanted to cut off the sun from his eyes.

He looked bigger than Eben Pay had remembered him. Not First Sergeant Barry big, like a wooden chunk, but long big, all straight lines and square angles. And a face clean-shaven and with eyes reflecting the green of surrounding foliage. As he came closer, he began to smile, a rather grim smile turning up only the barest corners of his broad mouth.

"Well now," he said and extended his hand, a gesture unexpected and a little out of place. Eben Pay stood up and took it, feeling the texture of Dylan Price's fingers, like brass cartridge cases. "Mr. Pay, is it?"

"Yes, I see we're here together waiting for something to happen."

Joe Mountain snorted and Eben Pay shot a quick, glaring glance at the Osage, who wasn't even looking at him. Dylan Price appeared not to notice, although Eben Pay knew there were few things this man did not notice. The Welshman released Eben Pay's hand and looked off toward the sea.

"Our good navy lads," he said. "Blowing the rust out of their guns. I hope they hit something."

Then Dylan Price dismissed the whole war with a wave of his hand, sat down on the log, and swept off his hat. Eben Pay was surprised that he had so little hair.

"So Mr. Pay, once more we meet," Price said and patted the log beside him. "So sit with me because as with our first meeting, I have libation."

Eben Pay sat down. And immediately gave another start when Dylan Price turned toward the woodline and gave a great shout. Dear God, these army people push up such a great noise with their diaphragm, Eben Pay thought.

"Ulrich, you bloody sausage, bring that mucking bottle down here double-quick time."

And so they sat on this Cuban hillside drinking a very raw Cuban rum waiting for the afternoon Cuban downpour and really unaware that slowly the firing from far off sputtered out and was no more. A flight of flamingos went up the coast but they hardly noticed. It was one of those strange lulls in war that come often but are usually forgotten in the telling of it later. Just waiting. Waiting for Colonel Stoval to return and tell them what the hell was happening. Until then, there was nothing they could do about it, and so the war was put aside.

Early on, Dylan Price held the bottle back behind him without looking or saying anything and Joe Mountain took it, had a long drink, and returned it to the still outstretched hand. As the conversation went on, this strange ceremony did as well.

It was a semihostile yet respectful exchange, wordless, like two venomous spiders suddenly becoming aware of each other in the same web. Eben Pay was acutely conscious of it and noted that in Joe Mountain it produced a steely intensity of expression, very serious, but in Dylan Price an amused detachment.

"This place smells of old molasses," Dylan Price said. "Or maybe it's this mucking rum. Appropriated as it was from some unfortunate Cuban by one of my bloodthirsty soldiers!"

It was as though this Dylan Price, only having seen Eben Pay less than half a dozen times, could read the younger man's fascination with soldiers and was teasingly suggesting disenchantment with such base and crude mortals.

And Eben Pay was rather proud of himself for having suspected from the first that this was no common, ordinary enlisted soldier but one who ran deep in his thinking. Probably not from any formal education but rather from wide experience of the real world. And Eben Pay determined to find out more. After all, he thought grandly, a lawyer is expert in bringing forth information from witnesses!

"You've been in the army a long time?" Eben Pay asked.

Price shrugged. "A considerable time. But not in this army. Here only a hitch or two, memory cloudy on it. But starting as a lad in the ranks of Vickie's redcoats."

And that was, pointedly, the only thing Dylan Price wanted to explain about his past despite all the lawyer's expertise.

But it was not an unpleasant hour. They commented on the flights of colorful birds at the edge of the jungle and Dylan Price said he had noted a snow-white flamingo flying along the coast earlier. To the south, they could see the ragged line of tree canopy along the ridges that looked down on the sea. Eben Pay remarked that it was from a distance much like hills in the Ozarks.

"Where might that be?" asked Dylan Price.

And without being aware of it, Eben Pay spent the next few moments being enthusiastic about Fort Smith and the hills of northwest Arkansas. And through it all learning nothing about the Welshman.

"This Ozarks. How does one get there?"

"Railroads. Coach lines, although some of the roads are sometimes rough and dusty. Or a river steamer from New Orleans to the mouth of the Arkansas and up the river to Fort Smith. Then the hills are on both sides, north and south."

"Hills have always been of interest to me," said Price. "There seems a natural freedom there. This is a primitive place I take it."

"It isn't Boston, but it's not so wild."

"I've always heard there were many savage red men there," Price said, a glint of laughter in his eyes. Behind him Joe Mountain snorted again.

"The Indians are our friends," Eben said and laughed and Joe Mountain spoke for the first time.

"Some ain't!"

Dylan handed back the bottle once more, still not looking over his shoulder. Joe Mountain took it, had his sip, and slapped it back into Price's outstretched hand again.

"You have family there, Mr. Pay? In these Ozarks?"

"Only an uncle. I'm afraid I haven't seen him since I was a pup. He raises horses and owns a bank in a small town near Missouri."

"A man of means, then, is it?"

"Yes. For myself, I'm from Saint Louis but I expect to be in Fort Smith for the foreseeable future."

Dylan Price looked at the far ridgeline and there was a deep vacancy in his pale eyes, as though he were seeing some land well beyond Cuba.

"At least, you're close to starting place. It would be good, being close to starting place. Sometimes, when a man gets beyond them, his beginnings mean nothing anymore."

He heaved a great sigh and tilted the bottle to his mouth and Eben Pay watched the heavy muscles of his neck moving as he swallowed. Price made a little gag, smacked his lips, shook his head, and laughed.

"My enlistment runs its course very soon now. Perhaps I want to try and be something besides a soldier. Perhaps in these Ozarks of yours, Mr. Pay."

"Well, there's plenty for a man to do there."

Price laughed again. "I was thinking more in terms of doing as little as possible."

Joe Mountain snorted.

Dylan Price suddenly rose and moved quickly off toward the tree line where the men of his platoon were sprawled about in the shade, and Eben Pay was ready to scold Joe Mountain for his bad manners when he saw that it was not Joe Mountain who had caused Price's abrupt departure. Lieutenant Colonel John Stoval was riding into the clearing.

The officers of the regiment moved quickly to gather around him, as did Eben Pay and Joe Mountain, and he confirmed that which most of them had suspected. The gunfire was naval. The Spanish fleet had flown the coop and headed for the open sea. But he had no information as to the outcome. He saw Eben Pay and touched the brim of his hat with three fingers.

"Mr. Pay, it has been a bountiful day for the Fifth Corps," he said.

The Thirty-seventh Infantry would stay in place on this hill-side, no need for shuffling about, according to General Lawton, so let the men enjoy a ground not turned into muddy mush, at least for a few hours. The kitchens and what little supply train they had would be brought up and they could consider themselves in division reserve.

Stoval told Joe Mountain that the horse he rode was on loan and needed returning to Shafter's headquarters so it could be given back to some unknown but certainly unhorsed and as certainly fuming general officer, so to save another long walk, why didn't Eben Pay ride the horse back.

"Although," Colonel Stoval said with a smile, "I doubt this little plug can carry you both." And he looked at Joe Mountain.

"I'll walk," the Osage said.

They didn't talk, going back to Shafter's headquarters, Eben riding and the Indian walking behind. It wasn't a comfortable ride. This was a McClellan saddle, split bottom, and in his time at Fort Smith Eben Pay had become accustomed to the solid-seat working western saddle. He missed the horn, too.

But it was not uncomfortable enough to prevent his thinking

again of the Welsh soldier. There was some quality here that fascinated him. Eben Pay knew there was Welsh blood on his father's side of the family but there had never been much made of it and certainly Eben Pay's father did not speak in that strange, lilting cadence, or with a voice that evoked the sense of mist in the highlands of Wales.

There was more to it than that, of course, as Joe Mountain had perceived but never mentioned. Price was the only really professional enlisted soldier Eben had ever known. And it surprised him a little that there were many qualities here that he found in the men of Parker's court. Oscar Schiller and Heck Thomas and the other deputy marshals who enforced the law in Indian Nations.

Both classes of men, Eben Pay thought, stood with a foot on either side of the line that divided good and evil. And perhaps the most efficient of them were a tough, brutal lot, yet amazingly compassionate. With astonishing soft spots that allowed them to have sudden, unexplained gentle lights in their eyes. That perhaps forced on them, like it or not, an appreciation and recognition of the whole contradictory human condition.

Eben Pay could recall many times a peace officer from Parker's court becoming downright affectionate with some just apprehended murderer. And he suspected that Dylan Price and his kind would display the same sentiment to a conquered enemy.

But he remembered the Spaniard on Kettle Hill who had tried to surrender and been shot down, and thought that perhaps being conquered by these regulars and surviving required very special circumstances.

In either instance, with those marshals or with these old soldiers, there appeared to be rules of the game that were incomprehensible to an outsider.

Eben was sorry he had not had time for a few courses in philosophy at the University of Illinois. He was beginning to believe that a degree from some university went farther to verify a man's ignorance than it did to nullify it.

And he recalled Joe Mountain's snorts of derision at various times in the conversation with Price. And he resented it. So he kicked his horse a little and picked up the pace and soon the Osage had to trot behind to keep up. And Eben Pay nudged the horse in flank again, and then Joe Mountain had to run, but he still stayed close behind.

By the time they reached Shafter's headquarters and Eben Pay dismounted, the Osage was soaked with sweat and his black hair lay down across his forehead and his tattoo marks looked like bullet wounds. He was breathing heavily and he looked at Eben Pay with a brittle light in his eye but he said nothing and Eben Pay was in that moment furiously ashamed of himself for being such a spiteful ass.

His first impulse was to explain it away somehow, but looking at Joe Mountain's face, he knew no such thing could register as anything more than a charade. So he kept his mouth shut. As did the Osage.

Captain Malcomb greeted him with a long, somber face, a little unusual, Eben Pay thought, in view of the latest development on the Spanish fleet. Malcomb drew him aside, holding a number of flimsies in his hand, and spoke in low tones.

"There's a man at the Siboney beach," Malcomb said. "Just arrived from New York. His name is Granger. Norman Granger. They say he's a former United States deputy marshal. Do you know him?"

"Hell no, why should I know him?" Eben Pay asked, his disposition nothing but sharp edges as he looked from beneath the tent fly and saw Joe Mountain sweeping sweat from his face with his fingers.

"Well, you're a federal court man. I thought you might. Hell, you don't have to bite my head off. Anyway, he's a Pinkerton now. And he's down here looking for evidence on a murder."

"I wish the man luck," Eben Pay said sharply and started to turn away but Malcomb caught his sleeve.

"No you don't wish him luck. The man he's claiming did the murder is a large Indian. You hear? Joe Mountain!"

Joe Mountain

If Eben Pay wants to go around shaking hands and telling funny stories with some of these soldiers who are common as dirt, it's not any of my business. But I don't have to like it. And if Eben Pay gets his tail out of joint when he sees I don't like it, that's just too bad.

Eben Pay is a big man in the court at Fort Smith now. He can shake hands and tell funny stories with judges and lawyers and federal marshals and even some of these big army captains like Roosevelt and Shafter. But when he starts to get cozy with some of these men who are as common as dirt, it looks bad.

Hell, Eben Pay has helped send better men than that to Judge Parker's gallows!

But it ain't any of my business.

Eben Pay getting his tail out of joint don't bother me. He does it all the time. It's just something you have to put up with because it's part of being a friend with a white man.

The day Eben Pay tried to outrun me on that horse he got his tail back in joint real quick after Cap'n Malcomb talked to him. I never saw Eben Pay act the way he did that day. It was like he'd had too much of that awful rum of Dylan Price's. Except I'd seen Eben Pay when he drank a lot more than that and he never acted so crazy before.

He came out of that tent fly and grabbed my arm and led me off down into the woods away from everybody. And he said from here on in, I wasn't supposed to talk to anybody unless he was right there with me. And that I was supposed to stay close to him every minute, night and day.

Hell, that's what I'd been doing all along, I told him, even when he tried to run off from me on that horse.

I was sorry I said that last part because I saw it made him feel real bad so I just laughed and said it was a nice little run and I liked it but I don't think it made him feel a hell of a lot better.

Then Eben Pay told me what it was that made him so wild-eyed. This soldier I killed the day Juan Carlos Smith was shot come from one of those Yankee states and he had a father who owned a lot of railroads or banks or some such thing and was a friend with big men in Washington, maybe even President McKinley his ownself, and that this man was all in a snit about his son being killed the way he was and he had sent one of these jake-leg Pinkerton detectives to Cuba to find out all about it so somebody could be arrested and taken back to this Yankee state to be tried for murder.

He told me all the details. He said the man I'd killed was named Thomas van Carlton III and his family was plenty impor-tant.

So I said, hell, I don't care what his name was, the son of a bitch and all his friends had been shooting at us that day and I wasn't going to stand there and let them put holes in us no matter how important his family was or how many banks his father owned and if the same thing happened again right now I'd sure as hell shoot back again if they didn't get me first.

Eben Pay was beginning to lose his temper with me and he said to just shut my mouth and listen for a while. So I did and he said that he'd told Cap'n Malcomb about me shooting that man but that Cap'n Malcomb hadn't told Shafter yet because there had been so much going on, like the battles and everything, but now Shafter would have to be told that there was a Pinkerton nosing around in his army area. Especially because it seemed like this Pinkerton had newspaper writer's credentials right out of Washington and could very nearly go anywhere he wanted to go.

I said it was as sneaky as anything I ever heard of, a detective getting news writer credentials and acting like he was somebody that he wasn't and that back in Fort Smith all the deputy United States marshals always went around with their badges out where people could see them and didn't try to fool anybody.

So Eben Pay told me to shut my goddamned mouth and listen

and I did and he said this detective, whose name was Norman Granger, was probably back there at Siboney right now talking to all those National Guard soldiers in the outfit Thomas van Carlton III was serving in when I blew the hell out of him. And Eben Pay said this detective would likely be right here in the forward area before long and I wasn't supposed to talk to him or anybody else unless Eben Pay himself was standing right beside me. Because Eben Pay said the father of this Thomas van Carlton III was hell-bent on getting somebody tried for killing his son.

I told Eben Pay I never heard of anything so damned crazy in all my life. A man going off to war and his father too dumb to know that sometimes people get killed in wars.

Eben Pay got so mad, I thought he was going to hit me with his fist. He yelled that this whole thing was damned serious because I wasn't even in the army when I killed Thomas van Carlton III and he wasn't sure how jurisdiction worked in such a case.

Well, if Eben Pay didn't know, I sure as hell didn't!

CHAPTER 21

AFTERWARD, Captain V. M. Concas, a Spanish naval officer, wrote of the moment he ordered the guns of his cruiser *Teresa* to open fire on the American fleet as the Spaniards broke from Santiago Bay and made for the open sea because their admiral assumed that the United States Army was about to take the city:

"My bugles were the last echo of those which history tells were sounded in the taking of Granada from the Moors; it was also the signal that four centuries of Spanish grandeur were ended!"

It would be a long time before any citizen of the United States became aware of that magnificent epitaph for Spanish glory. And even had they read it on the instant, on that July 4, 1898, it would have done nothing to dampen their exhilaration or celebration. For more than a few of them now realized that Cuba Libre meant much more than driving the Spanish out of western waters and putting a period to the Iberian paragraph in history. It meant the beginning of imperial Columbia. It was no accident that the most popular tune played in bandstands across the country on that wonderful fourth was "Hail, Columbia." And now, by God, the sun would never set on Old Glory, and the damned British would have to do a little bowing and scraping as we had been doing for a hundred years. So they said.

Nor would it have dampened the spirit of victory to point out that the Spaniards had been outnumbered and outgunned, their shipboard cannons obsolete and one of their largest vessels without any main batteries at all, her ordnance being at the time in Spain for repair. Or that none of the Spanish ships were sunk, but because they still had wooden decks were set afire at the first American salvos and run aground.

But everyone was magnanimous. The press applauded the sailors from American vessels who helped rescue the Spaniards from the water, and of course, the news writers of Mr. Hearst in their own boat, following along with the fleet as it chased the fleeing Spanish ships, pitched in with the rescue effort once colors were struck, and received appropriate accolades on every front page.

It was a glorious day for all. Well, not all. For Admiral Sampson, it was terrible, because he hadn't been there to command the action. He would spend the rest of his life trying to prove, in the columns of various friendly newspapers, that he had indeed brought about the victory.

And from that moment on through his remaining few years of life, General William Shafter would chuckle and gloat inwardly about the discomfort of that little navy son of a bitch who had wanted good army soldiers to throw themselves on solid Spanish defenses while he kept his ships safe in the open sea.

"I will never be placed on the level with Sam Grant," Shafter said to Captain Malcomb. "But by God's living blood, neither will that little bastard Sampson be mentioned in the same breath with Dewey."

Perhaps it was a comforting thought that accompanied him to his deathbed.

So now it was time to reduce Santiago. Attack! Attack! said all the editorial writers, not having seen the barbed wire, not having any appreciation for the condition of Shafter's army. Charge the fortifications! So they wrote from one Manhattan to the other and beyond, and so thought the politicians and a few soldiers besides. Like General Nelson Miles.

Miles had organized a small army of some few regiments to

take Puerto Rico. After all, with the Spaniards on the run, they should take all they could get. But now he would turn aside from the smaller island and come to Cuba, take charge there and attack. Attack! Attack! No more of this pussyfooting! No more of this Fifth Corps dillydallying. Attack, and take Santiago now.

Of course, Shafter had other ideas. The idea, in fact, that he had had all along. Why use up the blood of his troops if there was a chance the Spaniards would surrender? He wanted to press negotiations now more than ever, more urgently than ever. Because now it was not only a race with the hurricane season and yellow fever, but a race with Miles as well.

"How long will it take the pretty boy to get here?" Shafter asked Captain Malcomb.

"A week," Malcomb said, shrugging. "Give or take a few days."

"By the holy beard of the living God Jehovah," Shafter shouted. "Why in hell can't I get a straight-out answer around here?"

Fighting down his illness, Shafter organized his team. Eben Pay was on it. Shafter knew by now about what Captain Malcomb called the Joe Mountain affair. And Shafter looked at Eben Pay and said, "We'll cross that bridge when we get to it. For now, we need a surrender from those people down there in Santiago. Everything else is secondary."

As Shafter had suspected, once their navy was gone, the garrison in Santiago was more than willing to call it stops. General José Toral was representative of the Spanish arms, having succeeded General Vara del Rey, who had been killed at El Caney. And in the meetings that came, Eben Pay noted that General Toral, and all his staff men, were gentlemen. Courtly and courteous, carrying the swords at their sides as thought these ancient weapons were a part of them, not like the awkward toothpicks that American officers generally tripped over and cursed.

But gentlemen though they were, the Spaniards were also procrastinators, which did not fit with General Shafter's need for haste. Even so, Eben Pay was impressed by these Spaniards.

They were neat and trim, clean-shaven except for mustaches. He had occasion to shake hands with a few of them, and always there was the delicate odor of lavender water. Much unlike the sweat smell that clung to the blue woollen shirts of the Americans. They were all surprisingly light-skinned, with only a slight hint of olive pigmentation.

Eben Pay couldn't help wondering if perhaps some of these aristocrats were descended from the families of Hapsburg monarchs, who had so long ruled from the throne of Spain.

The talks between Shafter and the Spaniards were almost unbearable in one respect. The Spanish officers were trim and ramrod straight, while Shafter sat like a great lump on the heavy wooden tubchair his staff had provided, leaning forward and dripping sweat and puffing and sniffing. But there was no question about who was in charge of this talk. It was the great, hulking Shafter.

After their first day of seeing the Spanish officers at close range, Joe Mountain said, "You know, Eben Pay, these Spaniards may hablar the same lingo as the Cubans and the Mexicans like we seen in Texas, but they don't look much alike."

It was amusing to hear it from a full blood Osage. People like that Mexican tad on the Austin depot platform who sold them fake tamales and Juan Carlos Smith may have boasted a drop of Andalusian blood but mostly they were a stew of African and Anglo and American Indian. Just like me, Eben Pay thought, except my stew comes from a different part of the world.

And it was a little startling to think this: Joe Mountain has a better idea of where he comes from than I do!

Joe Mountain, who gave no indication that he was the object of a manhunt, continued to accompany Eben Pay, and at the end of the first day, everyone tired and irritable, as General Shafter started to be lifted up onto his horse he glanced at the Osage and winked. At least, Eben Pay thought he did. And it made things a little better, what with having in the back of his mind all day the shadow image of a Pinkerton detective creeping about in the palm groves.

As was his usual habit, Eben Pay threw himself into the work of Shafter's staff, having been selected as one of the recorders of this historic event. But at night he lay awake listening to Joe

Mountain snore, trying to recall precedents he might use when the Osage was confronted with arrest. As Eben Pay knew he surely would be.

He suspected that this Norman Granger was dragging his feet, waiting for the next development on the Santiago front before making his accusation officially. Perhaps waiting for the arrival of General Nelson Miles. Because it was well known that Nelson Miles had various political aspirations to high office, very high office. It would be politic for such a man to curry favor with powerful eastern entrepreneurs. Such as this father of the deceased Thomas van Carlton III.

There was another vicious little angle that Captain Malcomb had pointed out, having as he did the duty in Shafter's headquarters of keeping track of newspapers and whatnot. The *New York World* had hired the famous novelist Stephen Crane as a news writer. Unfortunately for Mr. Pulitzer, about all Mr. Crane wrote had to do with a New York National Guard regiment, and his copy was as square to the truth as had been everything in his book *The Red Badge of Courage*.

It seems that when faced with the prospect of close combat with the Spaniards, many men of this particular regiment had remembered urgent business in the rear area and departed the battlefield posthaste.

Such scurrilous accusations written about New York heroes were considered in many quarters to be in very bad taste. Just down the street from the *Post,* in the offices of Mr. Hearst's *New York Journal,* it was called absolutely un-American.

As a result, there was a bloodthirsty longing in certain New York salons to vindicate socialite warriors by having somebody's head. So long as it couldn't be Mr. Pulitzer's or Mr. Crane's, then anybody available would have to do.

All of which made Joe Mountain's position look very spooky indeed.

But first, the surrender negotiations. Eben Pay sweated through each blistering morning, welcomed the afternoon downpour that the council tent canvas did nothing to keep out, and sweated again before the talks were finished by evening.

Now the rainstorms were not confined to daylight hours. Now there were near hurricanes at night with lightning flashes turning the Cuban landscape blue-white, thunder shaking the jungle canopy as no mere man-made artillery could. Rain came in torrents. The few miserable roads were quagmires and getting rations and good water to the troops from the Siboney beaches was increasingly a major problem.

As the talks continued, Eben Pay was amazed to learn that the Spanish garrison in Santiago was almost starving, was out of ammunition, and was completely dispirited. It took longer than it should have before General Toral finally gave in and hauled down the colors of Spain. Sunday, July 17.

On that day, as Shafter's party rode back through the trench system on San Juan Hill toward the El Pozo headquarters, the general seemed aware for the first time of what the morning report summaries had been telling him for two weeks.

"It doesn't appear there are as many troops along this line as there have been," Shafter said.

"Sir, these are present-for-duty soldiers," said Captain Malcomb.

"I know that, for God's sake. But where are the others?"

"In hospital, sir."

"In hospital?"

"Typhoid, dysentery, and fever, sir."

"Goddamnit," Shafter said. "We beat Miles but we couldn't beat the goddamned pestilence. I knew it, I knew it."

And that evening, before another furious storm broke over the hills above the coast of southern Cuba, Captain Malcomb said to Eben Pay, "And it's going to get one hell of a lot worse!"

Olaf Swenson

I never seen Sergeant Price so picayunish. And I been on a lot of Saturday inspections and Sunday parades back in the States when he was a corporal. Now he was a sergeant. And he said we was one of the honor guard outfits for the Spanish surrender, so it had better be right or he would have somebody's arse.

Weapons were all right. We always had them in good trim because if we didn't Sergeant Price would eat us alive. But the damned wool shirts were awful. They had all this old dirt and mud in them and they smelled like a wet goat. We squished them around in stream water and let them dry in the sun and then brushed them with our hands. We done the best we could.

Sergeant Price got some grease from the cooks and we used that to daub our shoes. They didn't shine too good, but they looked better than they had in a long time. That's if we didn't turn the bottoms up because some of the soles had big holes in 'em.

Our old squad was about gone. Reed and Vanic buried on that hill at El Caney. And now Telner and Ulrich in hospital with the green apple spurts. Only they never eat no green apples or any other kind. But they couldn't stop messing their underwear, even after spending a lot of time squatted with their britches down. They didn't neither one want to go to hospital, but Sergeant Price had them hauled off anyway because they was both weak as that Polish guy in Milwaukee I knew whose wife hit him with a meat mallet. Pale as dead men, and they smelled pretty bad too, and not none of us smelled like rosebushes. When they started puking along with the spurts, Sergeant Price said that was the end of it and he had them hauled off to hospital.

The old soldiers back in Plattsburg Barracks used to say it was bad to get an arm or leg wound and get taken off to hospital because those sawbones there would hack them right off. But I guess it was different with Telner and Ulrich going to hospital with pukes and spurts because what the hell can they cut off when you got that?

They still didn't want to go. I couldn't help thinking about Telner going into that blockhouse to kill all those Spanish guys, him and Ulrich both, and now there they were, weak as old soap and eyes all watery and everything.

Me, I felt fine except sometimes at night I got these chills. I thought maybe I'd caught a bad disease, Sergeant Price was always warning us about, from that Polish guy's wife in Milwaukee, but Sergeant Price told me it happened so long ago that if that's where I got something the whole bottom of my pants would have dropped out by now. I don't know where Sergeant Price got all this medical stuff he told us about. Anyway, I guess it was just the rain and the hot sun. All that damned raw bacon we had to eat probably didn't help too much, either. If I'd known back when I worked for that Polish guy in Milwaukee that I was gonna have to eat so much bacon in Cuba, I never would have helped him slaughter all those hogs.

So anyway, we were lined out to be an honor guard for the surrender. When Sergeant Price got the platoon into formation there wasn't very many of us. Some of the guys had been wounded or killed at El Caney but most of them was sick in hospital like Telner and Ulrich.

We formed up in two ranks at order arms and counted off and when the count got to seven, it stopped. Which meant there were fourteen of us. And Sergeant Price. That made fifteen. We didn't have an officer. The lieutenant had been hit with one of those long-range bullets the Spanish were shooting at us when we came up on San Juan Hill after El Caney. Before they sent us back to that big meeting that never took place because the navy guy who was supposed to be there got all tied up in some kind of fight out in the ocean.

We heard the lieutenant died in hospital. It was a gut shot, which Sergeant Price said is never too good. He said it was a shame, a fine officer taking one like that from so far away the guy who pulled the trigger would look like a speck if you could see him at all. Like getting shot by a damned chicken mite, Sergeant Price said.

We heard the lieutenant had a real hard time dying because they didn't have much to give him to stop the pain. And because he was gut shot, they couldn't give him no water to drink. Sergeant Price said it would have been better if they'd just shot him in the head with a pistol as soon as he got back there in hospital and they seen they couldn't do anything to save him. All the old soldiers were saying, "Yeah, that's what they shoulda done." And they meant it, too. God, these army guys are hard to understand sometimes.

Well, none of the other platoons were any bigger than ours was and the whole regiment looked about the size of a couple of full strength rifle companies.

But we marched right out there between the lines. Up ahead was all the officers on horseback and we could tell which one was General Shafter because of his size. That horse of his looked fagged after the first ten minutes.

We moved out of column and right in line beside a couple of cavalry outfits. Of course, they still didn't have no horses. Everybody stood at parade rest until the Spaniards came out. The Spanish officers were all spic-and-span in their white uniforms and they had some good-looking horses. Right behind the Spanish officers came some troops, I guess infantry. They all had on straw hats and were carrying Mauser rifles.

Then we were called to attention and the Spanish troops were at attention and this Spaniard on a big red horse handed General Shafter a sword and the Spanish troops came to present arms and we did, too, and we really slapped those rifle slings so they sort of popped because we'd won this thing and by God we wanted those guys to know we were regulars.

Hell, I don't know. That kind of stuff gets into a man after he's been in the army awhile I guess. "Come up to present arms and let's hear hands slap those slings," Sergeant Price always said, and we did it, too, and there was this loud pop all down the line, everybody together.

So all our officers were shaking hands with all their officers and their officers were holding their hats in their hands. And all the officers were leaning over in their saddles to shake hands. And we were standing at present arms for a while.

Hell, it was nice, getting to be a part of a big surrender like that. And we knew this war was over and we didn't have to worry anymore about getting our ass shot off. Not in this war anyway.

The Spanish officers rode back to Santiago and their troops marching along behind, and then General Shafter and all his guys on horses and then us marching behind them.

But I never got to Santiago. It was right down below us and we could see it all stretched out to the bay. But I never got there. All of a sudden, I was hot as a four-bit pistol and things were spinning in front of my eyes and my damned rifle felt like it was a seventy-pound chunk of red-hot pig iron.

I tried. But my feet stopped working and the next thing I knew my chin hit Cuba square on and I heard Sergeant Price detailing two guys to haul me out of there and back across San Juan Hill and to the forward medical aid station at El Pozo.

God, then that trip in a damned wagon all the way back to Siboney and the fever hospital Clara Barton had set up and it was the worst trip I ever made. And I felt like hell because I didn't get to see the rest of the Spanish surrender or any of the señoritas in Santiago.

Maybe it was just as well. I never had much luck with women. Once, I thought it was pretty good when I'd go upstairs and visit that Polish guy's wife but then she went crazy and the whole business turned to shit. Sergeant Price always said I'd be better off if I just stuck to other soldier stuff, like drinking and gambling and cussing and leave the women to him.

CHAPTER 22

WHEN they went into Santiago de Cuba, the wisdom of General Shafter's thinking was brought home dramatically because they had to pass through the defenses that the navy and General Miles and most of the Washington crowd had been insisting they should reduce by frontal assault.

The Spanish position was organized in depth with four successive lines, each with an elaborate trench system, each covered to the front by a fantastic tangle of barbed wire, and each aligned so that defending troops could provide mutual support to one another by direct fire. Added to which would have been surveyed concentrations of shrapnel and high explosive from the Spanish artillery. Added to which were a peppering of blockhouses with embrasures commanding approaches.

Riding through all that, closely behind the generals, Captain Malcomb turned to Eben Pay and Joe Mountain, both of whom were mounted for the occasion on scrawny Cuban horses, and said, "Why, it's even stronger than we thought."

And Captain Malcomb had no conception of just how strong it was, never having been required in his military experience to storm such a position. But ahead and behind him were those who could truly appreciate those Spanish works.

General Wheeler, riding beside General Shafter, likely recalled the wire strung by the Yankees in many set-piece battle sites during the Tennessee campaigns of 1864, and he shuddered.

Dylan Price and his men, marching behind the mounted staff, had only recently had a taste of that Spanish barbed wire.

At shoulder arms they marched through the defensive lines and as they did Price ground his teeth thinking of what it would have been like. In ranks, Private Hermann Mittelberg said aloud, "Holy Mother, look what the bastards had waiting for us!"

And Sergeant Dylan Price, still gritting his teeth, faced in toward his marching men and said with some force, "One more sound from any man in this formation and all of you will be extra duty mucking out latrines for the rest of your bloody enlistment!"

Then they were into the city, and along the streets were Cuban faces appearing in window and door, tentative, eyes bright, frightened, yet inquisitive, faces glistening with sweat. The walls along these narrow streets seemed to be suffering from psoriasis, whitewash and green paint flaking off to reveal straw-laced tan adobe. The whole place smelled of sunbaked rock and open sewers. And as the men marched, the flies searched out their eyes and mouths.

Into the plaza, the steel shod hooves of the horses ringing on the paving stones set down in the time when Sir Francis Drake was lying off the shore to plunder Spanish ships, stones replacing here the packed sand and clay of outlying streets. And behind that unrhythmic clatter, the solid, steady, thirty-steps-a-minute thump of infantry feet.

There was an arsenal, a rather imposing building of limestone, with barred windows. Before it were rows of the hated Mauser rifles, in pyramid stacks. There was a small cathedral and the official residence of the governor of the province.

Each of the people who did business in these places was waiting, as were a great many citizens of Santiago, in a ring around the plaza, watching, silently. As all the troops moved into lines, both Spanish and American, General Shafter and his officers moved to these Spanish officials. And the archbishop and the governor and General Toral invited the conquering commander into a cool room of the governor's palace for lunch.

The lunch took about forty minutes. Later, Eben Pay, who

was there, said that it was not worthy of note. Except at the end, they were served slices of lime pie. And this, Eben Pay claimed, was pie of such magnitude that it should have been mentioned in every history of the Cuban war. When he thought of all the stories of starvation in Santiago he wondered where those limes had come from and finally decided that starvation applied to somebody other than the governor and the archbishop.

Joe Mountain, who had ridden into the city with Eben Pay, was naturally excluded from this luncheon, as he had expected, but at least he could stand in the shade of the porch of the governor's palace and watch the troops still aligned on the square sweating as they stood at parade rest waiting for whatever was about to happen next.

What happened next was the glorious spectacle. Having finished their lime pie, all the dignitaries walked out of the governor's palace and made the short trek to the steps of the cathedral. A great deal more handshaking took place. Then the military people, the Spaniards in their whites, the Americans in their dark blue, moved each to their respective formation of troops. Remaining on the steps of the church were the governor, whose stiff little beard was beginning to wilt with sweat, and the archbishop, who stood with downcast eyes, hands clasped before his white dalmatic as though he were about to celebrate mass.

General Toral took station before his troops. As did General Shafter. Close beside him was a small honor guard of soldiers from the Thirty-seventh Infantry Regiment. The regimental lines faced one another across the width of the square. The people of Santiago watched.

The white banner of Spain still fluttered from the flagpole atop the governor's palace. Now it would come down and Old Glory would go up. Each operation would be performed by a color guard made up of men from each of the two armies. Below, the troops were brought to attention by the sharp command of officers. On the roof of the palace, the men stood like statues.

It became very still in this great plaza. Even the breeze from Santiago Bay seemed to pause. Somewhere back toward San Juan Hill, a mule brayed. The archbishop frowned. The governor lifted misty eyes to the emblem of his nation flying above the palace for the last moment.

The cathedral clock began to strike, the brass clang making vibrations against the walls of the square and startling a flock of pigeons that flew out of the belfry and across the assembled troops, their wings making a fluttery, frantic whisper. The clock struck again and again. Twelve times. It was noon in Santiago de Cuba and everyone in the plaza was rigid in their places.

It was at this precise moment that Mr. Clement Eggmont, newspaper writer, saw his opportunity to enter into history. The Signal Corps had a number of cameras to record the great event. What better way to establish his place down the ages, Mr. Clement Eggmont reasoned, than to be caught on film at the base of the flagpole on that roof at the exact moment of official capitulation?

He ran to the front of the governor's palace and began to climb the lattice and balcony grillwork, like a great, slender monkey.

"Oh my God," Captain Malcomb whispered.

"Get the man down," General Shafter said as quietly as he was capable of speaking.

Mr. Clement Eggmont was on the roof. Some of the Sixth Cavalry color guard standing at the base of the flagpole made a number of coarse remarks. Mr. Clement Eggmont remained in his position. The lieutenant in charge of the color ceremony called down, a pained expression on his face.

"What should I do, sir?"

There was some controversy about exactly what General Shafter said. Years later, Eben Pay in relating the incident said the general exclaimed in a loud voice, "Throw the son of a bitch off."

Exercising uncommon judgment, the officer in charge of the roof detail assigned his two largest men to escort Mr. Clement Eggmont down the exterior stairs at rear of the palace. Escort, of course, is the wrong word. Manhandle is the right word.

The troops, still at attention in the plaza below, could see General Shafter's back lift and sag as he heaved a great sigh. Perhaps of relief. If so, it was short-lived. For Mr. Clement Eggmont was not to be so easily denied.

The red-faced news writer, seething with the indignity of

having been touched by common soldiers, ran around the governor's palace, across the plaza, and stationed himself in front of General Shafter and began in a loud voice to detail all his rights under the Constitution and other documents, some of which General Shafter had never heard. Once again, there were conflicting reports of the exchange. General Shafter, in his official report, would only say that "one word led to another." Indeed. Eben Pay said he heard the general say *bastard* once, *son of a bitch* three times, and *pissant* too numerous to count.

Whatever it was Shafter said, it was enough to convince Mr. Clement Eggmont that a slander had been committed against him personally, his family, and the profession of journalism.

Whereupon, Mr. Clement Eggmont balled his fist and threw a punch at the face of the commanding general of the Fifth United States Army Corps while that gentleman was attempting to accept the surrender of the representatives of the Spanish government in the Western Hemisphere. The fact that the blow missed could not be credited to any elusive action by the commanding general, Eben Pay would say, because Shafter could hardly avoid a slow-moving mule train seen well in advance. So it must have been the result of Mr. Clement Eggmont's absolute incompetence as a box fighter that saved what little face the United States had left as the governor, the archbishop, the Spanish troops, the American troops, and half the population of Santiago looked on aghast and mouths hanging open.

The news writer did not get a second chance. First Sergeant Maurice Barry and four of his men immediately had Mr. Eggmont in hand, in very rough hand as a matter of fact, and dragged him off to the far side of the square so the ceremonies could continue.

In later years, Eben Pay was to say that he was sure he heard General Shafter mutter loud enough to be heard all the way back to Siboney, "By God's holy blood, this is the damnedest war I've ever been in!"

But the ceremony went on.

Spain's flag came down. Red white and blue went up. The American troops were ordered to present arms. The Spanish troops rendered a hand salute, having then no arms to present.

As the banner of stars and stripes lifted up, so did the Caribbean breeze once more, and the sacred cloth danced out against the brilliant sky and the Sixth Cavalry band broke into a stirring tune. "Hail, Columbia." Of course.

It was a fine ceremony.

Except for Mr. Clement Eggmont, in his far corner of the plaza. He was still seething. But now he was held by First Sergeant Maurice Barry, a massive hand clutching the shirtfront of the news writer as though it were a wad of wastepaper.

"Well, now, lads," Barry asked his four soldiers standing close about with rifles and fixed bayonets. "What must we do with this gentle pussy?"

Mr. Clement Eggmont then made what was perhaps the worst mistake of his young life to that point. He attempted to launch another blow. But this one was even less effective than his first because even as he balled his fist, First Sergeant Barry yanked him forward with such violence that his teeth rattled and Mr. Clement Eggmont found his face within a quarter inch of a wild animal. And held there.

"Bucko," said First Sergeant Barry in a very calm voice, "the next sound that issues from that asshole you call a mouth will be the end of you. I will break your arms and jaw and other things and they will be scraping you off these walls with a shoe brush. You have made all the mark on these fine ceremonies that you will ever make, so now shut your face."

And Mr. Clement Eggmont did.

In that corner of the square there was a small stone pedestal upon which had been the statue of a great Spanish hero long since thrown down by Cuban patriots. So now the pedestal stood empty, five feet high and ideal for the purpose to which First Sergeant Barry now put it. He had his men hoist the unprotesting Mr. Clement Eggmont onto the pedestal, where the news writer had to stand like a statue himself because there was no room on the platform to do much footwork. Beneath him were the four soldiers, grinning, holding rifles ready, the points of the bayonets dangerously close to Mr. Eggmont's body. Then First Sergeant Barry's final instructions.

"Men, if this dog-pecker gnat attempts to dismount from his perch," said Barry, "I expect to find four bayonets stuck in his butt by the time I get to him. Are there any questions?"

"No questions, First Sergeant."

Barry then turned to observe the rest of the surrender ceremony.

Actually, there wasn't anything more to watch. As with all impressive rituals, once the last amen was said everything dissolved into afterglow. And just as Barry turned to observe, the archbishop was saying the last amen.

The city would be occupied by American troops. Their duty would be to watch the Spanish soldiers, who had now officially become prisoners of war. This was a simple duty because the Spaniards were certainly not going anywhere and were content to remain passive until they could be hauled away to Spain. The other duty of the occupying forces was to keep an eye on the Cuban population, who, now that the Spanish army was no longer in a position of power, might decide it was a good time to revenge themselves on past masters for whatever wrongs had been done them, either real or imagined.

The Thirty-seventh Infantry Regiment and two of the cavalry regiments stayed in the city, finding almost at once, as soldiers will always do, places that could provide strong drink and women. They attempted to conduct themselves, with somewhat limited success, as gentlemanly representatives of the world's newest imperialist power, the United States of America.

For the soldiers, it was an extremely elemental exercise. For General Shafter it was somewhat more complex. For no sooner had the surrender been accomplished than a number of Mr. Hearst's newspaper correspondents began going through the streets pasting placards to the sides of buildings. These placards were lettered in red, white, and blue with the message: Remember the *Maine!*

Back on his cot at the El Pozo headquarters when he first heard of this, General Shafter became profanely and obscenely furious.

"The general," Captain Malcomb said to Eben Pay, "is putting the island of Cuba off limits to all news writers. It will create a storm of protest."

"Can he do that?"

"Of course he can," said Malcomb. "General Shafter is boss on this island right now. Even Nelson Miles has taken his troops over to subdue Puerto Rico."

"I heard him screaming about the navy again."

"Oh yes, that hasn't helped his disposition. The navy claims all the small Spanish ships caught in the harbor are their prizes of war. Naturally, General Shafter has informed them that this is not true. Those vessels are the army's prizes of war because the army got there first. After all, the general had practically pleaded with Admiral Sampson to force his way into the harbor. The admiral declined, but now wants the booty. General Shafter has left instructions with our harbor people to repel navy personnel from those vessels with force where necessary."

"It sounds like a brand-new war."

"It is."

Eben Pay looked closely at Captain Malcomb's face. He was pale and his skin was dry with almost a translucent appearance.

"Are you feeling all right?"

"Of course," Malcomb said, but he was holding onto one of his chart tables for support.

Just afterward, as they moved off to their sleeping tent, Joe Mountain said Eben Pay didn't look too good, either.

"I'm just tired, damned tired. I need sleep."

"What you need is a hot bath in Fort Smith and your own feather bed to sleep in."

"We'll see this thing through," said Eben Pay. "Oh God, Joe, I'd almost forgotten about that damned Pinkerton in all the excitement."

"My grandfather always said not to worry about the Kiowas all the time. There would be plenty to worry about when they came."

"This man may be worse than a Kiowa."

"There ain't nothing worse than a Kiowa, my grandfather always said."

Back in Santiago, the harbor was aglow with the lights of ships. The Red Cross *State of Texas* was prominent among them. Clara Barton's people had been unloading supplies and setting up soup kitchens all over the city to provide beans and rice and bread for the hungry population. The troops in the city were eating better than they had since leaving Tampa Bay because now rations came ashore across the docks just down the street. There was no longer that vicious struggle to move wagons over the Siboney road. Not for them, anyway. The troops still around San Juan Hill and El Pozo were not so fortunate.

The Spanish officers kept close control of their men. The white-clad soldiers stayed in their barracks mostly but a few were allowed out in the evening to fraternize with the Yanqui. It was a peaceful, friendly arrangement.

The men of Thirty-seventh Infantry found their Spanish counterparts to be foursquare, a good lot. It was nice to sit with them in the *restaurante* near their barracks, to sip warm cerveza. A great many of the Spanish soldiers could speak a little English. A good many of them had been in Cuba a long time. Almost all said they had come into the army and volunteered for Cuban service to get away from Spain, where there was so much turmoil now, the possibility of a revolution constant.

The Cubans? Well, most of Shafter's men found the Cubans to be sullen sons of bitches, as they phrased it. To be avoided where possible.

And so in Santiago de Cuba the Americans who escaped the fever and the dysentery found themselves making friends with recent enemies and trying to elude still-current allies.

As usually happened, the units of the American army in the city found their own off-duty roosts. E Company's was a small, unpretentious cantina only a short walk along the street from the old banana warehouse where the regiment was billeted. It was infantry country and none of Wheeler's cavalrymen allowed themselves to be caught there after dark.

There were other areas of the city that were cavalry country. The infantry stayed clear of those. Because, as with all armies, combat soldiers who might have been dying for one another only recently were willing with the onset of calm to exhibit the skill and science of fists to impress anybody who wore a uniform with different-colored piping than their own.

"Old Mother Army breeds a strange lot," said Sergeant Dylan Price. "As soon as the last shot is heard against the common foe, the bloody soldier starts for a donny with one of his own.

"I could raise your hair with the story of seven Welsh Borderers defending a whorehouse in Durban from the encroachment of a whole mucking company of Kent sappers. Or maybe they were Herefordshire. No matter. In either case they were bleeding Englishmen."

The E Company saloon was very small. Dirt floored. Lighted only with candles. There were half a dozen rough wooden tables with stools, like milking stools. There was a short bar across the rear of the dark room, presided over by a one-eyed Cuban who wore a filthy white shirt with ruffles across the front. He maintained a fat candle in a niche in the adobe wall that cast a blue flame upon a crudely carved statue of the Virgin. The name of the place was La Colmena. The Beehive.

Young ladies dropped in each evening, wearing brightly flowered dresses cut low in the front. Some were not so young. Some were not ladies. Usually an old man came in and sat in one corner and played a twelve string guitar. Sometimes one of the ladies would sing as the old man played. These were always slow, sad songs. About love and death and the difficulty of getting rid of crab lice.

In La Colmena, First Sergeant Maurice Barry and Platoon Sergeant Dylan Price staked out their own territory, a table at the front beneath the cantina's only window, which had no glass but only wooden shutters with movable slats. When they walked in, alone or together, any soldiers sitting at that table quickly rose and moved elsewhere.

Often, a few of the ladies would visit the table for a glass of rum or cerveza. Always, as soon as the sergeants were in place, the bartender with the ruffled shirt would come over and lay a fistful of Havana cigars on the table.

"Stay away from those two when they're drinking," the old soldiers said. "That's a short fuse and it's already lit."

When they were there, staring into the candle flame, the cigar smoke thick, the smell of old beer strong, their voices were subdued. But others in the place could hear some of it. Enough to know that the time had come to make bets on who would win when it finally came to taw.

"I'll give eight to five on the first sergeant."

"The Welshman will take him."

"How much?"

"Paymaster coming?"

"That's the rumor. But I'll take your marker."

"My five to your eight. I've got Price."

"You're on."

The two men at the front table remained oblivious to all this, or at least seemed to. The first sergeant was usually smiling broadly, the very devil showing across his ruddy Irish cheeks. Price was more somber. But now and again he smiled, that taut little smile that only gently tugged at the corners of his wide mouth.

"Maybe not so good a war for you, Dylan Darlin'," said Barry. "Not like those where you shot down the poor heathern niggers in Africa."

"Nor so pleasant for you, Maurice, as in your glory days of killing red savages armed only with bows and arrows."

Barry laughed and slapped the table, but there was a grind of steel in his laughter. They looked at one another through the candle shine and the three women who had come to join them stood up silently and moved away for these were all women who had come to know how danger smelled.

"Isn't it about time, Dylan Darlin'?" Barry asked, leaning across the table.

"Soon, now, you Irish pig. After you've called me that just a few more times."

Again the first sergeant laughed and slapped the table. "Yes, by God, almost time, then. Almost time, Dylan Darlin'."

Dylan ap Rhys ap Llewellyn

The little white powder. What a blessing for the old British army while serving in Africa and India. The memories of that time. Like a child remembering school days.

When a man is not yet really a man but only a large boy who wears the uniform of service but is considered a man on the official rolls because he has the strength and stamina and skill to kill some enemy who is indeed a man, he will see certain of his officers as gods. Only after mature years will he see many of them for what they really were: an arrogant, self-centered, stupid lot allowed to lead only by virtue of a queen's seal on paper and a single ribbon on the tunic won most generally at somebody else's expense.

Those who were real leaders leap out of time's pages and it is most dumbfounding that so many of these seemed such ordinary mortals at the moment. None of the head back, chest up, teeth shining assurance to all who would listen that they were a genius of warfare, knowing more about such things than Napoleon did. Here is the authority, according to himself, of everything from cannon to cocktail, please don't bruise the gin by violent stirring.

There are these kinds of officers in every army. The quiet ones. Not the stupidly silent ones, but the calmly intelligent ones who do not care a damn about proving their aristocratic lineage with shouts about bruising the gin.

In the old queen's army, the enlisted soldier saw them in garrison. While on parade. Standing guard mount. Acting as batman or punch attendant at the quarterly colonel's ball. And the enlisted soldier lived or died with them on the battlefield, in the dust and blood and noise and puke. And the enlisted soldier after a while came to know who were the fakes and who the real officers.

And not only such a distinction among line officers but among service corps officers as well.

Take the medicals. Those generally malcontent, misplaced fugitives from the requirements of medicine in public practice. Who sometimes subsisted, it seemed, on their own supply of hospital alcohol.

Yet here, too, as in the line, there were a few. A precious few.

In Natal it was Surgeon Major J. H. Reynolds, Army Medical Department, who won the Victoria Cross at Rorke's Drift. He it was who explained to me the little white powder.

My dear departed father, son of a bitch that he was, would spit on Surgeon Major J. H. Reynolds because the man was an Englishman. Or a Saxon, as my da would say. But that same dear da had not the problem of malaria fever through most of his life as I did while wearing the queen's red coat in tropic climes. And once you have it, this malaria, you always have it, lurking and waiting to lay you low.

We do not know, said Surgeon Major Reynolds, exactly what malaria is or from whence it comes. But in Peru, a long time before the conquistadores of Portugal and Spain arrived, the heathen Indians found a tree called cinchona and this tree had bitter bark. Somehow, as has happened through the ages by accident or some twist of brain, these Indians discovered that if this bark were ground into a powder, it would halt the lethargy and final death of the malaria. Not cure it, mind, but stay its course.

This white powder we call quinine. And if the young soldier takes his daily portion of it, safe he is from sick report due to the malaria and so can go about his sworn duties as the soldier should.

It is not by chance or taste that British colonial officers and their wives, if wives are about, make the tradition of an afternoon respite to sip gigantic quantities of gin and quinine water. Of course, the common British soldier has no opportunity for afternoon respite when he might sit on a shaded veranda and sip gin and quinine water. And even if he did, no respectable British common soldier would muck up his gin with that foul tasting cinchona bark. So the common British soldier, as I knew him and was one myself, stirred his spoonful of white powder into a canteen cup of lukewarm water and gagged it down each morning after kipper.

Or else didn't and surely then fell as though hit by rifle fire in the liver.

While in Her Majesty's service, there was always in my kit a metal snuff box filled with the white powder. It was my reserve when the army's supply system broke down. Coming to the United States, I only retained the snuff box as memento of past times, thinking that surely its use was ended. But then as the news writers began to hint of invasions of Cuba, where I knew palm trees grew and that such things do not grow along the Arctic Circle but in malaria places, I dug out my little snuff box and traveled to the nearest Plattsburg druggist, who thought I was daft. Perhaps from my pronunciation of *quinine*.

But no matter. I came into Cuba with my little metal snuff box packed with the wonderful white powder. And had my bitter draft each day. Which was more than my men had because as usual the army medical support was responding to need only after it had been illustrated. It gave me some shame. But there was not enough to share.

It was some small consolation that my first casualties came from Spanish bullets and dysentery. But then the Swede went down. Laid low, that dumb, childlike, beautiful man with the innocence of a morning violet.

Here was a bad time without reckoning. One of the best soldiers I had seen, Reed, gone down in Cuban soil. At least with a small wee bit of teaching he would have been one of the finest soldiers I had seen. And Telner, his life perhaps flowing out of him in the bloody flux. And then the Swede. The sweet Swede.

A low time it was. Perhaps on the heavy side, too, my beloved enemy First Sergeant Maurice Barry, Irish devil. A man much admired yet much hated. Not hated by myself, even though my dear old father turns in his moldering grave because I did not, Barry being Irish as he most certainly was, but hated by the troops.

For me, there was some other emotion than hatred. Some

irritating rub against the soul. Perhaps it was because Barry gave me the most dreadfully forceful challenge I had ever had, even though he may not have meant to.

Oh the hell he didn't. He knew. And he knew that to open some strange door and let out the demon of my rage and fury against being a soldier, I would meet that challenge.

Yes, Old Mother Army, whether on this side of oceans or on the other, raises a brood of singular and savage children. But God love them, I always said, for doing the work they had been born to do.

A few people had heard of Walter Reed. Mostly army surgeons because he was head of the Army Medical Museum and in 1890 his interest was typhoid fever. There was a lot of typhoid, not only in Cuba but in all the staging areas where troops had been brought to prepare for it. And a great many were still there, mostly volunteer regiments, considered because of their lack of training and equipment not ready for combat. One such place was Camp Thomas in Chattanooga.

Now that news writers had been banned from Cuba, they began to concentrate on other places. And the flush of patriotic fervor was gone. Now they were finally seeing things they should have seen before.

The army, and somehow General Shafter, was taking a beating in the pages of the newspapers, because of the fever.

★

"Eben, you don't look so good," said Captain Malcomb two days after the surrender in Santiago.

"It's the damned heat. You don't look so good yourself."

"Like you said. The heat. We've got a couple of cases of yellow fever reported. Everything up to now has been malaria. The newspapers in the States are raising hell. Most of the ports along the Atlantic seaboard are saying they don't want any of these troops shipped back there. Because all these soldiers are supposed to spread pestilence among their citizens."

"Wonderful," said Eben Pay. "Speaking of news writers, when the general banned them from Cuba, did that Pinkerton get thrown out?"

"I'm afraid not," said Malcomb. "He just threw aside his press credentials, apparently, and started using his badge and New York influence. He's still in Siboney."

★

Only in the future would anyone understand that these fevers were spread by mosquitoes. Mostly, everyone thought they were like smallpox, transmitted from one person to another through bedding or clothing or close personal contact.

Nobody knew anything about hog cholera. That's what Yellow Jack was, a vicious little offshoot of hog cholera, spread by mosquitoes biting a human with the virus, because that's what it was, or a monkey so infected, and then sliding that long needle nose into someone else.

Nobody suspected mosquitoes. Well, maybe Walter Reed did. But it would be a few years before he proved what a Cuban named Carlos Finlay had said a decade before: that yellow fever and malaria were spread by insects. But Finlay couldn't make it stick. Walter Reed did. But far too late for Fifth Corps. Far too late for General Shafter to comprehend that what had destroyed a fighting force was mosquitoes!

Well, mosquitoes and other things as well. Bad water. Which explained the typhoid and dysentery. And bad food. And maybe too much booze in an island where rum was more plentiful than clear water, at least along the coasts.

Three days after the Stars and Stripes went up over the governor's palace in Santiago, for every combat casualty thus far suffered in Shafter's army, there were five down with disease. He'd been right about that, too. "We'd better get this job done fast," he'd said, "before the tropic maladies destroy us!" And he'd just barely made it. Because now he had an army mostly in hospital beds. Well, mostly on the ground because there weren't enough beds to handle all of them, even with the great Red Cross support.

★

"Eben Pay," said Joe Mountain on the fourth day after the surrender. "You're yellow as a punkin. I'm gonna carry you off down there to that hospital of Clara Barton's."

"No you're not," Eben Pay said. "I'm staying right here. Where's Malcomb?"

"He ain't in his tent. They taken him off today."

"Taken him off where?"

"Hospital."

"Aw, for God's sake!"

"There's a bunch of new people. Cap'n Shafter brought 'em in to take up where his old officers left off when they went to hospital. Malcomb ain't the only one went. Cap'n Shafter, he's started sweatin' again and he's not getting weaker, he's getting stouter. There's a hell of a man, Eben Pay."

"What's the matter with Malcomb?"

"Just a little fever they say."

They were in their sleeping tent. Only them now, with three empty cots. Eben Pay lay back in the dim shine of the lantern hanging from the ridgepole.

"God, I'm so tired, Joe, I'm just tired, that's all."

He was asleep almost at once and Joe Mountain sat on the cot across the tent from Eben Pay, a cot not nearly large enough for him and the canvas and wood creaking under his weight, and he watched Eben Pay's face.

"Why the hell'd we ever leave Fort Smith," he said aloud.

★

Malaria: chills, fever, enlarged spleen. Yellow Jack: headache, backache, fever, vomiting, nose and throat bleeding. Typhoid: quick high fever, diarrhea. Dysentery: bowels gone to mush, vomiting, fever, bloody discharge.

[317]

"Well," Shafter's best surgeon said to him, "all of this is aggravated by their interminable diet of hardtack, bacon, coffee, and sugar."

Only now, after the surrender, the supply system was beginning to catch up. Commissary details were delivering their first issue of beef in Cuba. It had been five weeks since any soldier in Fifth Corps had tasted fresh meat. Five weeks! And no fresh vegetables even now.

Someone would estimate later that with battle casualties and sickness, at one time or another perhaps 70 percent of this command had been unfit for duty.

There were some who escaped. Most especially those troops occupying Santiago, who now, compared to the past month or more, were eating like kings. And two of these were First Sergeant Maurice Barry and Platoon Sergeant Dylan Price.

Who, on this evening four days after the surrender, were sitting at the front table of La Colmena, drinking and sharing a bowl of beans and rice brought in that same day from the Red Cross *State of Texas* people. Eating casually, slowly. Sipping beer as they went. Smoking fat Havana cigars.

"Almost like officers," said Barry.

"Never like officers," said Dylan Price.

The old man was there, playing on his twelve string guitar. But none of the women were singing. Everyone, even the other soldiers, was back along the bar, in the gloomy darkness there, watching. Every other table was empty. All the people in this place standing back close to the blue-flame candle of the Virgin, watching, talking only softly if at all.

Another woman came in, saw the arrangement, and moved quickly to the cluster of people along the bar. Question in her eyes. "The sergeants," someone whispered, and that was all, and she knew and stayed there with the others, watching the two at the front table.

There was electricity in this room. As sharp-edged as that outside, where the evening storm had arrived and the lightning and rain was already creating a new world of violence in the streets, the cool air from it sweeping in through the door and through the shuttered window above the front table to make the candle flames dance and sputter in protest.

Barry and Price sat eating their beans and rice with wooden spoons. The old man kept playing his guitar. The soldiers and the Cuban women sipped their beer and rum and watched, waiting. Thunder shook the earth. A soldier dashed in, drenched with rain, laughing, saw the two men sitting at the front table, and was silent, moving back to take his place among the others at the bar, where the one-eyed man in dirty ruffled shirt passed him out a china cup of rum.

There was a corrugated roof on this place and the rain made a drumbeat on it. The chords from the guitar, with their gentle whisper, only emphasized the crash of water coming down.

There was a candle between them, drooling gray wax down along the bottle that held it. There were still half a dozen cigars scattered across the tabletop. They finished their eating and leaned on their elbows, the smoke of the cigars lifting across their faces like blue spider webs.

Finally, the rain outside began to slacken. They seemed to listen, not speaking. Heads cocked. A draft of air came through the window shutters and fluttered the candle flame again. First Sergeant Maurice Barry began to smile.

The thunder rolled off toward the mountains in the north. The roar of rain on the sheet iron roof grew softer, became a whisper. The old man strummed his twelve string guitar. Other than his hands on the strings and frets, there was no movement in this room except for the lifting of hands now and then bringing rum or beer to lips.

"Old Mother Army," Dylan Price said. "She breeds a strange lot."

He puffed his cigar, his eyes on the candle flame. But Barry was looking at him, puffing his Havana, holding it with the tip of thumb and forefinger, in a hand massive as a sledgehammer head.

"Yes," he said. "A strange lot indeed, Dylan Darlin'."

Price lifted his head only slightly and his eyes looked into those of the first sergeant and the small smile touched his mouth. Barry looked back, unblinking, still grinning.

"Was that the last time, Dylan Darlin'?"

"And you just said it once again, and once too often."

He thrust his cigar, fire first, into the bowl of beans and rice. And Barry did the same so the two Havanas stood like wooden tombstones in the bowl, wooden tombstones on a white gravel grave.

"Now?" asked Barry.

"I think so."

"I've been looking forward to it."

"The army is a strange mother!"

"Yes!"

Barry rose with a loud grunt and moved toward the man in the ruffled shirt and the women and soldiers quickly stood aside for him. He tossed down a silver coin and it made a little chiming sound on the hardwood bar. He spoke very softly, but everyone heard him.

"Sergeant Dylan Price and meself will now take a short walk in the cool of evening to discuss matters of interest to noncommissioned officers. We would both be very upset if anyone tried to follow and hear what we're saying."

Outside in the street the two of them paused before the doors of La Colmena and sniffed the air. The rain, as usual, had suddenly moved into the mountains north of Santiago, where thunder was still muttering. Already in the city there was a freshening wind and it scattered the clouds like silver fleece beneath a bright moon. There was the smell of salt water and behind them they could hear the old man playing his twelve string guitar.

"A peaceful time," said First Sergeant Barry.

They heard the sudden squalling of a cat in some sort of cat agony and toward the docks the shouts of a drunken soldier.

"Yes. As in a sleeping zoo," said Price.

"So, where?" asked the first sergeant.

"A nice, private alley."

"There are plenty of those around."

"Big enough for maneuver."

Barry laughed.

It was a wide alley, as Santiago alleys went, not far from La Colmena. Barry looked back along the street to see that no one had followed. They hadn't. The moon was turning it all to blue-white snowscape, the few clouds left hurrying north across the black sky as though running to catch up with the storm that had left them behind.

They dropped their hats then slowly peeled off their shirts, dropped those as well on the wet paving stones. Price scuffed the soles of his shoes on the alley surface, testing the footing. Barry turned aside and blew his nose with thumb and forefinger.

There were no further words or other preamble. Barry, still wiping one hand on his trousers, squared to Price, stepped closer, and launched the first blow, a right. Price slipped it easily and threw a left hook to Barry's eyes and a following right for the chin but Barry's head ducked quickly and Price felt the right fist smash into the hard ridge of bone across the first sergeant's forehead. Price hit Barry with another flicking left above the eyes once more and it made a soft, popping sound. As he stepped back, avoiding another right fist, Price could see the liquid running down Barry's face, black and shining in the moonlight, and gleaming through that, the ivory glow of Barry's teeth. Barry rushed in, still grinning.

Price sidestepped but not without taking a right to the short ribs and although it was only a glancing blow, it snapped the wind out of his lungs in a sharp gasp. Barry spun, moving faster now, and bore in and Price hit him three times in the head, high up, and took another blow to the body, felt the alley wall against his back and quickly avoided being pinned there.

Most of Barry's blows were easy to dodge but the few that landed hurt. And each time Price tried for jaw or chin, Barry's head tucked in between his shoulders and all that Price found was hard bone above the eyes, across the forehead, above the ears. Now with each charge, coming one after another, Barry tried to press the taller man against an alley wall and Price danced aside, lefts and rights hooking into the lowered head.

Then Price took a blow below the heart and everything spun

for a second and he lashed out blindly, standing face-to-face with the first sergeant now, both punching, and Price felt only hard bone at the end of each jab and hook and then Barry hit him with a right above the ear and Price saw little stars exploding in his brain and pushed himself away, staggering, and Barry was after him, grinning.

Price hit him three, four times, high in the head and Barry dug another right to Price's ribs and Price felt something give. An overhand right, square between Barry's eyes, and took another punch to the belly, stepped aside, then in quickly for two chopping lefts and a right into those shining teeth and realized this was the first time he had come even close to the first sergeant's chin.

They circled each other, hands up, breathing like winded horses, and Barry was reaching out with his left, fingers extended, as though trying to touch Price while holding the right cocked. Barry came again, blindly, and Price slipped aside but took a punch in the kidney and threw a hard, vicious left to Barry's ear and then a right, crashing into solid cheekbone.

Barry seemed to hesitate, his head turning from side to side, and Price stepped in, using both hands, aiming for the eyes now. But Barry hit him over the heart and Price felt his knees buckle, Barry feeling for him with the left, throwing the right to the body, Price snapping both fists into the first sergeant's face, and then Barry plunged a left under Price's ribs and Price was against the wall and took another right, low in the belly, and all his wind went out and he slid down the wall and sat there, legs out before him, trembling.

Barry was bent forward, moonlight on his face. Gleaming with blood. Price gasped for air, his hands held limp in his lap.

"Dylan?" First Sergeant Barry asked. "Where are you? I'm having a mite of trouble seein' you. You've closed me eyes."

"I'm here," Price said, sitting in the moonshadow of the alley wall.

"You're down, are you?"

"Yes."

"Are you gonna rise up, Dylan?"

[322]

"No," Dylan Price said. "Both my hands are broken."

"Damn!"

First Sergeant Barry reached out, groping.

"Where the hell are you, Dylan?"

"The army's a strange mother," Price said and lifted one arm so Barry could take it in his hand, and as Barry's fingers clasped his wrist, Price could feel the pain shooting up through his knuckles.

"Let me help you up," Barry said. "Jesus and Joseph, Dylan, you hit faster than anybody I ever saw."

Dylan Price had enough wind back in his lungs now to laugh.

"And you've got the hardest bloody head in this whole mucking army!"

Barry laughed with him then and pulled him to his feet.

"We'll do that again sometime," Barry said.

"Like hell we will!"

★

All bets had to be canceled. Because nobody ever learned what had happened in that alley.

First Sergeant Maurice Barry, not wanting to advertise his condition to any more American army personnel than necessary, took advantage of the friendly Spanish medical dispensary and had his face appropriately sutured. The next morning he was present for duty, but having to hold his head back in order to see through the puffed, blackened slits that were his eyes. Nobody dared question him because he appeared to be in foul temper. Even Lieutenant Beaster, the company commander, stayed clear of him.

But Platoon Sergeant Dylan Price had no such option. With those hands, he had to report to the Fifth Corps forward aid station in Santiago and from there shipped back by the morning ambulance wagon to more elaborate facilities at El Pozo, where his fractures could be properly bandaged.

It would mean Bad Time. It would mean that for each day lost to duty, Dylan Price would not be paid and might expect company punishment or even a court-martial for fistfighting. Because fistfighting seemed all right for a common enlisted soldier so long as he wasn't caught at it by proper authority and the result didn't render him unfit for duty. It would be a long while before Dylan Price would be fit for duty, and that would be Bad Time.

Except that First Sergeant Maurice Barry was still the kind of noncommissioned officer who believed that what the commissioned officers didn't know couldn't harm them. And so on that day, after seeing that Price's personal effects were bagged and sent back to him, entered in the morning report as follows: "Plat. Sgt. Dylan Price. Evacuated to hospital for fever."

He thought a moment, gnawing his pencil, his head tilted back so he could see the neat lines on the morning report form. Then added for good measure, "And dysentery."

Major General William R. Shafter

By the holy blood of Jehovah! Poor Ed Malcomb off to that hospital Clara Barton has at Siboney and from all reports he's got the Yellow Jack. Not many cases of that, actually, not yet anyway, but the sawbones tells me Ed has it. He's bleeding at the throat, not a good sign.

No need to blame myself for not having him evacuated sooner. They can't do much for him on this island and it was likely better for him to remain on duty as long as he could. What he needs, as do all those poor men back there, is rest and good food in a cool climate. Away from this infernal heat and humidity.

The man who has taken Ed's place as my adjutant, Major Thelmon Causie, would not make a good wart on Ed Malcomb's posterior.

But little time to worry about one man, even a good one like Ed Malcomb. There is too much else to worry about. This whole pitiful army, sweltering here in this terrible place.

I am so enervated with fever there is hardly enough strength left to cuss properly. My old troopers on the Texas frontier would find that impossible to believe. But this damned Cuba has taken a lot out of many strong men.

Dear merciful Christ, have mercy. Does it never end? With my soldiers dropping like flies, word arrives from the secretary of war, the Right Honorable Russell A. Alger, that we cannot evacuate the troops to any Atlantic seaboard cities because councils and mayors and citizens are in such a snit about catching something from them and therefore refuse to allow them into their ports.

Those are the same idiots who only two months ago were leaping and shouting like insane dervishes with the enthusiasm of Cuba Libre. And now will not take home those very soldiers who accomplished the task.

It is goddamned sickening! I have been furious with inept upper management many times during this campaign but I never imagined even in my darkest moments that I would have cause to question anyone's compassion. I am ashamed of my countrymen.

Mr. Alger informs that he has found a remote section of Long Island called Montauk Point where an encampment can be established for this army. A place which can be quarantined, as though we were all lepers! But then he pussyfoots as usual and wires that no fever victims can be brought there until the fever has subsided.

Great bleeding soul of God, are we to leave them here in their thousands to die? Because they surely would. It is the fever victims who need evacuation first.

I sent my most powerfully worded message of this war. I told Mr. Alger that if we didn't move this entire army out of Cuba at once, the number of deaths as a result would be a national disgrace!

I must admit to having in the back of my mind the elections coming up this year and the last thing President McKinley wants is a national disaster. The Democrats would be on that like a duck on a June bug from now to November. The Lord God help me for playing politician, but I would play the devil himself if it would help get these suffering soldiers to safety.

The results of that message were immediate, I must say, the only time in recent memory that the War Department responded to my reports. Mr. Alger ordered us out as soon as possible, all to Long Island, fever or not. Fresh, well-supported troops will be sent here to carry on occupation duties.

But such a happy decision, in this damned muddle of a war, could not go unclouded. Even as I was sending my official message, unbeknownst to me at the time, the leader of the Rough Riders was sending his own through communications designed to reach Congress and the newspapers before it ever came to the attention of Mr. Alger. Roosevelt, whom the Washington ass patters have elevated to brigadier general, wrote even more ominous threats of consequences than I had done. And on the very day, the very goddamned *day*, that the secretary of war issued his decision in a telegram to me, and before the news writers had knowledge of his order, Roosevelt's message appeared on every front page across the country. Thus, when Alger did make his decision public it appeared, regardless of what he might have said, to have been a result of the Rough Rider's plea.

And so in the end, Roosevelt has received the credit. Roosevelt is the hero once more. If my heart was not strong it would have exploded in wrath. But frankly, I am past caring so long as we can get these troops out of Cuba.

I fear this damned fever has sapped much of my capacity for rage. Even though the timing of Roosevelt's message has made it appear that I am incapable of moving the War Department to appropriate action and only he has that power. Beard of God!

So now we load them out on all ships available and send them off to Long Island. Good! As I explained to Alger, there is not really much Yellow Jack here now, only hysteria at the thought of it. But there will be plenty soon if we stay. And the weather gets worse every day.

However, a few tangles of business must first be untangled. Like that goddamned Pinkerton detective who has been sniffing around Siboney. He has finally come out of his gopher hole and wants to present his case. If we are lucky, a nervous sentry will shoot him on his way to headquarters.

Wishful thinking. Why should something as beneficial as that happen now after our record of such dreadful chaos in Cuba?

CHAPTER 24

HREE of them came to Fifth Corps headquarters. Pinkerton detective Norman Granger, Colonel Claude McBride, and Lieutenant Pierpont Lang.

Granger was a small man with pinched features and a mustache much too large and bellicose for his tiny face. He wore a strangely out-of-place brown bowler hat and a white seersucker suit.

Colonel McBride was the typical commander of a socialite regiment in the National Guard, rather plump, muttonchop whiskers, a uniform carefully tailored to his rotund figure, and with a saber carried by his great-grandfather in the Battle of Long Island in 1776. As he was quick to explain, his family had a long history of martial achievement, displayed mostly, one would suspect, in various full-dress fetes and masquerade balls in the National Guard armory.

Lieutenant Lang was bright eyed, pink faced, as well tailored as his colonel, his mustache closely trimmed, and his white cork British East Africa helmet unstained by mud or sweat. He displayed a jaunty air and self-confidence completely out of keeping with his deportment in that jungle clearing the day his men shot Captain Juan Carlos Smith to death.

When they arrived on horseback at General Shafter's headquarters it was early evening. There was still a faint afterglow of sun in the orange streak across the western sky, but to the south a purple cloud bank could be seen gathering on the horizon, forming into ranks for the nightly assault on Cuba's coast.

The visitors were escorted into the commanding general's operations tent. It was a rather large tent, only recently arrived, with a number of folding tables and canvas chairs, map charts on easels, hanging kerosene lanterns and behind the general's table, which acted as his desk for such meetings, was a squat rum barrel upon which the general always sat.

The visitors were asked to be seated, all in a group, and were offered lemonade courtesy of the Red Cross, which they all declined. The two officers squirmed with nervousness but the Pinkerton detective seemed perfectly rigid with confidence.

When Major Thelmon Causie came into the tent, the general close behind, the visitors stood up, Colonel McBride's saber rattling like tin cans tossed about in a burlap bag. Shafter sat down with a labored sigh on the rum keg and glared about with bloodshot eyes. Major Causie did introductions, referring to a slip of paper. The commanding general made no move to shake hands, acknowledging each name with an abrupt nod of his great, perspiring head.

"What's your business, gentlemen?" the general asked and everyone in the tent knew that General Shafter knew what the business was.

Detective Norman Granger presented a number of documents purporting to be representations of a federal district court in the city of New York, alleging the crime of homicide committed by one American Indian named Joe Mountain for the untimely and unprovoked death of a soldier of the National Guard regiment of Colonel Claude McBride, the deceased being one Private Thomas van Carlton, a former resident of Dutchess County, New York.

Further, that one Mr. Norman Granger, Esq., had been retained by certain members of said court to investigate the allegations, take Mr. Mountain into custody, and return him to the city of New York to answer questions before a grand jury, and where, if appropriate, he would be tried for murder.

And finally a list of witnesses who had made depositions regarding the alleged crime and a summary of their testimony. Chief among these was Lieutenant Pierpont Lang, of Larchmont, New York.

General Shafter hardly glanced at the papers before stacking them carefully on the edge of his table, and then cleared his throat.

"Thelmon?"

"Sir?"

"Fetch Mr. Mountain."

"Yes, sir."

Major Causie found Joe Mountain in his tent, sitting on a cot, smoking a cigar and looking at Eben Pay, who was lying on a cot opposite with his arm across his eyes, his face dry of sweat and very red, and his breathing coming in short gasps.

As Causie entered the tent, the Indian looked up. The single pale-burning lantern on the ridgepole sent a shiver of blue light across his hair. The tattooed marks along his right cheek in this light looked as purple as the clouds gathering to the south.

"The general wants you in his headquarters tent."

"What for?" Joe Mountain asked.

"It's a matter he wishes to discuss."

"You tell Cap'n Shafter Eben Pay's sick and I ain't leaving this tent," said Joe Mountain.

Causie had visions of trying to find half a dozen healthy and strong soldiers physically able to move this gigantic Indian off that cot.

"All right," Eben Pay said. "It's all right, Joe."

He sat up on his cot, head down.

"Eben Pay, you ain't in any condition to be wandering around in the night air."

"It's all right. We'll get this thing settled." He looked at Causie. "It is the Pinkerton, isn't it?"

"Yes."

"All right. I've been thinking about that. We'll get it cleared up."

"If you say so," Joe Mountain said. "But I still ain't moving out of this tent unless you promise me that as soon as we get it cleared up, you'll find us a way out of here and back to Fort Smith."

Eben Pay wiped his face with the palm of one hand. He seemed to feel his forehead.

"Yeah, you still got fever," Joe Mountain said.

"All right, Joe, I promise," Eben Pay said.

"Back to Fort Smith."

"Yes. Back to Fort Smith."

The Osage rose and looked at Causie and he was grinning but Causie knew there was neither mirth nor good fellowship in that expression. It signaled anything but a gentle disposition at the moment.

"You tell Cap'n Shafter we'll be along," Joe Mountain said.

The major backed out of the tent, obviously relieved, and stumbled away through the darkness that had fallen, cursing as he kicked through old palm fronds.

Eben Pay took his hat from the floor beside his cot but then tossed it aside. He pulled a canvas valise from beneath the cot and took from that a fat, walletlike folder and slipped it into a hip pocket.

"I'm not going to wear a coat, if that won't embarrass you too much."

"Hell, Eben Pay, them suspenders over your underwear looks fine to me."

"Gimme your hand," Eben Pay said.

The Osage helped him to his feet and Eben Pay stood for a long moment, holding Joe Mountain's hand tightly, breathing deeply.

"A little light-headed," he said. "Now remember, Joe, when we get over there, you don't open your mouth."

"If that's what you want."

Eben Pay freed his hand, squared his shoulders with a visible effort, and said, "I'm ready."

When Eben Pay entered General Shafter's tent, the three visitors hardly glanced at him because they were staring at Joe Mountain just behind. The Osage had to stoop to avoid brushing his head against the ridgepole. Detective Granger grunted, staring with triumphant eyes at that line of tattoos down Joe Mountain's cheek, and muttered, "Uh-huh. Uh-huh," as though those dark dots were proof of guilt beyond any doubt.

"That's him," Lieutenant Lang whispered loud enough for all to hear and General Shafter shot a wicked glance in his direction.

"Have seats," the general said.

"Cap'n, there ain't a chair in here would hold me," said Joe Mountain. "Now that you already got that keg."

The visitors looked startled, Eben Pay impatiently waved Joe Mountain to silence, and General Shafter chuckled.

"Very well, then, whatever," said the general.

Major Causie repeated introductions but nobody offered to shake hands and the visitors remained seated. Now that the moment he had been dreading had arrived, Eben Pay's fever-warped vision seemed to clear and his head stopped spinning. He fixed a glassy stare on Lieutenant Lang's face.

"We meet again," he said.

There was a harsh, metallic ring in Eben Pay's voice not caused by any fever and Joe Mountain's grin was broader as he settled into a squat beside General Shafter's table.

"Just like court in Fort Smith," Joe Mountain said softly and this time Eben Pay ignored him. The Osage began to trace designs in the sand between his feet, head down, still grinning.

General Shafter offered the documents Norman Granger had brought and Eben Pay began to leaf through them.

"Who is this man?" Granger asked.

"A member of my staff," said Shafter, glaring. Then, glancing at Eben Pay, said softly, "There's an allegation of murder here against Mr. Mountain."

The Osage looked up from his sand tracings, a little startled. It was the first time anybody in Cuba had called him mister. But immediately went back to his finger drawings.

Now Eben Pay was the only one standing in the tent. The others watched him—except for Joe Mountain, who was intent on his etchings across the face of Cuba—the general from his rum keg, Major Causie seated just behind the general, the three visitors all in a row. Like the monkeys, Eben Pay thought, seeing, hearing, saying no evil. Finally, he had seen enough.

"There is no legal basis for this," Eben Pay said, seemingly to General Shafter, but Detective Granger responded at once and with some shrill heat.

"Aw, but there is. You have failed to read the representation of the Federal Court for the Southern District of New York."

"I saw no signature of a sitting jurist."

"It is an official representation from officers of that court."

"May I see your commission?"

"My what?"

"Your commission, your commission," said Eben Pay. His voice was rising, but he quickly controlled it. "Perhaps you are unaware that you have no authority to make arrests in the name of that court unless you are a duly appointed United States deputy marshal with a properly sealed commission."

"Look here . . ." Granger produced from his pocket another document. Eben Pay stepped across the tent to take it and unfold it and read it. Quickly.

"It is a John Doe warrant," he said. "But you have no commission to serve it."

I am not at all sure of my ground here, Eben Pay thought, but I think these bastards are even less sure.

"Now look here—" Colonel McBride started but Eben Pay cut in sharply even though he maintained control of his voice.

"Sir, do *you* have so-called representations from this court in . . . where was it? New York?"

"Why, no . . ."

"I would suggest, sir, that any authority you have or responsibility to speak in the present situation is only that delegated by your superior officer, who is sitting immediately behind me. Who, in case it has eluded you, sir, is the commanding general of all military forces in Cuba."

Color rose slowly from around Colonel McBride's collar, soon reaching all the way to his forehead, until his face was as red as Eben Pay's, who now bent slightly toward McBride and spoke even more softly.

"I would suggest, sir, that anything you feel is relevant here should be said under oath and you may certainly be sworn by the adjutant general of this corps."

McBride's mouth opened. Then closed, like a large goldfish about to blow bubbles on the surface of his pond.

Eben Pay turned back to Norman Granger, still holding the John Doe warrant in his hand. General Shafter suddenly slapped his neck and muttered about the goddamned mosquitoes.

"This paper is useless," Eben Pay said and allowed the John Doe to flutter from his fingers and before Granger's frantic grab for it was unsuccessful, Eben Pay turned back to his original position, there faced the visitors once more, steadying himself with one hand behind him on the table.

"Now," he began. "Let me advise you, Mr. Granger, that it is doubtful a federal court has jurisdiction in this case because the incident alleged occurred on the sovereign soil of another country. But much more importantly, because it was an accident of war. All the principals involved were men serving under direction and within the structure of a military command in the posture of an invading army. Therefore, that command, Fifth Army Corps, would naturally have original jurisdiction to cause trial for any crime or misdemeanor.

"I am sure your military advisers there"—and Eben Pay waved a hand in the general direction of Colonel McBride and Lieutenant Lang—"have explained to you that a military organization under these circumstances has authority delegated by act of Congress to conduct investigations, file charges, cause trial, convict or acquit, and when appropriate pass sentence. Therefore, it is perfectly obvious that original jurisdiction rests with Fifth Corps."

"The fact is," said Norman Granger coldly, "that a crime did occur. A most serious crime. But the commanding general, for whatever his own reasons, has chosen to ignore it."

Eben Pay heard a sharp intake of breath from behind him but Shafter said nothing. Beautiful beautiful, Eben Pay thought, the dumb son of a bitch is bearding the old lion right in his den. He struggled to avoid smiling.

Instead he looked at one of the lamps, sighed, and asked for a drink of water. Major Causie was away and back at once with an army white china coffee mug filled with water. Eben Pay drank about half of it and placed the cup gently on Shafter's table and turned back to these visitors.

"Very well, then, let us consider this so-called crime of itself," he said. "I cannot assume, considering your demonstrated ignorance in such matters, that you gentlemen know what the terms *act of war* or *accident of war* mean. I will attempt to explain it in the simplest terms possible so that you may be able to grasp it."

He drew a deep breath, aware that all three of the men before him were puffed with anger at his words. He thought he heard Joe Mountain chuckling.

"In a time of great danger and violence, when all parties to such a scene are armed and capable of deadly force, individuals cannot be held responsible for random lethal results. In other words, metal flying about in a combat or war zone situation cannot distinguish between friend and foe. Nor can men be expected to remain docile when they are endangered. They will naturally use their weapons. Thus, often, and I repeat *often*, men are killed or wounded by friendly fire. That's the case here."

"No it isn't," Lieutenant Lang shouted, his voice high-pitched. He pointed toward Joe Mountain, who was still scribbling in the sand with his finger. "He shot Mr. van Carlton without cause."

Everyone except Eben Pay was startled at Lang's outburst, most of all Lang. Eben Pay showed no change of expression, his face almost pulsating red but calm. He took more water from the white china cup. In the silence, they could hear the grumble of thunder to the south.

"So much for the general case of act or accident of war. Now to the specific case of Mr. Mountain."

The Osage lifted his head once more, grinning.

"He was fired on. He was on an ordered and authorized military mission and he was fired on from ambush, and we *both* returned that fire."

"Both?" asked Granger, popeyed.

"Why Mr. Granger, I was there, you know. Lieutenant Lang knows I was there. Surely in all this great stack of hogwash you have collected there is somewhere, somehow mention of the fact that Joe Mountain was not alone." Now Eben Pay's voice rose. "And there was in fact a third party. A Cuban patriot named Captain Juan Carlos Smith, who was killed by Lieutenant Lang's troops when they fired from ambush."

"He shot first," Lang shouted, a note of hysteria in his voice that Eben Pay could recall from that jungle clearing in the rain, with Juan Carlos Smith's body lying wet and soggy on the ground at their feet.

Eben Pay began to smile. In the lantern light, his feverish eyes took on a devilish glint as he looked at Lieutenant Lang. His voice was calm once more.

"Lieutenant Lang, you are a liar!"

"I protest," McBride shouted. "I protest this—this man abusing one of my officers!"

"Abuse or no, Colonel McBride, your officer is a liar!"

"Now look here," McBride started but for the second time in this tent was cut off, now by the commanding general.

"Colonel, keep still," Shafter said.

Eben Pay had a moment of pride for the Old Man, who despite having been slandered by this bunch had refrained from exhibiting some of his most explosive purple obscenities. There was a moment of dizziness, but it quickly passed and Eben Pay glanced at Joe Mountain, who was watching him closely, and smiled.

"Gentlemen," Eben Pay said, still leaning, perhaps more heavily now, on Shafter's table. "Allow me to summarize so we can finish with this ridiculous proceeding.

"First, it is obvious to any rational man even remotely acquainted with the conduct of war that no crime has been committed here.

"Second, on the chance that a crime *has* been committed, then we are thrown back on the question of who makes determination. Obviously, the sovereign authority holding original jurisdiction,

Fifth Army Corps, has determined in its wisdom that no crime has occurred.

"However, if there is still doubt as to whether or not there was a crime, then one of those sovereigns with secondary jurisdiction, such as a federal court, might carry the case to its conclusion. Although to my knowledge there is no precedent for such a thing in an act or accident of war situation. But it could be done."

Granger's face began to brighten, as though a sudden sun had passed over it. His eyes glinted.

"Then, by God, you admit that this savage can be brought to trial in New York," he said, his teeth grinding with delight. He was leaning forward, hands on knees, elbows askew like a rooster trying to take flight. It suddenly occurred to Eben Pay that these politically motivated vultures were trying, actually trying, to take Joe Mountain back to New York and strap him with a murder charge. There, Eben Pay was sure, a jury would find him guilty and likely send him to the rope or that new electric chair they had. The boiling rage and fury that came up into his throat at that thought made him gasp for breath, but his dizziness was abruptly gone. The tremble in his voice was mistaken by Joe Mountain and General Shafter for a result of the fever, but it was not.

"No, by God, I say no such thing," Eben Pay said, still in a low voice. "I state categorically that such a thing cannot be. Because, you see, Mr. Granger, you are too late!"

"Too late?"

"Too late, Mr. Granger. This savage, as you have characterized him, is already in custody of a federal court. I have myself arrested him this very night."

There was a row of three gaped mouths. Granger found his voice first.

"You? You? What kind of tomfoolery is this?"

"No foolery of any kind, Mr. Granger," said Eben Pay. He slid from his pocket the fat wallet, took from it a folded, triple-paged document, unfolded it, and held it before the eyes of Mr. Granger, who tried to take it in his hand.

"Just read it, Mr. Granger. Some time ago, if you recall, I asked for your credentials from a federal court."

And Eben Pay waved his documents before Mr. Granger and Colonel McBride was bent forward trying to read it but Lieutenant Lang looked as though he were ready to cry. "You were unable to produce same. Now I produce mine. It is my warrant as an officer of the Federal Court, Western District of Arkansas, at Fort Smith. You will see it was signed and sealed by the Honorable Judge Isaac Parker, now deceased, and the first endorsement is a similiar authority signed and sealed by the presently sitting jurist of that court, the Honorable Winthrow P. Plowers. I am, sir, an assistant United States attorney. And I intend to take this savage back to Fort Smith, Arkansas, where this case will be duly heard."

Granger sat staring at the parchment before him, and as McBride tried to lean closer, pushed him back with a violent grunt. Eben Pay folded the papers, replaced them in his wallet, and returned it all to his hip pocket. He stood back, thumbs hooked in his suspenders. Joe Mountain was obviously chuckling now, and Eben Pay suspected that he heard General Shafter doing the same.

"In view of which, I also take custody of these representations you have made," he said, turning to Shafter's table and scooping up Granger's stack of papers, stuffing them somewhat haphazardly into the same pocket with the wallet.

"You can't *do* this," Granger whispered.

"Yes he can," the commanding general said.

"Further, you may advise all those who gave depositions that they likely can expect subpoenas, orders to appear in Judge Flowers's court. Judge Flowers is unalterably opposed to taking depositions in testimony so long as respondents are still alive, no matter how far away they may be. I realize that a trip from New York to Fort Smith would be hard, but one does not lightly dismiss a federal judge's foibles.

"I expect, Lieutenant Lang, that Judge Flowers will be most anxious to have a subpoena issued for your appearance, due to the nature of your expected testimony. And once you have given that testimony under oath in a court of law, I expect to indict you for perjury for which I am sure a Fort Smith jury will convict you, so you may look forward to serving seven to twenty years in the federal penitentiary at Detroit. Another of Judge Flowers's foibles is that he despises people who lie, particularly under oath."

Eben Pay turned to General Shafter and made a slight bow, as though to a jury in Fort Smith.

"Sir," he said, "if there is nothing more, I propose to take my prisoner to his billets where I will hold him in close arrest until we can arrange passage to the United States of America."

"I believe it is appropriate that you do so," said the commanding general.

Eben Pay turned now to Joe Mountain.

"Mr. Mountain, are you ready to come peaceably?"

"Oh, hell yes, Eben Pay!"

They were almost out into the now crashing and suddenly brilliant flashing night when Norman Granger leapt to his feet.

"Just a minute here," he shouted.

Eben Pay wheeled about and over his shoulder they could see the beaming face of the Osage, his teeth bared.

"Oh yes, I almost forgot you, Mr. Granger. I am so sorry. Let me assure you that you will also receive a subpoena. I intend to bring you to Fort Smith, and once this act of war case is resolved, you will be brought before a grand jury, and knowing Fort Smith grand juries, I am sure you can expect them to return a true bill against you for impersonating a federal officer. Perhaps you and that boneheaded son of a bitch over there in the cork hat can share adjoining cells in Detroit for a few years where you can reminisce about the wonderful times you had in Cuba. Good night, gentlemen. Good night, General Shafter."

"Good night, Mr. Pay," Shafter boomed.

Behind them they left three stunned visitors and a commanding general who felt better than he had in days, rising now from his rum keg seat. And Norman Granger, who was the only one of them who had the courage to speak still, ran to General Shafter's table, his hands out.

"General, you can't allow such a thing to happen. Don't you know there are large and influential forces involved in the state of New York?"

"The only large and influential forces you need worry about here, sir, is me," Shafter said.

"But general!" Granger yelled, red faced, his eyes beady, his lips slack, almost slobbering.

"Enough," Shafter bellowed, and against his great lungs the detective had no chance of being heard. "Now get your ass out of my headquarters, and if you are still here in one minute from now, I will have you taken out physically."

"Sir," Major Causie said from behind him, "I have a squad of armed infantry just outside, thinking they might be useful!"

By God, General Shafter thought, this Causie has some qualities I hadn't recognized.

Down the slope, in the night now accented with the more and more frequent flares of blinding lightning, Joe Mountain was almost dancing beside Eben Pay as they moved to their tent.

"I never saw you better," the Osage shouted above the thunder. "Eben Pay, old Judge Parker would have enjoyed that more than hanging the Rufus Buck gang."

"Joe, take my hand. I don't know if I can make it."

Suddenly Eben Pay felt himself lifted in Joe Mountain's arms, like a child.

"For God's sake, Joe, you don't have to carry me!"

"You're light as a bottle cork," Joe Mountain shouted, laughing. "Wait 'til I tell Blue Foot about this. Am I gonna be in custody all the way to Fort Smith?"

"Yes," Eben Pay said and he relaxed, allowing himself to go limp in Joe Mountain's arms. He was spent, and it felt good to be cradled. "In custody, all the way to Fort Smith."

"God, Blue Foot ain't gonna believe I been arrested," and Joe Mountain laughed and it was as loud as the thunder.

V.
MEMORIES.

Brigadier General John Stoval

After all these many years, after the horror of a real war in France, why in my old age does memory still carry me back to Cuba? Why can I see in mind's eye the faces of men at El Caney and recall in mind's ear the sound of their names, when it is difficult to remember many of my recent comrades in the Argonne Forest?

I suspect it is because an infantry officer always treasures his first command of a rifle company, which most will say is the best assignment of all in a whole career of military service. And the sentimental attachment to one's first regiment.

The old Thirty-seventh was shattered before the army was embarked from Cuba to that camp in Long Island. There were the combat casualties, of course, but mostly the sickness. In all areas of the Spanish war, our army suffered about 2,000 battle casualties, of whom 379 men died. But our nation lost 5,462 soldiers to typhoid, dysentery, and various tropic fevers.

By the time we came to France, we knew better how to control disease. But it was too late for Cuba.

The old Thirty-seventh suffered its proportional share of that harvest. And so by August, although the regiment still existed on paper, most of its troops were either in the ground or on their backs in hospital.

In those final days on that wretched island, I was promoted colonel and received orders to report to the United States Military Academy at West Point, where I would assume the duties of an assistant commandant in charge of infantry tactics and discipline. It was a noteworthy promotion and my wife sent me three telegraph messages expressing her hysterical joy. Oh Lord!

In the little time I had left on the island, I made an effort to visit all my men in hospital, but with the regiment on occupation duty in Santiago and most of the sick at Siboney, it was very difficult. It was, in fact, impossible.

But I did manage to get back to Clara Barton's hospital once, and had the opportunity to see many of my men before they were carried by steam launch to waiting ships, and thence to Montauk Point, Long Island.

It was a clear and shining day, the rain seeming to hold off until the poor soldiers were across the beach. There was a stream of them moving down to the shore, either litter borne or else walking with assistance from medical personnel or one of the Red Cross people. The engineers had constructed a few short metal docks where the steam launches could take on our casualties. It was most certainly a contrast to the wild confusion on the same beach the night we landed there under glare of naval searchlights.

I moved along the columns of men, speaking to them, shaking their hands, patting them on the shoulder. They moved down the beach in bright sunlight. It was a peaceful scene, the palm trees and jungle beyond green and moving gently in the sea breeze, the sky a deep blue, birds gliding on motionless white wings in the currents of air off the ocean.

Then I saw Dylan Price, sitting on an old abandoned packing case, smoking a cigar and smiling at me with his small, noncommittal smile. His hands were encased in heavy bandages from which only the ends of his fingers protruded like long sausages, which appeared to be mobile enough at least to hold a cigar.

I walked over to him and stood with hands on hips, as an indignant colonel is supposed to do.

"I'd heard you were in this hospital for fever," I said.

"Yes sir, fever of the hands."

"Dylan," I said. "If it weren't for a war just finished, I'd have your butt!"

"Yes sir, I know," he said, still smiling. "It's why the foolish things I do are always at the end of wars instead of at their beginnings."

"I don't suppose you'd tell me who the other man was, just so I might lay flowers on his grave."

He laughed. I had known his smile often, but it was the first time I'd ever heard him laugh. Actually laugh.

"Oh no, Colonel, it's a matter of honor."

"I suspected so." I laughed, too, and then we were silent for a moment. "It's a shame the whole regiment can't go off together, back to the United States. But the ones in Santiago will embark from there."

"A logical thing," he said, still smiling and taking a puff on the cigar held in those fingertips beyond the white bandages. "I'd heard you were promoted, and I see it's true by the fine eagles on your collar."

"Yes, and reassigned as well. So it's parting of the ways for us now, Dylan. But you'll be back soon in Plattsburg Barracks, training new men for the regiment."

He stopped smiling and looked out toward the bay where the steam launches were discharging hospital patients into ship's cargo doors, open safely now in the calm sea.

"No," he said. "My time has run."

"But surely you'll re-enlist, a sergeant now."

"No," he said. He dropped the half-smoked cigar in the sand and stood from the old packing crate, still not looking at me.

"I had supposed you were a contented soldier," I said.

"It has nothing to do with the regiment, sir. It was a bloody grand regiment." Now he turned his head and looked me square in the eye. "And you've been a bloody fine officer, John!"

I could only quickly grip Dylan Price by each arm with my hands and then as quickly move away and leave him without further words. For words at that moment would have been impossible.

As I walked up the sandy beach to my horse, I could feel his gaze on my back. And it passed through my mind that someone once said an army blunts the sharp edge of its savage vocation with massive displays of sentimentality. And it's true. On that day on Siboney beach, as I walked away from Dylan Price, and in effect away from my regiment, it was as though I left behind the warm, protective fireside of my dearest family.

Carlina Bessaford Newton

We cannot afford to take a newspaper. But one can hardly help but hear of the horrors visited on the soldiers in that Long Island camp. Horrors, horrors, horrors. One after another. Why do men become soldiers?

Mother, poor soul, comes in each afternoon from tending her peonies in the back alley where all her neighborhood friends congregate and talk with her about Cuba. They know nothing of Cuba. Only I know of Cuba. My sleep each night is disturbed with the red dreams of Cuba.

I say nothing. I go about my task of watching Father in his bed. A stroke, the doctor says, and now there is no more the strident voice in this house. He lies with eyes open day and night and I have to moisten them with drops of warm water and mineral oil.

Sometimes I read to him. In the morning, usually, with the curtains drawn back so the eastern light comes in and I think of the leaves in New Hampshire turning gold and orange. I read mostly from the Old Testament. Or an occasional verse from Revelations.

I don't go out of the house. It is terrible to see people, imagining their limbs cut off, knowing the color of their life's blood and how their flesh would appear if slashed open. A legacy of Cuba.

Sometimes I think of Clara Barton and wonder if she still lives. I dream of her. Drowning in a sea of crimson, palm trees ringing all about. Sometimes I can smell the sea as it was that day we left Tampa Bay. Sometimes I remember a kiss.

Often, when Mother is at her peonies, I sit beside Father's bed and tell him of my dreams of Cuba. And perhaps he hears.

Dylan ap Rhys ap Llewellyn

There must be something in this world besides a soldier.

Once the Montauk Point encampment behind, three months' back pay in pocket, a whole wide country before me, who knows?

A soldier's life is a good life, so long as responsibilities are taken on by someone else. These three stripes on my sleeve became heavy on my arm. Oh, there are those who relish the weight of accountability, who yearn for the power over others, who delight in giving orders.

But I was born to be a private soldier. And from my first promotion to those final days in Cuba with a platoon of men looking to me for their well-being, the load steadily increased until it felt as though I carried the whole bloody army on my back.

A private soldier, me! With no cares or worries. Drinking and gambling and whoring. Fed and sheltered and clothed. As my old Welsh comrades at Rorke's Drift said when we heard the Zulus were coming in their thousands, "Let the sergeants worry about it. Just have the ammunition ready." That's the whole thing, in the worst of all things: worry only about having the ammunition ready.

I have been a private soldier too long. A private soldier is not made of unthinking clay. He learns. As years go down, he learns, until he knows as much as the sergeants do, and though tries to hide it, cannot, and so the bloody officers make *him* a sergeant. And there's the end of carefree. There's the end of hell-raising on pay night in the canteen. There's the end of overstaying pass while in the perfumed arms of Aphrodite, who may in fact be nothing more than a goat-scented Turk in a Constantinople whorehouse.

The wonderful life is gone. Replaced by *responsibility*. To the common private soldier, the only word in the language worse than responsibility is sobriety.

But some like the press of this monster, responsiblity. Some seek it.

Me? Born to be a private soldier.

I am too old now to be a private soldier any longer. Sergeants do not enjoy having under their tutelage common soldiers who refer to them as "Sonny."

So, with back pay and shoulders freed of weight of seeing good men go down, dead in battle, dead in sickness, perhaps now there will be something other than marching bands, bugle calls when colors are lowered, flash of ranked bayonets on parade, standing in ranks all spit and polish. Something besides the regiment, the regiment, the regiment.

But what could take the place of that?

Well, perhaps there is in this world something besides a soldier.

Olaf Swenson

Plattsburg Barracks sure ain't the same. Reed and Vanic dead, Telner dead, Ulrich a corporal over in A Company, and Mittelberg's enlistment run out and he went back to Germany where he said they was a big army and besides he wanted to see his sister again. I guess he'll see his sister and then enlist in that kraut army.

First Sergeant Barry went up to regiment to be the sergeant major. This army is all worked up over reorganizing and changing stuff because one of the guys in Cuba is a general now and hangs a lot of weight. His name is Leonard Wood. I never seen him in Cuba.

But I seen this Roosevelt once. With his crazy little eye specs. And they say he may be governor of New York now, or maybe something else important.

You can't ever tell from what somebody reads in the newspapers. Like they said all kinds of bad stuff about Montauk Point and the bad grub we got there, but it was pretty good. Them guys who wrote that stuff should have seen what we eat in Cuba.

I don't get to ask Sergeant Price all about these things anymore because he left. After we was at Montauk Point and then come back to Plattsburg, he just up and left.

He came around his last day on post and he sure looked strange in that civilian suit he had on, but his hands were pretty well healed up from that coconut tree he said fell on 'em in Cuba.

He said he figured with bad hands he'd never make any jump at Bob Fitzsimmons, who had whipped Corbett in 'ninety-seven. Hell, I always figured Sergeant Price could likely whale hell out of most of those box fighters.

Anyway, we went down to the tavern just outside the main

gate of the post and had some beer and talked about the guys we knew and ate a lot of that hot sausage and pickled eggs. The kind of stuff that makes you pass wind all the time.

Then I just walked back on post to barracks, about three quarters drunk from all the beer Sergeant Price had bought me, and I never seen him again.

I don't know what I'm gonna do about it. There's a couple more years on my enlistment and this squad leader we got now don't know any more about being a soldier than I do. He don't know any more about being a soldier than the wife of that Polish guy in Milwaukee knew about being a soldier, which I don't think was very much.

Maybe I'll just run out my time and go back to Milwaukee and see if the police has forgot about what that woman said I done.

Without Sergeant Price here to explain stuff to me, it's not too easy.

Major General William R. Shafter

I suppose it doesn't matter that the press has crucified me. Blundering through one way or another, we did in Cuba what we were sent to do.

There is the bitterness of gall in my throat when I think of all those who contributed to those blunders but whose names have never been mentioned by Richard Harding Davis or Clement Eggmont.

But now it is all past. There are many things I wish I could recall. There are many things I am proud of accomplishing. My one hope is that at least a few of the soldiers who served on the island of Cuba will have a kind word for me when they describe their war to grandchildren.

Goddamn! I am so tired!

Joe Mountain

It's hard to understand these white men. Me and Eben Pay go off to some island where everybody's thrashing around in the mud and shooting at one another from a long way off, and so the other people say they had enough, and then we say we got Cuba and Puerto Rico and Guam and Hawaii and the Philippines, wherever the hell all those places are.

Eben Pay tried to explain to me that a couple of those places are way to hell and gone out in the biggest ocean we got on earth and puts the United States of America right cheek-by-jowl with China and Japan.

Washita River is far enough away for me. I can't get too excited about this China or Japan. I remember once me and four deputy United States marshals had to ride down to a place called Odessa, Texas, to pick up a prisoner and it took us two weeks just to get there on good horses. That's as far away from Fort Smith as I want to think about and Eben Pay is trying to tell me about this China and Japan.

So he stopped trying to explain it.

One day Eben Pay come out of Judge Flowers's chambers and he had this long face. I didn't know why because I'd just been in the courtroom a while ago and watched Eben Pay do a good case and convict two Creeks for murder over in Salisaw. But he had this long face and he showed me a newspaper Judge Flowers had give him and it said Major General William R. Shafter had died.

Why, I said, that's old fat belly Cap'n Shafter from Cuba, and Eben Pay said yes, it was. So him and me sat there in his office and talked about Cap'n Shafter and Cuba and how Cap'n Shafter got called an idiot by a lot of people in newspapers who didn't know what was happening. We looked out the window and saw the sun go down over in the Nations, all red and orange. Sometimes we did that, me and Eben Pay, him just sitting there without saying anything, watching the sun go down, and me with him.

I never got much of a jolt out of watching the sun go down because it happened every day, but sometimes Eben Pay acted like it was the most wonderful thing in the world. But I never bothered him when he wanted to watch the sun go down, I'd just sit with him in case he needed me for anything.

By the time we heard about Cap'n Shafter dying, Eben Pay was the United States attorney in the federal court at Fort Smith. He had this office in old Judge Parker's courthouse there on Rogers Avenue with that window facing over the river and we could sit there and look across into the Indian Nations when we wanted to.

When we came back from Cuba it didn't take Eben Pay's fever long to go away. His little son Barton was growing and looking more like Missy Bishop every day. Even though I never been too big for Cherokees, I had to admit young Barton was a nice little man. I started teaching him a few Osage words. I tried, anyway, but little Barton wasn't really old enough to learn about words I guess.

There wasn't any more posse duty, me and some deputy marshal going off into the Nations after somebody who had done crime. Everything was getting civilized and there was even a lot of talk about Oklahoma Territory and the Indian Nations going together and getting into the United States union as a single state.

Hell, it sounded all right to me.

But I still kept old Smoker Chubee's Colt pistol under my coat all the time. Just in case. Even though about the most dangerous thing I ever did anymore was go over on Rogers Avenue and buy me and Eben Pay a meat loaf sandwich at noon every day, or maybe one of them little chocolate tarts the Jews over there make.

We never did subpoena that New York bunch. Me and Eben Pay told Judge Flowers about those National Guard sons of bitches shooting at us in Cuba and me killing that soldier and about those men who wanted to take me off for murder. Judge Flowers laughed like hell. Not because of those two dead men, van What's-His-Name and Juan Carlos Smith, but because they tried to get me up to New York on murder.

Judge Flowers said I could just consider the case had been reviewed in chambers and there was no basis to proceed and we'd just wait and see if that New York bunch called Eben Pay's bet. That's what Judge Flowers said. And the New York bunch didn't!

But Eben Pay told me to stay out of New York.

Hell, I ain't even interested in going to Cassville, Missouri, much less New York.

I told my brother Blue Foot all about Cuba. I don't think he believed half of it. Blue Foot's just an old-line Osage. Hell, he still roaches his hair!